The Tolling

The Epitome of Science Trilogy

Ali Ives

Literary Wanderlust | Denver, Colorado

The Tolling is a work of fiction. Names, characters, places and incidents are either the product of the author's imagination or are used fictitiously, and any resemblance to actual persons, living or dead, business establishments, event or locales is entirely coincidental.

Published in the United States by Literary Wanderlust LLC, Denver, Colorado. www.LiteraryWanderlust.com

ISBN print: 978-1-956615-52-4
ISBN digital: 978-1-956615-53-1

Printed in the United States of America

Dedication

To the people who make a house a home.
Mum, whose love and wisdom have shaped me into who I am.
Your guidance and friendship bring so much light to my life.
Kate, the greatest partner I could ever wish for. Your laughter,
your kindness and your creativity mean so much.
Jed, the best dog in the whole wide world. (In my opinion.)
Dipper, feline scoundrel. (This one's just a fact.)

Other Works by the Author

The Ticking
The Winding

Prologue

Frettchen

Seven days ago, but also kind of always.

For all the timeless places in the universe, of which there are many, just as many exist where time is immutable. It is an undeniable element of these places, no matter how intangible it may be. Time cannot be touched or caught in a bell jar or seen in any one given moment by the naked eye. Like speed, it can only be experienced through other forces. The ticking hands of a clock, the wrinkles on a person's skin, and the frozen moments caught in photographs all lend time a quantifiable existence in the same way motion and distance allow speed to be understood. Untouchable, yet always there.

The city-state of Frettchen, largest nation of the Lower Lands, is one such place where time reigns supreme. Or rather, it *should* be. In fact, it *was* just that, up until a week before this final act of our story begins.

And then time in Frettchen stopped. Which makes things complicated.

The timeless places in the universe, the Pockets of the gods, exist on their separate planes, enveloped by the great Void Between Worlds, a swirling realm of nothingness and chaos. Time cannot simply cease to exist without this buffering vacuum. Yet it has in Frettchen. Only in Frettchen. Though the clocks in the city have all stopped, time carries on in the rest of the Lower Lands. Indeed, the human world remains unaffected beyond the great city's borders. For now.

So, the city sleeps, caught between a world run by the invisible hands of time and a power that defies it. Its clocks are broken, its citizens lost, the sky overhead clouded in darkness.

Two beings move through the silence. They roam the streets and sky, as lost as the sleeping city, but far more restless. Fire and shadow.

And hidden, frightened, something else lurks. A quiet breath of laughter in the dark.

So begins an ending.

Chapter 1

The Woman in the Dream

Sunlight sparkled off the waves rolling into the harbor of Trident's Point. It was a bright, mid-spring day, and in the South Cities that meant *hot*. This region of the Lower Lands, caught between the ocean and the Eastern deserts, stayed warm even in the wintertime, and now, as the days progressed ever closer to the summer months, it was getting to be sweltering.

The locals were well accustomed to the heat. It was, after all, an everyday part of life. As the southernmost of the South Cities, any less-than-warm day in Trident's Point was considered peculiar. Most of the citizens went about their days thinking nothing more of the weather than whether it was raining or not, or if the wind was carrying the salt of the sea or pollen from the scrubby farmlands to the north.

For Mikalai Gloucester, such a laidback disposition toward the weather was not so easy to achieve.

On a street down near the waterfront, the buzz of his motorcycle cut through the air, reminiscent of a cicada's call. Like the perpetual engines powering the cars around it, the machine's clockwork mechanism wasn't overtly loud, but it was still enough to drown out the ambient sounds of the seaside. The distraction was a welcome one. Gloucester had set out that day in search of escape. Not from the city itself nor the oppressive heat—though he would happily leave both behind if he could—but from a far more insidious enemy.

His own thoughts.

The mind is a difficult thing to outrun, unfortunately, even on a motorcycle. Though he'd been touring around Trident's Point for the better part of the morning, the motor's hum in his ears was the closest he'd gotten to peace of mind.

He'd had the dream again. The same one he'd had for several nights in a row. It always started the same way. Frettchen, frozen in time. Streets swallowed in darkness as a gigantic shadow carved a path through the turbulent sky. A towering figure of fire stalking the silent buildings like a ghost haunting a graveyard.

Once upon a time, not even very long ago, such a dream would have felt like nonsense. A strange conglomeration of metaphors at most. He might have entertained himself with idle consideration of what each image could mean. No question of that now. The dream was no metaphor. Frettchen was lost—temporarily, he hoped—and if they wanted to save it, not to mention spare the rest of the world from the same fate, they would have to find a way to fight the darkness which had overtaken it. And the being behind it all.

Which sounded very heroic, but was phenomenally easier said than done. The task felt as formidable now as it had a week before, when Gloucester and his friends first arrived in Trident's Point after narrowly escaping the downfall of Frettchen. As the citizens of Trident's Point went about their day, his thoughts stubbornly returned to his own city. Every sunny avenue he turned onto reminded him of Frettchen's streets, no matter the differences in architecture and design. He imagined the faces of its people superimposed over each innocent passerby, like ghosts haunting his every movement.

Frettchen's fate came to pass like the largest and heaviest in a long line of dominoes falling. First were the assassination attempts on the high minister. The investigation into that had won Gloucester his freedom from prison, but things quickly got out of hand.

Out of hand. Now there was an understatement if ever he'd heard one. Gloucester's eyes narrowed behind the visor of his helmet, the high minister's stern face flashing through his mind. Because of the politician's schemes, Gloucester had been thrown into a world of magic and conspiracy and kidnapping.

And things only got worse with the high minister's death. Soon they were dealing with monsters roaming Frettchen's streets and the out-of-control fury of Denken, the immortal personification of Thought. In a desperate attempt to stop Denken and his creations, Gloucester and his friends had banded together with Denken's kin, the Gambler, personification of Choice, and the goddess Purpurrot, mother of creation. In theory, they ought to have had good odds of success.

Only everything had gone wrong. Just when they thought the battle was won, Denken's power unexpectedly surged. If not for Purpurrot's last-minute Transportation spell, they would have been caught in the city as it fell into its current state: frozen in time and shadow.

So here he was, in Trident's Point. The sun beat down on the back of his head as he slowed his motorcycle and pulled over to the curb, in the shade of a café's awning. Removing his helmet, he swiped a hand across the back of his neck, where his curly black hair was slick with sweat. He'd parked on one of the city's quieter streets, away from its bustling center where the day's heat seemed multiplied by the sheer volume of people, but it was still uncomfortably warm. Taking a moment to catch his breath, he allowed himself to dwell on the dream.

Though it had begun as it always did, it ended differently this time, which was what made it stick in his thoughts. He'd walked the same silent, shadowy streets, and hidden from the same nightmare figures, but then something new appeared. Some*one* new. Gloucester had rounded a corner, ducking away from the spectral form of Denken's massive shadow shark, only to find himself unexpectedly face to face with a woman.

Stocky and a head shorter than Gloucester, she didn't look like someone who ought to be imposing. Chin-length hair fell around her face in vibrant orange ringlets.

Gloucester skidded to a halt at the sight of her. She smiled.

That smile was burned into his memory more than anything else. Now *that* was imposing. Calm, gentle, and starkly out of place. The sort of smile you offered a relative or a good friend when they seemed down. It felt like she knew him. Knew everything. In the city full of darkness, she was colorful, almost glowing, and Gloucester somehow knew she wasn't like the rest of the dream.

She was real.

"Mikalai Gloucester," she said, her voice warm and unfazed. "We need you to go home."

He'd woken up as soon as these words left the mysterious woman's lips. Blinking awake in the gloom of the motel room—his makeshift home for the past week—her instructions remained as clear in his memory as if the woman had carved them into the inside of his skull: *We need you to go home.*

But where was home? Gloucester's life had been in turmoil for a long time now, and all of the places he'd come to think of as home felt unreachable. Did she mean Frettchen, where he'd built a life for himself, now lost to shadow and madness? The apartment he once shared with his boyfriend Jeb had ceased to be his home even before Denken took the city. He'd lost that part of his life when the high minister locked him away for stumbling upon his secrets, leaving Jeb to think the worst and eventually move on.

Perhaps she meant an even older home than that. Gloucester was born and raised in the Nordlands, in the foothills of the mountains far to the north of Frettchen. Was that what the mysterious woman meant? What good could he do up there, though?

He was a questioning soul by nature, and now, with this fresh mystery to contemplate, his mind whirled, trying to find answers. The restlessness built up until he couldn't stand it any longer, and so he fled the motel, as if he might somehow be able to leave the questions behind as well.

Which hadn't worked, of course, but the motorcycle ride *was* helping. Ever since his six months of solitary confinement, Gloucester found cars almost unbearably cramped. Motorcycles turned out to be a very fitting alternative. He'd never mentioned his claustrophobia to his companions, but perhaps he wasn't as good at hiding it as he hoped, for it had been one of his friends who got the machine for him.

Three days after their unexpected arrival in Trident's Point, Gloucester was called from the motel room by Cassus Finch, who sounded suspiciously cheerful. He found the tall red-headed magician in the parking lot, looking extremely pleased with himself as he leaned on a parked motorcycle.

"Ta-dah!" he crowed, stepping back and sweeping his arms out like a game show host displaying the big prize. "What do you think?"

"It's nice," Gloucester said, nonplussed. "What's it for?"

"What's it for?" Finch repeated, a frown crinkling his tattooed brow, the skin there marked with the simple design of a sun, half-hidden by his hairline. With his perennially confident demeanor and jaunty West Isles accent, disappointment didn't suit him. "That's your response? It's a present. For you!"

"Why?" asked Gloucester, more confused than ever. "I mean, thank you, obviously," he added, because it wasn't every day he was gifted something so grandiose. "But, uh, why?"

Finch patted the motorcycle's leather seat. "I know you're not big on cars, so I thought this might suit you better. Beats sitting around this dump all day."

He'd left it at that, beyond adding that the motorcycle was only a rental, since they couldn't very well take it with them when they left the city. Which they would have to do soon; Gloucester knew that even before receiving the dream woman's strange instructions. They were of no use to anyone here in Trident's Point. By the time Denken's spreading influence reached this place, it would surely be much too late to stop it. Something they were determined to do.

The biggest question was how. It was one thing to pledge to save the world and another entirely to work out how to actually do that. Gloucester, Zane, and Finch, stranded together in Trident's Point by Purpurrot's Transportation spell, had spent the last few days gathering whatever information they could and then piecing it together into a plan of attack.

So far it went like this:

Denken had taken control of the city-state of Frettchen in a misguided attempt to recreate his timeless pocket dimension in the human world. For some reason, his influence had yet to extend past the city limits, but there was no guarantee that would last, so they had to act as quickly as possible. Purpurrot and the Gambler had been convinced that getting Denken back to the Maze, his actual home, would stabilize his powers and return him to sanity—or the closest thing to it that any of them could hope for when it came to Denken.

This, Gloucester, Zane, and Finch agreed, remained the best course of action. Which meant they needed the other immortals back on their side, as they couldn't hope to access the Maze without them.

With the Gambler apparently stranded in Frettchen, that left Purpurrot. Who was...somewhere.

Not so much a plan, as of yet. It was more a handful of goals, all seemingly impossible to attain. Still, Gloucester told himself, it was better than nothing. Better than having no clue at all what to do. Better than giving up.

And now there were the words of the woman from his dream: *go home*. It hadn't felt like she was telling him to give up. It felt like an order. Instructions. A plan.

He knew he was putting off talking about it with the others. Zane would scoff and Finch would grumble that it didn't help at all. Yet maybe together they could work out what it meant. Maybe it was the push they needed in the right direction.

It was time to return to the motel, then. He was just wasting time out here, dithering over his worries and sweating in the heat. Even in the shade, he could feel perspiration sliding down his back. At home in the Nordlands, hot springtimes and summers were rare, and the scorching sun of the south was nigh-on unheard of. He'd think better once he cooled off. He kicked the motorcycle back to life with a whirring of gears and pulled away from the quiet café.

Over the course of the drive, he tried his best to clear his head again, filling it with the sound of the bike's perpetual engine, as if the noise could take the place of riotous thought. Yet, like a jar of bees, once stirred up the worries were impossible to calm, and they buzzed around his skull, amplified instead of muted.

Reaching the motel was a relief. Gloucester had always possessed an unfortunate tendency to overthink problems. It would be helpful to work through the many questions filling his thoughts by voicing them aloud to others. His parents had filled that role when he was a child, replaced by friends in his teens and eventually Jeb, after he moved to Frettchen.

A few months ago, he never would have guessed that role would soon be filled by a short-tempered clockmaker and a flirtatious, semi-trustworthy magician. Then again, a few months ago, Gloucester wouldn't have been able to guess just about anything his future had in store.

Chapter 2

A Direction to Head In

Zane Zephyr was on the phone when Gloucester returned to the motel room. A round-faced young woman with dark skin and very curly hair, she'd tucked herself into the armchair opposite the beds, knees against her chest and lips curled into a frown.

"Yeah," she said into the room's landline receiver, waving a greeting to Gloucester as he walked through the door. He waved back at her and set his helmet down on the table by the window, but didn't interrupt her conversation. "Yeah," she said again, brows knitting together. "I know. But I've explained this to you already, Zara. Yeah, I have!"

Zara, Gloucester had learned, was Zane's older sister. That explained the exasperation, then.

"I told you and Dad, I can't come to you guys yet." She rolled her eyes melodramatically and tossed a smile Gloucester's way. "I'm nowhere near you, and the trains are mad right now."

Despite her air of sisterly annoyance, Gloucester knew she was happy to be talking to her family. She'd reached out to them the day after they ended up in the south. Zane's family had moved away from Frettchen a few years before, when her father retired and left his clock shop to his youngest daughter, and now they all lived in one of the South Cities, a mid-sized inland town called Mindel, several days north of Trident's Point. As soon as Zane assured them that she hadn't been in Frettchen when it fell, they'd clamored for her to come home to them, and she'd been dodging their continued demands ever since.

As Gloucester settled onto the edge of his bed, he could hear the faint sound of Zara's voice on the other end of the line. For a few minutes, the women's conversation filled the room. Gloucester fidgeted, trying not to eavesdrop. Dipping a hand into his pocket, he pulled out a pale shark's tooth and turned it distractedly between his fingers. It had become a bit of a habit in the last few days.

Across the room, Zane laughed at whatever her sister was saying.

"Course I want to meet your puppy—stop trying to tempt me! I told you, I'm visiting with friends. I'm not gonna just abandon them because you want to make me feel jealous over your dog. Give her a big cuddle from me. And say hi to Mum and Dad. I've gotta go, Zara." A pause, and Gloucester could see the longing in Zane's expression. "Yeah, I know. Love you too. I'll visit you guys as soon as I can. Yep. Bye, Zara."

She sighed as she placed the receiver back on its stand. "I hate lying to them," she said. "And I'm totally rubbish at it. I told them I'm staying with my friends Bleifrei and Lucienne. I'm glad they didn't push for any more information than that, 'cause I know I'd panic and blurt out something really stupid." She knuckled her forehead miserably, then threw herself onto the bed next to Gloucester. "And Zara has a new puppy. How unfair is that? I want a dog! Imagine, we could be playing with puppies. Instead, we're stuck brainstorming how to save the stupid world."

She blew a raspberry at the ceiling, making Gloucester laugh.

"I'm sorry I have no dogs to offer you." He played up an apologetic pout. "Would that I could."

"I'll try not to hold it against you." Zane rolled onto her side and propped her head on her hand, elbow digging into the floral-patterned sheet. "I'm surprised you still have that," she added.

Gloucester blinked down at her for a confused moment, before she pointed at the tooth still in his grip.

"It was Denken's, right? From when you punched him?" When Gloucester nodded, she said, "It's kind of amazing you haven't lost it, after everything."

"Just luck, I suppose."

The tooth had been in his pocket when they got teleported, along with the key to a storage unit holding all of his possessions. He'd held onto both. While the key was a reminder of his past and—perhaps more importantly—a hopeful promise of a future reunited with some remnants of his old life, he wasn't quite sure why he'd bothered keeping the demigod's tooth.

Zane held her hand out, and Gloucester dropped the tooth onto her palm. She eyed its jagged edges.

"Sort of gives a whole new meaning to the saying 'God's teeth,' doesn't it? It's funny, it really looks like a normal shark tooth. I would have expected it to, I dunno, *feel* different or something. But it just seems normal. Well, you know, for a shark." She passed the tooth back to him. "I suppose I get why you'd hold onto it, though. Not every day you get to knock a god's tooth out. I'd say you earned it as a keepsake."

Gloucester felt her watching as he idly rotated the tooth in his grip. When he glanced her way again, he saw an idea spark in her eyes. She lifted the pocketwatch that hung around her neck.

"I could put it on a cord for you, if you like. Might make it a little less easy to lose."

"I appreciate it, but no thanks. I think that'd feel too much like a taunt. Probably wouldn't help matters." Still, he stowed it safely back in his pocket with the key. He might not want to wear it like a trophy, but nor did he want to cast it aside. Zane was right; he had earned it.

Ready to change the subject, he pushed himself to his feet and regarded Zane seriously. "For what you were saying before, about the whole brainstorming thing, I think I might have a lead."

—

To Gloucester's surprise, his story wasn't met with the disbelief he'd expected.

"Home, eh?" said Zane when he finished explaining his dream, drumming her fingers on her knee. She'd pulled herself up to sit on a pillow, one leg crossed over the other, head cocked to the side. Her other hand played absently with the chain around her neck, sunlight from the window reflecting off the crystal of the dangling pocket-watch. "Does she mean Frettchen?"

"I don't think so," Finch interjected. He'd returned to the motel with sandwiches for the trio, just in time to save Gloucester having to recount his dream twice. Green-eyed and flame-haired, he wore an expression just as contemplative as Zane's. "Here's the thing, which I would've told you before if you'd not scarpered off so early this morning... She came to me in my dream too. Short lass, right? Red hair? Annoyingly knowing smile?"

"That sounds like Orange Ianto," said Zane, fingers halting their rhythmic motion as she sat up straighter. Her lunch sat half-eaten and now forgotten on her lap.

"The oracle?" Gloucester asked, dusting the last crumbs of his own sandwich from his fingertips. He'd been hungrier than he'd realized. "The one who called me about the prophecy?"

For someone who could apparently see the future, she had terrible timing. The call to warn them that Denken was about to unleash untold power over Frettchen had come too late to stop it from happening.

"That'd explain it, then." Finch rubbed his stubbly chin. "Oracles are really rare, but all of the ones I've met or read about have some dream-walking abilities. Explains how she was able to show up in both of our heads."

"And she told you to go home too?" Gloucester asked. Dream-walking was a new concept, but he suspected that asking about it would only lead to more confusion.

He glanced down at the rings on his right hand: three in total, linked by fine chains going from his thumb to his middle finger to his pinky. The jewelry had been a gift from a hedge witch, spelled with protective enchantments. He'd quickly learned that the world of magic was complex and there was much more to it than he could have ever guessed.

Finch shook his head. "Nah. She told me to listen to you."

"Wait, so she came to both of you? How come I didn't see her?" Zane pouted. "All I dreamt about last night was getting eaten by that bloody shadow shark. And then this other nightmare with zombie cats, but I don't think it meant anything..."

"I wouldn't take it too personally, if I were you," Finch told her. "Even for a magic-wielder as powerful as an oracle, projecting yourself into another's dreams is difficult. Only proper dream-walkers can do it with ease, and even then, most of them have to be touching the person. As a magician and a witch, my mind's already inclined to magic. Makes it easier to project into than a closed door like yours."

Zane clearly wasn't sure whether this was a compliment or not. She opened and shut her mouth a few times, then pointed at Gloucester. "Well, what about Gloucester, then? He's not magical either."

"Maybe not. But I reckon he's fairly magically inclined." Finch cracked a smile when Gloucester gaped at him in shock. "It would explain why Denken affects you so easily and why you're so good at channeling magic," he explained. "Most people wouldn't have been able to pull off a stunt like you did in the false Maze, siphoning my magic away from me like that. You have a sensitivity for magic, even with no training for what to do with it. I reckon you could've made a damn good magician, if you'd been taught when you were younger."

Gloucester fought the urge to defend his age. Twenty-six wasn't *old*, after all.

What did he know about magical training, though? Maybe it was like learning another language, something that became more and more difficult the older you got. He traced a finger along one of the enchanted rings, processing this new information.

He could have been a magician? He wondered if Finch could teach him a few tricks, age be damned. It might be nice to *wield* magic for once, rather than have it used on or through him. Back in the false Maze, when he'd managed to create that shield, it had been out of instinct and reckless desperation. What might he be able to do with even a little training? He squirreled the notion away for later contemplation.

"So I guess I'm just as mundane as they come." Zane sighed, so dejected that even Finch regarded her with sympathy.

"There's nothing wrong with being non-magical," he said. "Keeps you safer from Denken, for starters, if not by much."

"And I'd hardly say you're *mundane*," Gloucester added. "You're the one that introduced me to Antimony, after all. I'd still be thinking I was crazy if not for you."

Zane cheered up, eyes brightening. "I suppose that's true. And I guess I can't say I'm all that sorry people find it hard to break into my dreams." She stopped fidgeting with the pocket watch—it was enchanted, much like Gloucester's rings, as a protective amulet—and crossed her arms resolutely. "So...we're supposed to listen to Gloucester and head home. To where, though?"

She and Finch turned as one to look at him, and he frowned at the scrutiny.

"My best guess is the Nordlands," he said slowly. "If Orange Ianto meant Frettchen, she wouldn't have had any need to give Cassus a different message." It was still taking some getting used to, calling Finch by his first name, but Gloucester found he liked the sound of it. "So she must mean my old home. Where I grew up."

"Which is where?" Zane asked. "The Nordlands isn't exactly a small place."

An understatement. While Frettchen stood apart as the only truly independent city-state in the Lower Lands and the largest of the scattered metropolises, the Nordlands and the South Cities both took up far larger regions. The former spread from the northern limits of Frettchen and the eastern desert up to the impenetrable wall of mountains that marked the farthest edges of the Lower Lands. Beyond those mountains lay mystery, for no one had made it past them and returned in known history. If there was once an Upper Lands, it had long been lost to time.

A land of forests, long winters, and wide stretches of wilderness, the Nordlands was nonetheless a vibrant and essential part of the Lower Lands. The technological innovations of the Nordish people rivaled those of Frettchen and indeed often surpassed them. An inventor from the Nordlands had created the first perpetual engine, after all, and many of its cities were home to the best clockwork factories.

Gloucester had never spent much time in any of those cities, however. "I'm from Lalune," he answered.

As expected, Zane looked blank at the name. Finch nodded vaguely—he and Gloucester had briefly discussed their hometowns before—but he still followed it up with a shrug.

"Doesn't clear anything up for us, sorry."

"Unsurprising," Gloucester said. "It's a little village about two hours north of Tovak."

"Tovak I've heard of," Finch said. "That's way up there, isn't it? Near the mountains."

Gloucester nodded. "Lalune is hardly known even to Nordlanders. Most of the people there are woodsmen and farmers. I don't know what we're supposed to find there that'll help. Why couldn't this Orange Ianto woman have been more clear?"

What was the point of being able to see the future if you weren't going to explain yourself?

Zane frowned, apologetic. "Maybe she doesn't know herself. From what I've always gathered about her abilities, prophecies and future-telling are a complicated business."

"Yeah," Finch agreed, idly twisting a napkin between his fingers. "It's like when I dreamt about you being in trouble after Denken kidnapped you. I barely got that dream in time to do anything about it, let alone keep it from happening. Most of the time when it comes to prescience, by the time you figure the visions out, they've already come to pass. The oracle probably doesn't want to waste time deciphering everything before passing the message along."

These were hardly words of hope, yet where Gloucester's shoulders began to droop with defeat, Finch's squared with determination. Gloucester envied his ready optimism for any new heading, even one so paltry as this.

"Then again," Finch went on, rubbing his chin. "The rest of us, we aren't oracles. Someone like Orange Ianto, their predicting abilities are off the charts. Even if she doesn't know exactly what her visions mean, if she thinks we need to head for Lalune, then that's where we need to go. Beats sitting around in bloody Trident's Point, in any case."

This wry remark made Gloucester laugh and even brought a smile to Zane's lips.

"Whatever it is we're looking for," said Gloucester, "let's hope we know it when we see it."

"Yeah." Zane spread her hands before her. "Like a big sign that reads, 'Here's how you beat Denken and save the world!' That'd be handy."

Finch chuckled. "Now you're getting my hopes up." Tossing away his napkin, he took a cursory look around the small room. "Right, let's get packed." He grabbed his coat from the hook on the wall. "Aaaand that's me done. Ready to go?"

Chapter 3

Northward Bound

"Sorry, no more trains to Pell today. Come back in the morning."

Gloucester watched Zane turn away from the stern-faced ticket-master with a visible huff. She returned to where he and Finch waited on a nearby bench, shaking her head in disappointment.

The three friends had just arrived in Port Gnoll, the second to last city in a long string of train rides between Trident's Point and the southern border of Frettchennian territory. Where Trident's Point had been mostly flat, with hilly farmland and stony beaches leading out to the sea, here the terrain was much more dramatic. Monumental cliffs separated the water from the mainland, Port Gnoll emerging in a vertical architectural feat. Its white stone buildings appeared to climb the rocky heights, rising up from the sea into the rolling grasslands which stretched away from the coast.

The clocks struck ten. Gilded faces declared the time from every platform, while high above, the clocktower's massive movement tolled the hour, its melodious bellow carrying easily over the hubbub of people and trains.

Even at this late hour, the station bustled with activity. Passengers who had disembarked the same train as them crowded the building, milling about as they gathered their luggage and met up with friends and family before venturing forth into Port Gnoll. Gloucester remembered vacationing here with Jeb two years ago, though now it felt like a lifetime. He recalled how beautiful he'd found it then. How peaceful. He and Jeb spent a happy week exploring its cobbled streets, the city famous for its seaside culture and abundance of artists.

Now all he wanted was to get to the next city. They'd left Trident's Point four days prior, riding train after train as they made their way north, listening for any news on the situation in Frettchen.

They'd quickly learned that trains still weren't passing into or out of the city. None of the rail lines could cross onto Frettchennian soil. People had attempted to make their way by car as well, but the smaller machines fared no better, their engines inexplicably dying when they got too close.

Then came those who tried to finish the trip on foot. They vanished long before reaching even the outskirts of the city. Reports said they simply blinked out of existence, a distant figure one moment and then gone the next. Finch had bracingly told Zane and Gloucester that he was sure they weren't dead, just stricken by the enchantment cast over Frettchen. Gloucester tried to take some comfort in that, though doubt gnawed at the back of his mind. And it didn't solve the obstacle standing in their path.

Unlike the South Cities and the Nordlands, Frettchen stood alone as its own governing force, a city-state whose power lay in large part with its location. Situated between the sea to the west and the treacherous desert to the east, all trains between the South Cities and the Nordlands were forced to pass through it.

"Which is why we'll have to go by sea," Finch told them when they'd contemplated this problem on the second day. "We need to find a ship out of Pell to take us up along the coast."

Finding a ship to take them would be enough of a challenge under normal circumstances, let alone when it meant sailing by Frettchen as it was now. Tensions among the populace were rising as they got closer to the border, reminding Gloucester of Frettchen following the high minister's death. Perhaps that was Denken's influence spreading, a precursor of worse things to come. Frenzied rumors grew more plentiful and creative each day. Gloucester had heard other train passengers attribute the state of the city to everything from electrical storms to the wrath of any number of gods. He was tempted to tell those who perpetuated the latter theory just how close to the mark they really were.

Through it all, one thing became increasingly clear: They were running out of time.

Yet finding a ship would have to wait. Even if they wanted to try their luck here in Port Gnoll, it was too late in the evening to search for passage.

With paper-thin cheer, Zane gave a mocking toast. "Here's to another night in a dingy motel."

"At least a bed's more comfortable than a train compartment." Finch yawned. "Even if it's less convenient."

"I think I remember a couple of good places to stay," Gloucester said, rolling his shoulders as he got to his feet. "How much money do we have left?"

They'd had little on them when they woke up near Trident's Point, and their Frettchennian currency was of little use in most Southern cities. Luckily, Finch's magical abilities had proven useful once more—he'd managed to keep their pockets sufficiently lined from a few hours a day of busking back in Trident's Point, entertaining crowds with simple but showy magic tricks. Little were his impressed audiences to know the secret behind his illusions was *actual* magic.

"Not a lot," Finch replied. He pulled out his wallet and peered into it. "But it should be enough to get a decent room for the night. If we're going to bribe our way onto a ship in Pell, I'll need to put on a few more shows, though. Unless either of you want to earn some money."

Despite this ostensible burden, he didn't sound particularly peeved. Finch enjoyed being the center of attention and always flourished when given the opportunity to show off. Gloucester couldn't help but admire that confidence.

"Unless there's a load of people in need of clockwork repairs, I can't really help on the money front," Zane said. Unlike Finch, her frustration was evident. Zane hated feeling useless. Truth was, there was always work available for an expert in clockwork engineering like her, but it wasn't the sort of thing that earned quick cash.

"Leave him to his magic spells," Gloucester quipped, patting her gently on the shoulder. "He knows he loves being our hero."

"It has its rewards," Finch said with a wink. "Or so I continue to hope." He waggled his eyebrows at Gloucester for good measure.

"Ugh." Zane rolled her eyes. "Get a room."

"I intend to," Finch retorted. "And have been. Unfortunately, they keep coming with a grumpy clockmaker included, which really spoils the mood."

Now it was Gloucester's turn to roll his eyes. "Enough of that," he told them, a smile tugging at his lips. "Let's find a place to stay before midnight."

—

The moon was a sharp silver slice as they descended into the city. Carved out of an imposing cliff face, Port Gnoll wound its streets ever downward from the train station, which stood at the very top of the cliff, toward the water's edge far below. The whole city stretched out in a series of layered neighborhoods and districts. Finch strode forth, leading the trio onto the first of many tiers. Streetlamps dotted the impressive view before them like fireflies in the gathering dark.

Zane tugged on Gloucester's sleeve, urging him to pause. He raised his brows questioningly.

"All this flirting and stuff between you and him," she started, quietly enough that Finch wouldn't hear. "It's all right, I guess. Just...be careful, okay?"

She caught the look on his face and hurried on with a huff of exasperated laughter. "I mean, just don't give him all of your trust. Remember, he's hurt you in the past. Physically *and* emotionally. There's no guarantee he won't do it again."

Objectively, this was a valid point, but Gloucester wasn't sure he believed it to be completely fair. Yes, Finch had made significant mistakes in the past, but he was here now, doing what he could to make things right. And if they couldn't trust each other, who *could* they trust?

Trust no one. That had been his motto, his mantra after he was released from prison. *Trust no one.*

In the time since then, however, he'd met people who helped him even when it didn't benefit them to do so. People who had reached out and been kind. Who put their lives on the line for him and put their trust in him. Wasn't it only fair that Gloucester offer his trust in return?

"I'll be careful," he assured Zane. "Though, honestly, romance isn't exactly a priority at the moment."

"Seems to me it rarely should be," she said dryly. "Logically speaking. Doesn't stop it from throwing a wrench in the works of any given situation, far as I can usually tell."

He chuckled. "I promise not to put it ahead of saving the world."

Zane cracked a smile. "Good to hear." She turned her eyes to the city street ahead of them, watching people laugh and chatter with their friends, and the humor withered from her face. "In all fairness, all the stress and horror we've been through...it's got me thinking that maybe I want someone in my life too."

"Oh?"

"Yeah," she said contemplatively, the hint of a smile returning. "I'm thinking if we save the world and don't all die, I'll get myself a dog."

Following cobbled avenues and public staircases, the trio descended level by level. Now that they'd moved into the city proper, they kept an eye out for accommodations.

"City" was perhaps not the most accurate term, at least in comparison to the likes of Frettchen or Pell. Even Trident's Point was larger than Port Gnoll. Yet the beauty of the architecture and setting, as well as the rich culture, gave the place an unshakable sense of pride. Greenery dotted the white stone at seemingly every opportunity, and flowers adorned nearly every lamppost and balcony. It was considered a jewel among the South Cities, and its citizens were well aware of that.

"It shouldn't be hard to find somewhere to stay," Gloucester said, looking around as they reached the bottom of a wide stone staircase lined in lush potted ferns. "There are tons of tourists who come here. If we just follow the crowds, they should lead us to a place."

He was trying to remember where he and Jeb had stayed, but couldn't recall the exact name or location. It had been in one of the plazas, surrounded by elegant spires, the air filled with music from busking musicians and the enthusiastic hollering of shopkeepers hoping to lure tourists into their stores and restaurants. Port Gnoll was almost exclusively a pedestrian city, the steep, cobbled streets and plethora of steps restricting vehicles to only the top few levels, where roads from the clifftop hills connected with the city infrastructure.

Gloucester pointed at a bevy of young people weighed down by large bags. Their luggage, combined with the wide-eyed looks they cast around at the scenery, marked them as tourists. "They seem like a likely bunch."

They started after the chattering group. Port Gnoll bustled with nighttime frivolity, tourists and locals mixing together under the streetlamps lining its twisting streets. Despite the ebony sky above, the thoroughfares were bright. Restaurant doors were thrown open in welcome, music and pleasant smells drifting out.

"Zane!"

The call came as such a surprise that Gloucester didn't even register it right away, only to stop in his tracks a few steps later as realization dawned. Was someone calling out to a friend who just happened to share Zane's name?

But even as he turned to look, he knew this wasn't the case. The voice was a familiar one and, sure enough, he was greeted by the sight of an equally familiar face.

A slender woman stood in the doorway of a nearby restaurant. Though the light spilling out shadowed her face in contrast, her features were still easy to discern. With a narrow face and high cheekbones, she exuded a reserved, delicate air, her honey blonde hair woven into a braid hanging over one shoulder. An oversized knitted sweater draped over her plain skirt, its bottom hem stained with the dust that blew through Port Gnoll from the hills beyond the cliffs.

Antimony Jones.

She stared at them with open relief. Usually Antimony was difficult to read, hiding her emotions behind a default expression of benign apathy. Now, however, she hurried down the steps from the restaurant and swept a stunned Zane into a hug, smiling broadly. "I was so worried."

"Antimony?" said Zane, clearly dumbfounded. "I—It's great to see you! But...how? What are you doing here? What are the chances?"

She stepped back, not a rejection of the hug, but to get a better look at her friend. The last time the three of them had seen Antimony was when everything went wrong in Frettchen. They'd hoped that the scientist, along with their other companions, had also gotten out of the city safely, and while the confirmation of this was cause for celebration, Gloucester had to agree with Zane's sentiment. What were the chances they would run into her like this?

"Pretty good, actually," Antimony said. "When you have a dream visit from Orange Ianto telling you to be here. Luckily we were only a few towns in from the coast. That Transportation spell dumped us in a little farming village a day's drive from here."

"We?" Gloucester repeated.

"The government boys and myself," Antimony explained. "Hello, Mr. Gloucester. I'm glad to see you're all right. And you, Mr. Finch." Now past the initial joy of seeing Zane, she was back to her usual calm self.

"So Mulligan and Harrison are with you, eh?" Finch snorted. "You didn't exactly win the lottery for company, did you? I'm surprised Mulligan hasn't been making a fuss in the media."

"He's laying low. We thought it best to avoid the storm of reporters who would want to hear from Frettchen's leader in this time of crisis. And considering the state of things, Mr. Harrison is, shall we say, quite concerned about his employer's safety."

"He would be," Gloucester agreed. This was a security agent's worst nightmare. The city under siege from an enemy of immeasurable power and his charge essentially on the run, stripped of resources and the safety of a home base.

"No sign of Purpurrot?" Finch asked Antimony, who shook her head solemnly.

"When I woke up, it was just the four of us in a very confused farmer's front garden. I'd hoped that you might have a better idea."

"Nah," Finch said. "It was the same for us. Woke up in the middle of nowhere, just us three. We've been traveling for days just to get this far north. Wherever the old goddess is, seems she's not with either of our little parties."

A muscle in his unshaven jaw twitched, betraying his worry. Gloucester knew Finch was no fan of Purpurrot or her godly kin, but it was clear he didn't like losing track of her either.

"Hold on," Zane cut in suddenly. "Antimony, you said the *four* of you. You and the government fellows..." She looked questioningly at Antimony. "Is Gear with you?"

Gloucester noticed for the first time that Antimony was carrying a large rucksack on her back, and she shifted uncomfortably now, as if it were quite heavy.

"We should probably go somewhere more private," was all she said.

—

As it turned out, it was less than a ten-minute walk to the hotel where Antimony and the others were staying.

"Orange Ianto told me to go to the train station in Port Gnoll, so we figured it would be best to find someplace close by to keep an eye on things," Antimony said as she led them down the narrow streets toward a busy plaza. She pointed across the wide space to one of the buildings opposite. "We're staying just there."

"*Just* there?" Zane repeated. Her stupefaction was well-founded. The motel they'd holed up in back in Trident's Point paled in comparison to the grandiose building for which Antimony was making a beeline. Heavily embellished spires pierced the sky above a beautiful stone facade. It looked like it had been inspired by the architecture of Frettchen's oldest churches, perhaps even built in the same era, and it reigned over the plaza like a palace.

"Yeah," said Antimony lightly. "It turns out Mr. Mulligan has expensive tastes. Luckily, he was able to access his bank accounts from a local branch."

"So much for laying low," Finch sniggered.

"I think all of the magic and mayhem shook him a little," she said with a touch of sympathy. "He needed a taste of familiarity. Which apparently means five-star accommodations. As long as he's careful not to shout about who he is or let too many people see his face, I think we're all right. And I can't say I'm too sorry to sleep in a nice bed and enjoy room service."

"That spell dumped me with the wrong group," Zane muttered.

—

The hotel's décor matched the grandeur of its facade. Gloucester could tell two things from the moment he stepped through the handsome double doors: 1) he would never be able to afford the place, and 2) Mulligan might actually be a genius for choosing to stay there. No one would ever expect to find someone laying low in a place like this.

Not that Denken was even hunting for them, necessarily. Judging from the state of Frettchen, Gloucester suspected the demigod had bigger fish to fry. Antimony was probably right—Mulligan wasn't only trying to stay away from immortals, but also the confused citizens of the Lower Lands. If anyone found out that Frettchen's lord was out and about, instead of trapped in his city like all of his people, he would surely be hounded day and night by journalists and civilians alike, demanding answers.

Finch gave a low whistle as they crossed the foyer's marble floor. Columns of polished stone stood sentinel along the walls. Paintings in gold-leafed frames hung between each one, depicting proud portraits and beautiful landscapes.

"It's been ages since I stayed in a place like this," he commented. "Maybe we should put off going to Pell for a few more days."

"Pell?" Antimony asked, glancing back at him. "Is that the next move, then? You know there are no trains heading north out of Pell now, right?"

"Of course," said Finch shortly. "Everyone knows that. That's why we're going to take a boat."

"To Frettchen?" Antimony slowed her steps to fall in beside them. Her pale eyebrows drew together just enough to faintly crease her brow.

"No," said Gloucester. "We're going to the Nordlands. Didn't Orange Ianto tell you in her message?"

Antimony shook her head. "She just said to watch the train station in Port Gnoll. Nothing else. Dream-walking isn't her specialty, so it's not the easiest for her to stay in another person's dream for long. My guess is she hopped between all of our minds, delivering what messages she could."

They entered the elevator, and Antimony pressed the button for one of the topmost floors. Gloucester noted that Mulligan had at least shown enough restraint not to stay in the penthouse. Perhaps Harrison had put his foot down.

"Not to mention," she continued thoughtfully, as gears ground to life above their heads, moving the elevator upward. "If Ianto's relying on one of her visions, it's entirely possible she doesn't know much more than we do. I've known her for a long time now, long enough to know that prophecies are rarely simple. She could be guiding us into places we need to be, without even knowing herself what she's setting us up for."

"That sounds ominous." Zane sighed. "Maybe I'm glad I didn't get a dream visit after all."

Despite this declaration, she still sounded a little miffed to be left out. Antimony laid a gentle hand on her arm.

"Maybe she knew you didn't need it," she told her. Gloucester guessed that this was little more than bracing words to make her feel better, but Zane smiled nonetheless.

The elevator dinged and slowed to a stop. The doors slid open to reveal a hallway lined in tasteful wallpaper and red-and-gold carpet. Closed doors trailed away in both directions. Antimony led them to the right, her footsteps muffled into silence by the thick carpet. Walking right behind her,

Gloucester thought he could hear a muted ticking of clockwork from the bag she carried.

"Anyway," Antimony was saying. "Clearly I was sent here so that I would run into you three. I suppose we're to head to the Nordlands together. For whatever reason. Not much of a game plan, really, but better to be walking forward blindly than standing still."

"Tell that to someone on a cliffside," Finch said. "But I agree. If the oracle's guiding us based on a vision, then we should be on the right path. Running into you tonight proves that. If we just follow her instructions, they'll lead us where we need to go."

Zane eyed Finch with raised brows. "That's a shockingly optimistic view from you."

"It's magic," he said simply. "I trust it."

Saints above, my life is weird, Gloucester thought. It wasn't until the others laughed that he realized he must have said the words aloud.

—

The hotel room was as nice as the rest of the place. Nowhere to be found were the generic landscapes that adorned the walls of the Trident's Point motel. In their place were eye-catching photographs of woodlands, which matched the color scheme of the room perfectly, all earthy tones of green, brown, and gray.

There were two good-sized beds made up neatly with plush blankets and a smaller third one that looked out of place, as if it had been added upon request. If Gloucester were to hazard a guess, he would say that bed was Harrison's. It was hard to imagine either Mulligan or Antimony giving up a better bed. Then again, when it came to Antimony, it was difficult to say for certain.

On the bed closest to the wide balcony windows, a stern-faced man in his forties sat reading. Light from the bedside lamp reflected off his horn-rimmed glasses. He glanced up from his novel when he heard them enter, and in an instant his demeanor went from bored to bewildered.

"You found them," he said, setting his book aside so distractedly that he didn't even notice when it tumbled off the edge of the bed. "I don't believe it!"

"Trust in Orange Ianto, didn't I say, Mr. Mulligan?" Antimony replied, setting her rucksack down carefully on the other big bed. "Where's Mr. Harrison?"

Mulligan shrugged. "He went out for another walk. So much for the trained patience of the elite security agents." He sighed. Somehow Gloucester doubted the politician had concern for his bodyguard's well-being on his mind. "I'm sure he'll be back soon. Hopefully with food."

"You could go and get it yourself," Zane pointed out waspishly.

"Easier said than done when you're the leader of a city currently under magical lockdown," Mulligan snapped back at her. "All it would take is one person recognizing me and then I'd be swarmed by paparazzi, all hounding me for answers."

"He's not wrong," Gloucester told Zane, who glowered at him.

"I know," she said shortly. Gloucester kept his mouth shut this time. Zane was the closest thing he had to a best friend these days. Best not to put that in jeopardy defending someone like Mulligan.

"Right! Anyway. The gang's all back together." Finch clapped his hands, speaking loudly enough to cut through the burgeoning tension. "Well, more so than before. So where's your killer automaton?" he asked Antimony.

She offered him an unimpressed stare, which lasted just a few seconds longer than necessary, enough to make it clear that the tone of his question was not appreciated.

When they'd all first been introduced to Gear, the half-human, half-clockwork woman Antimony created, calling her a killer would have felt like a joke. She was the epitome of innocence, greeting every new face and experience with open curiosity. Antimony kept insisting Gear could be their secret weapon against Denken, as her metallic brain made her immune to the demigod's powers, yet imagining her as any sort of weapon had been practically laughable. She was like a little kid, experiencing everything for the first time and finding only joy in all of it.

Until the Gambler got hurt. Gear had quickly taken a shine to the personification of Choice, a fondness that appeared to be mutual, and when they'd found the demigod worse for wear after his battle with Denken, they'd all borne witness to a brand-new side of Gear. As she attacked Denken, her face, usually warm with a smile, had been cold as the metal click-clicking in her clockwork skull. With that memory engraved in all of their minds, "killer" seemed much more fitting now.

Antimony, however, obviously didn't share that feeling.

"That's where things are a little less celebratory," she told Finch coolly. She placed her hand on the rucksack. From the way it sank into the blanket, it weighed a lot. Gloucester could still hear ticking from within, and a sudden, horrible realization dawned on him.

"Oh no," he breathed. "Please tell me that's not..."

Mulligan grimaced, eyeing the bag with distaste. "I wish I could."

From the looks on Zane's and Finch's faces, they were reaching the same conclusion.

"Oh no," Zane echoed. "What happened?"

Antimony sighed. "The Teleportation spell. I think Gear must have been struggling against it a lot. And, well, you know how resistant she is to the immortals' magic. I suppose we should be relieved it worked on her at all."

"Are you sure 'relieved' is the right word?" Finch asked, managing wry humor despite the mild horror in his voice. He, like the rest of them, was staring at the rucksack as Antimony pulled it open. She reached in and pulled out—

"Oh, hello again!"

The head of Gear smiled at them from Antimony's hands, unfazed by the fact that it no longer had a body attached.

Chapter 4

In Pieces

"Aaarghh!" Zane yelped, leaping back so quickly she nearly fell. Next to her, Finch let out a string of profanities before erupting into laughter. Gloucester's stomach did an uncomfortable somersault and, like Zane, he took an involuntary step backward. No matter how much strangeness he witnessed, he didn't think he'd ever get to the point where a friendly greeting from a disembodied head would be anything other than extremely unsettling.

"Hello, er, Gear," he said.

Gear's eyes settled on him and her smile widened. "Gloucester! You're all okay! I'm glad. Antimony was really worried. I think Mr. Harrison and Mr. Mulligan were as well, though I don't get to talk to them often."

"You're not missing much," Antimony said. Mulligan sent her an affronted scowl, which she ignored.

She placed Gear's head down on a pillow with care. Gear beamed up at her, though her good cheer took on a strained edge as she cast her eyes around the room, accompanied by a noticeable uptick in the spinning gears inside her skull.

"Is the Gambler with you?" she asked the newcomers.

Gloucester shook his head, and her smile wilted. "Sorry, Gear. We think he's back in Frettchen." He didn't have the heart to describe the Gambler's current state to her.

To her credit, Gear was quick to put on a brave face. "Antimony said that too." She sighed. "But I still hoped..."

Zane moved toward the bed and gave Gear a gentle pat on the head, careful not to knock her from the pillow. "That's totally fair, Gear. Don't worry, we'll get to him somehow. You'll see him again."

She exchanged a quick, worried glance with Gloucester. Gear had been upset enough about the Gambler just being injured. How might she react to the form he was in now?

"You weren't joking when you said she didn't take to the Transportation spell well," Finch said, changing the subject. An unsteady warble shook his words, and when Gloucester looked over, it was apparent he was holding in more laughter. Gloucester elbowed him in the side and he cleared his throat, regaining some composure.

"It could have been a lot worse," Antimony said silkily. She reached into the bag again and pulled forth a large silver key on a string. "I believe this saved her. Lucienne's Protection spells are powerful. If Gear hadn't been wearing this, I don't think she would have survived the Transportation at all." She stowed the key back into the rucksack.

Finch eyed the bag. "Is there more of her in there?"

Antimony nodded, but thankfully didn't feel the need to show them. "We were able to scrounge up most of her pieces. Without the proper resources, though, putting her back together will be impossible. I need my lab. Which doesn't seem likely to be accessible any time soon." She dropped her gaze, hooded eyes downcast and lips twitching into a forlorn frown.

"I don't mind," Gear reassured her from her perch on the pillow. "It's not so bad. Though it does get a bit boring, being in the bag all the time."

"I can imagine," Gloucester said in heartfelt agreement. Solitary confinement had been terrible, but at least his head had still been attached to his body.

"We'll get you fixed." Antimony smiled down at Gear with renewed determination, before echoing Zane's earlier words: "Don't worry."

"All the more reason to set things right in Frettchen, then." Zane crossed her arms decisively. Eager to cheer Antimony up, she already looked much more composed than she had a few moments earlier. Gloucester admired her ability to roll with the weird punches. Then again, she'd had a lot more practice than he had, considering how long she'd known about magic.

"Yeah," added Finch with an enthusiasm too chipper to be genuine. "Just in case saving a whole city of people and quite possibly the entire world wasn't enough reason for any of us."

Gloucester rolled his eyes while Zane directed a rude gesture at Finch. On the far side of the room, Mulligan planted his hands on his hips, voice rising in a snarky retort. Antimony's reply to him was patient, but Gloucester wasn't paying attention to any of their actual words. They didn't have time to let their conversation dissolve into bickering.

"Enough!" he snapped. His single word was sharp enough to catch the attention of everyone in the room. "There's no point in us all standing around arguing like children. Orange Ianto told us to head north, so that's what we're doing. If she meant for you to meet us here, then you're supposed to come with us. We're all agreed on that, right?"

He looked from Finch and Zane to Mulligan, Gear, and finally Antimony, who offered a thin smile.

"I'm not sure what we're supposed to be looking for, but it'll be nice to be on the move," she said. "Waiting for you here has given me far too much time to think."

Mulligan sighed. "I can't say that this 'fly by the seat of our pants,' 'make it up as we go along' nonsense is okay with me, but I agree it's better than nothing. So..." He squinted shrewdly at Gloucester. "What's the next move?"

Why ask me? Gloucester wanted to demand. He wasn't the leader of their little crew. That job surely belonged with someone who knew what they were doing, even just a little. Like Finch, with his knowledge of all things magical, or Antimony, considering her connection with the immortals. Even Mulligan was probably a better choice, being an actual official head-of-state.

And yet, they were all watching him expectantly. Gloucester cleared his throat, befuddled and uncomfortable, and did his best to answer the question:

"No trains to Pell leave until morning, so we'll spend the night here," he said. "Once we get there, we have to find a ship to take us up the coast. If we play our cards right, that might be a handy time to let people know who you are," he added to Mulligan. The politician winced, displeased with the idea. "Even as the interim lord of Frettchen, people might listen to you. Possibly enough to let us onto their ship."

"Might?" repeated Mulligan indignantly. Gloucester ignored him.

"Or they might tear him apart for what happened to the city," Finch chimed in, suggesting the possibility with a notable amount of cheer. "It doesn't exactly look great, him somehow safe and sound while Frettchen's gone to hell in a handbasket. And with Denken's influence spreading, who knows what people might do."

"Fair point," Gloucester admitted, though he narrowed his eyes at Finch in wordless warning. "But not really helpful. We can see what sort of a state Pell is in before we decide on which approach to take."

"Yes, boss."

Finch was grinning. Gloucester wondered how one man could make him want to smack him and laugh at the same time.

"What's a ship?" Gear asked. Her eyes shone with eager curiosity, but there was no shaking how bizarre she looked on her pillow. Unable to turn her head, her gaze flicked over each of them in turn. "Is it like a car?"

As an automaton created in Antimony's lab, Gear didn't know about a great many things yet, but she was always excited to learn. It hadn't taken long for Gloucester to realize that confusing Gear's ignorance and naivety for stupidity was a mistake. She was quick to pick up on new concepts, and her excellent memory meant she made connections just as swiftly.

"Sort of," Antimony said. "It's another type of vehicle. Where cars allow you to travel across land, ships take you across water."

Gear's eyes widened. "Oooh, that's amazing." Her enthusiasm took its toll, and the shifting of her head as she bobbed in excitement made it topple from its perch. "Whoa!" she cried out, alarmed.

"This is us," Zane murmured, so quietly only Gloucester heard. "The dream team." Amusement and worry were at war in her eyes. She caught his glance and tried for a smile. "Things aren't looking great, are they?"

Gloucester shrugged. "We're better off than we were before. That should count for something."

—

It would have been a crowded hotel room that night, but Mulligan was so opposed to sharing the suite with all of them that he grudgingly paid for another room. Gloucester, Zane, and Finch were quick to note that it was significantly smaller and less ornate than the one he was sharing with his half of the party, but after the long train voyage, none of them felt like raising the issue.

It was still nicer than anywhere they could have afforded, anyway. A small but well-stocked kitchenette resided by the wide window. The bathroom was tiled in shining porcelain, with a vast claw-foot tub that called out tantalizingly to Gloucester, who couldn't remember the last time he'd had a bath. He made a mental note to take one in the morning, too tired now to think of much beyond falling into bed.

Therein lay the problem. There were only two beds.

In their previous lodgings, they'd found a small cot stowed in the closet and taken turns sleeping on this less-comfortable option. A quick inspection of their new room revealed no extra mattress, just some spare sheets, pillows, and duvets in the linen closet.

"I can take the floor," Gloucester offered, reaching into the closet for the extra bedclothes. "I don't mind."

"Nonsense," said Zane. "We all deserve a comfortable mattress after bumping about on trains for the last few days. You can share with one of us."

"I'm an excellent bed partner," Finch volunteered, waggling his brows. "Just putting that out there. In the most innocent sense, of course. I don't kick or flail or steal the blankets." He ticked his virtues off on his fingers.

Zane snorted. "Beats me on all fronts, then."

"In all not innocent senses, too," Finch added in a stage whisper. Zane rolled her eyes and Gloucester chuckled, though he glanced uncertainly at the clockmaker.

"Are you sure you're all right with it?" he asked.

She waved away his concern. "I'm asexual, not a prude. I'm not gonna have a heart attack because two men are sleeping in the same bed, long as you remember I'm right here in the room with you. Beats me having someone sleep in my bed with me. No offense."

"None taken," said Gloucester and Finch together.

As they took off their shoes and Finch disappeared into the bathroom, the brief joviality of the moment faded. Gloucester sat down on the edge of a bed and heaved a sigh.

"Gear seems back to her old self," he said to Zane. "Well, as old a self as she can have, I s'pose."

Zane frowned, mirroring him as she sat on the other bed. "Yeah. Makes it sort of hard to believe she went all murder-y, eh?"

"Do you think she'll get like that again? If we manage to get into Frettchen... I mean, it doesn't look like the Gambler's in a very good state, and if that's some sort of trigger for her..."

Zane echoed his sigh. "Good question. Wish I could answer it. Back in the Maze, I think Purpurrot was getting through to her, though. Maybe she did learn from it. Learning does seem to be her strong point."

Gloucester hummed in tentative agreement. Thinking back to the cold anger on Gear's face as she'd driven a knife into Denken's throat, he hoped Zane was right. That wasn't something he ever wanted to see again.

—

The beds were indeed comfortable. Gloucester had scarcely laid his head to rest on the soft pillow when sleep closed in. As the edges of his vision turned dark and his eyelids grew heavy, he turned his face toward Finch lying beside him.

In the moonlight from the window, he could see the magician clearly. He was sleeping on his back, his eyes closed and arms crossed loosely atop the sheet. Though Gloucester couldn't tell if he was already asleep or not, he looked more still than he ever was during the day. The pale light gave his fair skin a ghostly hue and turned his dark red hair almost black, a creature of highlight and shadow. A fitting description for the enigmatic magician, who was so often full of contrasts. Light and dark. Good and bad. Powerful and vulnerable.

Gloucester was tempted to reach out the short distance to touch him, to brush his fingertips lightly across his freckled cheek. It was something he'd often done with Jeb, back when he'd been a security agent and gotten home from a late shift. Jeb would already be asleep, and Gloucester would take a moment to marvel at his peaceful beauty.

Finch wasn't Jeb, though. And Gloucester himself had been different back then. That sort of casually loving touch had once felt natural and easy; now his guard came up when anyone touched him. After contemplating Finch's motionless face for a moment longer, he sighed quietly and closed his eyes.

—

The next morning, he awoke with the sun, which slanted through the windows to warm his face. It was pleasant at first, but after a few minutes the light was too bright in his eyes, even closed, and he sat up with a yawn.

Beside him, Finch remained asleep. There was no question of this now, as he was snoring lightly, even drooling a little onto his pillow. Gloucester wrinkled his nose, but found it more funny than disgusting. On the other bed, Zane was a motionless lump of blankets.

While his friends enjoyed having a lie-in, Gloucester had always been an early riser. He got out of bed as quietly as he could and moved to an open space of floor to do his morning stretches. He'd always enjoyed exercise, but it took his time in prison to shape his current routine. There hadn't been a lot of space in his cell, so he'd grown accustomed to stretches and conditioning he could do in a relatively cramped area: crunches, sit-ups, push-ups, and a series of arm, leg, and back stretches to keep him as limber and fit as possible.

For when I get out, he'd always told himself. Of course, as the days turned to weeks and then to months, the routine became less about freedom or escape and more to keep the boredom and despair at bay. To do *something*. It was one of the only ways to clear his head, and the habit had stuck even after his release.

Twenty minutes later, he'd worked up a light sweat and the other two were stirring from their slumber. Gloucester checked the clock on the table as he slid his protective rings back onto his hand: 6:45. Still quite early. Earlier than he imagined either Zane or Finch wanted to be awake, but their schedule over the last several days had involved catching the earliest trains they could in order to travel as far as they were able. Even the hotel's soft beds couldn't shake them from the urgency of their mission.

"Ugh." Zane glared with bleary resignation at the rosy sky through the window. "Just once I'd like morning not to bloody arrive."

"That sounds bleak," Gloucester joked, crossing the room to the small kitchenette. He had a feeling caffeine would be required shortly. Turning on the kettle, he then headed for the bathroom and the prospect of a luxurious, if quick, bath.

"Spoken like a morning person," Zane grumbled.

In the other bed, Finch was snoring again.

—

Despite his companions' begrudging awakenings, it wasn't long before Gloucester once again stood in Antimony's room, the day to come at the forefront of his mind. Less than an hour had passed, and though Finch and Zane were still yawning and grouchy, they stood alongside him. For his part, Gloucester felt more refreshed than he had in a while. Hair still damp from his bath, he held a glass of cool water in his hand. Outside, the morning was already warming into another sunny southern day.

Antimony sat on her bed, Gear's head on her lap. The only hint that she had been asleep recently was the haphazardness of her hair, which was twisted up into a messy bun. At the desk, Mulligan scowled at everyone over his steepled fingers.

Considering this attitude was typical of the politician, Gloucester paid him little mind.

One new addition to their company was Harrison, who had let them into the room and was now trying unsuccessfully to catch Zane's eye. The security agent had developed a soft spot for her from the first time they'd met. Whether intentionally or not, Zane hadn't seemed to notice.

"So it's agreed, then," Antimony said once they'd all exchanged their good-mornings. "We head for Pell."

"And from there, the Nordlands," Gloucester confirmed. He just wished he knew why.

"Whatever is there, I hope it works." Harrison gave up vying for a smile from Zane and turned his attention to the group as a whole. "Walking around last night... You can feel the anxiety in the people here. It feels like—"

"—like Frettchen," Finch finished. "Yeah. Consider it the first ripple of Denken's power spreading out. His anger and fear whispering into people's thoughts, even way out here. I reckon the cities closest to the border will soon see a fun little uptick in violence and crime, just like in Frettchen after the high minister died."

Uncomfortable silence filled the room.

"Right, then." Mulligan clapped his hands sharply as he got to his feet. "To the train station. Come on, chop chop!"

"Chop chop!" echoed Gear's head with a laugh.

Chapter 5

Kinsella

It was a four-hour train ride to the city of Pell, away from the tall cliffs of Port Gnoll and through rolling, grassy hills. They had a compartment to themselves, yet despite the privacy, none of them felt much like talking. Zane and Finch snoozed through most of the trip, leaving Gloucester in the less-than-talkative company of Antimony, Mulligan, and Harrison. He spent his time watching the Lower Lands' wilderness pass by outside, the steady rumble of the rails playing the same meditative role as the hum of his motorcycle.

Eventually the tracks brought them back to the coastline. Unlike the stone cliffs of the previous city, here the steep slope of hills led to sandy beaches and sprawling harbors.

Where Port Gnoll was a tourist town, Pell was a working city, bustling with trade and a roaring fishing industry. Like their previous stop, the train station was located near the top of a sloping cityscape, but instead of the streets zig-zagging sharply down a steep cliff-face, the roads here descended more gently toward the sea. The city itself extended far out onto the water, the harbor district like a miniature town on stilts. Long blocks of warehouses and shops stretched out to sea, the city's avenues of stone and pavement replaced by canals and bridges. Beyond these were the endless docks, to which hundreds of ships and boats of all sizes were moored.

This vast semi-aquatic metropolis was visible from almost everywhere in Pell. Gloucester found it difficult not to stare as they made their way toward it down the streets. Coming from a small, land-locked village, he'd always thought the harbor in Frettchen was amazing, but this place put it to shame. As he walked, he pulled Denken's tooth from his pocket, grounding himself with the gentle press of its serrated edges against his palm.

"If we can't find at least *one* ship down there that'll take us north, I think it might be a lost cause," he said, shading his eyes as he took in the view. The sun was near its peak, the light reflecting off the water utterly blinding.

"Then let's get down there and get this over with," Mulligan said brusquely.

The lord of Frettchen had forsaken his usual sharp suit in favor of a more pragmatic outfit, for both the weather and the endeavor to attract less attention. In place of a jacket and tie, he wore a light button-down in an airy fabric. A line of tiny embroidered parrots flapped colorful wings across the front.

The effect of seeing him in such casual attire was quite jarring. When he'd met them in the hotel lobby earlier that morning, Gloucester had to resist a laugh. It was just so strikingly unlike him that it felt rather like seeing a fish walk on land. Taking in the outfits worn by the locals, however, he could appreciate that Mulligan had made a good choice, as most of the people they passed were dressed in much the same fashion. Gloucester himself had long since packed away the long-sleeved shirt Antimony lent him back in Frettchen and stuck instead to a loose T-shirt he'd picked up in Trident's Point, along with lightweight trousers that breathed far more easily than jeans.

Harrison had also deigned to dress more casually. Unfortunately, being taller and brawnier than almost everyone around him made it difficult to fade into the background, no matter how much he might try. He did his best to stay close to Mulligan without making his role as a bodyguard obvious.

"Off we go, then," Antimony said, striding forward to lead the way. "The Old Harbor has the most northbound ships, if I remember correctly."

She pointed down toward the water directly in front of them. The canals there were lined with buildings made mostly of stone, instead of wood or brick. Gloucester spotted the bell tower of a church, its walls striped in different-colored stone, lending it a decorative appearance.

"You've been to Pell before?" he asked, as she had spoken with a sense of familiarity. Sure enough, she nodded.

"I've been to a lot of places, Mr. Gloucester. But I lived in Pell for a number of years." She spoke with gentle fondness and a touch of wistfulness. "My girlfriend at the time and I lived just on the edge of the Old Harbor. It really is a beautiful city."

Antimony led the way down toward the water, Mulligan at her flank, with Harrison walking alongside him. Zane fell into step beside Antimony, chatting with her quietly. From the bag slung across Antimony's back emanated the faint clicking of Gear's clockwork.

This left Gloucester and Finch to take up the rear. They walked in companionable silence, interrupted only by a gentle tune Finch whistled to himself.

Though Gloucester was growing reaccustomed to the hustle and bustle of daily life, excesses of noise and activity still tended to overwhelm him. Tuning it all out just created a sort of vacuum in his mind, however, demanding to be filled with questions and worries and unwanted thoughts. So he was doing his best to combat such over-stimulation by engaging with it on his own terms. Instead of letting his senses be drowned in a great confusing wave of sights and sounds and smells, he tried to pick up on details: the scent of the ocean, the colorful clothing of a passerby, the snippet of conversation outside a shop.

Unfortunately, this did little to help his nerves. Uneasiness slunk through the city like an invisible force, sliding into every conversation Gloucester overheard and each interaction he witnessed. Enough people were speaking Frettchennian for him to pick up on the latest news amidst all the gossip, and little of it was good. Several people fretted over strange nightmares, voices laden with palpable anxiety. Gloucester heard more than one person weeping, lamenting loved ones lost in Frettchen. Worse still, people were now vanishing further and further away from Frettchen's border. Just that morning, the newspapers reported an entire village an hour south of the city had gone silent, unreachable by any attempted means. The danger was spreading.

"It is a beautiful city," Finch said, abandoning his whistled song and pulling Gloucester from his fretful thoughts.

"Have you been here before?" he asked.

"A few times, yeah. Never for very long. There's a city a few hours inland where we lived for a year or two. We used to do business here from time to time. Leastways, that was Dad's excuse. He had an on-again, off-again thing going with a witch in the fish market district." Finch laughed, but his smile quickly grew wan.

Gloucester could guess why. Finch's whole life had been just him and his father, whose death was still all too recent. He hesitated, then laid a hand on Finch's arm.

"Zane told me the other day that her parents and sister live in one of the inland cities here in the south," he said, hoping to distract Finch with conversation. "I'm starting to feel like the only one who's out of his element." He made a face and added, "Well, I say that, but I've felt out of my element for ages now. Being the only one without a clue is sort of becoming my thing."

His self-deprecating laugh was carried on a sigh. He couldn't say it was a feeling he enjoyed.

It was Finch's turn to offer a pat on the shoulder. "If it's any consolation, I think you have the charming Toby Mulligan up there as company," he said, emphatically sincere. His sober expression soon broke into a smile. "Gods help you."

"That saying has a whole new meaning now."

As they neared the docks, Gloucester became grateful for the sea breeze blowing in, keeping the worst of the heat at bay. They reached the Old Harbor under a cloudless blue sky marked by wheeling seabirds. The gulls' cries pierced the air, interspersed with the creaking of ships and the gentle lapping of water. In dockside markets, fishermen and their families regarded those who passed their stalls with the same sharp gaze as the birds soaring above, calling out their prices in a mish-mash of languages and dialects, hoping to make good money off their catches.

Business wasn't the only thing on people's tongues. Here, too, gossip pervaded. In one stall they passed, a man with more grizzled beard than discernible face was trying to explain to a burly, tattooed woman in a wide-brimmed hat how a freak electrical storm caused the strange Frettchennian blackout. A young boy tugged on his sleeve, asking if giant flying sharks were real.

Hardly bothering to look up from the fish she gutted, the woman countered that it was a disease outbreak, coupled with some sort of government cover-up. It made for a strange mix, these people going about their daily lives under the weight of this unprecedented strangeness.

They made their way along the docks until they reached the largest ships, moored the furthest out from land. They steered clear of the freighters, who would have little interest in taking on passengers even at the best of times, and decided to try their luck first with the big fishing boats, privately owned yachts, and mid-range trade ships.

After hollering up at several to no response, or receiving impatient dismissals from suspicious sailors, they came upon a promising cargo ship. A Nordish flag hung from its bow, depicting golden mountains set against a field of blue. Gloucester recognized it as the flag of Thormund-Dul, a coastal metropolis that dealt heavily in trade with the South Cities and Frettchen alike. Beneath the flag, the head of a fluffy black cat was painted on the hull near the prow, its yellow eyes mischievous and its mouth open in a feline grin. Gloucester wondered if it was an ode to a particular cat or just a symbol for good fortune. Cats were plentiful and well-liked in the Nordlands, considered to be lucky.

"Ho there!" Finch called up to the deck, hands cupped around his mouth.

"Ho there?" echoed Zane, snickering.

Finch brushed aside her mockery with ease. "Nothing wrong with changing it up a bit. I've got a good feeling about this one." He returned his attention to the ship. "Is anyone aboard?" he shouted.

There was a long pause, then they heard the repetitive thud of approaching footsteps. "There's always someone aboard," came a voice from above. "Who's asking?"

A moment later, a head came into view, followed by shoulders and a pair of arms as the sailor leaned against the ship's railing. The woman, perhaps in her mid-thirties, had a sun-weathered face behind a pair of thick-framed glasses and coppery brown hair, mostly hidden beneath a wide-brimmed hat that shaded her face. She eyed them all with cautious curiosity.

"We're looking for passage to the Nordlands. Any of the coastal cities will do. Is your ship taking passengers?" Finch asked.

Out of all of them, he was the most at ease on the docks, so the others kept quiet and allowed him to do the talking. The only one irked by this was Mulligan. All it took was one look at his pinched frown for Gloucester to know the new lord of Frettchen was struggling with the temptation to take control of the conversation. Antimony sent him a stern look, however, and to Gloucester's surprise, Mulligan kept his mouth shut.

"Mayhaps," said the sailor. "Depends on the passengers. And how heavy their wallets are." Her words carried a similar accent to Finch's, marking her as a West Islander.

At the mention of money, Mulligan did speak up. "They feel very heavy at the moment," he said dryly. "I imagine they'll be nice and light by the time we reach our destination."

"Mayhaps," said the woman again, accompanied by a laugh this time. "Come aboard. We'll talk business."

"Are you the captain?" Finch asked. "We don't want to end up stowaways."

The sailor's hearty guffaw defied her slim frame. "Not to worry, chum. You're looking at the captain of this sorry tub."

As she spoke, she waved her hand in a beckoning motion. She guided them toward the ship's gangway and met them at the top of it.

"Captain Remy Kinsella," she said, sticking out her hand toward Finch, who was the first to step foot onto the deck.

Up close, Captain Kinsella's build, which had merely appeared lean from the dock, was revealed to be diminutive. Gloucester would be surprised if she measured at more than an even five feet tall. She was hardly what his mind conjured up when he imagined a hardy sea captain.

"Cassus Finch," the magician replied, shaking her hand. "A pleasure to meet you. And this is Mikalai Gloucester, Zane Zephyr, Antimony Jones, Anthony Harrison, and Jeremiah Montague."

He pointed to each of his companions in turn, ending with Mulligan, who covered his surprise at the false name with admirable swiftness. Gloucester wondered if Finch had come up with the moniker on the train ride or if he was simply that good at inventing lies on the spot. Neither case would surprise him.

As for Harrison, Gloucester realized he had no idea if the first name Finch had given was another lie or not, as he'd never heard Harrison referred to as anything other than his surname. It was possible that Finch, who had worked for the high minister alongside his father for over a year, might know more about the other security agent than Gloucester did.

"A pleasure to meet all of you," said Captain Kinsella, letting go of Finch's hand and offering the rest of them a friendly tilt of the head in greeting. Her smile soon faded, however. "And what business do you lot have in the Nordlands?"

Finch and Mulligan exchanged a glance, but Gloucester spoke up before either of them could devise a suitable lie.

"Heading home," he said. "I'm from there. Normally we'd just take the trains, but..." He let his explanation end there, knowing further details weren't necessary.

Sure enough, Kinsella nodded gravely. She fixed him with a scrutinizing look, and for a moment he caught a glimpse of a serious mind behind the captain's friendliness and disarming stature. "Aye," she said finally. "I can hear the accent. Not very strong, though. Been away from home a long time?"

"Too long." Bilingualism meant his accent in both Nordish and Frettchennian had always been slight, but Gloucester didn't think that mattered enough to explain to someone they'd just met. Anyway, it really did feel like too long since he'd last been home.

Kinsella's gaze softened into sympathy. "Well, they say going home isn't easy, but right now it might just be impossible." She grimaced at their disappointed expressions. "I'd love to help you out, really. I'm dead curious what a rag-tag bunch like you is all headed home for, too. Can't say it looks like a family reunion, all considered. But I've not taken *The Jem* northward since the fall of Frettchen, and I can't say I will until whatever it is what's happening in the city passes. To be honest, you'll be hard-pressed to find anyone who will. Seafolk are a superstitious bunch. People reckon Frettchen is cursed, and no one wants to have that carried onto their ship for passing too close."

Zane made a noise in the back of her throat somewhere between a scoff and a groan, and Harrison sighed, but Finch merely cocked his head to one side. He considered Kinsella keenly.

"Must be hard on business," he said. He pointed toward the bow of the ship, where the Nordish flag swayed in the breeze. "Cut off from your supply route. Sooner or later you're going to have to take the risk or lose all Nordish business. Can't imagine that's easy to afford."

"Nah, it isn't," Captain Kinsella agreed, matching the glint in Finch's eye with one of her own. "But my business is hardly your concern. You're all mighty desperate to get home. Why is that?"

"It's home," said Gloucester. "And if you need more reason than that, well, my family is there, with a great whopping city under some sort of a curse between them and me."

The words came out with rather more vehemence than he intended, but the passion wasn't without reward: Kinsella blinked owlishly at him, then raised her hands in gentle defeat.

"Fair enough," she said. "I'm still curious about the entourage, but I'll buy that you want to get back to your family. Unfortunately, none of that changes the fact that I don't want to risk my crew or my ship, sailing it past the fallen city."

"What would it cost to mitigate that risk, Captain?" Mulligan asked.

Kinsella turned her gaze on him, and for a prolonged moment she said nothing. Gloucester held his breath, waiting for recognition to spark in the tiny woman's eyes and for a volley of accusations to fly through the air.

Yet none came. Instead, the moment passed and a sweet smile spread across Kinsella's features. "Are you asking me to name my price?" she asked.

Already Mulligan looked full of regret. "Within reason. There are other ship captains we could ask, after all."

"Who would charge you much the same, mate," she countered. "Or just rob you blind. I'll not demand what I'm not due for the risk I'd be taking. Fair is fair is fair."

Finch chuckled. "Fair is fair is fair," he echoed. "My dad used to say that all the time."

Captain Kinsella regarded him with notably more warmth than Mulligan had received. "Aye, you've the Islands in your voice. Whereabouts are you from, then?"

He grinned. "Cyclops Stone. Wee little place. Chances are you haven't even—"

"—heard of it," she finished with a laugh. "Nah, can't say I have. Then again, you could sail through the Islands all your life and never see them all. Shock as it may be to Mainlanders," she added, twinkling eyes darting toward the rest of the group.

It was a fair point. The Western Isles were a series of islands off the coast of the Lower Lands, ranging in size and importance. Little was known about them on the mainland, from how many there were to all of their names. The Isles depended on the Lower Lands to survive, but most people in Frettchen and the outlying regions paid them little mind.

"Judging from the accent, I'm going to hazard a guess and say you're from Bestin," Finch said, rubbing his chin shrewdly. "One of the biggest islands," he added as an aside to the others. "Close as you get to a big city out on the sea."

"And what a shining city it is." Kinsella laughed. "Got it in one. Can't help that I've a more refined way with words than you yokels from the wee rocks."

"Yokels with rich friends," he reminded her. "So? D'you think you could be persuaded to risk the curse? You could always go further out to sea. You know, if you're scared."

Kinsella's eyes narrowed behind her glasses. Gloucester guessed there was a battle of interests going on in her head. Finally she sighed, a short, sharp sound of defeat.

"I know when I'm being goaded," she said. "Just like I know when I'm being bribed. I'd like to say no just for that, but truth is I don't want to turn my back on good money. 'Specially with a hold full of salted fish and silks the southerners aren't about to buy right back from me. The crew will appreciate the bonus, too, even if they grumble about it. Grumbling is what they do best, anyway. This curse thing is just giving them a solid excuse for it."

"This better be a small crew," Mulligan muttered. Despite his own grumbling, he looked resigned to the idea of parting with a lot of his money. "I hope you know a good bank nearby."

"Surely do," she assured him with a puckish grin. "I'll escort you myself before we head out to sea. This is going to be a 'payment first' sort of deal."

He clicked his tongue in an indignant manner, as if aghast she would suggest foul play on his part, but otherwise his composure didn't falter. "Fine. We're in a hurry, though, and want to set out as soon as possible. If you've nothing better to do at the moment than take my money, let's get this over with."

Kinsella stepped forward and slung a jovial arm around Mulligan's back, steering him back toward the gangway and the dock below. "Righty-o, Mr. Montague! To the bank we go. And on the way, let's talk numbers."

Chapter 6

Like Old Times

An afternoon of forced patience followed. Zane Zephyr hated it. She wasn't, in her own opinion, an impatient sort of person generally, but the unshakable feeling of what her father called "hurry up and wait" was doing her head in. It felt awful, just sitting around while the fate of the world hung in the balance, even if she knew there wasn't anything she could do to speed things up.

She could tell the others felt the same. In the wake of their meeting with Captain Kinsella, Finch announced he was going busking, to earn what money he could by entertaining tourists and fishermen in the Old Harbor with showy magic tricks. Zane expected Gloucester to accompany him, as he seemed to enjoy watching the magician in his element. He'd certainly looked tempted, dark eyes lingering on Finch's back as the other man peeled away from the group and headed for the hubbub of the dockside market. He didn't follow, however, and she hadn't bothered asking him why. She could hazard a guess. Finch had far greater tolerance for crowds than Gloucester did. She suspected he was eager to find somewhere quiet to collect his thoughts.

While Harrison and Mulligan went off with Kinsella to arrange payment for their upcoming voyage, Zane, Gloucester, and Antimony were left with the task of finding overnight lodgings. Antimony claimed to know a good place and gave the others directions to follow once their business was completed.

The inn was noticeably less grandiose than the previous hotel, but Zane decided she much preferred it. It was a relatively small building, with white brick walls swathed in ivy, and the welcoming smile of the innkeeper that came for free. Here, at least, she didn't feel like they might get tossed out for not wearing the right designer socks or something.

After an hour, restlessness pulled Gloucester back to his feet and out into the city. He excused himself politely, slipping from the hotel room with the quick excuse of going for a walk. Zane watched him go from where she and Antimony huddled together over Gear's disassembled body. All of the body pieces Antimony had been able to find were laid out across one of the bedspreads, so that they could inventory what remained and what was salvageable.

"Be careful," she called after Gloucester. She was tempted to urge him to stay—it was safe here in the room, and she hadn't forgotten the time Denken snatched him off the street in Frettchen when he'd gone wandering—but she bit her tongue. He needed his space. She also hadn't forgotten the accusations Finch had thrown her way, claiming she was doing Gloucester no favors with her overbearing protectiveness. Much of that had been Denken's influence ramping up her worries, but she still bore it in mind. Gloucester was her friend, but he was also an adult, capable of making his own choices.

So she left him to it. Saints knew she had enough on her own mind to deal with. The problem of Gear provided excellent distraction, and she was keen to do *something* useful. She turned her thoughts away from one friend and back onto another.

"Well, Gear's secondary movement is definitely kaput," she told Antimony. "I reckon we'll be able to salvage a good amount of its parts, but the balance wheel is done for and a lot of the gears are missing."

"Is that bad?" Propped up on a pillow, Gear's head watched Zane and Antimony with wide eyes. "Am I going to be okay?"

Antimony ran a comforting hand through Gear's short brown hair. "You'll be fine. We just have to get a sense of what's needed to fix you, that's all." Despite the reassurance, a muscle twitched in the scientist's jaw, betraying her own worries.

"Exactly," said Zane, eager to ease both of their minds. "The important thing is that your central movement is intact." She pointed at the complex mechanism encased within Gear's skull. "If that had gotten broken, we'd be in a much worse spot!"

An understatement. If her cerebral clockwork had been destroyed, Zane was positive the automaton wouldn't have survived. Even if they rebuilt her, there would be no guarantee she'd return as the same person.

"I think Lucienne's enchanted key is to thank for that," Antimony mused, some of the tension leaving her face. "Having it around Gear's neck like that. I'll have to remember to thank her when all's said and done."

That is, if *all gets said and done. If we don't fail.* These words went unspoken. Antimony's jaw twitched again. Zane didn't think she'd have noticed if she didn't know her so well.

"Setting aside all the, you know, potential apocalypse stuff, this feels a bit like old times," she said, with as much joviality as she could scrounge up. "Me and you working on clockwork together. Figuring things out. Only this time Gear gets to weigh in too."

She smiled at Gear, who grinned back at her, previous concerns forgotten.

"I don't understand it much," Gear said. "But it's very interesting to see how I work. Do people often get to see all their bits and pieces like this?"

Zane snorted. "Hopefully not! The rest of us aren't as hard to break as you are. Speaking of, Antimony, what about her organic parts? The skin and other tissues?"

Antimony had managed to find quite a bit of Gear's body, but she was far from complete. One hand was missing, as was most of her left leg and a good chunk of her lower torso. The remaining patchwork skin was ragged, its neat stitching torn in dozens of places.

Surprisingly, Antimony didn't seem too worried about that. "Her organic components are all lab-grown. Once I have access to my workspace again, it won't be difficult to create the necessary replacements. It's the clockwork I'm more concerned about." The smile she offered Zane was warm and far more familiar than any expression she adopted in the presence of others, unless aimed at Gear. "I'm glad that you're here to take a look at her. You're right, it does feel a bit like old times."

Long before any of the current madness, long before Mikalai Gloucester stumbled into Zane's life, she and Antimony had worked together on the project that would one day become the cheerful automaton watching them from a pillow.

Antimony had reached out to Zane for her expertise in clockwork. In so doing, she'd introduced her to the hidden world of magic lurking in the shadows of the mundane world. With a creation like Gear, born of science and spellwork together, letting her in on the secret had been necessary. Zane recalled the disbelief on Gloucester's face when Antimony first explained the existence of the supernatural to him—she remembered feeling that same confoundment, hand in hand with a flattered pride that, of all the clock technicians in the city, Antimony had chosen to share this secret with her. That she had proven herself worthy, in skill and trust. Since then, magic had become, well, not *normal*, but an unquestionable part of her world.

Working with Antimony had been amazing and fascinating, and they'd made a lot of progress together. Yet slowly, Zane had begun to doubt the possibility of their success. Behind Antimony's brilliance and drive lurked grief, years old but ever-present. The loss of her husband haunted the project, a melancholy ghost clinging to the work. Zane wondered if the scientist's ambition was less about creating life and more about defeating mortality. This suspicion made the work feel like a private, impossible goal, a pipe dream she was intruding on, no matter how welcoming Antimony was. Ultimately the pragmatist in Zane pushed her to return to her shop and the tangible, attainable work she could do there.

Maybe nothing is impossible, she thought now, listening to Gear hum a jolly tune.

"I'm sorry for leaving before, Antimony," she said. "For not believing that Gear could work. I'm glad you proved me wrong."

Antimony shrugged one of her narrow shoulders. The movement dislodged her braid, sending the long golden line of it sweeping across her back like a pendulum. "I don't blame you. And I...I'm sorry if there was anything I did...anything I said that made you uncomfortable. That pushed you away."

Her eyes were on the mess of gears and limbs on the bedsheet, her face serene, but a faint tremor laced the apology, spider-silk cracks in her stoic facade. Zane blinked, surprised. Her heart clenched as memories spilled across her mind's eye.

"Antimony," she said quietly. "That wasn't why I left. I promise. I know I couldn't give you what you wanted, but you never made it a...a *thing*. Never blamed me or acted like I was wrong for how I am. I always really appreciated that. I left because I didn't think there was anything else I could do to help you. And because I had my own work to get back to. I wouldn't ever want you to think it had anything to do with the way you felt."

For a moment Antimony said nothing. She sat still as a statue, her eyes downcast, sunlight from the window painting delicate shadows of her lashes across her cheeks. Zane waited. Finally, Antimony drew in a gentle breath and looked up. If there was a slight gleam in her eyes, Zane wasn't about to point it out.

"In the end, there are many different kinds of love. I'm happy to have whatever sort you have to offer, Zane. That's what matters." She reached across the bedspread and took Zane's hand. "I'm delighted to be your friend. That's a wonderful kind of love."

Zane squeezed her hand, smiling back at her. "It is. I do love you, Antimony Jones."

"And I you, Zane Zephyr."

Gear, who had been quiet throughout this exchange, could no longer resist taking part. "And I love you both! I think I understand that. It's that happy feeling you get when you see someone special, isn't it? Or even when you just think of them." Her smile faltered, and Zane could guess who she was thinking of. "And sometimes you worry about them a lot," she added, confirming Zane's suspicions.

"That's love," Antimony agreed, stroking Gear's hair again.

For a while they fell into comfortable quiet, Zane sorting through the clockwork for what was still usable and what wasn't, while Antimony jotted neat notes down on a pad of paper. Gear went back to humming.

Eventually, worry niggled past the familiar calm of work.

"D'you think he's all right?" Zane asked. She set aside the bulk of Gear's torso, which had housed the now-defunct secondary movement, and glanced over at the clock on the wall. "Gloucester, I mean. He's been gone for ages."

Mulligan and Harrison had stopped by the room a quarter of an hour earlier, just to get their key to the room across the hall, and Finch would likely be out until evening, but Zane felt

Gloucester's absence weighing on her more as the afternoon drew on.

Antimony stowed the notepad in the front pocket of her rucksack. The paper was packed with minuscule notes in her tidy handwriting. Plans for Gear's reconstruction. She offered Zane a reassuring smile as she packed Gear's pieces away. "I'm sure he's fine. You'd know better than I, of course, but I think he just needed some time with his thoughts."

"Why would I know better?"

"Seems to me that the pair of you understand each other well, that's all. You're more perceptive than I think you give yourself credit for, Zane. You have a way of seeing past people's defenses."

Zane helped load Gear's torso back into the bag. "Says the most inscrutable person I know."

Antimony's laugh wasn't something Zane got to hear often, and she enjoyed it, like a well-earned prize. "Surely not the *most* inscrutable."

She thought about that. "Okay, maybe the most inscrutable *human* I know. In any case, I'll take the compliment. I'll try and trust my gut and believe that any moment now, Gloucester's going to pop through the door and suggest we get something to eat. All while managing to look incomprehensibly melancholy. I—oh!"

The door opened and Gloucester stuck his head through, relief darting across his solemn face when he saw Zane, Antimony, and Gear. "Oh, good, right room. How are things going here? Do you want to grab some food in the pub downstairs?" His brows drew together. "What's so funny?"

Chapter 7

Recognition

The next day dawned gloomy, the rising sun sluggish. It remained shy throughout the morning, half-hidden by great puffy clouds that threatened rain. Despite the inclement weather, it felt like a new day in more than just the literal sense. Perhaps it was the change of pace their imminent boat ride would provide, but Gloucester awoke feeling more confident than he had in days. They were finally getting somewhere.

His good mood was quickly put to the test.

After a short breakfast in the hotel dining room, the group left for the docks, yawning and brushing toast crumbs from their clothes. Mulligan led the way, frowning up at the clouds and bossily ordering everyone to hurry up. Gloucester was just weighing the pros and cons of pointing out that none of them were dragging their feet, when a cry reached his ears.

"Mr. Mulligan! That's Toby Mulligan, isn't it?"

Up ahead, a brawny shopkeeper, holding a broom in one hand and pointing accusingly with the other, moved across the cobblestones from a café to their left in order to block Mulligan's path. The politician was forced to stop short.

"You are, aren't you," the man said in accented Frettchennian, his voice carrying. A few passersby stopped, curious.

"Ah, shit," Harrison murmured under his breath. He squared his stance almost imperceptibly.

Mulligan recovered his composure with remarkable ease. "Don't know what you're talking about," he said with a shrug. He tried for a chuckle, but the laughter didn't reach his eyes. "Name's Montague, not whatever it was you said."

"Nah, nah." The shopkeeper shook his head, gripping the broom like a weapon. "I definitely recognize you. You were in the papers. You took over Frettchen after the old high minister kicked it. I'm right, yeah?"

He looked around at the other people on the street. Several had gathered, reeled in by the growing bluster. A few of them shrugged or murmured their uncertainty, but Gloucester noted a few nodding as well. Quite a few eyes narrowed in Mulligan's direction.

"I'm right," the shopkeeper said again, clearly hoping for someone to offer solid confirmation.

"You're *not*," Harrison told him. "My mate Montague, in charge of a city? As if! That's a good one." He gave a passably convincing laugh, which Gloucester and the others hurried to join in on. A few passersby tittered accommodatingly, but far too many considering stares still lingered on Mulligan's features.

"We need to get out of here," Antimony said in an undertone.

The shopkeeper took a step closer, still in Mulligan's path. "Issa!" he called to someone inside the café, never taking his eyes from Mulligan. "Do we still have that stack of old newspapers? Grab them for me, would you?"

Somewhere within, another voice called back in a Southern language Gloucester didn't recognize, but the words sounded worryingly like agreement.

"Look, er, mate," said Mulligan, sweat shining on his brow. He was still trying valiantly to seem amused, but the way he adjusted his glasses and dragged a hand through his hair came off as much more anxious than unfazed. "This is ridiculous. If you're trying for some sort of joke, it's not funny, so just leave us be."

He made to move around his accuser, but the brawny man grabbed hold of his arm. In an instant, Harrison was on him, one big hand latching onto the shopkeeper's wrist and prying Mulligan's arm free. Face dangerously calm, he gave the man a gentle but firm push back. Gloucester realized belatedly that he, too, had taken a sharp step forward, hand half-raised toward his hip, where once he would have carried his firearm. Now, that place was empty, the gun Finch had given him stowed away in the small bag slung over his shoulder, not within easy reach. He wasn't too upset about that; the last thing they needed was to escalate the situation.

Though the shopkeeper was broad-shouldered and burly, he was dwarfed by Harrison, who, abandoning all pretense of cheerfulness, loomed between him and Mulligan. "Montague told you he isn't who you're thinking of. I'd advise you do as he says and leave us be."

"Look, mate," the man echoed, his mockery shaded with barely contained anger. "I think you're all full of it. Whatever's happening in Frettchen, it's no good. I've friends in that city. Friends I can't get a hold of now. I don't know if they're okay or not. Yet here you are, bonny as a sunny day. And I want answers."

Gloucester risked a look around. Several more passersby had stopped, watching with curious eyes as those who had witnessed the whole interaction whispered in their ears. Anxiety tightened his chest, tangling into a knot behind his sternum. On one side of him, Zane drew in a breath that carried the hint of an unhappy moan. On his other side, Finch was muttering to himself.

Or whispering a spell... The faint brush of magic stirred against Gloucester. A moment later, something crashed inside the shop, followed by the same voice they'd heard before, raised now in disgruntled alarm.

That pulled the shopkeeper's attention. Distracted at long last from his scrutiny of Mulligan, he turned to holler a question through the doorway, using the same dialect as the other voice. Gloucester didn't need Finch's tug on his arm to recognize the distraction for the opportunity it was.

Whether or not the rest of their group noticed the accident had been magically incited, they were all quick to take advantage. As the man peered back into his shop to survey the damage, they hurried away, making a show of their renewed amusement at the idea of "good old Montague" being in charge of Frettchen. They strode as casually as they could in the direction of the docks.

Behind them, the man shouted angrily for his employee to forget the broken dishes and find the newspapers. The gathered crowd, uncertain one way or the other, let Gloucester and the others pass. Their stares followed the group, encouraging them to hasten their steps as much as they could without looking any more suspicious than they already did.

"The sooner we're out of Pell, the better," Gloucester said. As they rounded a street corner, he heard the shopkeeper's raised voice sound out again, distinctly triumphant, followed by an excited hubbub. Gloucester swore. "C'mon, Montague, let's get you out of here before they find their pitchforks."

Mulligan, a bead of sweat running down the side of his face, didn't argue as he broke into a run.

—

Ten minutes later, Captain Kinsella met them at the gangplank of her ship. Weak morning sunlight shone off the hull, where white block letters proclaimed the ship's name: *The Jem.* Curiosity tugged at Gloucester's inquisitive mind, but he was too out-of-breath from their hurried escape to pay it any mind. They'd earned more prying eyes on their way to the docks and hadn't risked stopping to find out if more people recognized Mulligan or if they were just alarmed by the small group of people running through the Old Harbor.

"Morning, passengers," Captain Kinsella greeted them. She was a lot keener to have them aboard this morning, no doubt thanks to Mulligan's money making its way into her bank account. She grinned at him first, which he ignored in favor of clutching at a stitch in his side, leaning heavily on Harrison.

Zane panted a hello and Antimony smiled, fanning herself with a pale hand, but Finch simply jogged up the gangplank with no more than a perfunctory nod to the captain.

"Ready when you are. Which I hope is now," he told her, beckoning impatiently for the others to follow him onto the ship.

Kinsella's brows rose. "Eager, are you? Got a reason to hurry out of Pell?"

Once again her eyes lingered on Mulligan. Her smile didn't waver, but it took on what Gloucester's imagination painted as a knowing edge. On the shore, beyond the long stretch of docks, he could swear he heard raised voices coming from the fish market. His heart stuttered, fear rushing through his veins, but then Kinsella merely shrugged.

"Lucky for you lot, then, we're just about ready. Was just waiting on my charming passengers to arrive. Welcome aboard and all that." She spun on her heel, turning her back on the city. "I'll have someone show you to your cabins."

—

Luckily everyone's moods improved once they were underway. By the time the noon hour arrived, Pell had long disappeared from sight. The coast, now a few miles off their starboard side, showed nothing but a tall line of gray cliffs draped in greenery. Sunlight shone down on sparkling water. The morning clouds had vanished, turning the day into another of spectacular fair weather. Only the white specks of distant gulls marred the clear blue of the sky. This change in scenery temporarily chased worries away.

Gloucester leaned against the railing mid-deck and breathed a deep sigh of satisfaction. This was his first venture onto the open sea, and he was finding it distinctly to his liking. The wide space and fresh air worked wonders to clear his mind.

As he watched the slow procession of the distant coastline, he let his thoughts wander. For once he didn't dwell on the dangers lying ahead or the regrets that had led him here. In fact, he didn't think about very much at all, an exercise he was rather enjoying until footsteps stirred him from his meditation.

He looked over to see Zane making her way toward him, a little green in the face.

"You all right?" he asked. He shuffled to one side, in case it was the railing she was squeamishly aiming for and not his company.

"I bloody well hate boats," Zane groused in return. She leaned against the railing beside him and squinted unhappily at the view.

"I've never been on one before," he admitted.

This got her attention. "Never? Really?"

"Not one like this. A real proper ship. I've been in canoes, small boats and the like. Out on ponds and lakes. But I've never been on anything big before. Or the ocean." He gestured at the water that surrounded them.

"Huh," said Zane. Then she smiled, though she was still pallid and sweaty. "What do you think of it so far? You look like you're enjoying it a fair bit more than I am."

Gloucester chuckled. "Not exactly a high bar to clear, that one." He dodged the lazy swat of her hand with a grin. "I like how open it is. And I like the constant movement. Back and forth."

"Funny." Zane let out a long breath, more *harrumph* than sigh. "That's exactly what I hate about it. I feel like someone put a curse on my stomach and now it hates me."

His smile turned into a sympathetic wince.

Past Zane's head, he spotted Antimony approaching, her swaying gait uninhibited by the waves beneath the hull. She still carried the bag containing Gear across her back. Gloucester guessed that she was reluctant to leave it anywhere out of her sight, even in the privacy of the cabins Captain Kinsella had allocated to them. He marveled at how much physical effort she had to be putting into it. The bag was clearly heavy, and she wasn't a sturdily built person.

If she struggled under the strain, however, she didn't show it. Then again, Gloucester suspected Antimony could lose an actual limb and only offer the barest of reactions.

"There's a storm ahead," she told them in lieu of a greeting. She pointed to the sky further up the coast. There, the bright blue they were sailing under darkened into turbulent storm clouds.

"Huh, that's sudden," Zane murmured. She shaded her eyes as she scrutinized the oncoming change in the weather. "Looks to be a few hours off still. Is that—?"

"Frettchen. Yes." Antimony regarded the horizon gravely.

Gloucester watched the distant clouds as they scudded across the sky. It looked windy, but if that was the case, wouldn't they feel some vestige of that here on the boat? Unease prickled down his spine.

“No wonder the crew thinks it’s a curse,” he said. “Even someone who isn’t superstitious would have to admit how weird this is.”

“Luckily their love for money was stronger than their fear of curses,” Zane replied.

“What are we talking about?” asked a muffled voice from Antimony’s bag. “Can I come out and see?”

Antimony cast a fond look over her shoulder and reached around to give the bag a gentle pat. “Not yet, Gear. I’m sorry. We’ll go back to the cabin and you can see the sights from the window there.”

“Aw, the cabin’s boring,” Gear protested. Gloucester could imagine her crestfallen pout. “I’ve seen everything in it already.”

Antimony gave her another sympathetic pat. Turning to leave, she paused and looked back at Gloucester and Zane. “Brace yourselves,” she told them. “I don’t think it’s going to be pretty when we hit that storm.”

Chapter 8

The Storm

Over the next couple of hours, the waters grew rougher, white-crested waves crashing against the hull of *The Jem*. Zane had long since fled green-faced to her cabin, unable to handle the increased rocking of the ship as it plowed ever forward. The cliffs of the coast had given way to rocky shores, and through the rapidly waning sunshine, they could see the skyline of Frettchen ahead.

The clouds over the city were now nearly black, highlighted every few seconds by flashes of lightning lancing across the sky. No man-made lights shone in Frettchen, its normally glittering skyscrapers dark. An eerie silence hung in the air, despite the strong winds whipping at their hair and clothes.

Several of the crew—which comprised no more than a dozen people, to the relief of Mulligan and his wallet—gathered on deck to take in the sight, mouths agape. One of them swore in Nordish, and Gloucester murmured a fervent agreement.

Within the city's silhouetted skyline, searing light moved amongst the skyscrapers. At first Gloucester thought it was just the lightning, but he quickly realized it was something closer to the ground and far less fleeting. The light was too consistent. Too warm. Like fire.

He thought of all the stories they'd heard over the last two weeks, coupled with the now-famous photograph reprinted in every newspaper. Taken by some brave soul who had gotten as close to the city as possible, it depicted Frettchen under the same tumultuous sky they were witnessing now. What had captured everyone's attention, however, were the two specters haunting the shrouded city: a shark composed of living shadows and a giant engulfed in flames.

When Gloucester first met the Gambler, he had looked almost human, appearing in the form of a slender young man with brown skin and blond hair. There had been plenty of odd details to set him apart from humanity, of course: his eternally bleeding knees and bare feet, which left a trail of red footprints wherever he went; his voice, imbued with countless centuries of history and heartache; his eyeless stare, where smooth skin stretched over empty sockets and yet he still seemed to see into the very souls of those around him.

What stalked through the city now made the Gambler's usual form downright mundane by comparison. Dwarfing all but the very tallest skyscrapers, there was little beyond the vaguely human shape recognizable as the demigod. A figure of fire, the Gambler burned so brightly it hurt to look at him. If Gloucester hadn't seen him in a similar—albeit significantly smaller—fiery state when he fought Denken, he never would have believed this was the same being.

His thoughts went to Gear, down in Antimony's cabin. He hoped that Antimony was distracting her away from the sight on the shore.

"Makes you wonder if there'll even be a city to save, with him tromping about like that."

Finch joined Gloucester and the members of Kinsella's crew crowded at the railing, moving across the rocking deck with ease. He'd done his fair share of traveling across the Lower Lands, not to mention his childhood on the Western Isles, so it didn't surprise Gloucester to see him so comfortable aboard a ship. Finch gestured derisively at the Gambler's burning form.

"Half of Frettchen's probably ash at this point." The disgust curling his lip made him seem more like someone deriding a messy neighbor than contemplating a dangerous immortal.

"I'm going to file that under 'Bridges to Cross When We Get to Them.'"

Gloucester had to admit he made a worrying point, though. What state would Frettchen be in when—*if*—they managed to wake it up?

The wind picked up again. Everyone struggled to keep their balance. Then the unnatural silence popped like a balloon, replaced by the roar of the gathering gale. The shift made them all stumble in alarm, several of the crew clamping hands over their ears or making gestures of protection. They'd clearly crossed the threshold of the magic that bound Frettchen, despite the distance the ship maintained from shore.

"Here comes the other one," Finch said, raising his voice over the storm's howling. His green eyes narrowed.

Through the roiling clouds came a shadow darker than the rest. It moved like a living thing, sweeping through the air above Frettchen. A gargantuan shark, gathered of the very absence of light, ethereal and terrifying. Gloucester felt like he had been pulled into some nightmare trench in the ocean's depths, where monsters lurked in the impenetrable blackness, waiting for an unsuspecting victim. Around him, the sailors brayed their horror.

"It's just like in my dreams!" one cried, knuckles white where he clutched the rail, his eyes wide and locked on the shark. "Swimming in shadows, bringing death to us all." Several of his crewmates shouted fearful commiseration.

"Everyone in that city is dead," moaned another, close enough for Gloucester to hear over the shrieking gale. "Lost souls, the lot of them. And we're next..."

"Crew!"

For such a small person, Captain Kinsella had a set of lungs suited to her job, her bellow able to cut through the roar of the wind and the distraction of her crew's fear. She emerged from the bridge, arms braced on the doorframe and her glare so thunderous it put the storm to shame.

"Back to work! Now!" she barked. "You want this storm to sink us? No? Then do your bloody jobs! We'll have time for nightmares later."

Her words worked like the click of a hypnotist's fingers. The crew members who had been staring in wide-eyed horror at Frettchen and its monsters shook themselves from their misery and focused instead on their captain. Gloucester could only admire their loyalty and Kinsella's leadership as they called out their understanding and dispersed to their proper positions.

A heavy rain started to fall, carried on the gusting wind to pound against their faces at an almost sideways angle. They were all soaked in seconds, squinting in the face of the deluge. Lightning split the sky, closer than before, followed almost immediately by a crash of thunder so loud it rumbled in their very bones.

"Anyone who isn't crew, get your arses to your cabins," Kinsella hollered over the noise. In her order was laughter, raucous and wild. "This is a witchy storm. If there's a god you believe in, pray to that bastard now!"

"C'mon!"

Gloucester could barely hear Finch over the wind and the thunder, but he felt the tug on his arm. He turned to the other man. Short hair plastered to his brow, Finch looked ghostly in the uneven light—no humor in his eyes, only pinched worry. He gave Gloucester's sleeve another tug and pulled him in the direction of the companionway. Gloucester hurried after him.

Drenched and shivering, they made their way belowdecks, jostled by crewmembers rushing down the corridors in the opposite direction.

At the door to the cabin claimed by Antimony and Zane, Gloucester glanced over his shoulder to see Finch starting back the way they'd come.

"Where are you going?" he yelled, bracing against the doorframe as angry swells rocked the ship.

"Just want a word with the captain! No worries!" Finch shouted back over his shoulder. He waved Gloucester away when he made to follow. "I'll be back in a tick. Make sure the others are okay."

Before he could protest, Finch raced out of sight. Gloucester hesitated, but the sound of retching from the cabin behind him drew his attention, along with Antimony asking for help finding a bucket. He would just have to trust Finch not to get washed overboard.

—

Waves crashed over the rails of *The Jem,* sweeping across the deck. Cassus Finch tried not to let his feet slide out from under him as he darted out of sight of the bridge, wishing he was anywhere other than where he was.

Well, almost anywhere, he amended. He reached the starboard guardrail and squinted through the torrential downpour at Frettchen's dark skyline. A pang of guilt passed through him for lying to Mikalai about why he'd turned back, but he dismissed it. Explaining the actual reason would have been too complicated. Or too stupid, maybe. He just needed to see it. The storm. The city. The damned shark. It was still visible, though he only recognized its shape because he knew what to look for. Little more than a black smudge, Denken's fearsome apparition swirled through the clouds. Finch glared at it, ignoring the rain leaking through his clothes and the distant shouting of Kinsella's crew as they struggled to keep the ship on course. For a moment all that existed was the shark. The source of all this.

And somehow, we have to stop it. The immensity of that thought pulled him back into the present. Back into his soaked clothes and chilled skin. The wind roared up to full volume in his ears, buffeting him a step off-balance. Slipping, he caught himself on the rail, white-knuckled and swearing. He ought to have just gone into the cabins with the others. He wasn't sure what he hoped to gain from this surreptitious look at Frettchen. Some sort of inspiration, maybe, some idea of what the hell they could possibly do to fix this mess.

Or maybe he just liked making himself miserable. That would explain a lot. Before everything had gone to shit, when it had been him and his dad, they had always looked out for each other and that was it. Simple. You took care of yourself, your family, and didn't worry about the rest. That simplicity was the road to happiness.

So how in all the Saints' bloody names had he ended up here?

His first thought—half frustrated and half wildly, stupidly fond—was that it was all Mikalai Gloucester's fault. His second was far more sober. Mikalai wasn't to blame for any of this. And as much as he wanted to rage at the shark swimming through the storm clouds, he knew Denken wasn't solely at fault either.

We did this, Dad. You and me. We broke the fucking world.

He was saved from his miserable, rain-drenched self-pity by a flurry of frightened shouts. Off to his right, a quartet of crewmembers had gathered along the rail, swathed in heavy raincoats, hats, and hoods. They hollered to each other over the cacophony of the angry sea, pointing down at the roiling waves. None of them had noticed him yet. Reluctant to get in the way and risk attracting the wrath of *The Jem*'s tiny captain, Finch made to head back to his cabin. Only to stop when he saw what had attracted the crew's attention.

Something moved in the water, too solid to be a trick of the dim light or the natural motion of the waves. Thick coils of dark-scaled skin cut through the water's surface just off the side of the ship. A fin like a sail slipped in and out of view.

Sea serpents weren't unheard of in this region, though they usually avoided ships and shallows, making them a rare sight. This one must have been pulled to the surface by the storm. As Finch moved closer, fascinated in spite of himself, the creature's head briefly came into view. A pale eye the size of a dinner plate glared balefully up at the crew. The serpent's snout was blunt, more akin to a fish than a snake.

As quickly as it appeared, it vanished again, though its immense writhing body was still visible. Whether intentional or not, it was keeping up with *The Jem*'s forward movement.

"It's not natural, one of them acting like this!" shouted a crewmember. Despite this fearful declaration, they were dangling so far over the rail with a morbid fascination that one of the others had to bodily pull them back.

"No, it bloody isn't. So, what are you playing at, trying to dive into its mouth?" their rescuer demanded with a half-mad laugh. "It's been stirred up by the witch storm, sure as anything. Sent to try to sink us!"

Finch bit his tongue to keep from scoffing aloud. The serpent was enormous, but hardly capable of sinking a cargo ship like *The Jem*. The beast was probably disoriented and as afraid as the humans on deck.

Not that it didn't make the bastard dangerous. The crewmembers lurched backward with cries of alarm as the sea serpent's head lunged out of the water once more, this time with far more aggression. Its attention caught by the activity at the railing, it drew itself up out of the waves to a formidable height, snapping needle-thin teeth at the sailors. Momentum and the constant movement of the waves worked against this attack, sending the serpent back into the water as it missed its target by several meters. It was more than enough to scare the sailors, however, who yammered their fright in an ear-splitting chorus. The serpent lunged again, closer this time.

Before he knew what he was doing, magic swirled through Finch. There was plenty in the air to draw from. Kinsella's crew was right about the unnatural state of the storm, just wrong about the sort of magic behind it. It felt different than what Finch was accustomed to, nothing like his own, but it still flowed into him when he reached for it. He drew from within as well, hoping to lessen some of the unfamiliarity by using the magic in his own blood, the birthright from his mother. The two intertwined, and he pulled in a deep breath, mentally running through all of his spells to settle on the best one to ward off angry monsters—

"Dark magic! That's what it is!"

The shout, shrill with terror, made Finch look up. He half-expected to be met with accusing eyes, but the sailor in question was pointing down at the creature in the water. The group still had yet to even notice that he was there.

But the fearful cry gave him pause. These people were already superstitious, already afraid. Over and over they'd—rightly—attributed Frettchen's wretched state to magic. What might they do if they glanced over and saw him casting a spell?

Right. Going with the subtle approach, then.

As the serpent reared its head for a third attack, Finch moved back to the railing and gripped the cold metal with both hands. Spellcasting without the usual accompanying hand movements was a pain in the ass, requiring a lot more concentration and mental precision. The key was maintaining a constant visual on the target, which was easier said than done when the target was a great bloody fish that wouldn't stop moving.

"C'mon, you bastard," he whispered, unsure if he was talking to the monster in the water or himself. Trying not to focus on all the ways this could go wrong, he drew in more magic and settled on a spell.

Under normal circumstances, it wouldn't be a difficult one. He didn't want to kill the beast, just get it far enough away from *The Jem* that it wouldn't continue its assault. A Roping spell ought to do the trick. In theory. But without using his hands, not to mention keeping the incantation out of earshot of the crew, he might as well be casting the spell blindfolded.

Excuses, excuses. Just do the damned thing or don't but stop griping.

Saints, I sound like my father.

Swallowing a growl that contained too many emotions to count, Finch launched into the incantation. He dared not raise his voice above a murmur, despite the roaring wind. He locked his eyes on the sea serpent's twisting coils and visualized a long cord of magic reaching out from him to the creature. Imagined it wrapping around the scaly body. He poured all of his concentration into it, until he could *feel* the tautness of the line, the grip of its cords against the serpent's cold, slick scales. He could *hear* the creak of the rope as it became a physical thing, tightening around the creature's flesh, not enough to wound but secure enough to keep it from slipping free.

In his mind's eye, Finch threw his end of the rope down into the depths, far below the waves, where the sea was cold and still. Where beasts as strange as the serpent lurked, untouched by the storm howling so far above. The spell drew the serpent down with it, slowly and surely. Away from the rampaging waves and the gusting winds and shouting, fearful humans. Back to the quiet places of the black deep that was its home. He could almost feel its confusion, soothing slowly into relief as it was pulled away from the fury of the surface world and its own anguished rage—

"You all right, mate?"

Finch opened his eyes. He didn't remember closing them. A sailor stood at his side, her eyes wide with concern under her rain-soaked hood. Seeing him blink back to reality, she grinned.

"Scared you silly, eh? Don't worry, the beastie's gone now." She gestured down the length of the guardrail to where the serpent had tried lunging at the crew. Though waves still crashed against the ship's hull, within them remained no sign of scales or fins. "It dove back down. Got tired of us, I s'pose. That's when I saw you over here, gripping the rail like your life depended on it. And mayhaps it did, seeing as you're standing out in the middle of a damned storm with your eyes squeezed shut, you daft bastard."

There wasn't any real annoyance in the admonishment, relieved as she blatantly was by the sea serpent's disappearance. She laughed and made a shooing motion at him. "Get back to the cabins with the rest of your friends. If Kinsella catches a passenger out here in this weather, she'll toss you overboard herself!"

You're welcome, thought Finch. *Only saved your stupid life.*

Maybe Mikalai and his do-gooder friends really were rubbing off on him, though, because he didn't find it that hard to bite his tongue on a retort. Instead, he nodded once and made for the nearest door below deck. He'd had more than enough of the weather.

Chapter 9

Fears

The storm went on for hours. They waited it out in their cabins, as rain beat against the portholes and waves crashed against *The Jem*'s sides like an angry horde battering to get in. Antimony—and the still-hidden Gear—stayed with a violently seasick Zane, who sat hunched over a bucket and swore at anyone who came too close.

Finding Zane well-attended, and leery of her cabin's tense atmosphere, Gloucester eventually departed in favor of his and Finch's quarters. He found Finch there, pulling on a dry shirt.

"Did you have your word with the captain?" he asked, surreptitiously enjoying the brief glimpse of Finch's bare chest before it vanished from view. "What was it about?"

"Nothing important. And nah, she was too busy. Just ended up helping some of the crew with a wee problem on deck before they chased me back down here. Not that I'm too bothered. It's a bit damp out there."

The magician seemed at ease where he leaned against the porthole, staring out at the chaos. Despite the dry clothes he'd changed into, his hair was still wet, ruffled into unruly angles. He didn't seem in a talkative mood, though, so Gloucester resisted the urge to tease and instead reclined on one of the beds, trying to think of anything other than Frettchen and the nightmare it had become. Beyond the porthole, the storm raged on.

After a while, Finch spoke, his voice quiet and matter of fact. "I hate them."

"Storms?" asked Gloucester, whose quest to think about other things had left him ill-prepared for a conversation. He'd been reminiscing about a garden back home in the Nordlands, where they sold lilies and peonies of all colors. It was the sort of random memory that snuck in whenever he tried to clear his mind. The garden was a beautiful place, and about as far from their current surroundings as he could possibly imagine.

"No," said Finch, looking amused for a scant moment. Then the clouds darkened in his eyes again. "Gods. Immortals. Whatever you want to call them."

"Oh." Gloucester blinked away visions of flowers. "I suppose you've got a lot of reason to. Though, they've also got a decent bit of reason not to like you, either."

This made Finch laugh. It was a rich, pleasant sound, and it made the storm outside feel suddenly much further away. "Fair point," he conceded. He shifted against the wall of the cabin, half-turning to face Gloucester.

They fell into silence again. Until—

"I know he wasn't a very good person, but my dad was...he was my dad." Finch looked down at his hands, twisting one of his rings between his fingers. "He was the only family I had. And I know...I know he made his own bed, but I can't help but hate the immortals for what happened to him."

Gloucester considered this. He could point out that only Denken was to blame for the elder Finch's death at the hands of a woman driven mad by his influence, that the Gambler and Purpurrot hadn't any fault to bear. He could remind him that the Finches had made the first move of aggression when they captured the Gambler in the first place. But these were things Finch already knew. Grief and logic were rarely amiable companions.

"Tell me about him," he said instead. "What was he like?"

Finch eyed him for a moment, as if surprised. Then he offered a tiny smile. "He was brilliant. And maddening. Tenacious to a damned fault and completely obsessed with magic."

Gloucester hummed. "Must have been difficult, what with you being so different, then."

This earned him another short laugh. "I am my father's son. What can I say? Not like I really had anyone else to influence me much growing up. After Mum died, it was always just the two of us. Dad did the best he could, I think, in his own way. He was never really the parenting type. I was always more an apprentice in his eyes than a son." He tapped the tattoo on his brow. "He gave me this when I was thirteen. I'd started showing more signs of my mother's witchy abilities and he wanted to see if a channeling rune would make my magic stronger."

"Oh," said Gloucester, brows drawing together. Tattooing your child as part of a magical experiment sounded to him like pretty terrible parenting. Finch didn't seem cross at the memory, though. "And, um, did it?"

"Probably. Sort of hard to know, since I can't say for certain what I might've been capable of without it. Comes in handy, whatever the case. But that was Dad for you. Always wanting to learn, always pushing his abilities and mine. Always wanting to know more about the mysteries of magic. It was why the Brothers fascinated him so much. Why he couldn't say no to the opportunity the high minister offered him. So yeah, he was a bastard, but...I miss him. Whether they were justified or not, he's gone because of Denken and his lot."

His expression hardened again, and he turned his face back toward the porthole. Silence fell over the cabin.

As he listened to the crash of waves and thunder, Gloucester thought about family.

"Mighty brave of you," he said eventually, avoiding Finch's eyes when he looked his way and staring up at the ceiling instead. He hoped he appeared nonchalant, rather than abruptly and staggeringly nervous.

"Oh? What's that, then?" There was the whisper of a laugh in Finch's question. Gloucester's hopes of an easygoing facade wilted.

He shrugged, trying for a breezy action ruined as much by his own self-consciousness as by the unpredictable rocking of the ship. "Facing your fear. It's very heroic of you."

A small grin worked its way onto his face as he shot a look over at Finch.

Finch laughed again and took a joking bow. "Why thank you, kind sir. Though I will have you know that I did *not* say that I was afraid of them. Just that I didn't like them."

Gloucester offered him a disbelieving glance. Finch sighed and ducked his head in good-natured defeat. Humor kept the storms at bay, literal and emotional both, pulling their thoughts away from the haunting sight of the city across the water and the pain of grief.

"Fine, all right, they scare me silly. Happy now? What about you, eh? I guess a big, brave security agent isn't supposed to be afraid of anything."

"Everyone's afraid of something," Gloucester argued lightly.

Finch pushed away from the wall and crossed the cabin, maintaining his immunity to the floor's movement beneath his feet. Coming to a halt directly in front of where Gloucester sat, he stared down at him with a fond sort of curiosity, as if Gloucester were a puzzle that was turning out to be an enjoyable challenge.

"What are you afraid of, then, Secret Agent Man?" he asked.

Far too many things, Gloucester thought.

"Beetles," he said aloud. "Can't stand them. Dunno why, either. Spiders? Like 'em. Worms? Fine. But beetles? Ugh, no thanks."

Finch stared at him for a long moment, then laughed when it became clear Gloucester wasn't joking. Gloucester expected teasing, but when Finch spoke, it was to say, "Fair enough," with an understanding wink. "I'm not one to admit to my faults, as a rule, but I think I can make an exception for you, so here's the thing that gets me: clustered dots."

It was Gloucester's turn to wait, but Finch appeared to be finished. "Um," he said. "What, uh, what about them?"

"I just don't like them. They freak me out."

"Clustered dots," Gloucester repeated skeptically, "freak you out."

Finch pulled a face. "Yeah, always have. They make me think of bugs. Or bug eggs, to be specific. Burrowing into things. Like skin, you know? It's just—" He broke off with a shudder. "Yeah, so I know it sounds silly, but there you have it. Scared of dots."

"You must have a tough time looking in the mirror, then," Gloucester said innocently. Finch was one of the most freckled people he'd ever met.

"Oi! Cheek!" Finch laughed, pressing a hand to his chest in mock dismay.

"Still," said Gloucester, laughing as well. "Thank you for sharing your, um, one fault with me. That must have taken a lot of courage."

Finch's laughter ceased, replaced with an admirably straight face. "It did," he said, closing his eyes melodramatically. "But I feel better for it. And so, so close to you now."

As if to illustrate his point, he sat down beside Gloucester on the narrow bed. Their shoulders brushed against each other as the ship rocked.

"Though, you know," he added, fingers playing with the charmed rings on Gloucester's hand. "If you tell anyone my secret, I'll have to come after you. Got a reputation to uphold and all."

"Not to mention all those enemies who would know your weakness," Gloucester teased. "The power of magic at your fingertips, only to be defeated by the pips on a die. Tragic."

"All right, all right, it's not that bad." Finch used the thin chains connecting the rings to lift Gloucester's hand and brushed his lips against his knuckles, light as a butterfly's wings. "Still, best not to go blabbing."

"Ah, 'blabbing.' Such a romantic word."

Despite the levity in Gloucester's tone, he couldn't help but wonder if they were getting a bit carried away. He thought of Zane's warning. Now wasn't the time for romance.

Devil's advocate here, he thought, as Finch pulled him closer with a smile. *Maybe in a private cabin on a ship sailing through a vicious god-storm towards an uncertain future is a perfectly fine time. Zane can mind her own business.*

—

The storm outside continued, high winds buffeting *The Jem* as if it were a tiny rowboat. Rain battered the windows, like a thousand angry hands slapping against the glass. Several times the entire ship tipped so much to one side or the other that Gloucester, lying on the narrow bed in his and Finch's cabin, thought they were surely about to capsize.

When at last the tempest ended, the silence was as jarring as the storm. Gloucester and Finch got dressed and left the cabin to investigate.

They emerged on deck to a world of darkness.

It was not, however, the foreboding black of unnatural storm clouds. Instead, they were greeted with a clear night sky. The moon shone brightly overhead, casting just enough silver light to make out the black line of the coast. Frettchen was nowhere to be seen.

"We survived!"

The voice pulled Gloucester's attention. Zane was walking toward them. She looked very unsteady, but her broad smile became apparent as she reached them.

"It's finally over," she said jubilantly.

Finch opened his mouth, but Gloucester, who was becoming quite accustomed to both of his friends' tendencies, put a hand on his wrist in silent warning. Finch glanced over at him and apparently rethought whatever comment he'd been about to make.

"You disappeared from the cabin earlier," Zane said, her smile turning apologetic. "Sorry if I scared you off."

"You're fine," he assured her. "It was just a bit too crowded."

Zane looked from him to Finch. "So, you spent the storm with Finch."

"*Less* crowded," he said, feeling foolish for the faint embarrassment twisting in his chest.

"I'll bet."

"Where's Captain Kinsella?" asked Finch, rather loudly. "I wouldn't mind knowing whereabouts we are."

"The captain's asleep," a nearby sailor told him. "She was on the bridge all through that devil storm." Admiration rang clear as a bell in her voice. "Don't worry, though. The worst is behind us. We'll be in the Nordlands by morning."

"Hear that?" Finch chuckled to Zane and Gloucester. "The worst is behind us."

Gloucester smiled grimly. "If only."

Chapter 10

Back on Land

In the wake of the storm, their journey turned to smooth sailing. The next morning dawned clear, the sky once more an egg-shell blue with nary a cloud in sight, Frettchen's dire skyline replaced by the rocky shores of the Nordlands. Unlike the cliffs of the south, however, the land beyond the water was instead edged in forests and long stretches of barren flatland. It was as if the tempest never happened. The only hint at *The Jem*'s ordeal lurked on the horizon behind them, where bare hints of angry gray crept above the long line of the coast. Before long, even that was swallowed up by the curves of tall, water-carved stone and evergreen trees.

Away from the unnatural weather, the crew's mood improved greatly. They went about their duties with a vigor and cheerfulness born of relief. A chorus of singing filled the air as they worked, the music amateur but practiced in the way of people accustomed to being together.

Captain Kinsella, for all her hard work the night before, was not one for sleeping in. By dawn's break she was up, making her way through the sailors, checking on how they were faring and, on occasion, telling them off for slacking. Gloucester watched with quiet amusement from where he leaned against the rail. Despite her brashness, it was clear the tiny captain was well-respected by her crew.

Chatting with the ship's cook as he cast the remnants of day-old stew overboard, Kinsella noticed Gloucester's gaze. She excused herself from the conversation and made her way over to him. Like Finch, she walked across the ship's deck as if walking on solid land.

"Morning, landlubber," she called out, grinning toothily at him. Gloucester chuckled at the gentle insult.

"First time being called that," he said once she was close enough, he didn't need to raise his voice to be heard. "On account of never being at sea before."

"You're better at hiding it than some of your friends." Kinsella shook her head. "Zephyr's a lot less pretty when she's that particular shade of green. And 'Montague' looks like death warmed over."

The quotations she placed around the name were audible. Gloucester's stomach tightened. He'd quite forgotten about Mulligan and Harrison, and the knowing way Kinsella regarded the former on the docks of Pell. He glanced around, seeking out some sign of the politician and his bodyguard, but they weren't on deck. He'd seen neither hide nor hair of them since before the storm.

Catching the look on his face, Kinsella correctly guessed what was causing it and said, "Those two shut themselves away almost as soon as we left the harbor. I'd think they were getting intimate, if only I didn't suspect it was something much more intriguing. You lot are a mysterious bunch."

Gloucester laughed uneasily, because that was easier than offering an explanation. He kept waiting for the other shoe to drop, but he wasn't about to pull it down by the laces himself. He feigned nonchalance. "We are who we are."

"Indeed." Kinsella looked out over the water with a pensive hum. "It's who you are that's the mysterious bit. And what you might be up to. We've all got our reasons for doing things, I suppose, eh? Like if I were, say, the leader of a city-state what fell under a curse that I somehow escaped, I'm wondering what I might do, you know?" She slanted her gaze back to Gloucester. "Me and my mysterious friends."

He thought very carefully. "I think you'd do what you could to try to fix it," he said. Beneath them, waves rocked *The Jem* back and forth, but he held Kinsella's gaze steadily. "However mysterious it might seem to others."

She didn't say anything for a long moment. Then she chuckled and shook her head. "Good answer. Doesn't actually answer anything, course, but I'll take it. I like you, Gloucester."

Relief swept through him like one of the waves below, and he let out a laugh of his own. "Thanks," he said.

Then, in the lightness of the moment, a thought occurred. "Wait, if those two have been in a cabin since Pell, how do you know what Montague looked like after the storm?"

"Poked my head in, of course." She didn't appear ashamed in the slightest. "Just in case they were getting intimate." Peering at his face, she guffawed. "I say, are you blushing?"

"No," said Gloucester quickly, thinking how lucky he and Finch were that Kinsella hadn't come nosing around their own cabin.

Kinsella clicked her tongue in amusement. "Wouldn't have taken you for a prude."

Her jovial teasing reminded Gloucester of Bleifrei, the chef back at Purpurrot's Pie Shop. He spared a moment to wonder if she and her wife had gotten out of Frettchen in time. He hoped so.

"To be honest, I'm not sure what to take you for." Perhaps the captain had taken his silence for indignation, because she sounded faintly apologetic as she went on. “At first, I thought you were the least interesting. I mean, that’d be Montague, only we both know why that isn’t the case. The tall fellow is clearly his bodyguard. Your Islander friend is all kinds of mysterious under that roguish charm act he obviously likes so much. And the ladies definitely have some sort of secret in that rucksack. And then there’s you. The other one.”

“Thanks.” Gloucester wasn’t sure if he ought to be concerned about Kinsella’s perceptiveness or hurt that he’d been dubbed the boring one of the group.

“Only you’re not just some tag-along, are you, Gloucester.” She leaned against the rail beside him, the rolling waves of the sea at her back. “See, I’ve been a lot of places. Seen a lot of different people. Got an eye for noticing things, you know? Like a landlubber carrying around a shark’s tooth, clutching it like it means a whole lot. Gift from someone special, was it?”

Gloucester looked down. Sure enough, Denken’s tooth was in his hand. He hadn’t even noticed he’d been fidgeting with it. He tucked it back into his pocket, alongside his key. “I guess you could call it that.”

Sunlight reflecting up from the water below cast dancing patterns across Kinsella’s face as she regarded him. “See, that’s interesting. And it’s not just that, either. You don’t last long as a captain without learning to tell things about people. The way someone walks or talks or stands. It all says more about them than they mean to say. And you, Gloucester, you’re saying a lot.”

“Another thing no one’s ever said about me before,” he joked, hoping to deflect her curiosity.

To no end. Her eyes were sharp behind her glasses. “The way you stand says you’ve got training. The way you move says you’re restless. Worried. And eyes rarely lie, and yours say you’re scared.”

“It’s a scary time,” Gloucester said, finally abandoning the unsuccessful shield of humor. “That storm was terrifying. What’s happening to Frettchen scares me to death.”

"Hm," grunted the captain.

She eyed him a moment longer, then nodded and walked away. Gloucester watched her go, thinking she wasn't the only one who didn't know what to make of the person in front of them.

—

The rest of the day passed in quiet uneventfulness. Gloucester and the others were glad for the lack of excitement, their thoughts on the challenges ahead. No one knew what waited for them in the Nordlands, nor how whatever it was might aid them in the inevitable fight coming. Gloucester couldn't get the image of Frettchen out of his head. What could possibly combat the supernatural forces they'd witnessed at the heart of the storm?

Purpurrot came to mind, of course, but where was she? The fretful, pessimistic voice in the back of his head wondered if she'd even survived the showdown in the false Maze. Had the botched Transportation spell been her final act?

No, he didn't think so. Somehow, he felt certain they would know if the mother of creation had died. Perhaps she had simply used up the powers she so recently regained and fled somewhere to recuperate. Could she be what they were looking for in the Nordlands?

That had to be it, he decided. Gloucester couldn't think of any other reason the oracle would send them up to this end of the Lower Lands. Purpurrot had to be here. If they could find a way to get her back to full strength, maybe they could win this. Maybe.

—

The next day, *The Jem*'s course turned toward the coast, and they sailed into a city most called the Hartland. This wasn't its true name. Payis-Chasse was one of the oldest cities in the Nordlands, perhaps in all of the Lower Lands, but its given name was scarcely used by anyone not raised within its borders. It translated roughly to "land full of hunter's game," and so the nickname of Hartland had long ago been born, made all the more suitable as it was the most popular Nordish port and was by and large considered the friendliest city in the region, as well as its cultural center.

Despite this, Gloucester had only been there on a handful of occasions. In addition to being a port, the Hartland was one of the few cities connected directly to Frettchen by rail, and he'd passed through it a few times since moving to the central city-state. He'd never spent any real time there, however.

As the last of the group to step off the gangplank and back onto solid ground, he paused to take in the sight of the great city. Behind them, Kinsella and her crew bustled around, preparing to unload cargo.

Like the South Cities, those of the Nordlands were all varied and unique, but they bore certain similarities which united the far-flung locales within their interconnected culture and history. Unlike the south's laidback character and open architecture, the Hartland was fortified against harsh northern weather and potential enemy attacks.

Stories told of how the last tyrannical empress had attacked the Hartland in Frettchen-of-Old's final stand. Armies marched on Payis-Chasse from the southern grasslands while a naval fleet bore down on its harbor. It had been the strength of the city's walls as much as its own forces that held the invaders at bay. Their fortifications had been built over centuries, designed to repel hurricanes and the great winter beasts that came down from the mountains with the snows. The Southern armies had woefully underestimated the strength that required.

All these centuries later, the walls remained. Once upon a time, they would have been manned with constant patrols, but now it was sprawling displays of flowers and exploring tourists who stood sentinel. Gloucester spotted several large wall-top gardens just from where he stood on the docks, distant spots of trailing green ivy, fruit trees, and colorful blooms. The people of the Hartland took great pride in the walls—no matter where he looked, not a single mighty stone showed its age, each one a polished, pale gray. The horticultural achievements crowning the walls mitigated this austere effect, but it was still a far cry from the vibrancy of the South Cities.

Emotion twinged in Gloucester's stomach at the sight. Jittering nerves and...happiness? This wasn't his city, but it was his homeland, and it felt like a long time since he'd been here.

"I always thought the Nordlands would be colder," Zane said.

Her words shook Gloucester from his thoughts, and he turned to see her looking around speculatively. While it wasn't nearly as warm as it had been in Pell, the temperature was pleasant enough for short sleeves, especially with the sun beating down. He raised his eyebrows.

"It's almost summer," he pointed out with a smile. He led the way down the docks toward land, away from the hubbub aboard *The Jem*. "What did you expect? It's not winter year-round here, you know. Especially not this far from the mountains."

"Can't say I'm too sorry about that." Antimony came to walk beside them. She shaded her eyes with one slender hand as she gazed out over the city. Beyond the docks, a park shaded by trees acted as a buffer between the harbor and busy city streets. On the boardwalk further ahead to their left, several people were fishing, gazing down at the water from beneath wide-brimmed sunhats. Cats of all different colors sauntered around them, hopeful for a snack. "I've never been here before. It's nothing like Frettchen or the south, is it? It feels much...quieter, I suppose."

Gloucester shrugged. The city might not be his own, but the region was, and none of it felt odd to him. It was always strange to hear other people comment on things he simply considered normal. He supposed it was much how his Frettchennian coworkers must have felt when he first moved south.

"The Hartland's a nice enough place," he said. "But we shouldn't stay long if we want to make good time to Lalune."

"Can I see?" came Gear's voice from the bag slung across Antimony's back. "I want to see where we are."

"Sorry, Gear," Zane whispered. "We can't really risk you being seen. People are already on edge. I'd hate to see what they might do if they came across a talking head."

The bag squirmed, as if Gear were rolling around in displeasure. "All heads talk," she said.

"Most are attached to bodies, though," Gloucester told her. "That's sort of a vital part of the equation."

"I don't know what that means." Gear sounded distinctly sullen now.

"We're just trying to keep you safe," soothed Antimony. "I promise I'll fix you as soon as I can."

All well and good to say so, but when would that actually be? Setting aside the time it would surely take to rebuild the automaton, where would Antimony find a lab to do so? There were plenty of clockwork factories in any given Nordish city, of course—the Nordlands boasted a reputation as a region of innovators—but Gear was undeniably a special case. How would they explain her existence to anyone they spoke to about using a lab? They didn't have time to fend off curious inventors and anyone else who might be intrigued by Gear's one-of-a-kind nature.

Perhaps Zane was thinking along the same lines, because she hurried to change the subject. "Well, here we are in the Nordlands. Now what? Go to the train station?"

"I think we should take a short breather first," Gloucester suggested. During his security training, he'd had a teacher who insisted that lightning fast wasn't always better than slow and methodical. *Conserve your strength*, she told her students over and over. *You can't protect anyone if you're exhausted. Not even yourself.*

"We've been at sea for a few days," he explained. "Better if we get our feet under us on solid ground again. And get something to eat. I'm starving."

Zane eyed him in mild surprise. "I would have expected you to be the one most eager to leave," she said. "Seeing as it's your home we're heading for and all."

"There's too much at stake for us not to be a little bit prudent," he said. "Orange Ianto didn't tell us why we have to head north, after all. We've got to be ready for anything. And that's a hell of a lot easier if we're not dead on our feet."

That was the logical reason. Lurking behind it, in the back of his mind, was the illogical one. The fear.

Not of the uncertainty of the oracle's instructions, nor even of Denken and his spreading disaster. No, this trepidation was more personal and more deeply set in his heart of hearts. It was the fear of going home.

What would happen when they got to Lalune? His parents thought he was dead. That was what Jeb had been told, and what he'd said Gloucester's parents believed as well. How would they react, finding out their only child was alive? They would be happy, surely, but would they believe his story? He had Finch with him, who could certainly prove magic was real. Not to mention Gear. But proof like that might be overwhelming. Would it be too much for them? The existence of magic probably wasn't a simple concept to swallow if you'd spent the last fifty years never knowing about it. Should he really do that to them?

All questions to which he didn't know the right answers. He didn't know if there even *were* right answers. Still, he knew when it came down to it, he would offer them the truth. They were his parents, and he owed them that much. Whether they accepted magic's existence or not... He supposed he would find out.

Either way, at least he wouldn't be lying to them. Everyone else had lied to them: that he had died while on a mission, that there was nothing left of him to even bury.

No more lies.

All of this mental turmoil rumbled through Gloucester's thoughts in an instant, his companions none the wiser. He turned his attention back to them as they bickered over where to find rooms for the night.

They ended up relying on Captain Kinsella once more. It turned out that, as one of the main ports she traded in, the Hartland was a city the minuscule woman knew very well. Once they managed to pull her attention away from the unloading of her ship, she was happy to point them in the direction of a decent hotel. It had none of the overt splendor of their Port Gnoll accommodations, but the room Gloucester shared that night with Finch was spacious and clean. He didn't think he could ask for more, even if Mulligan was affronted. Whether the politician's displeasure stemmed from the understated décor or the fact he was still paying for everything was hard to say. Gloucester was happy to ignore him either way.

He fell asleep to a blessedly cool breeze stirring through the open window, bringing with it the faint strains of music from a nearby club and the muted hubbub of a city that never quite slept.

—

The next morning brought disappointment, as they discovered there were no outbound trains scheduled. It turned out being cut off from Frettchen and its constant stream of travelers had greatly disrupted the flow of traffic into and out of the Hartland. No matter how Mulligan tried to cajole, berate, and eventually bribe the train conductors, he always got the same answer: Not today. Tomorrow.

"Bloody Nords," he huffed, having stormed back to the group after a fourth unsuccessful attempt.

They were all sitting in the shade of several large umbrellas outside a café. The name on its sign was in Nordish, a slanting, elegant alphabet, and the letters were entangled in painted white and pink flowers. Gloucester translated for those who didn't know the language: *The Magnolia Café*. A suitable name, considering the magnolia trees planted around the outdoor seating, their buds not yet flourished into full blossoms. It was a pleasant little establishment, filled with cozy booths and squashy armchairs, but the sunny weather had led them out onto the patio as they ate a late breakfast and waited for Mulligan to sort their train tickets.

"Stubborn as oxen." Mulligan braced his hands on his hips, narrowed eyes lingering on the station across the road.

"They're employees," Gloucester retorted, picking apart a sticky bun and scarcely gracing Mulligan with a glance. One of the city's many cats had curled up under the table, and he stroked it lightly with the toe of his shoe. Its satisfied purring added to the morning's peacefulness. "They can't change the trains just for one small group of people."

As much as he wanted to be on the move again, he couldn't help himself from arguing with Mulligan. *I guess that makes me a stubborn Nord.* The thought sent a pang of home pride through him. As far as he was concerned, there were much worse things to be.

"Considering how we don't even know what it is we're looking for, I think one more day of rest won't kill us," Finch added. "Worse comes to worst, we'll rent a car and drive ourselves."

He didn't sound the least bit bothered by this latest hitch in their plans. In fact, he was smiling as he looked from Mulligan to Gloucester, seemingly quite amused. Then again, Gloucester knew Finch's jovial demeanor didn't always mean much. He showed only what he wanted to show. Beneath the smirking nonchalance, he was surely as worried as the rest of them.

"Sorry," said Mulligan, in the thorny tone of someone about to explain why they weren't actually sorry in the slightest. "But did you all happen to forget what we saw on our way here? The state Frettchen is in? Did you not hear the news back in Pell? That madness is spreading! And we've no idea how fast it'll move as it does."

"Working ourselves into a frenzy isn't going to help stop it," Gloucester said.

It was strange; Mulligan's concerns were the very same ones that had been pounding through his own skull ever since they set out, yet while the former chief advisor grew more agitated, Gloucester felt calmer than he had in days. In the sunlight of the Magnolia Café's patio, the storm raging over Frettchen felt wonderfully distant. Perhaps it was simply the comfort of being back in his homeland or the opportunity to rest long enough to catch their breath. Secretly, he suspected it was mostly because they had a goal. A task to fulfill. Orders to follow, enigmatic as they were.

Once a security agent, always a security agent.

Mulligan *hmph*ed but didn't argue further, instead stomping into the café to buy himself a croissant. The cat under the table yawned widely and went to sleep.

Zane grinned over at Gloucester. "Look at you, all calm and condescending," she praised, giving his shoulder a cheerful clap. Clearly, he wasn't the only one finding himself in a better mood that day.

"I'm not condescending," he argued, though he couldn't hold back a chuckle.

"You were a bit." Antimony's thin lips quirked in a smile over the rim of her teacup. She'd donned one of the broad-brimmed hats that were popular here, protecting her pale complexion from the morning sunshine. "But he sort of deserves it, so I don't think any of us will judge you too much. Except maybe Mr. Harrison," she added, tossing her head in the tall agent's direction.

Harrison stood a short distance away, his eyes latched onto Mulligan's back through the café window. *I'm not the only one who's a security agent through and through*, Gloucester thought.

Yet Harrison surprised him.

"No," he said in his slow and measured way. "You probably have earned a bit of condescending, all considered."

Zane laughed, which made Harrison's eyes flicker toward her, a smile twitching his lips.

"There you go, then," she told Gloucester. She sat back in her chair, radiating satisfaction. "Not even the bodyguard is judging you, so feel free to enjoy it."

Chapter 11

Angus

It took Gloucester the better part of a day to recognize something was strange about the Hartland. It niggled at his mind, not so much a worry as the nagging sensation of a thought unrealized, a mental itch growing more and more noticeable.

Finally, it dawned on him: none of the citizens seemed worried. This was one of the closest major cities to Frettchen, and yet tension didn't pervade the streets as it had in Pell or Port Gnoll. Even cities much further removed from the stricken region had felt more upset than the people here. Certainly, everyone in the Hartland knew about it—newspaper headlines proclaimed all the latest developments from their street-corner stands—yet for the most part, everything appeared to be business as usual. Other than the interrupted flow of traffic into and out of the city, everyone went about their day as if nothing were wrong. There was laughter, even, an especially rare sound of late.

Having come to this realization, Gloucester reflected that he ought to be bothered by it. Rather than feeling unsettled, however, he found the Hartland's high spirits infectious, and by the time late afternoon rolled around, he was in too good of a mood to worry very much at all. Even the news that the trains were delayed again didn't bother him.

Evening fell, and he watched the sky darken with a sense of peacefulness.

The others were in similarly good moods. Zane and Finch hardly bickered all day, even trading jokes a few times; Antimony was smiling and chatting with Gear whenever they were safely away from the eyes and ears of passersby. Even Mulligan's fretful mood eased over the course of the afternoon, and though he was still reluctant to have much to do with the rest of them, he spoke easily with Harrison, whose stern calm had been replaced with contentment.

Nightfall failed to chase away their levity. Most of them weren't keen to retire to their hotel, so as the clocks tolled later and later hours, they sat out in the warm night air, in a small park beside a lively club. A glittering sign spelled out *The Garden*, its letters entwined with vines and flowers. Music drifted through the club's closed doors, accompanied by the sounds of laughter and merry making.

"For possibly the end of the world, today has been a really nice day," Zane said.

Perched on a swing, her legs moved idly to sway her back and forth. Antimony sat on the swing next to her, Gear's bag down in the sand and the automaton's head on her lap.

"No kidding." Finch leaned against the swing set's metal frame, out of danger of getting kicked. He drummed his fingers to the beat of the club's music. Gloucester, leaning next to him, murmured a lazy agreement. The entire day had been a much-needed respite.

"Maybe it's just the air in this place, but I've gotta say, I'm liking the Hartland," Finch went on, slinging his arm around Gloucester's shoulders with a grin.

"It's certainly refreshing," Antimony mused. "Even Mr. Mulligan and Mr. Harrison seemed chipper."

The politician and his bodyguard had returned to the hotel an hour or so earlier. Still, Antimony wasn't wrong: even Mulligan's ill temper had been soothed by the unexpected day off from their mission. When they'd parted ways, Mulligan and Harrison were cheerfully discussing what they would get for room service, sounding more like friends than an employer and employee.

"Chipper," repeated Zane. "Not a word I would have thought to describe either of them, but I like it." She laughed, the sound open and girlish.

In contrast, Finch's was a low rumble. Gloucester could feel it as much as hear it, making him realize how close he and the magician were standing. Finch's arm traveled down from Gloucester's shoulders to his waist, a notably forward display of affection from him, considering the public space. A happy warmth spread through Gloucester. His own hand brushed Finch's leg.

The music changed to a different song, one with an upbeat tempo difficult to ignore even from a distance. Gear began to hum along. Antimony tapped her foot, and Finch laughed lowly again as he pulled Gloucester closer.

Zane got to her feet, leaping smoothly from the swing and landing in the sand. "I feel like dancing," she declared.

She pointed at the club. Light spilled from its doors as some newcomers entered, and for a moment the music sounded louder, as if beckoning them inside.

Gloucester looked at the club, then back at Zane. "Seriously?"

Were he to make a list of the things he'd thought he might do tonight, dancing wouldn't be on it. He hadn't been to a club in a long time. That sort of carefree activity belonged to the old Gloucester, the one who hadn't yet been imprisoned or betrayed, who didn't know all the dangerous things he knew now. He knew he ought to be scoffing at the very idea, especially considering everything going on. But he didn't want to drag anyone's high spirits down, including his own.

He opened his mouth to agree, feeling the warmth of Finch's breath on his neck, but it was Antimony who spoke.

"Something isn't right."

She said it vaguely, a smile on her face. Yet the words hung in the air, and Gloucester watched as the cheerful look fell away from her features. Just as he knew it fell from his own. Realization was dawning, and with it came a slinking unease.

"Nah." Zane laughed. "It's all right!"

But it was in her voice, too. Anxiety and doubt growing beneath a gaiety that abruptly felt forced.

"Nothing's wrong with a good day," she said. The insistence sounded like she was trying to convince herself more than anyone else.

Gloucester shook his head slowly. While he was reluctant to let go of the good mood, it was starting to seem more like a haze. The untrustworthy cheer of inebriation. Something in it felt all too familiar, now that he was properly focused on it.

"Fuck," he heard Finch mutter, drawing away from him as if he'd only just realized how close they were. No one was smiling now, except for Gear, who stared around at them from Antimony's lap.

"What's wrong?" she asked. "Everyone was happy."

"Exactly," Finch growled, rubbing his temples. "Someone's messing with our heads."

"Denken?" suggested Gloucester. The thought of the rogue demigod invading his mind again chased away any remaining joy, like a cold shower. Had Denken somehow sensed them passing by Frettchen and followed them?

Thankfully, Finch shook his head. "This isn't him. Even if he was here somehow and had gotten past my spells, this doesn't feel...the same. Not exactly. It's almost like..."

His halting words were cut off by another curse, but not from him. It was Antimony, who stood up so quickly that she almost dumped Gear's head into the sand beneath her feet. She caught it at the last minute.

"*Angus*," she said.

Zane and Finch groaned. Gloucester looked from one to the other, at a loss.

"Who?" he asked. He felt hot in the face, his embarrassment a combination of confusion and the surefire knowledge that he was once again being played. And, as usual, he remained the only one out of the loop.

"Remember how we said that there are three Brothers?" Finch asked through gritted teeth.

"Yeah," said Gloucester, who had forgotten this fact entirely.

"Angus is number three. The personification of Love."

Gloucester wanted to clamp his hands over his ears and squeeze his eyes shut. Hold at bay the revelation of yet another troublesome immortal being.

Instead, he said, "Oh." He thought about it a bit. "Is he...affecting us, then? Did he make us..."

He was blushing now more than ever, much to his annoyance, as he thought about how close he and Finch had been to some rather public displays of affection. He cleared his throat. "What makes you think this is him? What are his powers? Couldn't it be, I dunno, Denken's effects spreading or something?"

Antimony shook her head. "Like Mr. Finch said, this is different."

She clutched Gear's head protectively to her chest, as if afraid this new god might burst from the shadows to attack them at any moment. Which was a threatening possibility

Gloucester hadn't thought of until that moment. He cursed his frustratingly active imagination. It wasn't helping matters.

"Care to elaborate?" Zane demanded. It was uncommon for her to be short-tempered with Antimony, so her sharpness betrayed how rattled she was. Their good moods were nothing more than distant memories. "For those of us who haven't actually met Angus before?"

"Denken controls thoughts. That's his domain," Antimony explained. "It's what he personifies. Angus...well, they call him the personification of Love, but he has power over emotions in general. Think about it. Love drives so many other emotions. It makes us happy. Or it makes us sad. Angry. Joyful. It can lift you up—"

"—or destroy you." Finch pinched the bridge of his nose. "Great. But what is he doing here?" He waved an arm around at the nighttime city. "His brothers are wreaking havoc in the south, and Angus is just, what, hanging out in the Hartland?"

Antimony tapped her chin in thought. She was the only one having any success in recovering her composure. "I don't know him well," she admitted. "I've only met him a couple of times. He doesn't like humans very much."

"Oh good," said Zane faintly. "That's promising."

"Mostly, he just avoids us when he can. He stays in his Pocket more than the Gambler or Denken have ever cared to remain in their spaces. The Gambler always says that even when he is here in our world, he tends to keep...well, not a distance, *per se*, but...reservations."

"Whatever that means." Gloucester liked Antimony, but this explanation was leaving him with as many new questions as answers. "Is he dangerous?"

She shrugged. "Only if he wants to be."

"I guess we'll soon find out." Finch stared grim-faced at the dance club. "I doubt we ended up in the same city as him by accident. Let's follow the siren's song."

—

They approached *The Garden* warily. Somehow, all of them knew that if this new, mysterious god really was in the city, this was where they would find him.

"I should have known," Antimony murmured. When Gloucester eyed her questioningly, she pointed at the verdant imagery adorning the sign on the building's front. "The Garden is the name of Angus's Pocket. It doesn't feel like a coincidence."

What does he want with us? Gloucester fretted. Antimony's description didn't bode all that well. There was no sense in running now, however; whatever this Angus was after, he would be hard to stop. Better to deal with the situation when it still might be on friendly terms.

A bouncer stopped them at the door, asking for the entrance fee and their IDs. Finch stepped forward and laid a soft hand on the brawny man's bicep. The air whispered with magic, and then, smiling, the bouncer stepped aside. A line of sweat beaded on Finch's brow as he waved them all through the door.

"Tough spell?" Gloucester murmured in his ear. Finch cocked an eyebrow, but he seemed to understand that the question hadn't been meant as a jab.

"Only for some," he answered. Inside, the music was much louder, and he had to lean in close to be heard. "If I was an enchanter, that sort of magic would be child's play. Emotional manipulation and illusions are their specialty. We magicians have to work a lot harder at it."

"Well, it's appreciated," Gloucester told him. Finch's face was quite close to his, and he thought suddenly of kissing him. He resisted. How much of what he was feeling now was real and how much was Angus? The uncertainty made him feel vulnerable and manipulated. The hypocrisy—considering how they'd gotten past the bouncer—wasn't lost on him, and he frowned, uneasy with the whole situation.

"Gods are assholes," he grumbled.

"Agreed," Finch said without hesitation. "I can only guess at the thought process leading to that statement. So, let's go give one a piece of our mind."

The dance floor was a riot of noise and movement. Confetti floated through the air, glittering in the flashing lights. The scent of alcohol and sweat assaulted Gloucester's nose. Countless bodies moved to the music's beat, caught up in the moment and the emotions running wild. Gloucester knew everyone here was feeling as he and the others had been. The only difference being that no one here knew they were in someone else's thrall.

It made him all the more angry. Of his two brothers, Gloucester already knew which one Angus reminded him of.

They threaded through the crowd, trying not to lose sight of each other. The intangible pull was more difficult to depend on now that they were inside, muddled up with the cacophony of sound and emotion. Angus's presence was impossible to accurately describe, but Gloucester could feel it all around them, permeating the large room as surely as the cloying scent of sweat.

It reminded him of something Zane once told him about magic. She'd said it was a matter of noticing it, of discovering its existence, and then you started to see it everywhere. Having realized they were being affected by a demigod's powers, he could begin separating that from his genuine feelings. His mounting anger helped considerably. It made Angus's presence much easier to detect.

Just not when it came to actually spotting the god himself.

"Does anyone know what he looks like?" he asked, raising his voice over the music.

Zane and Finch shook their heads, but Antimony nodded. She'd stowed Gear safely back in her bag, which she now held close to her chest, no doubt worried her creation might be jostled by one of the dancers if she wasn't careful.

"White hair," she called back. An upbeat Nordish rock ballad full of raucous guitar and enthusiastic vocals boomed out of countless speakers, the bass line thudding like a second heartbeat in their chests. "Pale skin and a gap-toothed smile. Or, well, that's how he looked the last time I saw him. They can change their appearances at will, but they tend to stick to certain looks. Personal preferences. And some things can't change."

Gloucester thought of Denken, shivering as he recalled the way he'd been able to change his face—to a degree. He'd shifted forms to look like Finch, but the black eyes and shark teeth had remained, making the imitation all the more unsettling.

Who was to say whether Angus would be the same? They could be looking for anyone. Gloucester searched the faces of nearby dancers, looking for some sign of godliness.

By the time they made it a few steps into the crowd, he started to sense something was wrong. A wayward elbow grazed his ribs, and he winced around an instinctive, "Careful!"

"*Watch it!*" the culprit snarled back in Nordish. The vehemence of the reply caught Gloucester off-guard.

So did the shove the dancer gave him. He stumbled into Zane's shoulder, only to find her gaping at another angry clubber. The young woman, sparkling with glitter and perspiration, was baring her teeth at Zane.

"*Get out of my way,*" she snapped, whirling away again.

"I don't speak Nordish, but that sounded uncalled-for," Zane said.

Gloucester slowed to a halt and observed the crowd pressing in on them from all sides. "I do, and yeah. Can't help but sense a change in the mood here."

Though music filled the club with a major key, the dancers' faces were no longer blissful. Smiles and laughter hardened into glares. Voices raised in accompanying song began to holler angrily. The movement of dance now felt distinctly more like the onset of an all-out brawl.

"It's Angus," Finch said. "The personification of Love messes with emotions. Everyone stick close together, and let's try to get through this without getting punched in the nose."

Easier said than done. Though no fights had broken out yet, as far as Gloucester could tell, it definitely felt imminent. Every step forward earned them a yowled protest from someone who suddenly found them to be in their way.

Soon they were more or less trapped in the mob, unable to see a clear path through. Over to their left, near the bar, shouts rose in volume over the pounding beat, and the crowd descended into a flurry of violence. People on all sides roared in response and moved as an angry herd toward the fight, buffeting Gloucester and the others.

"This is impossible," Zane cried, holding her arms up defensively to shield her face. "Snap out of it, people!"

Her words fell on deaf ears, other than a fellow right beside her, who spat a derisive curse before Gloucester shoved him away.

"If Angus is this powerful, how come we're not falling for it?" Zane asked. "How come we were able to resist?"

She threw a protective arm across Antimony's back. The scientist had curled her slim frame around her bag, blatantly fearful for Gear within.

"Not to brag, but I think the Blocking spells I cast on everyone are doing a lot of legwork here," said Finch, none-too-gently pushing aside a burly club-goer who had just swung his meaty fist at the magician. "That, and we know we're being played. These poor idiots don't have a clue."

He swatted another of the "poor idiots" across the face as she lunged for Gloucester, her makeup streaked and her eyes glinting with a fury not her own.

"We can't hurt them," Gloucester said, feeling rather hypocritical as he was immediately forced to shove back another would-be attacker. The man fell and was swiftly trampled by the crowd. At this rate, someone was going to be seriously injured, if they hadn't been already. Fresh anger flared through Gloucester's chest. "This isn't their fault; they aren't in control. We have to find Angus."

"Right," grunted Finch. "Hold on."

He shouted an incantation and spun on his heel with a dancer's grace. As he moved, his hands brushed over each of his companions. There was a loud popping noise, and then suddenly the din of the club was muted. Flailing limbs were no longer in Gloucester's face, pushed back by a gauzy, rose-hued wall that curved out around him and his friends. They stood in the center of a large pink bubble, approximately six feet around.

"Oh, thank the Saints," Zane huffed.

"Or the magician who actually did it," Finch said. "And it isn't an ideal fix, so let's get a move on. Those louts can't get through to us, but neither can fresh air, so I recommend getting out of here and finding Angus before we run out of oxygen."

They hurried through the crowd, trying not to breathe too deeply. The bubble moved with them. Through the film of it, Gloucester could see clubbers rebound off its sides. The whole experience was so bizarre that he had to hold in a laugh.

By the time the bubble's air became dangerously stale, they'd crossed the dance floor. On the other side was a buffer of tables between the dancers and the stage, which Gloucester presumed hosted musical acts and the like. Along the walls, dimly lit booths and sofas provided more intimate seating. The space here was much less occupied, so Finch risked letting the bubble disappear.

It did so with a sprightly pop. Gloucester and the others gasped in relief, fresh air filling their lungs as the sounds of the club rushed back to full volume.

To Gloucester's surprise, the vitriolic fervor of moments before had gone. The song changed to a slower beat, and with it, the mood shifted. Looking back out at the dance floor, he watched people gawp around in open confusion, help each other to their feet and, in more than a few cases, apologize tearfully to both friends and strangers.

"I guess whatever point Angus was making is made," Antimony said. For once she sounded as unimpressed with an immortal as Finch. Gloucester nodded mutely, turning back toward the booths and tables.

And there he found who they were looking for.

The moment his eyes landed on the pale youth lounging on a sofa, he knew this was the demigod, Angus. Like the Gambler, Denken, and Purpurrot, they possessed a presence larger than themself, charging the air like a human-shaped thundercloud. And if that weren't enough to convince him, the demigod's appearance did the rest.

Like the other immortals, Angus looked young but ageless all at once. At first glance, Gloucester would have placed them in their mid-twenties, but the longer he looked, the more that didn't feel right. All of the demigods hid eternity behind a thin facade of humanity, making a small detail like age irrelevant.

Beyond that, they held little in common physically with their kin. In contrast with Denken's slim build and the Gambler's angular features, the personification of Love was stocky and round-faced, residing in androgynous limbo between masculine and feminine. They put Gloucester immediately in mind of the cherubs featured in the Blue Church of the Nordlands's religious imagery. If one of those chubby baby angels were to grow up, this was surely how they would look.

Their hair was a mop of curls, a white-blond so light as to be almost colorless. Their cheeks were rosy, and their mouth formed a full-lipped smile, decidedly smug. From the short sleeves of their cowl-necked shirt, Gloucester saw black lines of a tattoo spreading down both of their thick arms from their shoulders. It looked like feathers.

Angel wings, he thought. *Maybe the cherub thing is intentional.*

Or maybe it was the other way around. Perhaps it wasn't Angus who had gotten inspiration from the church, but rather the church that had spent the last thousand years trying to depict a god they didn't even realize existed.

As with their kin, Angus's eyes did the most to separate them from humans. Where Denken's were black and Purpurrot's violet, and while the Gambler simply had no eyes in his head at all, Angus's were a pearly white. Pupil and iris alike were even paler than their hair, set against an ebony where the whites of human eyes would be. They sparkled in the club's strobing lights, and as the group drew closer, Gloucester realized Angus was crying. Tears tracked stains down the demigod's round cheeks in a silent, unending stream. The sight instilled a melancholy in his soul as surely as the Gambler's voice always did.

The group approached Angus in a shared, cautious daze, staring wordlessly. Angus stared back, smile unwavering. Slowly, they rose to their feet.

They were deceptively tall, standing several inches taller than Finch. It was still nothing compared to Purpurrot's looming height, but more than Gloucester had been anticipating. He shied back an involuntary step, waiting for the demigod to make the first move. For a moment, they all stood frozen, a tableau of expectation.

Finally, Angus opened their mouth. From his experience with the other immortals, Gloucester expected their voice to be overwhelming. He resisted the urge to cover his ears in preparation.

Sure enough, it was as unearthly as all the others. Low and melodic as Purpurrot's, with a sadness reminiscent of the Gambler. There was an allure to it as well, echoing Denken.

"Fuck's sake," they said. "About time. I've been waiting here for flaming ages. Get yourselves together, idiots!"

Chapter 12

Love God, Hate Humanity

As far as godly wisdom went, this left something to be desired.

"Er," said Zane. "What?"

"I've been *waiting*," Angus drawled, eyes rolling upward for the barest of moments. "You do know the fate of the world is at stake, right? You didn't miss that memo?"

"Wow, Love's a bitch." Finch didn't bother lowering his voice. "What were you playing at anyway, with that chaos back there?"

He jammed a thumb over his shoulder in the direction of the dance floor, where people were still picking themselves up. As far as Gloucester could tell, no one appeared in too-rough shape.

"Takes one to know one," Angus retorted, turning their pearly glare onto the magician. "And I wanted to see what you were capable of. If you couldn't handle a few rowdy humans, why should I believe you'd be any use at all against my brothers?"

Whatever Gloucester had been expecting from this meeting, this certainly wasn't it. "All right," he said loudly. "Are we all done bickering now?"

"Barely started," Finch said, but his expression softened as he turned to Gloucester. "But I get your point. Gotta say, though, I'm a little underwhelmed. The oracle sent us all this way for *this*?" He gestured at Angus in disgust. "I'm assuming this meeting is why she sent us north. *This* is the third Brother?"

"I don't care for that title anymore," the Love god cut in. "It doesn't suit me these days. Sibling would be preferred. And trust me, I wasn't exactly tickled pink when Yanni talked to me, either."

"Yanni?" Zane asked.

"Orange Ianto," Antimony clarified. She was the only one unfazed by Angus's prickly behavior, though she offered them a piercing look. "You've spoken to her? In person?"

"Antimony! Nice to see you again." To Gloucester's surprise, Angus actually sounded sincere. The cynical curl of their lip disappeared, and they spread their arms to her in welcome, the lines of their tattoo on further display. "Glad to know someone here is worth talking to. And no, I didn't. Not face to face, at least. She came as an astral projection. I imagine it took a lot of effort on her part, all considering."

"All considering what?" Gloucester asked.

"Considering she's stuck in the Sleeping City." Angus's waspishness returned in an instant. "Obviously. She said she came to all of you in your dreams. She couldn't well do the same with me, since I don't sleep." A hint of smugness coated these words, as if this were a clear mark of superiority.

"Obviously," repeated Finch in a sardonic undertone.

"What else did she say?" Antimony asked. "She wasn't able to tell any of us much. Was she able to speak freely with you?"

"Not as well as either of us would have liked," Angus said. Gloucester was beginning to suspect that the best way to keep this conversation going smoothly would be to bite his tongue and let Antimony carry out their side of things. Whatever disdain the demigod bore for the rest of them, they clearly didn't feel it for Antimony. "She couldn't hold the projection for long. Just enough to tell me I was in the right place and to wait here for the heroes." They regarded them all once again and pulled a very ungodly face. "Her words, not mine."

"Hey now, be kind," Antimony chided gently.

"Blonde scientists aside," they amended. "You've got to admit, Anty, this isn't exactly an awe-inspiring team."

"We are who we are," Gloucester said, going against his own unspoken plan to keep quiet. Out of the corner of his eye, he caught Zane incredulously mouthing the word "*Anty*." "We're trying our best here. You want heroes of legend? Tough. We're what you have, what we all have, so we'll just have to do what we can."

Angus regarded him in silence for an uncomfortably long moment. Their strange eyes and tear-stained face made their expression as difficult to read as those of their eyeless brother.

When finally they spoke again, their voice was level and untainted by impatience. "Interesting," they said, and nothing more.

Again, Gloucester found himself reminded of Purpurrot. The goddess's melodious voice always carried notes of contradiction, beautiful and terrible all at once. In a single phrase, she could evoke the echoes of war drums and the peaceful hum of bumblebees on a summer day. Angus's intonation was much the same. Even in this single, enigmatic word, Gloucester heard more than he could hope to convey in his whole lifetime.

He gave his head a hard shake. The gods were exhausting to be around. He needed to focus.

Whatever Angus meant by their single-worded observation, they didn't appear interested in explaining further, so there wasn't much point in pushing the matter. Not with far more important things to discuss.

"So, Orange Ianto wanted all of us to meet. I'm guessing Finch is right—that's why she sent us to the Nordlands. For this right here."

He tried to ignore his sinking disappointment at the realization that he'd never been meant to return all the way home. From the knowing look Angus sent him, the demigod could read his emotions as easily as Denken could read his thoughts. He tried to ignore this, too.

"Probably," Antimony agreed. She looked at Angus. "The question is...now what? What do you make of the situation in Frettchen?"

Angus ran their hands through their hair with a heavy sigh. The sides were trimmed short in a stylish cut. "My brothers are idiots, that's what I make of it. C'mon, let's go somewhere quieter to talk."

They gestured for everyone to follow them deeper into the club.

Angus led them away from the clamor of the dance floor and up a flight of stairs. At the far end of the second-floor corridor was another lounge area—the VIP section, Gloucester presumed—and it was empty. He thought this would be their destination, but instead, Angus took them inside a richly decorated office on the other side of the hallway. The spacious room was lit with soft, warm light, which reflected off the leaves of dozens of potted plants. The gentle scent of greenery filled the air. Away from the music and movement, this part of the club was starkly quiet.

"Whose office is this?" Gloucester asked. It wouldn't do to have some poor manager burst in while they discussed their plans to save the world from rabid gods.

Luckily, this concern turned out to be unnecessary.

"Mine," Angus answered. They sat down on the edge of the handsome desk that took up a large portion of the room. "I own this club. Have done for years."

The group stared at them. Even Antimony looked surprised, caught off-guard by something she hadn't known about one of the demigods.

"Um," said Zane. She sounded like she was trying to decide what to ask first. She eventually settled on simplicity. "Why?"

"Why not?" Angus countered. Their attention wandered to an intricately pruned miniature tree on the corner of their desk, pinching off a few stray leaves.

"Because of your obvious disdain for humanity as a whole perhaps?" Finch suggested airily. "You act like you can't even stand to be around us. I was told you avoid the human world as much as possible. So why would you own a nightclub in the Hartland?"

The demigod shrugged, not looking up from the plant. They stretched across the desk and pulled a small watering can out from behind it. "I find all of you more tolerable when drunk."

Zane frowned. "When *we're* drunk or when *you're*—"

"Is that really important right now?" Antimony cut in, a little sharply. "Angus, do you have any idea what our next move should be? Can *you* enter Frettchen?"

Tiny tree apparently tended to their satisfaction, Angus set the watering can aside and scratched their chin thoughtfully. Gloucester suspected this was more for show than actual consideration. Surely Angus would have thought all of this through many times over already. They pulled their legs up onto the desk, sitting cross-legged with their elbows on their knees. Everyone stood in a loose semi-circle in front of them, uncomfortable and expectant.

"I think so," Angus said. "It's become like our Pockets. Timeless. Not totally separate, as a Pocket ought to be, but not quite a part of this dimension any longer. It's why no mortals can enter it freely."

"So why haven't you gone in?" Gloucester asked. "Couldn't you talk to your brothers? Calm them down?"

He'd expected sarcasm or a snarky barb in response, but Angus merely shrugged again, unfazed. "Yanni told me to wait."

Part of Gloucester was curious about this strange confidence and loyalty the demigod showed toward the oracle. Especially considering how little they clearly cared for humanity in general. Was it Orange Ianto's power granting her exemption from their disdain? Finch said oracles were as rare as they were powerful, so perhaps Angus saw a kindred unearthly spirit in her.

Whatever the reason might be, this wasn't the time to be postulating about it. If he was lucky, there would be plenty of time to ask later.

"Do you think you could bring us with you if you went into Frettchen?" he asked. "Denken was able to bring us into the Maze before. If Frettchen is sort of like a Pocket now, it should work similarly, I'd imagine."

Angus blinked at him, surprised. Gloucester wasn't sure if this was because they'd not thought of that themself or if they simply hadn't expected Gloucester to think of it too. He doubted they had much faith in the intelligence of humans.

"Perhaps," they said.

Nettled, Gloucester held in the pithy reply that tried to escape him. Arguing with Angus didn't seem like the best idea. If their powers lay in the realm of emotions, who knew what they might be capable of when angry. The world already had enough out-of-control immortals to deal with.

Finch, it turned out, didn't share his concerns.

"Do you have a better plan?" he asked, wagging an accusatory finger in Angus's direction. "If so, consider us agog to hear all about it. I—"

Then a very odd thing happened. Finch opened his mouth, clearly not finished with the disgruntled tirade he was embarking upon, only to stop very suddenly. He flinched. Angus stared at him flatly. Whatever pain or discomfort Finch felt, there could be no question of what—or rather, who—the source was.

The strangest part wasn't any of this, however. It was a sound, on the very edge of Gloucester's hearing. The roaring of fire and the rustling of wings.

"*Angus.*"

Antimony's warning cut like a knife through the tense moment. The sound ceased as suddenly as it had started, but Gloucester knew better than to believe he'd only imagined it. He just wished he knew what it meant. His skin prickled with gooseflesh, the hair on the back of his neck standing up. It had felt like a warning, one he hoped Finch might heed. Then again, considering this was Finch, those hopes weren't high.

"'Perhaps' is better than 'no,'" he said quickly, endeavoring to intercept any further arguments before they could get going. "And if it's the only plan we have, then we'll just have to hope for the best."

Angus turned to him and laughed. To Gloucester's surprise, it wasn't derisive. It sent relief flooding through him, soothing as the touch of cool water on a burn.

"I like your optimism, Mikalai," Angus said. "So 'perhaps' it is."

"*Perhaps* we'll live. *Perhaps* we'll all die horribly." Zane sighed. "I hate 'perhaps.'"

—

They left Angus in their club and headed back to the hotel. Gloucester wasn't quite sure what to make of the third Brother. *Sibling*, he corrected himself mentally. On the one hand, they were as bizarre and unworldly as the Gambler, while on the other, they made Denken's casual attitude seem practically gracious.

"They certainly don't like people much, do they?" he commented to Finch as they made their way through the nighttime streets. A few steps ahead of them, Antimony and Zane had their heads together, chatting quietly. "Or, you know, at all."

"Gods rarely do." Finch had been closed-mouthed and sour since Angus silenced him earlier. Still, he attempted a smile and clapped Gloucester on the back. "But you're right—they are *not* our biggest fan. Some god of Love they are. Talk about irony! No wonder so many love songs are full of bitterness and pain, with that prick personifying things." He shook his head, then cast an amused look at Gloucester. "They seemed to like you well enough, though."

"Not sure why," he said. "If they're gonna judge humanity so harshly, I'm hardly special enough to earn an exception. Antimony's friends with Purpurrot and the Gambler, so it makes sense that Angus might have grown to like her, but why me?"

Finch's amusement tempered. "I mean," he said seriously, "you did save their brother. And attempted to once before that, even when you didn't know the Gambler at all, and paid pretty damn dearly for it. Maybe Angus knows that."

He shrugged and laughed again, his bad mood easing away the further they got from Angus's club. "Or maybe they just like your handsome face."

—

Sitting in the hotel room an hour later, Gloucester was still dwelling on this conversation. Beside him, Finch slept peacefully. Perhaps when you had seen and done as much as he had, it took a lot more to cause unrest. Gloucester, however, couldn't quiet his mind enough to sleep.

Did Angus really hate humans as much as they claimed to? If so, were they a trustworthy ally? Then again, did that matter when they had little choice but to place their trust in them?

Amid all these questions chasing their tails through his thoughts, Finch's words echoed: *They seemed to like you well enough.*

Gloucester had always enjoyed puzzles, but there was no annoyance quite like that of a piece which didn't fit. Twist and turn it every which way, and still it continued to defy, making the entire picture lack sense. He couldn't help but feel that's what he was. The piece that didn't fit.

He had no magic, no connection to the immortal personifications beyond that of mere circumstance. He'd felt in over his head since the moment Denken slunk into his thoughts to try and make him kill the high minister. He shouldn't even be there, let alone have others deferring to him as a leader or gods giving him a second glance. He just wished he knew what any of them saw when they looked at him.

Finch's guess made sense, he supposed, but it wasn't like he was the only one who'd been there, rescuing the Gambler. And anyway, wasn't that what most people would have done, had they been in his shoes?

If you spend all your time worrying about what other people are thinking, you'll drive yourself mad, his mother used to tell him. There would be a sad smile on her lips as she ruffled his hair. *Sometimes,* she'd add, *you just have to tell yourself it doesn't matter. People will think what they think. But if you do good, if you do what is right, what is kind, then you will win the hearts of those who truly matter.*

Sometimes the lesson would be shorter and simpler: *Try not to worry so much, Mikalai.*

Easier said than done, Mum, Gloucester thought now. Still, as he closed his eyes, he kept her words in mind. He tried to counter all of his questions with one simple piece of advice, tailored to fit:

Try not to worry. Do good. Do right.

Despite this mantra, the sleep he fell into was an uneasy one, haunted by specters of weeping gods and a city frozen in time.

Chapter 13

Dream-walking

As Gloucester drifted into a fitful sleep, beside him Cassus Finch was already in the midst of a nightmare. It was a particularly lucid one, which never boded well. For a magician, lucid dreams were often more than mere constructs of a sleeping imagination.

In it, he wandered through the well-maintained streets of Frettchen's Uptown. As nightmares went, things certainly could be worse, at least in terms of outright horror, but he didn't need monsters leaping out at him to know this wasn't going to be a pleasant dream.

The shops and restaurants stood abandoned, drenched in silence. More than simple quiet, this was the complete absence of sound. He could feel it pressing down on him, squeezing his chest, the hand of an invisible giant. No pigeons rustled or cooed from ledges above the storefronts. No bees hummed around the flower baskets hanging from streetlamps. No electricity hummed on the edge of his hearing. Cars and other vehicles filled the roads, but they stood empty and motionless, frozen in time. Overhead, dark clouds tumbled and swirled, but the roar of the storm was absent, swallowed by the all-encompassing silence.

Soundless, too, were the footfalls of the monstrosity that rounded the corner at the end of the street. Finch's peripheral vision burned, white spots chasing across his vision as he whirled about.

Most of the buildings in Uptown were no more than two stories tall, apart from the occasional clocktower or ambitious residential complex. The Gambler loomed above the architecture like a child walking through a village of dollhouses. Finch craned his neck as he stumbled back, searching for some discernable feature in the burning figure's distant face. There was none he could parse out. Just fire, white-hot. Every step the demigod took brought him meters closer. Finch tried to move, to run or hide, but his feet were rooted to the pavement.

"Oh, come on," he whispered, trying desperately to yank the soles of his boots free. "What is this, punishment? This is a bloody dream! What, is it my guilt manifesting or something? That's rubbish. I'm not going to give over to this...psychological self-flagellation, like some sort of whimpering idiot. So come on, me, *move*!"

But still, he couldn't budge. The Gambler was almost on top of him, silent stomping strides reverberating through Finch's very bones. The fire blistered his skin, burned the breath from his lungs. He felt like he was about to burst into flames himself.

Tears leaked from his eyes as he squeezed them shut, evaporating from his lashes in an instant. Was this just a nightmare? A prophecy? Was it somehow real?

What would happen if he died here? He was surely about to find out—

The heat vanished. Its sudden, jarring absence sent shivers convulsing across Finch's skin. His treacherous feet finally remembered how to move, and he fell clumsily to hands and knees, gasping for breath. Opening his eyes, he stared down at the backs of his hands, expecting to find them burnt and blistered.

The skin was unmarred by anything other than his usual freckles and the many minuscule scars earned over his lifetime.

Finch collapsed onto his side and rolled onto his back. He lay there for a long moment, trying to regain control over his spinning thoughts and thundering heart. No sign of the Gambler remained.

"Saints, I hate dreaming," he gasped up at the clouds once his lungs were no longer gasping for air. He didn't think it was a prophetic dream, at least. Just a nastily lucid nightmare. The two could appear dangerously similar, but this didn't have the same unexplainable feel of prophecy. Not yet at least. They sometimes had a way of sneaking up on him, interrupting his dreamscape with riddles and breadcrumbs to follow.

Finch wasn't surprised when his surroundings shifted suddenly, changing to a residential street. It was less as if he'd abruptly transported there and more like time had shivered and skipped, in the strange way it so often did in dreams. One moment he was lying on his back in Uptown, the next he was standing in the center of a completely different road. Two lines of brick townhouses faced each other from opposite sides of the street, their front gardens bursting with springtime greenery. Here, too, the same silence reigned. The same stillness.

"I know this place," he said.

Voicing things aloud helped him to remember his dreams after he woke up. And he had a feeling he would want to remember this one. Plus, it felt reassuring to organize his thoughts. Impose some sort of control over the dream, in whatever small way he could.

"This is where Antimony lives." He paused, looking around at the houses again, then amended, "Except not quite."

While the townhouse directly in front of him, with its painted blue door and large rhododendron, was certainly the home of Antimony Jones, Finch also recognized the house across the street. Enough to know that it wasn't there in real life.

It was the dilapidated old house Denken had settled in to build his new Maze in the human world. In reality, it existed across the city from Antimony's home. Yet here it was, ominous and ramshackle. Immediately behind it loomed the pale stone walls of All Saints Shrine, equally displaced. In direct contrast with the church's ornate facade, the house looked on the verge of collapse.

"I'm sensing symbolism here," Finch said to himself.

The door of the broken-down house creaked open. Other than his own voice, it was the first noise to break the silence. From the outside, the structure was unimpressive, an abandoned building in need of significant work or demolition. Inside lay a different story. Hidden within its crumbling walls was a pocket of powerful magic. A space between worlds.

One that appeared to be beckoning him in. In the church behind it, light flared to life through stained-glass windows.

Standing in the middle of the empty street, Finch hesitated. His dreams didn't usually present him with a choice like this. Even the visions generally guided him toward what he was supposed to see, whether he liked it or not. This felt different.

"Go in or stay out," he muttered, weighing his options. Nothing good had come of either place, and a self-opening door was spooky enough to be worrisome. Then again, the dream was clearly trying to show him something.

"Onward to glory." He sighed and took a step toward the buildings.

Only to freeze an instant later, the street's silence interrupted by something other than the sound of his own voice or the door's creak. Sharp peals of laughter cut through the air, ringing out behind him. Finch spun on his heel to face Antimony's house. No one was visible, but he narrowed his eyes, staring at the front window. For a moment, he thought he glimpsed something behind the glass. Something huge. Something that darted out of sight in an instant.

A shiver ran down his spine. He wasn't alone here.

It's just a dream, he reminded himself. *It can't hurt you.*

Caught between the two sides of the street, Finch hesitated again. Both seemed to beckon him, yet both seemed to warn him away. The still air of the city turned cold with menace.

"There you are! I've been looking all over for you."

Finch jumped, rattled by the sudden words, and turned sharply on his heels again. The street was still deserted. He searched the gardens, the parked cars in driveways, the shadowed porches, but couldn't spot anyone.

"I hate walking in magicians' dreams," someone said from right behind him. "You've all got slippery minds."

This time, when Finch spun around, he caught a glimpse of red hair and an apologetic grimace. Then a hand pressed flat against his sternum and *pushed*. Immediately, he was overtaken by the sensation of falling backward. Down, down, down into darkness. Three words were the last thing he heard:

"Sorry about this!"

Chapter 14

Possession is Nine-Tenths of the Law

Gloucester awoke to movement in the bed beside him. Finch sat up very suddenly, as if bolting awake from a nightmare.

"Everything all right?" Gloucester asked sleepily. Squinting bleary eyes at the hotel window, he saw a sky the indigo hue of early morning. The semi-distant light of a streetlamp left Finch more a silhouette than anything as he leaned forward, clutching his head. The pitter-patter of rain filtered in through the window's screen, accompanied by the buzzing of mosquitoes.

"I'm fine," Finch replied.

He didn't sound fine. Strain pulled the reply taut. Gloucester sat up, peering at Finch with some concern. Reaching across the rumpled sheets, he clicked on the bedside lamp, wanting a better look at him. Finch's face remained downturned, hidden by his hands. Caution whispered a warning in the back of Gloucester's mind. His enchanted rings were on the nightstand beside the lamp, and he quietly picked them up.

"You sure?" he pressed, sliding the rings onto his fingers. "You sound...off."

Finch huffed. It was a distinctly un-Finch-like sound. "Bloody hell. Fine. You got me."

Bizarre statement aside, there it was again: something about his voice was wrong.

Finally, it clicked. No accent. Or rather, in the place of Finch's West Islander lilt was a thoroughly Frettchennian accent. Which meant...

"You're not him," Gloucester accused, kicking away the blankets and leaping to his feet. Putting himself between the interloper and Zane's bed, he raised his hand with fingers splayed. Magic hummed faintly to life in the rings. There was only one being he knew for certain could take other people's forms.

"I'm not Denken!" Finch—or whoever the imposter was—said hurriedly. He raised his chin, finally making his face visible to Gloucester. He looked like himself, but Gloucester didn't lower his hand. "I'm guessing that's what you're thinking. Look!"

He hastily stuck a finger into the corner of his mouth to pull his lip back, displaying blunt human teeth. His eyes, wide and imploring, lacked Denken's inky hue.

From the other side of the room, Zane stirred, woken by the noise. "Wha's the matter?" she mumbled.

"I'm not sure yet," Gloucester said, never taking his eyes off the magician. His thoughts flickered to his gun, but it was stowed away in his paltry luggage, completely useless to him now. If he cast the Shield spell, he could maybe give himself the time to grab it, but then what? "If you're not Denken, then who are you? You're not Cassus!"

Finch winced as he disentangled himself from the bedsheets and turned to properly face Gloucester, apologetic frown almost a pout. Another expression unsuited to him at all. "I'm just borrowing him for a moment. And believe me, he's not happy about it. But magic-users as powerful as he is are more in touch with the dream world than most. Makes him a good conduit. And I needed to talk to you lot properly, rather than in snippets of dreams."

"Snippets of—" Gloucester stared. "*Orange Ianto*?"

The person in Finch's body ducked his head in acknowledgement. "The one and only. You'll have to tell him sorry from me after this. He is gonna be *furious*."

Gloucester could understand why. The idea of having his body hijacked, even by a relatively friendly person, was horrible. The look on his face must have conveyed as much, because Ianto-Finch dodged away from making eye contact, contrite.

"Yeah, I know, it's weird," she said. "And not exactly fun for me either, you know. But it's important. Things are getting worse in Frettchen. We don't have a lot of time left. Whatever you're seeing already is nothing compared to what will come if Denken's influence continues to spread. We're talking tidal waves of weirdness. Not just towns, but whole continents getting wiped into the same semi-existence as Frettchen, their people lost."

"Wait. Am I getting this straight?" Zane sat up and stared at them from her bed, still muzzily blinking away sleep. "This isn't, like, some really weird dream or something, is it?"

"Sorry, Zane," said Ianto-Finch. This, in Gloucester's opinion, proved the possession beyond a shadow of a doubt. The real Finch would never willingly apologize to Zane. "You'd best grab the others. You're in the Nordlands, right? I figured you had to be, since you're close enough to latch onto his mind."

"Yeah, um, okay." Zane got out of bed and shuffled to the door, blanket wrapped around her shoulders. She seemed too confused and sleepy to question the bizarre situation any further.

As the door clicked shut behind her, Gloucester rounded on Ianto-Finch with a glare.

"Is he awake in there?" he demanded. "Does he know what you're doing to him?"

"I'm not doing anything to him." Ianto had the grace to look guilty. "All right, well, I mean, yeah, I get what you mean. The answer is 'sort of.' He'll be groggy for a bit once I'm gone, but I reckon he'll remember it more or less. It's not like I do this very often," she said, rather defensively. "He isn't hurt or anything, though. I promise. I can sort of feel him moving around up here—" She tapped Finch's fingers against his temple. "—and he's not pleased at all."

Gloucester scoffed. Only now did he drop his hand back to his side, but he refused to relinquish his accusatory glare. "I wonder why!"

To Ianto's credit, she didn't snap back at him. Instead, she sighed. "I know it isn't a great thing. It wasn't nice of me. I'm a better dream-walker than most, but it isn't my specialty. And Cassus here is the only one among you who's powerful enough to walk solidly in the dream world. That's the only way I can contact you lot. You, you're close, just with magical sensitivity, but your mind is too unsettled."

Gloucester wasn't sure what to make of that. On the one hand, it was surprising to hear that Ianto considered him a close second to Finch when it came to magical inclination. On the other, he was immensely—and perhaps selfishly—relieved she *hadn't* chosen him. Being in Denken's thrall had been bad enough. The idea of someone stealing control of his whole body turned his stomach.

That, combined with what felt like a dig at his mental state, only fanned the flames of his anger. Perhaps the oracle sensed that—or foresaw it—because she hurried on before he had a chance to interject.

"I wouldn't have done this if I didn't think I had to, all right? And if we all live to see each other face to face, I promise I'll apologize."

Nothing about this was all right, as far as Gloucester was concerned. Still, he nodded grudgingly.

In a bid to calm his temper and nerves, he forced himself to take a seat on the edge of Zane's bed, drawing in a measured breath. For all the times magic dazzled him, there were as many times like this, when its power struck him as dangerous. A sinister and overbearing force, even in the hands of the well-intentioned. If this was what someone trying to do right was capable of, he didn't want to imagine what someone determined to do ill could manage.

He didn't have to, of course. The current state of Frettchen was already proof enough.

"It's just as well I didn't use you," Ianto went on. For a second time, she tapped her stolen temple. "You think you're angry? He would have killed me."

Gloucester was still processing that when the door reopened. Zane appeared, looking more awake and inquisitive now, followed by the others. Antimony even had Gear out of her bag. The automaton was the only unworried face in the room. Nor did she seem at all tired. She gazed around with the same bright-eyed interest as always.

"Is this a party?" she asked, before anyone else could speak.

"Er...no," said Gloucester.

Gear looked vaguely disappointed. "Oh," she said. "I've never been to one, but Murphy tried explaining them to me once."

Murphy, Antimony's housemate, had struck Gloucester as surprisingly accommodating of a sentient clockwork robot in the house. Living with Antimony Jones probably meant getting used to all sorts of strange things.

Gear's eyes landed on Ianto-Finch, and she gasped. "Oh!" she cried, enthusiasm renewed. "Who are you?"

They all stared. Gloucester glanced over at Zane, but she looked as dumbstruck as the rest of them.

"I didn't say anything," she promised, moving to sit next to him. "Just that we all needed to talk right away. I don't even know how I would explain this. Gear, how did you know that's not Finch?"

Gear's head twitched as she tried to shrug without the significant aid of shoulders. "He's just different. Usually, Finch is all...hmmm...sharp. Now he's soft."

"I am not!" Ianto protested with a pout.

"And his eyes are a different color," Gear added.

Gloucester looked more closely at Finch's face. Gear was right. His green eyes were now a stormy blue. The color of Ianto's eyes, he guessed.

He wasn't the only one to make that connection. Antimony leaned forward, peering at Finch with unusually open interest. After a moment, she asked, "Ianto? Is that you?"

Lingering by the door with Harrison, a disheveled Mulligan sighed. "Oh, what fresh hell is this?"

—

To Gloucester's chagrin, no one else took much offense to Orange Ianto's possession of Finch's body. Antimony in particular handled the odd circumstances as if they were completely ordinary, which Gloucester found entirely unsurprising but more than a little irritating. The others in the group simply looked on in sleepy shock and mounting intrigue.

The oracle was quick and matter-of-fact as she explained the situation, talking mostly to Antimony. Gloucester got the distinct impression she was avoiding looking him in the eye.

"How bad are things in Frettchen?" Antimony asked. She leaned against the chest of drawers near the end of Finch-Ianto's bed, Gear's head still cradled in her arms. "Do you know? Or are you..."

"Sleeping," Ianto finished. "Yes. But also, yes." She twisted Finch's lips in a frown. "I might be the only human in Frettchen who has any idea what's happening. Maybe some of the stronger dream-walkers, but it's hard to say. As far as I can tell, everyone's stuck in a sort of in-between space. It's hard to explain. I think it's better if you just see for yourselves. And, well, I suppose the Brothers are sort of aware. '*Sort of*' being the operative words. I've tried reaching out to both of them, but neither one is responding, so it's no good."

"So, what *do* you know?" Gloucester asked, rather sharply.

"What I see in my dreams." Perhaps Ianto was losing patience with his annoyance, because there was a testy edge to her voice to match. Still, she was quick to recognize this wasn't an exceedingly helpful answer and went on to explain: "I'm an oracle, so my dreams are more solid than other people's, even when they aren't actual prophecies. You know, like the one I was trying to warn you about before everything went pear-shaped."

She flung a pointed look at Antimony, who ducked her head slightly, apologetic at the subtle accusation. It had been her not answering her phone which led to them receiving Ianto's warning too late.

"Mostly I'm stuck in my own dreamscape," Ianto continued. "Which, admittedly, is more useful than most people's. I can reach out to folks, like I did with your dreams back in the South Cities. And I still get premonitions. And then there's this." She gestured at the body she wore. "I was lucky to find him while he was sleeping. It's not easy to locate dreamers when you're not physically close to them. Especially if you don't know them well."

Glancing around the room, Gloucester could see he wasn't the only one to whom this was all new information. Though Zane and Antimony nodded in understanding, Mulligan and Harrison gaped, openly sharing his bewilderment. Gear, accustomed to not knowing things, hummed cheerily to herself.

"All well and good...I think," said Mulligan. "But what good does telling us all this do?" Making use of the kitchenette to brew a pot of instant coffee, he waggled a spoon interrogatively at Ianto.

"Nothing." Ianto shrugged. "But I'm not *always* stuck in my dreamscape. Sometimes I find the right door. I've only managed it a few times, but sometimes I find my way into...*his*."

"Whose?" Gloucester demanded, in no mood for theatrical reveals.

For the first time, Ianto smiled. Even *that* looked different from the crooked grin Finch usually wore. This time, it was small and grim.

"The Gambler," she answered.

Gloucester gawped. Around him, everyone else did the same. Even Antimony blinked in muted astonishment.

"You've been in the Gambler's dreams?" Zane asked. "He's *sleeping*? But he's all..." She trailed off, but waved her arms in a vague way, pantomiming the dancing of flames as she pretended to take a few stomping steps. With the overly serious set of her face, it would have been a funny display under different circumstances.

"Ehhhh," Ianto said, as she waved Finch's hand in a mildly dismissive gesture. "Sort of. It's a little hard to explain. He's...stuck. Caught between our world and Denken's Pocket. Sort of the immortal version of being not quite awake, not quite asleep."

"Why's he stuck?" Gloucester asked. "Can you talk to him in his dreams? His dreamscape or whatever? Can he help us?"

Ianto raised Finch's hands in a *whoa there* motion. "One question at a time. He got stuck because of the rough shape he was in when Denken's power exploded. I reckon it was a self-defense thing. Instinct more than conscious choice. He took on his most powerful form to combat the blast of power, but now he's caught in it. Far as I can tell, it's taking up most of his consciousness just to contain his own raw power. One slip up and he could set half the Lower Lands ablaze."

"Comforting to know," Gloucester muttered. Zane made a noise of amusement, then shrugged when he glanced at her askance.

"Stole the words right out of my mouth," she said, before turning back to Ianto. "So, what did you see in his mind?"

"Fire," Ianto answered. "And fear."

"Seriously, Yanni?" said an uncanny voice. "Do try to be a little *more* enigmatic."

They all whirled to face the door. Leaning against the frame was Angus, looking for all the world like they'd been there all along. Gloucester swallowed an oath, his ringed hand half-raised in defense. A loud clatter and curse came from Mulligan's spot by the table, where he'd dropped the coffeepot in surprise.

"Saint's teeth, I wish you lot would wear bells," Zane snapped.

"Wow! Who's that?" Gear exclaimed from Antimony's arms. "Are you the person from the loud music place? You've got a very strange voice!"

Since Gear had been stowed away in Antimony's bag while they were at the club, it made sense that she would only know Angus by sound. The Love god blinked at her, their eerie eyes still leaking tears.

"Fuck, that's weird," they said. "Why've you got an extra head, Anty?"

Their amused curiosity then tightened to something shrewder. They swore again, very quietly, and regarded Antimony with a piercing stare. "Does Purpurrot know about her?"

"It's a long story, Angus." Antimony sounded as unfazed as ever, yet Gloucester noticed that she held Gear's head a little more snugly. "How long have you been listening in?"

Gloucester was quite sure there had been no sign of the demigod mere moments before they'd spoken up. Of course, that didn't mean they hadn't been lurking about. He was pretty sure the immortals could turn invisible on a whim.

"Not long," Angus said, giving their head a shake. White curls bounced around their ears. "I felt some odd magic stirring, so I came to find out what it was. It felt strangely familiar, and now I know why. How are you, Yanni? And why are you wearing the magician?"

Color flared in Finch's cheeks, and when Ianto spoke next, she sounded more than a little guilty again. She hugged Finch's arms around herself, shoulders rising unhappily. "I wish you wouldn't say it like that. It was a last resort, all right? I'm stuck in Frettchen. This was the best I could do."

"Hey, hey," Angus said with a laugh. "I'm not judging. He's much less annoying this way. I don't much care for magicians."

She snorted. "You don't much care for anyone."

Harrison cleared his throat loudly. "Can we stay on point here?"

"Yeah," Gloucester agreed. "Unless you plan on *never* giving Cassus his body back."

Ianto's frown deepened. It was clear that she felt bad about what she was doing, but Gloucester had little sympathy for her.

"Right, of course." She took a moment to compose herself, sitting up straighter and releasing a long breath. Like the man she was possessing, she acted at ease in the spotlight, in spite of her momentary bashfulness. Zane had once mentioned that Orange Ianto worked as a fortune-teller, so it made sense that she'd be accustomed to an audience.

"From what I can tell from his mind, the Gambler isn't totally aware of what's happening," she went on, shifting to sit cross-legged on the bed, like a camper launching into a ghost story. "He might look scary, but he's mostly just bumbling about, barely conscious. I think if you can get to him here in the waking world, you might be able to snap him out of it. With Angus's help, you should be able to enter the city without falling under its sway. Well, Angus and a bit of tricky mind magic. Cassus here should be able to perform that. I'm leaving it in his memory."

She said it all so casually that Gloucester couldn't help but stare. Oracles and other soothsayers were born with magic, Finch had explained to him. Like witches, as Finch's mother had been, magic ran in their blood, an innate part of them. Perhaps that was why she could talk about such impossible things without batting an eye.

"Cool," said Zane faintly. It came as a mild comfort that she looked rather stunned herself, despite her own lengthy history with magic. "I'm sure he'll appreciate that."

Gloucester guessed that she, like him, was anticipating a very grouchy Finch when he returned to his stolen senses.

"So, what happens if we wake the Gambler up?" he asked, looking from Ianto to Angus. The demigod merely shrugged. "What about Denken?" he pressed. "Is he the same way? Stuck?"

Ianto shook Finch's head. "Definitely not. Which makes it hard for me to know what's going on with him."

"My best guess is he's doing all he can to wrangle this newfound power of his," Angus supplied. For the first time since their appearance in the doorway, they grew serious. "He's unleashed in a way none of us have been before. Not since Purpurrot was at her full strength. When she was still the All-Mother."

It should have been difficult to reconcile the idea of an all-powerful goddess of creation with the owner of an Uptown pie shop, but Gloucester had met Purpurrot for himself and it really wasn't. Standing head and shoulders above everyone around her, she was as beautiful as a summer storm. He wouldn't soon forget the aura of power she wore, like anyone else would wear a coat. And that was Purpurrot at her weakest, drained of her powers by her prolonged stay in the human world.

All in all, that didn't make for a reassuring comparison when it came to Denken's newly unleashed power. Despite all of Orange Ianto's foretelling and instructions, Gloucester was starting to feel like this was an even more hopeless endeavor than they'd feared. Denken had the power of the universe on his side, and all they had were maybes and perchances.

"Don't feel that way," Angus told him, clapping a hand unexpectedly on his shoulder. Gloucester jumped. There had been no indication of Angus moving toward him. They'd been lounging in the doorway one moment and at his side the next. "It's really bumming me out."

"Thanks for the godly words of comfort," he snarled. Angus winked and gave his shoulder another pat.

"So let me get this straight," Zane cut in. "The plan to save the world goes like this... Walk into Frettchen—*maybe*—to wake up the Gambler—*maybe*—and then...what? The last time we confronted Denken, it didn't go super well, and that was with the Gambler *and* Purpurrot on our side. And he wasn't all-powerful."

Angus muttered something about being bummed out again and flickered over to sit on the bed next to Ianto. This seemed to be their preferred way of getting around, as if walking the short distance was too much effort. *Maybe it's simply too human*, Gloucester thought uncharitably.

Orange Ianto sighed. "I wish I could give you more straight answers. Fortune-telling is a tricky enough business when I'm awake. I'm a lucid dreamer, but I can't always control everything in my dreams. Less so than most, even in some ways. I see snippets of what-could-be's and what-might's, but no certainties. And nothing absolutely clearly. Just puzzle pieces. If I'm lucky, I get enough pieces that fit together to get a hint toward the bigger picture, the most probable future. Breadcrumbs is all I can give you."

She gestured around the room. "I see you lot. The Lost Boy at the center of it all." She pointed at Gloucester. "The Lover and the Friend." She tapped Finch's chest before pointing at Zane. Her finger continued to move from person to person. "The Scientist and her Creation. The Skeptic and the Loyal Man. And the Brothers."

"Siblings," Angus corrected. On the other side of the room, Mulligan muttered skeptically to an ever-patient Harrison about his assigned title.

"Siblings. Sorry. Regardless, you all need the Gambler and Angus at your side. They're in every vision I see. You can't defeat Denken without them."

"What about Purpurrot?" asked Antimony, with a note of what Gloucester thought might be concern.

Ianto gave Finch's head another shake. "I can't see her. Honestly, though, I never really can. Not in my visions. Even when her power was drained, she's not of this world. This world is of her."

Antimony and Angus each nodded in understanding. Gloucester exchanged looks of mutual puzzlement with Mulligan and Harrison, trying to wrap his head around the idea. He wasn't sure he would ever truly understand magic.

He could only hope there would be ample time in the future to dwell on the ongoing discoveries of this brand-new side of his world. They just had to first ensure there would *be* a future. And a world.

"Right, er, sure," he said. "No Purpurrot, then."

This was a difficult thing to set aside. He couldn't help but feel like their most powerful piece on the board had been lost.

Where are you, Purpurrot? he wondered. *We could really use you right now.*

"Don't worry," Angus told him lightly. "You'll have me. And the Gambler, if things go well. Denken won't stand a chance against us!"

With their words, a great wave of emotion swept over the room; relief, like a warm blanket, settled over their minds. Gloucester sighed, a heavy weight lifting from his shoulders. It wouldn't be until a few hours later, when the demigod's power ebbed out of his mind, that he would resent the intrusion.

"Oh shit," Orange Ianto muttered. Her words disturbed the pleasant silence that had fallen over them. "Cassus is waking up proper-like now. I'm out of time."

Gloucester blinked, emerging from the fog of calm. Looking at Finch's face, he saw the blue in his eyes morphing back into green.

"Right," said Ianto hurriedly, her Frettchennian accent beginning to shift back into Finch's Islander lilt. "Good luck!"

Finch took a great shuddering breath. A visible shiver ran through him.

Then he blinked. A deep crease furrowed between his brows as he stared around at everyone assembled in the room.

"Okay..." he said unsteadily. "What the ever-living hell was that?"

The Gambler's Interlude

Dreaming

Fire.

It was everything. All-consuming. Ever present. All he knew. Where possible futures had once filled his skull, shifting like sand, now only fire remained. No futures played out, snatches of could-be's and would-be's and their ever-changing odds. The absence of their cacophonous symphony was painful in a way fire alone could never be. A piece of him was missing, stolen by his own kin, an unmalicious cruelty that hadn't even been noticed by the perpetrator, let alone intended.

Loneliness and betrayal were for the realm of conscious thought, however. The full scope of their pain eluded him, niggling and nagging sensations flickering through his dim awareness like the flames consuming everything else. Never leaving him alone, never to be addressed. Fragments of self, crumbling to ash.

How long had he been this? An instant? An eternity? Even such questions were too concrete to grasp with his burning, drifting consciousness. Perhaps this was simply what had always been. Perhaps the rest was nothing more than a fleeting dream. Shards of memories. Half-remembered futures. Two impossible roads crossing under an endless sky. Eyes whirling free, truly Seeing. The smell of coffee. Peals of pleasant laughter and the ticking of gears. How could any of that be real, compared to the fire?

The inferno burned on, scorching away the faint calls of a name from the edges of his mind.

Chapter 15

In the Hands of Gods

As predicted, Finch was fuming in the wake of Orange Ianto's departure from his mind. The sudden addition of several new spells in his memory did little to appease his indignation, no matter how often he was assured it had been a necessary invasion of boundaries.

"That's a really pretty way of saying 'possession,'" he snapped at Antimony, when she offered this argument. Gloucester nodded in enthusiastic agreement. It earned him a scandalized look from Zane, who seemed to think he wasn't helping matters, but Gloucester for once didn't care what she thought. In his opinion, Finch's anger was well justified.

Angus had little patience for either side of the matter. "Enough," they said, injecting the single word with a flare of annoyance sharp enough to sting. "Meet me at the southernmost city gates at noon. We'll leave from there."

Before any of them had a chance to question this command, they vanished.

Gloucester sighed. “I really hate how they do that.”

A tense morning unfolded, a far cry from the carefree mood of the previous day. Outside, the sky was a glum echo of the temperaments inside the hotel, drab gray clouds threatening a return of the night’s rain. With Finch moody and waspish as he worked through Orange Ianto’s spells, Gloucester and Zane spent an hour tracking down breakfast for the group, eager to be away. The others were no better company: Mulligan and Harrison were antsy, unimpressed with the haphazard plan depending so heavily on the magic they both distrusted, while Antimony was even more distant and stoic than usual.

While they waited in line at a nearby coffee shop, Zane suggested it was the scientist’s own way of showing her stress.

“It probably doesn’t help having to carry Gear around all the time. Her back is probably killing her. I offered to carry the bag for a while, back on the boat, but she said no. When it comes to Gear, I think she doesn’t really trust anyone enough to hand her over to them.”

A whiff of hurt flitted across her face before she squinted up at the menu above the counter. “Do you think they have Frettchen fogs here?”

—

As the noon hour approached, Gloucester led the group toward the Hartland’s southern gates. Here the buildings were mostly houses, interspersed with the occasional corner shop or public park. The train station was a ten-minute walk west of their destination. Though it also had a city exit, it would only draw unwanted attention to them. The trains, after all, were neither coming nor going from the southern direction.

Therefore, they were headed for a smaller gate, where people came and went on foot or by car. A number of small towns and hamlets were nestled in the hills surrounding the

Hartland, and even the crisis in Frettchen couldn't stop the localized ebb and flow of day-to-day life.

They reached a street corner and paused. For the first time since their arrival, the city walls sat in full view before them. Though the gray stone was made more for function than aesthetics, the beauty of simplicity and grandeur of scale were compelling all the same, and Gloucester felt that the gardens softened the structure's harsh lines, adding a modern flair.

Finch leaned over to speak in his ear. "These walls were built with magic," he said, pointing up at the long line of stone.

Gloucester gaped at him. This was apparently the reaction Finch had been hoping for, as he grinned in a satisfied way. Considering how ill-tempered he'd been all morning, Gloucester wasn't about to complain.

Instead, he encouraged him. "What? How so?"

Distracting Finch from his bad mood was just a bonus. He was genuinely intrigued, and considering what they were heading into today, he could use a little distraction too. Anxiety had paced prickling steps up and down his spine for hours. In just a few minutes, they'd be facing the unknowable dangers of Denken's hold over Frettchen. He'd eagerly take a little light-hearted conversation in the meantime.

"Warding spells, mostly," Finch said. "For protection. To make them withstand time and wear and whatever else might try and get past them."

"Would Denken's power—?"

But Finch was already shaking his head before he could finish the question.

"Mayhaps the spells would slow it down some, maybe already are, even, but not enough. I don't reckon human magic alone would ever be enough to stop the wave of weirdness building up in Frettchen."

"You, of all people, should know better than to dismiss human magic so easily." Antimony fell into step with them on

Gloucester's other side. "It wasn't just magicians who built walls like these, after all. It was sorcerers."

Gloucester blinked at her. "What's the difference?"

Finch answered before Antimony could, reluctant as ever to share the spotlight. "There are a few. Sorcerers are rare, for one. As rare as oracles. I'd say maybe even more so, but I've only ever met Orange Ianto now—sort of." He paused for a moment to grimace. "I've met two sorcerers in my life that I know of. Though one of them might have been lying through his teeth to impress me."

"So, what can sorcerers do?" Gloucester asked.

The walls loomed higher and higher as they continued down the sidewalk. Ahead of them, Harrison seemed to have lucked into an amicable conversation with Zane. Gloucester guessed she was so worried about what lay ahead that she'd forgotten to snub him. Maybe he wasn't the only one open to a little distraction.

"If you listen to the legends, just about anything they want. Martial magic, shape-shifting, temporal phasing, you name it. The stories say that in the time of the Old Empire, there were sorcerers everywhere. Then they disappeared."

Gloucester's next question must have been apparent, because Finch addressed it before he could even open his mouth. "No one knows how or why. Theories abound, of course. Some say they all died, murdered by royals or maybe just by each other. Some say they had their magic stripped away for crossing the gods. And some say they simply left the Lower Lands. After all, if anyone had the power to cross the northern mountains, it would be the sorcerers of old. Maybe they found something better on the other side."

Gloucester stared up at the stone walls. Like so much in his life, they were now imbued with new meaning. Was magic really so entrenched in the Lower Lands? How had he spent so much of his life never noticing it?

"It's weird," he mused aloud. "I guess I really was blind to the world around me."

This earned him a chuckle and a pat on the back from Finch. "Magic's good at hiding."

Zane's voice drifted back to them. "Unless you're the personification of Love and just don't care."

She stopped, allowing everyone to catch up with her, and then pointed ahead, where they were greeted with a very strange sight.

They were approaching a small church, its white brick accented with blue paint at every opportunity: doors, window shutters, elaborate gables, roof tiles. These decorations marked it as part of the Blue Church, the most prevalent religion in the north.

Perched atop the church's short garden wall was Angus. They lounged with feline grace, propped up on one elbow, as they smoked a long wooden pipe. Fat white puffs swirled and danced unnaturally around their head and bare shoulders, sparkling like sunshine on snow. Several actual cats sprawled around them, batting lazily at the wisps of smoke. Though the gray sky hadn't lightened any, the air around Angus seemed brighter, projecting an aura of warm spring and sunshine. A breeze dancing down the street carried the scent of flowers. Half a dozen people were crowded around Angus, and from the glazed looks on everyone's faces, it was clear their overwhelming presence was getting the better of the humans.

Gloucester and the others moved forward hesitantly, wary of getting too close.

"No way I'm going near them if they're doing that to people," Gloucester said. It was bad enough being around a demigod who was behaving themself. The Gambler had never tried to manipulate him, and even his presence could be difficult to stand.

"Seconded." Zane eyed the scene with open scorn. "If you ever catch me looking at anyone like that, slap me upside the head."

"Will do." Finch sneered, but his derision wasn't aimed at Zane. "For someone who claims not to like people, they certainly enjoy being the center of attention. I'd be jealous, but it's not like any of the adoration is actually earned."

"Angus takes a lot of getting used to," Antimony said, crossing her arms and eyeing the spectacle impassively. "But they're not as bad as their first impression suggests. They're—"

"Please don't say 'complicated,'" Gloucester interjected.

She hummed, a quiet, polite sound, but layered in unspoken meaning. "A cliché, maybe, but true, nevertheless. Gods are complicated."

"*People* are complicated," Finch said. "Gods are chaos."

—

The cheery peacefulness left Angus's strange face the moment they spotted the group. Disdain swept across the street like a physical wave. Those people and cats flocking around the demigod scattered, darting away like startled minnows. Gloucester imagined he felt a tinge of warmth as Angus's gaze crossed his own. But when the demigod spoke, they sounded as unimpressed as their projected emotions suggested.

"About time," they said by way of greeting, straightening up in a languid motion. They flicked their wrist, the pipe in their hand vanishing. "I've been bored stiff."

As if to emphasize this, they yawned and stretched their arms over their head. Lines of black ink swirled across their pale biceps. Up close, Gloucester could make out additional details of the tattooed feathers in white. The intricate artwork seemed to move, wings ruffling in the breeze.

"You've probably been here five minutes," Antimony chided, the only one among them not staring at Angus in open annoyance. "And we're right on time."

There was *definitely* warmth when Angus looked at Antimony. "Yeah, well," they said. "I get bored fast. So, let's go."

Gloucester was quite certain that if it were anyone other than Antimony admonishing them, the demigod wouldn't be so civil. He wondered how well the pair knew each other. He'd noticed Antimony got along with all of the immortals. Even Denken had seemed fond of her before all hell broke loose. What was it about Antimony Jones that raised her so far above other humans in the eyes of Purpurrot and the Siblings?

Gloucester pushed the question to the back of his mind before it could become more than idle curiosity. He'd ask Zane about it later.

Providing we survive.

That thought was less than comforting, stirring up his nerves anew. He drew in a long, steadying breath. The last thing he needed was to go into Frettchen in the spirals of an anxiety attack.

"Wait!"

The protest came from the back of the group. Mulligan was glaring at Angus. Though objectively dwarfed by Harrison, who stood next to him, he drew himself up with every ounce of imperious command he possessed. Up against journalists or politicians, it was probably an effective display of authority.

"You still haven't explained what exactly we're doing."

Angus stared at him flatly. "We're going to Frettchen," they said, the words slow and deliberate. If it weren't for the twitch of amusement Gloucester could feel tickling the back of his consciousness, he would have bought Angus genuinely thinking Mulligan was an idiot.

Mulligan's fists braced against his hips. "Yes, *obviously*. But how? The city's impenetrable."

"No, it's not. It's just locked away. And some of us have a key." They smiled as they spoke, blatantly pleased with themself. Unlike Denken's wide, sharp-toothed grin, Angus's was smaller and distinctly smirking, with a noticeable gap between their front teeth and a dimple tucked into their rosy cheek. It was a smile that ought to have accentuated a youthful appearance. Yet the cupid's smile held an ancient edge.

"And what does that mean for the rest of us who don't?" Gloucester asked. "*Is* this going to be like when Denken took us to the Maze?"

That was the impression he'd gotten, but now that the trip was imminent, he really wanted to be certain. The mind-bending weirdness of Denken's home dimension wasn't something he would forget anytime soon.

Yet the journey between worlds was a chaotic blur. He had no memories at all of the trip to the Pocket, seduced as he had been by Denken's hypnosis, but he'd been perfectly conscious for his return to the human world. All he could recall was a whirlwind of sound, color, and sensation, with only Denken's grip on his arm keeping him from getting torn to shreds. It wasn't an experience he looked forward to reliving.

"Hm," said Angus. They turned their smile on Gloucester, and it suddenly felt more genuine. "A bit like that, yes. Frettchen is now essentially a Pocket of its own, so travel there will be...similar. We'll have to travel through the Void Between Worlds. Just a little more briefly. And it isn't as stable as the Pockets, especially not for humans, which is why Yanni needed to prep your magician with some new spells. Those'll keep all of your little human minds from skittering into the Void as we pass through it."

"Ugh. Can we not?" Zane lamented. She huffed a sigh and squared her shoulders, continuing on before anyone could answer. "I mean, obviously we have to. I just...ugh, don't want to. At all."

Antimony laid a sympathetic hand on her arm. "None of us do."

"But all of us will," said Angus, with the sort of cheerfulness that would have been blatantly false even without their emotions filling the air. The demigod held out their hands. “All right, everyone. Let’s get this little friendship circle going.”

Once they’d all gathered in a circle, Angus looked to Finch. Contempt weighed down the space between them. “Right, spellmaster, put yourself to use.”

Finch might not have been able to share his emotions the way Angus could, but they were still obvious as he glared at the demigod. He raised his hands, offering Angus an impolite gesture with each before gathering magic around them.

Chapter 16

Enemy Territory

The Void was worse than Gloucester remembered, even with Finch's spells guarding his mind. He clung to Angus's hand with white-knuckled fingers, grasping Zane's hand on his other side. It felt like they were walking through a hurricane. A hot wind whipped at Gloucester's face, and it was difficult to breathe. He wasn't sure if he even *could* breathe here in this in-between place.

Then again, he wasn't sure if he needed to. He felt disconnected from his own body. Maybe he didn't have a physical form here, and he somehow existed only as a consciousness being transported. That doubt made him squeeze the hands he held even harder, but then he wasn't sure *that* was real. He couldn't hear anyone else, and he dared not open his eyes. Like breathing, he didn't know if he even could.

For an eternity and an instant, he and the universe were entangled in an existential crisis. He imagined the spells Finch had cast like the bubble they'd used in the club, a safe barrier keeping the Void at bay. He didn't know if that was exactly how it worked, but it made for a comforting thought.

And then it was over. He was himself again, thankfully solid and certain. Air filled his lungs with reassuring ease, and he took great gulps of it, eyes watering and bleary in the newfound reality. He immediately let go of Angus's hand but held onto Zane's for a moment longer. He dimly realized that she was clutching his fingers just as tightly, and when he looked over at her, he saw his own relief and passing fear reflected in her wide brown eyes. Tears clung to her lashes, and she blinked them away in favor of a smile back at him.

A shoulder bumped his, and Gloucester looked away to find Finch staring down at him in concern. Finch's hand was on his arm, his touch grounding.

"Are you all right?" he asked.

Gloucester managed a smile. "I feel like someone put me through a tumble dryer, but I'll live. You?"

Reassured, Finch's cocksure grin was back in a flash of teeth. "Right as rain."

"And the rest of us are fine too, thanks very much for asking," said Mulligan from their right.

He didn't look fine. He and Harrison were leaning on each other, both winded and sweaty.

Mulligan slowly straightened up, adjusting his glasses. "Please tell me that hell was worth it and actually worked."

"Look around," Angus said, tossing their head like a proud horse. "See for yourself."

Gloucester took in their new surroundings. The drab gray sky of the Hartland was gone. Instead, the group stood beneath a ceiling of black storm clouds. Every few seconds, lightning threaded across the sky, a split-second freeze-frame of natural fury that did little to illuminate the shadowed city street where they now stood. What faint sunlight leaked through cast the city in perpetual twilight. Gloucester shivered.

A pale glow emanating from Angus only strengthened the eerie feeling.

The more that Gloucester looked at them, the more obvious it became that they weren't actually glowing. Rather, they were simply immune to the darkness, their colorless hair and rosy skin refusing to be shadowed, regardless of their surroundings.

"That's adorable," Finch said, following Gloucester's gaze and somewhat ruining the ethereal effect. "Like a little ray of sunshine."

"Fuck off, jealous," Angus retorted.

Gloucester barely heard their exchange. He was staring around the street still, trying to take it all in. It took him a moment to realize the location, silent and still, was a familiar one. Turning on the spot, he found himself facing a familiar window, beneath a sign declaring a familiar name. Zephyr Clocks. They had actually done it. They were in Frettchen again.

"This is spooky," Zane said, standing beside him as they stared into the empty clock shop. She splayed her hands against the window, peering inside. Through the glass, they could see hundreds of timepieces lining the shelves and walls, their many hands frozen. Behind their own reflected faces staring back at them, empty cars stood motionless on the road. "I've never been less happy to see my own home. It's like the whole city is abandoned. Actually..."

She frowned and glanced over at Angus. "Where is everyone? The city got frozen in time, didn't it? Shouldn't there be people all over the place? Just sort of..." She momentarily froze to demonstrate what she meant, widening her eyes in over-the-top surprise, her mouth forming the *O* of a silent gasp. "So where is everyone?" She approached the nearest car and peered in through the passenger side window. "Why's everything empty?"

Angus pulled a face. Combined with their perennial tears, the moue made for a tragic appearance. They reminded Gloucester of the statues of saints lining the walls of the High

Minister's Cathedral, carved faces depicting martyred dismay. He braced himself for terrible news.

"It's complicated. And before you all get uppity, I'm trying to figure out a way to word it so your little human brains can comprehend."

"How gracious," Mulligan muttered. He leaned back against the hood of the frozen car, arms crossed firmly over his chest and his shoulders up around his ears. His posture spoke more of anxious discomfort than his usual annoyance.

"Like I said before, Frettchen is essentially a Pocket now," Angus explained, after a moment longer of deliberation. "Like the Garden—my home—or the Crossroads or the Maze. A world outside of worlds. Outside of time. The main difference being it's still stuck where it is in space, smack dab in the middle of the Lower Lands. Not a true pocket dimension. Just enough of one to really mess with reality."

"I think I follow, but I'm not sure how this answers the question," Gloucester said, furrowing his brow.

Angus didn't roll their eyes, but it looked like they were tempted. "Humans have to be *brought* into a Pocket. You lot are creatures of time. You can't exist in a place without it unless willed there by someone like myself."

Gloucester stared, horrified. "So, everyone *ceased to exist*?"

"Saints," moaned Zane, as green in the face as she'd been during their sea voyage. Muffled by the bag, Gear cried out in dismay. Even the unflappable Antimony looked alarmed.

Angus laughed, the sound as inhuman as their brothers' amusement, horrible and beautiful all at once. Against the backdrop of the city's silence, it filled Gloucester with further unease.

"No, no, not anything like that," Angus said, waving their hand dismissively. They paused. "Well, mostly not like that. Everyone in the city exists *in potentia*, as it were. Nothing to worry about, as long as we get this all sorted out."

The more Gloucester got to know them, the more similarities he could see between Angus and Denken. He glared at the demigod, unimpressed.

"So everyone *potentially* ceased to exist," he gritted out.

Angus shrugged their agreement.

"Splitting hairs a bit there, mate," Finch told them. His hand returned as a warm presence on Gloucester's arm. He wasn't sure if this was a show of support or if Finch worried he would try and take a swing at Angus. It was tempting, even if he didn't fancy his chances in a fight.

For a being so built on emotions, it took Angus a long time to read the mood. Or perhaps they simply hadn't cared enough to bother. Either way, their smile vanished. This time they did roll their eyes, the eerie white of their irises and invisible pupils spinning like pearly marbles through an expanse of black.

"Fine. Don't get your knickers in a twist. It's not like anyone's in pain or anything. They're sort of just...in limbo. Neither here nor there."

"Here nor *where*?" asked Zane.

Angus ignored her. "If we manage to save the day, as I'm sure we stalwart heroes will, then all mortal things will pop right back like mushrooms in springtime," they said, with an exaggerated patience that grated at Gloucester's nerves.

"Hold on," Finch interrupted. "What about Orange Ianto?"

"What *about*—No, wait, I follow." Mulligan's face went from perplexed to full-fledged realization in an instant. Uncrossing his arms, he turned his frown on Angus. "That woman who possessed Finch, she said she was here, but stuck sleeping. So how does that work? Was she lying? She must have gotten out of the city before this all happened. What's she playing at—?"

"No." Angus's denial was firm. "Yanni doesn't lie. She's here and not here, just like the rest. But she's an oracle. A psychic as powerful as she is possesses a strong consciousness. Stronger than any human I've met since the sorcerers before the Fall. Her body is temporarily lost, but her mind lingers."

Gloucester shivered. So Orange Ianto was stuck here, disembodied, like a ghost in this empty city. He imagined her, an orange-haired apparition peering out from every window, immaterial and silent. Was she aware of the state she was in or did she merely think she was sleeping, unable to see the full truth of her situation? He thought that might be better. The alternative sounded terrible. And if she did know...

"No wonder she was desperate," he said. A surge of pity coursed through him, despite what she had done. Some of his misgivings toward her eased. What might he have done had he been in her position?

Finch pursed his lips. "It doesn't excuse body-snatching."

Still, Gloucester thought he didn't sound quite as scathing as he had before.

"Look," Angus cut in, nearly toppling all of them as impatience rushed over the group like a stiff wind. "We could stand here gabbing about this until one of my dumb brothers stumbles upon us—probably literally—or we could move along. Maybe find a spot to plan our next move, where we're not a big ol' group of sitting ducks?"

Harrison cleared his throat, speaking up for the first time since their arrival in Frettchen. "As much as I hate to agree with the god, they're right. Until we have a proper plan, we should find somewhere to lay low."

Gloucester agreed. Back when he'd been a security agent, it would have been his top priority to make sure his charge wasn't in a vulnerable position. Training and instinct alike were telling him to get out of the open.

"Where should we go?" he asked. "The clock shop? It's right there, after all."

"It seems a bit obvious," Zane said. "We don't know if Denken might have felt our arrival or something—*I don't know how it works*," she added hotly, when Angus made a scornful sound. "I just figured it might be somewhere he'd think to look for us, all right?"

"I think we should start with Purpurrot's Pies," said Antimony, laying a soothing hand on Zane's shoulder. Gear's clockwork ticked a steady beat from the bag on her back. "We don't know what happened to her when Denken's power surged, if she was stuck in the city. If she was—"

"That's where she'd go." Angus's scorn vanished. "Good idea."

Mulligan radiated doubt, arms akimbo. He'd recovered an admirable amount of haughtiness in the wake of their voyage through the Void. "Wouldn't Orange Ianto have mentioned if the goddess were here somewhere?"

"Maybe she doesn't know." Gloucester tried not to pay too much mind to the tiny ember of hope flaring to life in his chest. He didn't want to foster it only to have it quashed. Yet... "Ianto did say she can't sense Purpurrot very well, remember? Maybe..."

The hope grew treacherously brighter.

Angus smiled their smug little smile. "Only one way to find out."

Chapter 17

The Fox

Though both in Uptown, Zephyr Clocks and Purpurrot's Pies were not within easy walking distance of each other. The shopping district spanned a large section of the inner city, spreading out from the long stretch of the main thoroughfare in a network of well-maintained side streets. Under normal circumstances, the whole area would be busy with traffic of all sorts, from pedestrians and cyclists, to cars and city-run buses. Frettchen was famous for its ease of navigation.

Now, however...

"We could commandeer a car," Harrison suggested. He indicated the empty vehicles in the street. "There's no shortage of choice, after all. Though...would their engines work?" He raised his hand and tapped the timepiece on his wrist. "My watch has stopped, so maybe their clockwork won't work either."

"There's that, yeah, and also the issue of the drivers," Finch said. "The people who were in the cars when time stopped. If we're lucky enough to succeed in our little heroic mission here, presumably all those people will reappear in their cars. Can you imagine, you're driving along one street one minute, then suddenly time blips and oops!" He held his hands out in front of him, spinning an imaginary steering wheel in mimed panic. "You're on the other side of Uptown."

"An accident waiting to happen," Gloucester agreed, scratching his ear as he tried not to fret. "So, we walk, I guess. It's gonna take us a while, though. We'll be lucky if Denken or the Gambler don't find us before we get there. Or both of them."

"Ugh, yeah, I keep waiting for horrible sharky death to swoop down from above." Zane's eyes darted skyward, and she shivered.

Despite the severe weather, the sound of thunder was unnaturally distant, as if held at bay by some invisible force. It felt oddly suffocating, an all-too-fragile calm within the storm. The air was devoid of wind, of smells, of all the faint sounds and vibrations that were so hard to notice until they were gone. Frettchen didn't just feel empty, it felt like a vacuum. Besides far-off rumbles in the storm clouds, the only sound was the ticking of Gear's clockwork. This repetitive noise sparked a thought, and Gloucester turned a curious frown toward the automaton on Antimony's back.

"Hang on, if all the clockwork has stopped, how come Gear's still going? Not that it isn't great that you are," he added, raising his voice a little so Gear could hear through the bag.

Antimony's fond smile had a weary tilt. "Gear's primary movement—the clockwork in her head—has a lot of spellwork woven through it. In all honesty, she probably would be worse off if she wasn't in pieces, strange as that is to say. If her secondary movement—"

"That's the one in her torso," Zane interjected helpfully.

"Just so. If that had been up and running when we came here, it likely would have stopped like all the rest of the clockwork in Frettchen. She would have been incapable of moving, and a lot heavier and more difficult to carry than she is now." A gentle laugh escaped Antimony's lips, and lightning glinted off her glasses as she turned her face skyward. "Luck works in mysterious ways."

"At least it's *good* luck for once," Zane said. "That's a nice change."

"Yes, yes, it's lovely Gear didn't die. Well done. *Focus*, people," said Mulligan. He, too, was watching the sky. "Could we just teleport again? Not that I'm eager to relive that experience, but it's probably less terrible than being eaten by Denken's monster."

With a synchronicity that surely annoyed them both, Angus and Finch shook their heads.

"I wouldn't worry too much about the trip," Angus said. "Frettchen's a Pocket now. Well, more or less. Journeys only take ages in places with time."

"Oh great," grumbled Zane. "This is going to be some weird magic thing. I just know it."

"You bet your bottom dollar," they said with a gap-toothed grin. They were in distinctly better spirits since arriving in Frettchen, in spite of the dire circumstances. "Now just think about where you want to go. Focus on being there. Remember what it's like in dreams? When you go from being one place to being somewhere else completely different in the blink of an eye? It's like that. Easy."

Gloucester nodded slowly, but inside, his heart sank. It was one thing to say something was easy, but another to actually make the trick work. "Do we all have to, er, concentrate at once?"

"Please tell me we don't have to hold hands again," Mulligan said.

"Tempting to say yes, but no," Angus said. "All it really takes is one. Just walk forward with confidence that you'll get where you want to go."

Gloucester chewed his lip. His heart had now passed down beyond his stomach and was somewhere closer to his knees in its hopeless descent. Would magic still work if he *pretended* he had confidence in it?

To his great relief, he was saved from having to find out. Finch stepped forward, crooked grin fixed on his face.

"Confidence in magic and expertise in lucid dreaming? Sounds right up my alley." He cracked his knuckles and tossed a wink at Gloucester. "Watch and learn."

Gloucester grinned back at him, grateful. "Gladly."

Beside him, Zane rolled her eyes with an audible sigh. She didn't argue, however. Nor did anyone else. Looking supremely pleased to take center stage, Finch strode across the pavement. He navigated around the immobilized cars, slowing when he reached the clear space at the center of the road.

"Follow me," he called out. "It'd be a bit daft if I ended up leaving you all behind."

They all hurried to fall into step behind him. As Finch made his way down the road, the air thickened. Gloucester quickened his pace, tempted to reach out and grab hold of Finch's hand, lest whatever magic was gathering snatched him away from the group as he had warned. Doing that wouldn't help the others, though. They just had to stick close and hope for the best.

Despite the feeling of magic in the air, for a moment, Gloucester wasn't sure anything was actually happening. Then the street shimmered, a mirage wavering in the heat of the desert. It trembled, then changed in the blink of an eye.

He stumbled as the world resolidified, knees wobbly from the unnatural shift in scenery. Gone was Zane's shop, full of its time-frozen wares. In its place were the wide windows of Purpurrot's Pies, the name proclaiming itself from the glass in large block lettering. Its purple letters swam dizzyingly before

Gloucester's eyes, difficult to focus on. Unsure if it was an effect of their odd travel or the dreamlike state of the city, he looked away, nauseous.

"Oof," muttered Harrison, from his left. The security agent already had a steadying hand on Mulligan's elbow. "That was weird. I get the dream comparison, but still. Weird."

"As if the rest of this has been so normal." Finch stood at the head of the group, hands on hips, surveying their new location with some satisfaction. "Nice one, me."

Gloucester humored him with a congratulatory clap on the arm, before moving past to inspect the darkened interior of the bakery. Unlike the words on the signage, it appeared solid enough. Its plush purple booths sat empty, the rotating pie display by the front counter motionless.

"I don't see any sign of Purpurrot," he said, cupping his hands around his eyes. "Though I suppose it's a bit much to expect she might be sitting front and center with a big grin and a welcome banner."

"Now there's an image." Antimony leaned against the glass beside him, mirroring his stance as she too searched the pie shop for some trace of its proprietor.

"What image? Can I see?" Gear asked. Antimony tilted her head back with a quiet breath of laughter.

"It's a saying, not an actual image to look at." Her smile diminished. "Gear, if we do find Purpurrot, I think it would be best if you stayed quiet. Things will be stressful enough for her without..." Her words trailed off, clearly determining the kindest way to word her point. "It might just make things easier."

The bag was silent for a stretch, save for Gear's clockwork. The ever-present ticking sped up, then came a notable click, louder than the rest, as Gear reached the end of a train of thought.

"All right," she said. Gloucester heard a note of disappointment in the agreement, but she didn't argue. "If you think it'll help."

"Thank you, Gear." Antimony returned to searching the bakery through the window. Her sigh painted the glass with an ephemeral fog. "I can't see anything helpful."

"Yeah, we might actually have to go and look for her, imagine that." Angus's interjection was slightly muffled by the window pane, as they had appeared suddenly on the other side of the glass, their face inches from Gloucester's. He reared back. This elicited a broad smile from the demigod, who wandered jauntily over to the front door and unlocked it.

"Come in, one and all," they said, sweeping their arm in a mock gesture of welcome.

Despite their seeming good cheer, a trepidation permeated the air that Gloucester knew wasn't just his own.

No wonder Angus avoids people, he thought. *They can't ever hide what they're feeling*. A constant vulnerability of that sort would probably lead him to shy away from others as well.

As an unexpected pang of sympathy crossed his mind, he caught Angus watching him. Their head cocked to one side, eyes narrowed. Tears gathered in their pale lashes, sparkling in a flash of lightning. Then the moment passed, and they turned to the group at large.

"Right, heroes of legend. Let's see if we can find ourselves a goddess."

Inside the pie shop, the distant thunder no longer reached their ears. Instead, they were drenched in a silence heavy and cloying. The shop contained no remnants of people who had fallen into limbo, no half-eaten meals or abandoned belongings—Purpurrot had locked up before their ill-fated venture into the false Maze.

The group moved through the dimly lit front room, picking their way past tables and neatly stacked chairs. Their best source of light came from Zane, whose enchanted pocket watch emitted silvery illumination. She lifted it from around her neck and held it aloft like a lantern. At the swinging doors to the kitchen, Angus paused, blocking the way for everyone else. Their hand splayed on the door.

Antimony touched their tattooed arm. "She'll be okay. I'm sure of it."

She was doubtlessly lying—how could any of them be sure of that?—but Angus nodded their silent thanks. Gratitude flitted through their projected worry like a breath of fresh air.

Angus pushed the door open and led them into the hallway beyond.

The last time Gloucester walked this corridor was a couple of weeks ago, on the day when everything went wrong. Again. He recalled his dread and uncertainty, the unfamiliar sensation of the enchanted rings on his fingers—something he scarcely even noticed now—and Finch's smile as he asked what he was thinking. The mounting anxiety he'd felt then had been his alone.

"Can you sense if she's here?" he whispered, as they paused for Angus to stick their head through the first doorway they encountered. A supply closet, it held a wide assortment of cleaning items and bins, but no goddess of creation.

"This whole place feels like her," Angus said, shutting the closet door and continuing on. "Makes it difficult to tell. Honestly, I usually avoid coming here."

Zane's brow furrowed. "Why? Isn't she your mum?"

Irritation rippled through the air. Angus didn't look away from the corridor ahead. Though their whole body seemed to repel shadow, the mood emanating from them was as dark as their surroundings. "Yeah, she is. My mother who walked away from her Pocket and her powers in favor of living here, making pies for humans. She walked away from who she was."

And from her children. The words hung unspoken in the quiet hallway, as palpable yet intangible as the demigod's emotions. Zane murmured an almost inaudible apology, cowed, and no one knew what else to say. Finally, Angus gave themself a little shake, pulling themself together.

"So yeah, the place has weird vibes for me. Come on, let's search her office."

They pressed forward, shoulders stiff. On the edge of his hearing, Gloucester caught the rustling of wings. He fell back a step, cautious of being too close to the demigod and their temper.

Purpurrot's office lay beyond the empty kitchen. Its heavy wooden door stood ajar. Angus hesitated minutely, then nudged it open further. It swung wide on silent hinges.

On the far wall inside the office, a large window looked out over the parking lot behind the bakery, framed by flowers in a planter on the sill. Just enough light filtered through to cast the room in dim illumination. At first glance, it looked as empty as the rest of the premises.

Then something moved.

A shape stirred in the shadows behind Purpurrot's elegantly carved desk, the half-light brushing against fur and reflecting off a pair of bright purple eyes.

"Angus? Antimony?"

The voice was unmistakable, wild and beautiful as nature itself. Yet as what he expected to be Purpurrot straightened up into view, Gloucester heard his own gasp echo through the rest of the group.

It was a fox. Large for its kind, it didn't look like the scrawny foxes occasionally spotted in Frettchen, rooting through compost bins or unattended recycling. This one was the size of a retriever, with a rich red coat, thick and healthy. It brought Gloucester back to the wilds of home, to forests and creatures far-flung from city streets and the trappings of humanity.

"Oh, Purpa..." Antimony slipped between Gloucester and Angus to approach the creature. "What's happened to you?"

The fox sighed, a very strange sound to hear from such a beast. "It's a complicated story," it said in Purpurrot's voice.

"Oh boy," muttered Finch.

The rest of the group pressed up against Gloucester, Angus, and Antimony, gaping at Purpurrot's strange form from the doorway.

"Is the, uh, the fox a good thing?" Gloucester asked no one in particular. "Is this her...her true form or..."

"It is *a* form," chastised the goddess-turned-fox. Her eyes flicked between each of the newcomers, lingering on Angus for a long moment, before settling back on Gloucester. "I have many, none of them more true than another. Such as it is, to be what I am. This form is one I am not unfamiliar with. When Denken's power overwhelmed me, I returned to a simpler state. I am lucky to have even this body." Her bushy tail flicked back and forth. "I had little time to react. Most of my power went into the Transportation spell."

"Thank you, Purpa," said Antimony. "You saved our lives with that."

Finch scoffed. "Yeah, sure, it was great. Maybe you want to tell us what's happened since then?"

"Once I *re-corporealized*, I had no choice but to escape Denken's false Maze." Purpurrot's voice was definitely sharp now, a canine growl lining every word. "The magic there was too wild, even with all of Denken's creatures returned to their doors. If I had stayed, even this form would have been destroyed, pulled apart by the magic latching onto me. I needed to regain my strength, so I came back here."

"And have you?" Finch's bullish tone met Purpurrot's anger head on. "Regained your strength? It doesn't really look like it."

Gloucester cast him a warning look, but deep down he couldn't help but agree. Disappointment twisted in his chest. Purpurrot had been their best hope, but if she couldn't even manage a human form...

Better a weakened goddess than no goddess at all.

"Ignore him," he said hurriedly. "We're glad you're okay, Purpurrot. And like Antimony said, thank you for saving our lives back there."

"Suck up," muttered Finch, but he relented.

The fox turned her long snout in Gloucester's direction. The bristling hackles on her back smoothed down. "I'm glad it worked. And that you're here, which means Angus helped you return."

"For better or for worse." Angus's sneer made it clear which one they suspected it to be. They turned a cold stare onto Purpurrot.

"Hello, Mum. Long time, no see, and all that. Nice tail."

Though this greeting was delivered with their usual sarcasm, the energy in the room was charged with anxiety, putting Gloucester in mind of the storm raging outside. He wondered if the goddess was feeling as tentative as her child. Her long, pointed ears twitched, but he wasn't sure what that might mean. Foxes weren't really known for their easy-to-decipher expressions.

How long might it be before an outburst just as deadly as lightning struck here?

"It's good to see you, Angus," Purpurrot said. Her words were steady, guarded in the wake of her earlier growls. "Thank you for bringing them. And for coming."

"Yes, yes, we're all thankful." Mulligan squeezed his way into the room. "Now that we've found you, what's next? What do you need to do to fix this?"

Purpurrot's hackles ruffled again, and her tail swished, but when she spoke, it lacked her earlier vehemence.

"Nothing."

Chapter 18

Hopeless

They waited. Gear's muffled clicking counted the frozen seconds steadily, while outside the window, lightning flashed.

"Pardon?" asked Zane.

The fox sighed, turning her head to look out the window. "I cannot fix this. If Denken is to be stopped, you must be the ones to do it. I...cannot."

"Is it because of what you said about the false Maze?" Antimony asked. If she felt any of the same disappointment currently hollowing out Gloucester's chest, she didn't show it. "We spoke to Orange Ianto—sort of—and she says Denken's consciousness is in the shark, so we might not have to return there—"

"I cannot!"

At the goddess's sharp bark, Antimony took a startled step away. Purpurrot bounded up on her hind feet, front paws braced on the desk, scattering a mug full of pens and gouging deep scratches into the wood. She bared her teeth. Mulligan snapped an oath as Harrison pulled him bodily through the open door and into the hallway, safe behind him. Finch's hands came up in a defensive flinch, though he resisted uttering a spell. Even Angus drew back.

The goddess's rage was fleeting. As quickly as she'd leapt up, she retreated.

Ears tucked back, she dropped her paws to the floor and laid down. The white tip of her tail swept over her nose as she curled in on herself.

"I cannot help," came her quiet admission. "All I've ever done is make everything worse. I thought I was saving him. Saving everyone. And now everything could be destroyed. Because of me."

"Shit, Mum." For once, Angus moved like a human, stepping around the side of the desk and crouching beside their mother. They laid a hand on her flank. "No need to tear our heads off. Denken's already happy to do that."

"Not funny, child," grumbled the fox.

"So, what are we supposed to do?" Zane's hand shook, trembling the light from the watch. Whether she was asking Purpurrot or Angus or just the room at large was unclear.

Purpurrot flicked her tail. "If Orange Ianto sent you back here, then there is hope. You can do what I cannot."

"Or *you* can do what you *don't want to*." Furious, Finch pushed forward, leaning across the desk. Gloucester tried to pull him back, Purpurrot's burst of rage still fresh in his mind. Finch shook him off. "No! She's just making excuses. You expect us to believe that we have any hope in stopping Denken if *you* can't? That's bullshit. You just can't be bothered. What's one little world to a goddess? You can just—"

"Cassus. Shut up."

Finch's tirade stuttered to a halt, knocked off course by Gloucester's firm interjection. Purpurrot hadn't moved under the brunt of the magician's accusations. Gloucester nudged him away from the desk and moved to take his place.

Over the last month, he'd seen and done a lot of things he never would have expected. Never would have believed. He'd met gods and monsters. He'd felt magic first-hand. He'd faced down death time and time again. Yet he didn't think any of that could prepare him for this.

He took a deep breath.

"Purpurrot, I'm sorry. What Cassus said isn't right...but it isn't entirely wrong, either." Behind him, Zane drew in an audible breath of protest, but he ignored her. Ignored everyone but the hopeless, lost goddess curled up on the floor. "I think you *are* afraid. And that's okay. It'd be mad if you weren't, honestly. We all are. And you...you created this world. Of course you fear losing it. What happened back in the false Maze...none of us knew it would go down like that. And yeah, the day wasn't saved, like we hoped it would be, but the world didn't end either. Not yet. If we all work together—all of us—I *know* we can make it right. Even if we're terrified. Even if we made mistakes. Together, we can do this."

He paused for breath more than anything. In the wake of his words, silence held sway, and he began to feel a bit silly. Impassioned speeches were hardly his thing. And here he was, giving one to the creator of the world. He probably sounded ridiculous. But what else could he do?

Purpurrot's ear twitched, her only sign of movement. Gloucester tried to brush aside his second guesses and mounting self-consciousness, tried to think of something else he could say to inspire her—

"You don't understand." Purpurrot rose slowly to her feet, leveling a steady gaze at him over the expanse of the desk. "It's not just the world I could lose. It's not just the world I let down."

Her eyes moved to Angus. "You are my child. As is Denken, lost out there in the storm. The Gambler, too. If I had been better...if I had been there, when everything started going wrong, maybe things would be different. Maybe none of this would have happened. My children suffered and continue to suffer because of my failings. And if I fail again, I won't only lose everything—every*one*—I've ever created and loved, there would be no denying that *I* destroyed them. You're right, Mikalai Gloucester, I am afraid. But courage alone would not make me the one to undo what's been done."

Defeat weighed heavy, pulling her back down to the floor.

Angus stared at her, eyes bright with more tears than ever. "Mum..." they whispered. A hard-to-place emotion filled the air, the painful tug of desperation and despair. "Please. I don't know if we can do this alone."

But Purpurrot was done talking, it would seem. She closed her violet eyes, head resting on her paws. "I'm sorry," was all she said.

Gloucester didn't know if foxes could cry, but he expected if they could, Purpurrot would be weeping as much as her child. Hopelessness threatened to overwhelm him. This couldn't be how it ended, after everything...

"Fine."

The simmering, unhappy emotion emanating from Angus sharpened into something Gloucester recognized as betrayal. And, woven inseparably into it, fresh determination.

The personification of Love lurched to their feet. The tattoos along their broad shoulders and arms seemed to bristle. "We'll do it without you." Without waiting for Purpurrot to respond, they flitted away, reappearing behind Mulligan and Harrison in the hallway. "Come on, humans. There's nothing for us here."

Their derision was hard to resist, but so was their sadness. Gloucester's heart was a stone in his chest. He tried to catch Purpurrot's gaze for one last appeal, but she didn't look up, didn't open her eyes.

Out in the corridor, Mulligan and Harrison reluctantly followed Angus, who stalked out of sight. Finch moved after them, with Zane trailing a step behind. Only Gloucester,

Antimony, and the hidden Gear remained. The inquisitive automaton stayed true to her word, keeping silent despite all the questions Gloucester was sure she had.

Antimony gripped the straps of her bag, back unbent despite the burden. Whether it was the weight of carrying Gear or what they had just heard that required fortifying herself, Gloucester could only guess.

"I hope you change your mind, Purpa," the scientist said. She brushed her fingertips across the surface of Purpurrot's desk, carefully righting the toppled mug of pens, but made no other move toward her friend. She drew in a nearly silent breath, then turned away. "Come along, Mr. Gloucester. There's much to do."

—

Outside the shop, Frettchen's eerie stillness and stormy sky felt more oppressive than ever. The group stood in silence, unsure what to do. Angus was stone-faced and unapproachable, pointedly not looking back at Purpurrot's Pies. The demigod's emotions swirled around them all, making it difficult for Gloucester to process his own. He sat down on the curb, chin in his hands.

His head hurt—not due to the unnatural influence of an immortal, but rather the very human trait of being thoroughly overwhelmed. Finding Purpurrot should have been the key. It should have been a victory. Instead, everything felt a thousand times more daunting. What could they do, when even someone as powerful as a goddess felt hopeless? He knuckled his brow, trying to wrestle down his worries before they turned into a full-blown panic attack.

To his relief, Zane broke the silence and pulled him from his spiraling thoughts.

"Well, that sucked. But we can't just stand around here, feeling sorry for ourselves." She tugged distractedly on the hem of her sleeve, then noticed the anxious tic and crossed her arms.

"If Purpurrot can't help us, then we figure out what to do ourselves."

A touch of relief soothed the riot in Gloucester's head. He was glad for Zane's calm, forced as it might be. They needed to focus on what they could do, not lose themselves to panic.

"Right," he said. "But where should we go? Where else could be safe?"

Zane tapped her foot as she thought, looking up and down the street. "Maybe we could go back to—Hold on, what was that?"

She abruptly cut herself off and hushed the rest of them when they started to question what had caught her attention.

"Listen," she hissed.

They all fell silent, holding their collective breath. At first Gloucester didn't understand what he was supposed to be listening for. The ghost city seemed as devoid of sound as it had been since they arrived.

Then he heard it.

It would have been quiet, too quiet to make out, had it not been for the sheer silence of the rest of the city. An echoing, uneven sound. Laughter.

Gloucester got to his feet, exchanging a nervous look with Zane before glancing around at the others.

Mulligan and Harrison stood as still as statues, a matching set of deep lines furrowed between their brows and heads cocked to one side, listening. Finch's lips moved silently as he prepped a spell—Gloucester could feel the magic gathering in the air—and even Antimony looked openly uneasy. She raised her fists and metal glinted around her right hand in the low light, the brass knuckles Lucienne had given her, enchanted with combat and protection spells.

Gloucester raised his own hand, the rings a comforting defense. With his other, he reached for his gun. He'd finally unpacked it before they left the Hartland, strapping it in its holster under his arm, hidden by a jacket he'd picked up in Pell.

The laughter was getting louder.

Closer.

Please don't be a giant shadow shark. Had he ever heard Denken's spectral form make any noise? He didn't think so, but what else could it be? Purpurrot had claimed the monsters from the Maze were sent back to their home, leaving only their master behind.

He stared down the length of the street, past empty cars and frozen bicycles. Was it just him or did the road seem to undulate oddly, too long and too short all at once? He narrowed his eyes at the optical illusion, trying to catch any sign of movement, of danger.

"Hey!"

Even muffled, Gear's sudden cry made them all jump. Gloucester nearly bit his tongue as he swallowed down the urge to swear. Beside him, neither Zane nor Finch felt the same inclination to hold back.

Antimony, uncharacteristically startled, craned her neck to look at the bag. "Gear?" she said. "What's wrong?"

"I hear my friend," came the reply. The bag moved, Gear's head rolling around in excitement. "Can I come out? I want to see them!"

"Your friend?" Baffled, Antimony slipped the straps from her shoulders and swung the bag around. Crouching down, she opened the top and pulled Gear's head free. The clockwork girl was smiling eagerly. "What friend?"

"The big, tall, laughy one." Gear wrinkled her nose. "I don't know their name, because they don't talk. But they were really nice, and I can hear them now."

Realization cascaded over Gloucester. "*Hyena*?"

He'd completely forgotten about the creature who escaped with him from Denken's captivity. The mammoth beast was frightening to behold, hulking over even the tallest of men. Their long skeletal limbs and neck of stretched, exposed muscle were topped off with a six-eyed, skull-like head resembling that of a monstrous horse. However, Gloucester had soon found that the creature's fearsome appearance masked a helpful and courageous personality. He'd named the beast Hyena, due to their constant laughter, and they hadn't seemed to mind the moniker.

The last time he saw Hyena, they'd all been leaving Antimony's house to face Denken and stop his plan to recreate the Maze. Hyena remained behind, hiding out in Antimony's basement, and all thought of them had completely fled Gloucester's mind since.

"Who are we talking about now?" Angus asked, sounding annoyed by their own confusion.

The others paid them no mind.

"What're they doing here?" Finch demanded. "All of them went back to the real Maze when things went sideways. That was supposed to be the one bloody thing that actually went right!"

"We'll just have to ask them," Angus said.

They gestured down the street, head cocked to one side and teary eyes focused in that direction. Their resigned anger and newfound confusion had been joined by amusement. Gloucester followed their pointing finger. Something huge was lumbering down the dim, still street. It barreled through the uncanny warping of physical space without hesitation, heading straight for the group.

Even recognizing Hyena's bizarre, gangling form, they made for a frightening sight. Gloucester heard Mulligan gasp somewhere behind him.

"It's okay," Gloucester told him, not bothering to glance his way. "Believe it or not, they're a friend."

Hyena's laughter grew louder as the thought-beast drew close, until they came to a halt, looming over them. They giggled what Gloucester guessed was a giddy greeting. As he looked up at the giant creature, he surprised himself with the grin spreading across his face. He hadn't realized until now how relieved he was to see that Hyena was all right.

"Long time, no see," he told them, the words far warmer than when Angus had aimed them at Purpurrot. Hyena cackled an agreement, their long head bobbing enthusiastically up and down.

"Somehow, it doesn't surprise me that you're friends with this," Angus said.

Gloucester turned to glare at them, nettled by what he took to be a slight against both him and Hyena. But Angus was smiling. Not snidely, either. If anything, they looked sincerely pleased.

"We went through a lot together," he said, unsure if he ought to be defending himself or not. Hyena laughed in what he took to be another agreement.

"So, they say," Angus remarked.

"You can understand them?" A very pale Mulligan stared up at Hyena with wide eyes. They'd kept Hyena a secret from Mulligan and his agents, and Gloucester supposed this was probably a bit overwhelming for him and Harrison both.

He wasn't shocked, however, to learn Angus could understand the beast. Of course they could. Really, being able to glean meaning from the raucous laughter of a creature made of raw imagination was one of the *less* bizarre abilities he'd witnessed from one of the Siblings.

"Good," said Antimony. "Because I think Hyena must have quite the story to tell."

Chapter 19

Hyena's Tale

Two weeks earlier

Everything had gone suddenly wrong.

This was saying a lot, because the creature recently dubbed Hyena found that the human world already had plenty wrong with it. Ever since they were pulled through their door in the Maze and sent spiraling into this strange place, they had struggled to make sense of their new surroundings. Their newfound corporeality was bad enough—not to mention this pesky new level of sentience that went along with it—but the world made everything ten times worse. The very *air* felt wrong.

Yet, somehow, the worst of it all was the Guardian. Yes, he was mischievous and mercurial, but he was the keeper of all the creatures of imagination, their protector, and he had always taken that duty seriously. Hyena had been relieved to find themself in the same place as the Guardian when they ended up in this world.

Only to have that relief quickly wither. The Guardian was filled with only rage and wild emotion now. It turned him cruel and violently unpredictable. He would lash out. He would hurt. And perhaps worst of all, he would laugh in the face of Hyena's fear. He was no longer a protector, but a tormentor. The new Maze that the Guardian was building felt like a prison, devoid of all comfort. And yet Hyena feared to leave it, terrified of the strange new world and its inhabitants.

And then Gloucester came along. Tiny and helpless and as strange as any human. But different from what Hyena expected. The Guardian had ranted about the viciousness of mortals, of their malice and heartless crimes. Gloucester wasn't like that. He helped Hyena, brought them to freedom at his side and even gave them a name.

Hyena had never had a friend before.

No sooner had they gained one, however, than they were destined to lose him. Hyena was terrified when Gloucester and the others left to face the Guardian. Too terrified to join them. Too terrified to heed the call tugging at their essence to congregate with the rest of their kin, where their false home was gaining strength and purchase. Too terrified to do anything other than hide.

But there was no hiding from what happened next.

One moment they were curled up in the basement of the house where they'd been allowed to stay, trying their hand at sleeping and failing quite spectacularly. The next, the tug they had been ignoring became a sharp yank, sudden and painful. It felt like something was attempting to drag them away by their very soul, if they possessed such a thing.

And so they did the only thing they could. They resisted.

No easy feat. Every strand of their being was pulled on, drawn against their will toward their master. Whatever was happening, they knew the Guardian was at the center of it. And

Hyena had promised themself one thing: they would never again be at the Guardian's mercy. They wanted to stay right here, in this place that, in spite of its strangeness, felt safe. Where the people, tiny and odd-mannered as they were, treated them with kindness and even respect.

When Hyena met Gloucester, they did something they never had before. They made a choice for themself. They acted against the Guardian's orders and helped the human escape.

Now they made another choice. With all of their might, Hyena chose rebellion.

To their amazement, it worked. For a stretched-out moment, they thought they would be torn apart by the Guardian's violent pull, but then, as suddenly as the sensation had struck, it ceased.

The basement was quiet in the aftermath. Hyena had thought it was so before, but now a different silence filled the air. The gentle ticking of the many clockwork devices lining the shelves and walls stopped. The muted hum of miniature perpetual engines died. Even the distant scurrying of mice in the walls vanished from Hyena's keen hearing. All that reached their ears was silence.

Sitting up on the floor, they laughed, just to hear something. The sound wasn't loud, but its mere existence came as a comfort. Hyena laughed again out of sheer relief.

The feeling was short-lived. Something was wrong. Very, very wrong. And somehow, the Guardian was the cause.

Hyena got to their feet slowly. They left the silent laboratory and crept up the stairs. The rest of the house was as quiet as the basement. No one had been home before, but plenty of ambient noise had breathed life into the place, from insects buzzing in the windows to electricity humming through wires in the walls. That breath of life was gone. Outside, no birds sang in the garden. No cats meowed from neighbors' windowsills. No children called out as they played in their yards. Silence.

And stillness. That took longer to dawn on Hyena than the simple lack of sound. Nothing was moving. No people in the street. No vehicles passing by.

They stared into the glass-fronted case of the clock on the corridor's wall, its delicate hands unmoving on its cross-stitched face. As if time itself had stopped.

That couldn't be right, could it? Hyena had spent eternity in the timelessness of the Maze, and one of the strangest things they'd struggled to comprehend since tumbling out of the Pocket was the way time progressed here in the world. Things aged and grew and withered. It was fascinating and terrifying all at once.

And now it was no more. Hyena chuckled a question, but no one was there to answer.

Lumbering to the front door, they tentatively pushed it open. Getting through the opening was a bit of a squeeze, but they managed, the porch boards creaking beneath their weight. As the first instance of sound other than their own laughter since this frightening shift in reality occurred, the noise was a welcome one.

The street before them was as still and abandoned as the house behind. Hyena craned their long neck, looking up and down the road, but caught no sign of life, neither human nor any other creature. Their unease grew. They stretched out their consciousness, searching the city for the familiar spirits of their kin. Unease quickly turned to panic as they found nothing. No other thought-creatures reached back to their psychic calls. Not in all of Frettchen. Not anywhere.

Hyena sat back heavily on their bony haunches. This time, the creak of the porch boards brought no comfort. They were well and truly alone.

Spurred very much by emotion and very little by thought, Hyena lurched back to their feet and onto the road. They ran for several blocks before they really knew where they were headed, dodging around empty cars and impossibly balanced bicycles.

No pedestrians stared as they charged through the city streets, no onlookers from shop windows gaped.

The only movement other than Hyena themself was the roiling clouds in the sky, interspersed with violent strings of lightning. This light refracted from the windows of colossal skyscrapers, like shards of falling glass, and the buildings themselves twisted and turned unnaturally, nightmarish optical illusions far over Hyena's head. Every now and then, out of the corner of their many eyes, they thought they spotted a glimpse of something bright and in motion. But whenever they turned their head, they found nothing.

Finally, they reached their destination. The derelict house looked the same as it had before, nothing about its outward appearance hinting at the Guardian's new Maze within. The last time Hyena saw it, the door had hung off its hinges, revealing an impossibly large interior and lurking horrors.

That was the only difference now. The door stood shut and distinctly intact.

Hyena approached cautiously, trying to quiet their laughter carried on every panting breath. Cold fingers of fear settled once more over their jagged shoulders, their previous haste forgotten. They reached toward the doorknob as if it were a venomous snake threatening to strike with deadly fangs if Hyena moved too quickly.

Before they could touch the door, something stirred in their peripheral vision, stopping them short. A huge shape moved at the end of the street, too close and consistent to be the restless clouds. They turned slowly, terrified at what they might see.

What rounded the corner of the deserted street wasn't the Guardian, as Hyena had feared. In the place of expected shadow was blazing light, an enormous figure forged of flame so hot it burned white. Each step carried it forward by humongous strides, and Hyena knew there would be no chance of dodging out of sight in time. They squeezed all six of their eyes shut and awaited fiery death. The heat of the burning figure was tangible, growing stronger with each passing second...

And then it was fading. Slowly but surely, the air began to cool again. The scent of fire, so briefly overpowering, dissipated. And death didn't seem to have struck Hyena down. They were fairly certain they would have noticed.

They cracked open the eyes on one side of their head and squinted around.

Darkness filled the street once more. Hyena opened the rest of their eyes and turned in time to watch the cast light of the burning figure disappear around a corner. Its head and shoulders remained visible over the rooftops even as it lumbered further and further away.

Hyena released a barely audible whine of laughter.

If they didn't know better, they would think they'd just crossed paths with one of their kin. But they *did* know better. The walking nightmare that had narrowly avoided trampling them shared more in common with the Guardian than any mere creature of imagination. It practically thrummed with power. Hyena didn't know what to make of it, but it scared them to their core. They dashed the rest of the way to the door and yanked it open.

The hinges gave way without protest, swinging open so easily Hyena nearly lost their balance. Recovering clumsily, they made their way into the house.

Inside, the magic still held strong. Walls stretched upward to impossibly high ceilings obscured in gloom. Hyena hoped this was a good sign. Considering they had no idea what was happening, they couldn't really say for certain one way or the other. Picking a direction at random, they began their search.

That, at least, had a clear goal. They knew what they were looking for. *Who* they were looking for. If Gloucester was here and in danger, Hyena wanted to help.

No more hiding.

—

Their newfound courage was in vain. No amount of searching revealed any sign of Gloucester or the other humans anywhere within the twisting halls. After what would have been hours—maybe even days—had time not ground to a stand-still, Hyena gave up. Whatever had happened here, Gloucester and his friends were no longer around.

What *had* happened? The Guardian had been Hyena's keeper for as long as the beast had existed, yet they'd never experienced anything like this before. Then again, there was much about the Guardian and his powers that had changed since their unexpected invasion of the human realm.

Eventually, Hyena left the false Maze and wandered back into Frettchen's empty streets. The storm clouds looked thicker than ever, churning and gray as wet ashes. Wishing they were a lot smaller than they were, Hyena ducked their head low and scurried back toward Antimony's house. It was the only place in the city where they felt safe, and they needed some of that security now. Despite its emptiness, Frettchen felt anything but safe.

And what about beyond Frettchen? Hyena had no idea what lay past the city limits, what the wide mortal world was like even under normal circumstances. Now, that unknown was even greater. How far did the consequences of the Guardian's actions extend? Was the whole world lost to this deserted, timeless fate?

Hyena thought of running until they reached Frettchen's edges, of escaping the urban landscape in search of whatever lay beyond.

But again, fear stood in their way. Not only was the greater human world a frightful mystery, but when they peered toward the direction of the city's borders, they found a curtain of darkness lurking there. No, not just darkness. What encircled

Frettchen was deeper than any night or shadow. It was a void. When they stared at it too long, it pulled at them.

They would stay in the city. Frettchen might not feel safe, but anything felt safer than *that*.

Much to their relief, they reached Antimony's house without incident. Several times there had been close calls, either from the mysterious lumbering giant or, once, the all-too-familiar shadow of a leviathan cutting through the clouded sky like murky water. Hyena swiftly hid from both. They had no desire to battle monsters on their own.

Time passed. Or rather, didn't. Hyena was all too familiar with the sensation of temporal suspension draped over the city. It reminded them of home, where everything instead existed in a state of ever-present. That familiarity ought to have been a comfort.

It wasn't.

More accurate to say, then, that *existence* passed. Hyena hid in Antimony's home and wondered what to do. Often, they wondered if the entirety of the human world had turned to this, but there was no way to know without venturing outside Frettchen and through that terrible void. The thought turned their stomach. Hyena couldn't bring themself to leave the house again, let alone the city. They were relatively new to emotions and were quite boggled by how overwhelming they could be. Fear alone was terrible, making their eyes roll and fingers twitch.

But the hopelessness was even worse. It tangled itself up with the fear and married it with sadness until Hyena felt too heavy and weary to move. They didn't dare try and navigate the streets again. So instead, they hid and told themself they were waiting. They didn't know for what. Hope, perhaps.

Before hope came confusion, in the form of a strange visitor.

Hyena was curled up in Antimony's sitting room, languishing in misery, when movement skittered through their peripheral vision. Cautiously, they raised their head, turning it so the eyes on the right side could get a good look into the hallway. A figure stood beneath the doorframe, shimmering in and out of sight, but undeniably there. Hyena turned their head the other way, giving their other eyes a chance to double-check things, but the figure remained.

"Oof," said the apparition. "You've got the strangest consciousness I've ever encountered."

This didn't feel like an overtly threatening introduction. Hyena chuckled a question.

"Sorry," said the newcomer. "I don't speak thought-beast. I'm surprised to find you here, though. Why didn't you go back to the Maze with the rest?" The figure solidified slightly, its details easier to pick out, though it still appeared translucent. A human, short and red-headed. She offered them a kind smile. "Hm, not that I would understand your answer... Would you mind if I tried something?"

She took a step closer.

Hyena hesitated. They didn't know this human. If she even was a human. How was she here, when every other living creature had vanished? She seemed friendly, but it could be a trick. Maybe the Guardian had cooked this up somehow, a ploy to lure Hyena back into his clutches. Thinking of the Guardian, however, and the state he was in, Hyena doubted that was the case.

They glanced out the window, eyes searching for fins in the murky clouds. Nothing. Tentatively, they glanced back at the specter and nodded.

"Thank you." The strange woman closed the distance between them, crossing the room in a sputtering, intangible motion. She raised her hands toward Hyena's head. They didn't expect her to be corporeal enough to touch, yet when they lowered their long face for her to reach, they felt the cool brush of her fingertips.

"Wow," she breathed, closing her eyes. "You *are* an odd one. Could you close your eyes too, please? It'll make this easier for both of us."

Hoping they weren't going to regret this, Hyena acquiesced.

The moment they did, color blossomed across the backs of their eyelids. A scene appeared: the same room they were in, but now brightly lit with warm, inviting light. The apparition stood before them, solid and no longer flickering. She smiled up at them, relieved.

"That's a lot better," she said. "Thanks for letting me in. I'm going to sort through your memories a bit, all right? See how it is you ended up where you are."

Not really waiting for a reply, she narrowed her eyes in concentration. Hyena sat back on their haunches as images and sensations suddenly washed over them. Glimpses of their arrival in the human world; the fear of facing the Guardian's wrath; meeting Gloucester and escaping at his side; their loneliness in the aftermath of whatever had happened to the human world.

Finally, it subsided. Hyena tittered unhappily, and the woman sighed.

"I'm sorry. For what happened to you and for making you relive it. I'm glad to have found you, though. As Denken's power grows, I'm losing my grip here. I don't think I'll be able to reach Gloucester and the others when they arrive. So, you'll have to find them. There's something I need you to tell them." Reaching out her hands again, she placed them tenderly on either side of Hyena's skull. "Let me show you."

Again, images overpowered their vision, but this time they weren't memories. Hyena saw a place they had never been, full of darkness and stone. A figure stumbled through the shadows, slim and unsteady on their feet. A tattered yellow scarf hung around their neck. The Guardian.

He collapsed to the stone floor amidst the strewn remains of broken ropes. Shadows black as pitch flooded from his body, consuming it. Out of that darkness stormed the shark, bursting free in a flurry of teeth and rage. It flew toward Hyena, who flinched away, terrified—

Only to find themself back in Antimony's house, dimly lit once more. The apparition stood before them, barely visible and fading fast.

"Tell the others," she said, words growing as faint as her visage. "Find them when they get here and tell them what you saw."

She disappeared, and Hyena was alone once more.

—

And then, finally, hope did come. It appeared suddenly and with no warning, a new presence slipping across Hyena's perception. One Hyena recognized. No, *several* they recognized.

They'd been stretched out across the floor of Antimony's kitchen, bored and forlorn in equal measure, and now they sat up, trying to pinpoint the source of the new presences. Then, like a hound following a scent, they were on the move.

They didn't know how Gloucester and the others had gotten into Frettchen. Nor did they care. They had never been a being to dwell on questions. Until very recently, they'd never really had need of them. All they knew—and all they cared about—was that something had changed. Gloucester was here. A friend in the darkness. And they had something to tell him.

Chapter 20

A Key to the Past

"And that brought them here," Angus said, concluding their translation of Hyena's story. The tale had been related through Hyena's usual chorus of giggles and guffaws, accompanied by impressively effective hand gestures, and Angus had no problem understanding any of it.

Gloucester beamed up at Hyena. "I'm glad you're all right." Their attachment toward him was flattering, and he couldn't help but feel a great wave of fondness for the creature.

"You're not alone anymore," he assured them.

Hyena's responding laugh was heartfelt.

"All very touching and weird, but maybe we should move this reunion somewhere that isn't out in the open like this?" Mulligan suggested, still regarding Hyena with open skepticism. "From the sounds of it, we have a lot to figure out, and I'd rather do that somewhere relatively safe. Especially if that fox goddess isn't going to help."

Gloucester shot him a scowl out of habit, but didn't argue the point. It was a good one. While the Gambler might be oblivious in his wanderings, that didn't mean Denken was. Orange Ianto hadn't been able to assess the personification of Thought's state of mind, and it didn't sound like Hyena knew either. If they weren't staying here with Purpurrot, they needed to find safety elsewhere.

"We need somewhere to hunker down where no one would think to look for us." Harrison crossed his arms, standing protectively at Mulligan's side. His eyes kept going back to Hyena, as if drawn by a magnetic pull, and Gloucester could practically hear the questions and concerns simmering within him. He held them in, though, apparently choosing to trust the others when it came to this strange new addition to their group.

"We've the city to ourselves," Finch pointed out. "Seems to me we could go anywhere we want." He swept his arm over their surroundings. Brick-fronted shops lined the street on both sides, signs indicating a dozen different businesses. Many of the buildings here housed apartments on the second floors, either rented out or occupied by the shopkeepers. "Pick a building, any building."

Angus shook their head. "It's not going to be that easy, babe. You lot don't belong here, not in the way Hyena and I do. Mortals stick out like sore thumbs, especially in the minds of my brothers. Believe me, it's a miracle Denken's shark hasn't already found us."

Gloucester scanned the sky for suspicious movement, unease creeping along his spine. "What's stopping him?"

"Purpurrot, while we were in the bakery. She might not want to help, but her company is still its own sort of ward. And now? Them, probably," Angus said, laying a gentle hand on Hyena's arm. "As the last remaining imagination beast, their presence is pretty powerful. Like a strong smell covering up any other scents. No offense," they added, when Hyena gave an affronted giggle. "Eventually Denken will be able to see through it, though. Probably sooner than later."

"So what do we do?" Antimony asked.

Angus was quiet for a moment of indeterminable length. "Hide in plain sight," they said eventually. "What we need is somewhere that bears at least one of your presences without being somewhere obvious."

"Easier said than done." Zane worried at her lip. "I mean, our homes are the first places to come to mind, right? But that *would* be obvious... Where else is there?" She glanced at Gloucester, Mulligan, and Harrison. "Maybe the high minister's mansion? You were staying there for a while, right, Gloucester? And Mulligan and Harrison worked there."

"It would be a pretty long walk," Mulligan replied. "Though I suppose we can do the creepy dream-walking thing again. Is it accessible, though? It isn't within city limits. I know the effects have been spreading, so maybe—"

"I think I may have a better idea," Gloucester said, cutting in before Angus could answer. He stuck his hand in his pocket, fingers brushing past the jagged edges of Denken's tooth, and pulled out the key Jeb had given him. Small and brass, there was nothing particularly impressive about it. In fact, the looks he received were universally nonplussed, a sharp contrast with his own smile.

"What's that?" Mulligan asked, leaning forward and scrutinizing the key as if it held a great secret.

"It's a key," Gloucester said, because sometimes resisting the opportunity was impossible. Finch snorted, but nobody else seemed to find him funny, so he hurried on. "It's the key to the storage unit that's holding all of my stuff."

"Stuff?" repeated Zane. "What stuff? You have stuff?"

"Course I have stuff," he said, a little annoyed by the assumption that he was entirely without worldly possessions. "Everyone has stuff."

"Can we stop saying 'stuff,' please?" Harrison asked. "It's starting to not sound like a word anymore."

"First we've heard of it in your case, Mik," Finch said, not unkindly. "We all sort of assumed you lost everything when the whole prison thing happened."

This was fair, Gloucester grudgingly admitted. "When the minister's lot told him I was dead, Jeb put all of my things into storage," he explained, rummaging in his pocket again to find the slip of paper Jeb had written on. "He gave me the key, along with the address of the company, Fredson's Storage."

"Jeb...?" Finch echoed.

"My boyfriend." Gloucester could feel the blush spreading across his face. He coughed, fixing his eyes on his feet. "Ex-boyfriend," he amended.

This wasn't a conversation he wanted to have now. Or ever.

"Ah, Jeb!" crowed Finch, with notable gaiety. "When were you reunited with good old Jeb, then?"

Gloucester offered him a reproachful look. "Right before I got kidnapped by Denken, if you must know. Right around the same time I found out he thought I was dead and had moved on with someone else."

"Yikes," said Angus in a melodramatic stage whisper.

Finch's expression appeared caught between glad and apologetic. "Right. Um. Not a great day, then."

"I've had better."

"Getting back on track," Mulligan said loudly. "Will Gloucester's storage unit work to hide us?"

The question was aimed squarely at Angus, and Mulligan's glare warned the rest of them off of further interruptions.

The demigod looked thoughtful. "If enough of his possessions are there. Things that mean a lot to him. Hold a lot of emotions, that sort of thing."

"You could say that," Gloucester confirmed, thinking of the life he'd built with Jeb. It didn't really feel real anymore, but that didn't mean any of it had lost its sentimental value. If anything, it made it all mean more, the priceless remnants of a lost civilization. He'd suggested the storage unit on a whim, but now he wondered if he was ready to face it.

A hand laid itself on his shoulder. To Gloucester's surprise, it didn't belong to Finch, or even Zane. Instead, Angus stared down at him. For once, the demigod's attitude wasn't flippant or impatient.

"The past is always hard to face. Trust me, I have a lot of it. But it might make you feel better."

"Might." Gloucester sighed. "That's a wobbly term from someone who's supposed to be an expert in emotions."

Angus laughed. Though still an overbearing sound, there was a definite pleasantness to it this time. Their hand on Gloucester's shoulder gave a light squeeze, and through the gesture, he could feel Angus's empathy. The emotion traveled through him, easing the tension in his spine.

Angus withdrew their hand and gave the tip of Gloucester's nose a playful tap with one finger. "Which is exactly what gives me the confidence to say that nothing is easy to predict when it comes to emotions. Just look at my brothers. One sees the futures and the other reads minds, but they're both still idiots when it comes to their feelings."

"Ah," said Gloucester, rubbing his tingling nose. He wasn't sure these words were as comforting as Angus believed they were. Still, it was compelling to know sibling dynamics transcended humanity. "Right. Thanks."

—

Though Gloucester himself didn't know the location of the storage facility, his companions were by and large more well-versed in the city than he was, and it didn't take much to narrow down where they ought to be headed based on its address. Finch gestured for everyone to follow him once more, as if drifting dreamlike through space was an everyday occurrence.

The strange form of travel had worked out fine before, but Gloucester still felt a trill of worry as the street began to shimmer. Hyena, standing at his side, noticed his nerves and laid one huge hand on the top of his head. Though the appendage was big enough to engulf his whole skull in its grasp, the touch was purposefully gentle.

Gloucester reached up to pat Hyena's thumb.

"I'm glad you're here," he told them as they stepped forward together into the shifting scenery. "Thank you for finding us."

At least one immortal being trapped in Frettchen was happy to see them.

By the time Hyena chortled their reply, Purpurrot's Pies and the empty shops of Uptown were gone, replaced by long, low buildings near the coast. They bore none of the welcoming décor of the shopping district. An industrial area of Frettchen, it ought to have been bustling with people and loud with machinery. The stark quiet was more unsettling than ever here. To the west, the ocean stretched out toward the horizon.

Or rather, it should have done. Instead, the distant water sank into a black void sprinkled with pinpricks of stars. The depth of it was compelling, silently calling out to Gloucester. He hurriedly looked away again.

"Not a bad way to get places, moving around like that. For once magic does something useful," Zane said with a nervous laugh. She, too, was pointedly avoiding looking out toward the ocean, her smile shaky. Gloucester sensed she was just trying to break the eerie silence and couldn't fault her in the slightest.

"I agree. Imagine the time you could save, never getting stuck in traffic."

Despite their need for noise, neither he nor Zane spoke louder than a whisper. No one wanted to attract too much attention.

"Oi, plenty of magic is useful," Finch said, sounding hurt. Judging from the twinkle in his eye, Gloucester suspected it was just for show. "Ungrateful cads."

Brushing imaginary dust from his hands, Finch swept his gaze over the group. "All right, everyone still with us? Mik, Zane, pragmatic bastards that you are. Antimony and the talking head, check. The besuited twins, gotcha—"

"Neither of us are wearing suits," Harrison said.

"And yet you knew who I meant," Finch countered, before continuing his roll call. "Got the Love god, got the laughing beast. Right, that's everyone. And now, Mik, it's on to you."

Gloucester blinked. "Me? Why?"

Why did everyone keep looking to him at moments like this?

Finch pointed at his hand. "Because you have the unit number and key." To his credit, he managed to keep any amusement out of the statement.

"Oh," said Gloucester, feeling rather dim. "Right."

He held up the scrap of paper and squinted at Jeb's neat handwriting. What had once been clear print was now a challenge to read, smudged by the time spent in his various pockets. The paper was crumpled and creased, beginning to rip along one of the folds.

"Fredson's Storage, 103 Peter Street," he reiterated first, just to be sure they'd landed in the correct spot. He glanced around for the nearest street sign. "Looks like we're in the right area."

"Definitely," Antimony said. She pointed at a large billboard further down the street, which proclaimed "Fredson's Storage" in large red print. Thankfully, it was in the opposite direction from the harbor and its abyss-like view.

"Then we're looking for unit 28," Gloucester concluded.

As they walked closer, they saw that the gates of the establishment stood open. Everyone wandered into the storage yard, eyes peeled for the right number, no employees around to question or stop them.

"Bit foreboding," Mulligan muttered.

"Not really." Finch shrugged. "Everyone just *poof*ed out of existence—sort of—remember? The place probably hadn't closed for the day when it happened."

"If you're looking for foreboding, though, I think we've got you covered."

The sharp note of warning made everyone look Angus's way. They were staring down the street, back the way they'd come. Blackness pooled in the sky there, devoid of all light. Gloucester's stomach clenched.

"He's coming," Angus said, and no one bothered asking who.

"First one to find unit 28 doesn't get eaten by a giant shadow shark," Gloucester whispered.

"Sounds like a game prize to me," Finch whispered back. There was a grim smile on his face as he took off toward the nearest unit. "C'mon!"

Chapter 21

Hideout

Luckily, whoever Fredson was, they had organized their lot in a regular, systemic fashion. Once the group located unit 1—logically placed closest to the main office—it was only a matter of following the increasing numbers to the twenty-eighth door. Their feet crunched on the gravel no louder than their hurried breaths, yet every sound echoed like a siren in their ears. Behind them, black clouds grew closer.

When they finally came upon the correct door, nothing set it apart from the other twenty-seven they'd passed save for the number 28 above the lock. About ten feet across, the unit's entrance was made of plain metal, designed to be pushed upward like a garage door. Gloucester stood before it, key in hand. On the other side lay everything remaining of his life here in Frettchen.

It was just stuff. He knew that. Just things. Possessions, unimportant to the mission they were on, or in the grand scheme of things in general. Yet it felt important.

"Can we hurry this up a little, please?" Mulligan demanded from somewhere behind him. "Before we get eaten by the terrifying shadow monster?"

"Right." Gloucester snapped himself out of his thoughts and hurried forward to fit the key into the lock. It clicked with little effort. With a final backward glance at the ominous black sky, he hefted the door upward enough to let them all duck through. "Get inside."

No one needed telling twice.

They shut the door again behind them, and for a moment the only points of light were Zane's glowing pocket watch and Angus's eerie immunity to darkness. Then Finch murmured an incantation, and soft golden light flared to life around both his hands. He flicked his wrists. Two orbs roughly the size of grapefruits floated upward to hover near the ceiling, illuminating the room.

"Is that safe?" Antimony's glasses reflected the new light source. "The magic won't attract attention?"

Finch shook his head. "It's a pretty small spell. Angus and Hyena's presence should be enough to cover it. I don't really fancy hanging out here in the gloom, do you? A bit nicer to see what we're dealing with."

The storage unit was sizable but cluttered enough that its precise dimensions were difficult to gauge. Several chairs and a sofa lined the nearest wall, while a small kitchen table and a desk filled the middle of the room. Gloucester spotted his chest of drawers against the back wall, along with a few smaller pieces of furniture and some framed artwork. Most of the remaining space was stacked with cardboard boxes.

It didn't leave much room for standing. Everyone picked their way through the maze of belongings to try and get out of each other's way.

Mulligan, panting from the hurried escape through the storage yard, claimed the most comfortable chair available and sank into it gratefully. Harrison took up his usual spot behind him, while Antimony moved with careful grace past the small army of boxes to sit at the desk, easing Gear's bag from her back and onto the floor. Angus flitted to the rear of the unit, reappearing on top of a stack of blankets by the dresser. Hyena, far too big for the cramped space, hunched their shoulders and ducked their head, trying not to bump it on the ceiling. They watched the magical orbs with interest, slitted eyes glittering in the light.

In this enclosed space, the sense of timelessness trapping the city was far less obvious. Some of the tension eased from Gloucester's shoulders and back as he closed his eyes, listening to the breathing of his companions, the tread of their footsteps, the ticking of Gear's clockwork. All quiet sounds, but tucked away together in the unit, they made for a grounding comfort. The unnatural silence consuming Frettchen was locked outside, just like the shark carried on the clouds.

"A Gloucester museum," Finch murmured.

Gloucester opened his eyes again. Beside him, the magician was peering around the room with obvious delight. He sighed a laugh.

"Don't call it that, please. It's just stuff. That said, I won't mind having my own clothes again." He looked down at the rolled-up cuffs of his trousers.

Antimony had been kind to give him her late husband's clothes to wear, but Mr. Jones had clearly been a taller man than Gloucester. Having to roll up his pant legs and the sleeves of all his shirts grew tiresome after a while. He'd picked up a few items of clothing while in the South Cities, but it would be nice to take a moment to sort through his belongings. And thinking of the danger lurking just outside, he was eager for the distraction.

"I think we're in the clear for now. Might as well see what you can find while we hide out in here," Zane whispered with a shrug. "I'll lend you a hand."

She pushed away from the door, where she had been leaning with her ear pressed against the segmented metal.

Finch snorted. "You're just saying that because you want to snoop through his stuff as much as I do."

"I do not!" Even in the low light of the unit, Zane's guilty expression gave her away. "All right, maybe a little. Sorry," she added to Gloucester. "But it beats thinking about that terror outside. And, well, it's not like we actually know that much about your life from...you know...before..."

"Before I was locked up for being in the wrong place at the wrong time?" Gloucester finished her sentence wryly. "You could just ask, you know."

"But snooping is so much more fun." Finch was already crouched on the floor, lifting the lid off one of the boxes. He began to sift through its contents.

"Can we maybe discuss our plan to save the world *while* you misbehave?" Mulligan asked, frowning at them from the armchair near the wall. "We're not here on a lark, need I remind you. There's just the world itself at stake, if you recall? And seeing as God herself isn't feeling helpful, I think we need to come up with a plan."

"Yeah, yeah." Zane knelt next to Finch and opened another of the boxes. "Don't worry. None of us have forgotten about—*Are you wearing eyeliner in this picture*?"

She held up a photograph. Stepping closer, Gloucester saw the box was full of them. The picture held between Zane's fingers was from two years ago. The night in question returned to him, vivid. He stood in a nighttime street filled with light, thousands of lanterns, candles, and fairy lights chasing away the darkness. Petals fell around him like colorful confetti. If he closed his eyes, he could still hear the music, smell the flowers, feel the warmth of the summer air. It was one of his fondest memories. And now it was here, stowed away in a box in the dark.

"Yeah," he said, as lightly as he could manage. "I was, yeah."

Finch shuffled over to take a look. He whistled low through his teeth. "It's a good look." He winked at Gloucester.

"Fate of the world?" Mulligan dared not speak too loudly, but the words were nonetheless a scathing stage-whisper.

"Some things are just as important," Finch told him silkily.

Gloucester rolled his eyes. He supposed he understood his friends' interest and amusement, but he couldn't help but agree with Mulligan, as much as that pained him to do. "I can tell you all about my fashion choices later. For now, Mulligan's got a point. Now that we're hidden—we are hidden, right?"

He glanced questioningly at Angus where the demigod was perched cross-legged atop the dresser. They'd draped one of the blankets across their lap and appeared quite comfortable.

They shrugged. "I'd say so. For the moment."

Despite their voiced nonchalance and cozy pose, Gloucester could feel their unease weighing heavy in the air.

"Now that we're hidden *for the moment*," he started again. "What's our next move? Seems to me it would be best to approach the Gambler first. If we can get him back on side, we'll have a way better chance against Denken."

The suggestion was met with general agreement. If they didn't have Purpurrot, the Gambler felt like the next best thing. Gear in particular, held in Antimony's arms so she could be included in the conversation, grinned in open relief.

"Yes!" she enthused. "Finally! Let's find him. Everything will be better once he's back with us."

Her cheer was refreshing, but not exactly infectious.

"If the Gambler's unaware of his surroundings, it'll be a trick getting through to him, though." Zane tugged at the hem of her sleeve, as she often did when she was fretting. A photo album lay open and forgotten across her knees.

"Well, they're his sibling, aren't they?" Harrison leaned against the back of Mulligan's chair and gestured at Angus with a tilt of his head. "Strikes me that if anyone can get through to him, it'll be family. Especially if it's a family member who didn't try to kill him."

"Not this time, anyway," Angus agreed. They enjoyed being the centerpiece of their forming plan, the emotion drifting off of them like a pleasant scent. "But the bodyguard is right. If I can't get through to the big flaming idiot, no one can. He might just need a jolt. A reminder of who he is. After all, it's not like he's struggling with the same level of raw power that Denken is."

"Do we know that for sure?" Mulligan asked shrewdly.

Angus shook their head—a denial, not to Mulligan's query, but of the unspoken fear behind it. "We'd know if he was. He might look scary, but he's relatively powerless at the moment. His fire isn't even destructive. Otherwise, the whole city would be ablaze at this point."

That was mildly comforting.

"What happens if—*when*—we get through to the Gambler?" Gloucester asked. "Will the two of you be enough to take Denken on? Do you have any idea how to undo what's been done?"

Angus held their hands up. "One thing at a time, Mikalai. Believe it or not, I've never really been in this sort of mess before. We've had some interesting scrapes in the past, my family and I, but nothing like this. I'm figuring things out as I go along here."

That was...less comforting.

Gloucester had barely opened his mouth to ask another question before Angus hushed him.

"Just...everyone give me some space here, right?" the demigod said. "I need to gather myself."

Whether they meant this figuratively or in some unknowable magical sense, they didn't say. Closing their eyes, they tuned out all of the following questions and concerns, until the rest of the group eventually backed off enough to give them their requested space.

—

"It is sort of interesting, seeing all this."

Gloucester looked up from the box of kitchen supplies he'd been staring aimlessly into while pondering, with a distant sort of misery, the sheer amount of his belongings filling up the unit. Realistically, he knew Jeb had probably found them too painful to be surrounded with, but petty insecurities whispered that he'd just used Gloucester's purported death as an excuse to buy all new things.

Of all people, Harrison stood in front of him, his calm stoicism softened by a smile. At Gloucester's questioning glance, he gestured at the boxes of paraphernalia.

"All of this," he explained. "Zane is certainly enjoying the photographs."

Gloucester followed his gaze over to where Zane and Finch were still huddled over the box of photos, sifting through them with apparent glee. He shook his head with a sigh.

"You'd think I dodged every question ever asked of me," he said, bemused. "It's not like I'm a closed book."

Harrison chuckled quietly. "Maybe it's just that none of us took the time to read the pages."

"What's that supposed to mean?" Gloucester demanded, unsure how he was supposed to take this comment.

Patient as ever, Harrison let Gloucester's peeved tone roll off him. "I suppose it's just easy to forget you had a life before all of this. Back when everything was normal."

"So did everyone."

"True enough." He shrugged. "But yours was just that, wasn't it? Normal. No magic, no big secrets, no friends with immortals, no...whatever that is."

He pointed at Hyena, who was trying to keep themself out of the way but only succeeding in appearing more nightmarish than ever as they loomed in one shadowy corner, chuckling. Beside them, Antimony sat primly on one of Gloucester's chairs, chatting with Gear's head. Her heavy rucksack was at her feet, and she massaged her shoulders idly as they talked.

Harrison eyed them for a long moment, then shook his head and refocused on Gloucester. "I guess it just makes me realize that out of everyone here, you're the one I have the most in common with."

Gloucester must have made a face, as Harrison laughed again and held his hands up placatingly. "Sorry, I know I'm not your favorite person. But even Mulligan knew about magic and the Brothers. Siblings, I mean. I was just as much in the dark as you were." He paused. "And to be honest, if I'd been in the same situation you'd been in...who knows? Maybe I'd have done the same. It could have been me in your shoes. You were a good agent, Gloucester. I'm sorry for what happened to you."

Gloucester stared. He wasn't sure what to say. He couldn't remember Harrison ever saying so much in one go, and he certainly hadn't expected an apology.

"You were doing your job," he said eventually. "Other than drugging me that time, I don't think you have that much to apologize about, but...thanks. That drugging thing *was* really messed up, though."

"I'm sorry," Harrison repeated. To his credit, he still seemed totally genuine.

"Oh, and you hit me in the face once, too," Gloucester added. A smile threatened to sneak past his purposefully stern accusation. "You can be sorry for that."

"I am," Harrison said.

"And for kidnapping me and Zane after that bomb—"

"Okay!" Harrison's voice had lost a fair amount of its trademark patience, but there was a smile on his face. "I get it." His gaze strayed over to Zane again and the smile shrank. "Do you think she holds it against me?"

Gloucester shook his head. "I doubt she's given it much thought, with everything else going on. And if she did have hard feelings, trust me, she'd let you know."

He hesitated. This entire conversation wasn't something he'd been prepared for. "I've gotta say, though, if you're hoping for...anything with her, erm, romantically, I mean... Well, you'd be barking up the wrong tree."

Harrison's composure slipped further, and he cleared his throat, gaze shifting quickly away from Zane again. "Is it that obvious?" he murmured.

"Yeah," Gloucester said emphatically. "Except maybe to her. And that's not because she's dumb or naive. She's aromantic. It just isn't something she's interested in. With anyone."

Harrison sighed. "Fair enough. Still...let's go back to thinking about the impending apocalypse to cheer me up a bit."

"That's the spirit," he said, clapping Harrison on the agent's brawny arm.

Chapter 22

Family Reunited

"Sky's encouragingly clear. As shark-free as a frog pond."

Angus's cheery declaration sounded loud in the silence of the storage lot. Gloucester had to stifle the urge to hush them as he ducked under the half-open door out of the unit. The moment he was out in the open again, the weight of timelessness settled heavy on his shoulders once more, pushing a sigh from his chest.

In truth, the demigod's words were spoken barely above a whisper. Probably for the best not to chide them, anyway. Gloucester wasn't sure he wanted to find out what would happen if he told the prickly demigod to be quiet.

"Hush," said Antimony, who apparently had no such qualms. "You'll bring him right back if you aren't careful."

For a moment, Gloucester thought Angus was going to stick their tongue out at the scientist, but in the end, they went for the slightly less childish option of rolling their eyes.

"Denken's far off, so we're in the clear for now. Don't you worry your little head. Either one of them."

They glanced over Antimony's shoulder, where the transparent back of Gear's head was now visible, reflecting distant flares of lightning. Though she was facing away from Angus, Gear offered up a smile. Behind its glass casing, the clockwork complications of her brain spun in excitement.

Both Gloucester and Zane had offered to take a turn carrying the heavy bag, but Antimony just waved them aside, unbothered. Instead, she'd adjusted her rucksack so that the automaton's head was strapped to the top of it, allowing Gear to see her surroundings. With no one else in the city, there remained no need for the automaton to hide. This new setup gave Antimony the eerie appearance of having a second head facing the opposite way, but both she and Gear seemed happy with the arrangement.

Gear in particular was delighted to be out of the bag. Everyone had warned her several times already that being quiet was of the utmost importance, but she kept letting out little gasps of excitement that she hastily swallowed.

"Well then, let's focus on the other Sibling," Mulligan was saying. He raised his arms, as if to clap his hands together decisively, and then wisely changed his mind and dropped them. In spite of Angus's assurances, they were all wary of making too much noise. Wincing at his near mistake, he asked Angus, "Are you feeling, er, all powered up?"

"As a freshly wound clock," the demigod told him. "If my grumpy fire-giant of a brother tries anything stupid, I'm ready to kick his stupid teeth in. Magically speaking, of course."

Gloucester believed them. The air around Angus was practically thrumming. Magic rippled out from them with every movement, brushing against Gloucester's skin like a tickling breeze. He rubbed his arms as goosebumps rose at the sensation. He didn't think any amount of sheltering nostalgia would disguise Angus's presence for long now.

"No bloody kidding," groused Finch.

Gloucester glanced his way. If *he* could feel the magic this blatantly, it must be nothing compared to what a trained magician felt. Sure enough, Finch pressed two fingers against his temple, brow furrowed as if battling a migraine. Gloucester reached out and took his free hand.

"Are you all right?" he asked quietly.

"No," Finch grunted in reply. Glancing at Gloucester, his scowl softened. "Sorry, it's just...I hate being around immortals. Even at the best of times. I don't think I'm going to have a clear head until this is all over, the way they make it ache."

His chuckle tumbled out on the breath of a sigh. Gloucester squeezed his hand sympathetically.

"When all this is over, you can go on holiday," he said. "Somewhere far away from all magical beings. I'd say I'd pay for it, but, you know..." He shrugged. "Guess I could pawn all my stuff," he joked half-heartedly, gesturing back at the storage unit. Hyena was the last one out, carefully lowering the door shut again, cutting off Gloucester's view of his possessions.

"Come with me and we'll call it even," Finch said. Gloucester searched his face for humor but found only rare sincerity.

"Deal," he told him.

They let Angus take the lead. It was the obvious choice for a multitude of reasons, not least of which was the confident way the demigod strode down the street, never once glancing back to see if anyone was following them. The group did so, minnows trailing after the bigger fish.

Gloucester took a single look back at the storage unit, wondering if the all-too-brief reunion with his worldly belongings would be the last time he ever saw them. To a lesser degree, this thought carried the same bitter sting as the realization that he'd never been meant to return all the way home. It felt like fate was mocking him with pieces of his old life, offering them up to him before snatching them away again.

Perhaps Finch saw something in his face, because he silently pressed a kiss to Gloucester's temple. Around them, the street shivered and changed.

—

Despite their nearly instantaneous shifts around Frettchen and the eerie sensation of stopped time, they didn't succeed right away. Angus led them from one part of the city to another, from wide highways lined with empty cars to tree-filled parks, never finding what they were looking for.

Gloucester couldn't imagine that the Gambler would be an easy thing to miss, yet wherever they went, only heavy clouds and lightning greeted them. A few times, he thought he spotted movement in his periphery, but whenever he turned to look, he found nothing more than shadows and the city's abandoned paraphernalia.

Often, the architecture and open spaces of Frettchen felt unnaturally warped, only adding to the dreamlike feeling of their surroundings. Signs jumbled their letters into unintelligible riddles. The doors and windows of houses swapped places. Graffiti depicted imagery of phantom sharks, the paint swirling and changing every time Gloucester turned his head away.

The unreal quality of it all reminded him of the Maze, both the real one and the fake. He supposed that made sense, as Denken's power and his attempt to remake his home there in Frettchen was the cause of all this. He did his best to ignore the way buildings bent oddly, and streets stretched on too long. From the shipyards to the business district to the shadow of the Old Cathedral the group went, but the fire of the Gambler's unleashed form was nowhere to be found.

"Maybe we should get to high ground," Finch suggested after the seventh empty street. "Go atop one of the skyscrapers. See if we can spot him from up there."

The suggestion, though logical, was delivered with syrupy sweetness. Angus's eyes narrowed. With dramatic pizzazz, they snapped their fingers.

The street vanished.

In the blink of an eye, they were all standing on the roof of one of the tallest skyscrapers in Frettchen. Zane swore, grabbing onto Antimony's elbow. Wind whipped at Gloucester's hair, and he shivered. The whole city stretched out below them. From here he could see the harbor to the west, water sparking with the white crests of angry waves. Out where the horizon ought to be, that looming void pulled at him again, calling out in its complete absence of all things.

Looking the other way, he could almost see the scrubland beyond the eastern edge of the city. There, too, the void held sway, swallowing up any view past Frettchen's borders. Gloucester darted his eyes away from it, which unfortunately brought his attention back to his more immediate surroundings. Though not normally fazed by heights, his stomach did an unhappy flip at the sudden change in altitude. The pressure in his ears throbbed, and he swallowed to get them to pop.

On Gloucester's other side, Finch shook off any surprise with admirable swiftness.

"I bet you anything they just hadn't thought of that themself," he whispered smugly.

"You're going to be the first person to ever be thrown off a building by the personification of Love," Zane warned, letting go of Antimony in order to lean around Gloucester and offer him a glare.

"That's assuming I've never done it before," Angus said. Busy scanning the view, they didn't bother tossing a look their way.

From this height, the reality-bent skyline was all the more obvious and unsettling. Gloucester's gaze lingered on the spires of the Old Cathedral, which curled and twisted before his very eyes. Struck by a wave of dizziness, he squeezed his eyes shut. He just hoped the effects were merely optical. He didn't really fancy being up this high if the building they were on decided to start twisting and turning like that.

"There," called Antimony, accompanied by a triumphant bark of laughter from Hyena. They were both pointing in the direction of Frettchen's northern border. "If you're not all too busy snarking at each other, I think that's our man. Or demigod, rather."

"Where?" cried Gear, facing the opposite way. "Show me, show me!"

As Gloucester followed the line of Antimony's and Hyena's pointing fingers, he thought Gear might want to reconsider her eagerness. Beyond the city's border rose a dark swell of wooded hills. The high minister's mansion, where all of this madness had started, stood somewhere among those trees.

While the big house wasn't visible from where they stood, something else was.

In the streets just below the forest's edge, a warm light radiated upward. From a distance it looked small, but Gloucester knew they could only see it because of the magnitude of its source.

"The Gambler," he murmured.

Until now, the concept of coming face to face with the personification of Choice in his current terrifying form was, well, just that. A concept. A hypothetical. It had just been an idea, harmless and intangible. Now, faced with the daunting reality that they would soon be confronting him, a shiver of uncertainty ran through Gloucester.

"Perfect," Angus said, a fresh determination to their voice. In it, Gloucester heard the echo of racing heartbeats and final breaths, and his foreboding grew stronger.

Without a moment of hesitation, Angus stepped off the edge of the roof. Gloucester's heart leapt into his throat, but before he had a chance to react, their environment shifted once more.

"—cking hell!" Zane said as the city reformed, finishing the only thought thundering through Gloucester's mind. "Do *not* do that."

No pithy retort came back her way. Angus raised a hand for silence, and it was granted immediately. The gravity of their emanating emotions made any further protests or commentary nigh on impossible.

Buildings surrounded them on all sides once more, brick and wood in the place of steel and glass. They were on a residential street, in the area Antimony and Hyena had just pointed out. Wooden houses painted in cheerful colors lined the road behind gardens full of spring flowers and lawn ornaments. It was a neighborhood called Garden Town, and its residents took that seriously.

Yet despite all of the blooms, there was a stark absence of scents, as if the flowers, though still there, didn't truly exist. Combined with the silence encompassing a place that ought to have been full of life, it accentuated the emptiness. Gloucester almost preferred the gut-twisting heights of their previous location. He knew that if he turned around, he'd be able to spot the skyscraper they'd just been standing on in the distance.

Which meant...

"Heads up," Finch murmured, eyes narrowed down the street. At the far end, the orange reflection of fire danced in the glass of many houses' windows. Breathing in uneasily, Gloucester smelled smoke.

Given the Gambler's current size, he expected thundering footsteps to herald his approach. Yet when the demigod lumbered into view a moment later, his tread was as silent as ever. That, along with the ever-shifting contours of the fire engulfing him, lent the Gambler a ghostly presence, like a fiery apparition instead of a physical being. Only the burning scent filling Gloucester's nose felt real.

"Oh," said Mulligan faintly. "I liked this idea so much more five minutes ago."

Gloucester agreed. Reasoning with the Gambler had sounded like a much better plan when he was able to picture the tall, solemn-faced man the demigod usually appeared to be. That image was difficult to bring to mind now.

Yet it was too late to change course.

"Right," he said, mustering his best encouraging voice and hoping the others wouldn't notice its unsteady waver. "You're up, Angus." He hesitated, then added, "You can do this."

It felt stupid offering a confidence boost to a god, but to his surprise, a wave of gratitude rolled over him when Angus met his eyes. For a moment, they seemed about to say something, but then they merely winked and turned away again.

The rest of the group fell back, watching Angus advance down the street. Ahead, the Gambler loomed. Angus looked tiny in comparison. Yet when the smaller sibling spoke, their words carried as much power as the sight of their brother's fiery, monstrous form.

"Brother, you need to wake up."

The words, though loud, held nothing but compassion. Gloucester could feel it, like the warmth of the Gambler's flames, but with none of the menace. This was the warmth of the sun on his face on a peaceful summer day. It was the unconditional love of his mother's kiss pressed against his brow. It was the gentle squeeze of Zane's hand in his when she knew they were both scared. The pride in Antimony's eyes when she looked at Gear. The crooked curve of Finch's smile when it softened just for Gloucester. It was love, in all its complex simplicity.

The Gambler ignored it. As though deaf and blind to the people before him, he continued his march forward, each infernal step bringing him closer.

Soon he was almost on top of them. Gloucester had to squint against the brightness and heat of the flames. He knew that the fire wasn't as hot as it should have been, nor was it setting anything else alight, but it was still intense. Beside him, Zane raised an arm to shield her face.

"It's not working!" she cried. "We've got to get out of here."

Mulligan and Harrison immediately started for the relative cover of a nearby garage, but Angus shouted, "No!" and the power of their command rooted them to the spot, captured by desperate and enduring hope.

"Joujou!" Angus called up to the Gambler.

It was a nickname Gloucester had heard the immortals use for the Gambler before, a strange reminder that beneath all of their otherworldliness, they remained bizarrely human. Perhaps Angus hoped using it now would stir that humanity up from where it was buried, deep within a heart of fire.

"Listen to me. You're stuck, Joujou," they said, arms spread imploringly. Firelight painted their tattoos in warm color. "You're caught in a nightmare. But I'm here now. You can wake up."

Still, the Gambler ignored them.

"I really don't think this is working," Gloucester whispered to the others, echoing Zane's words.

"I don't know," Antimony said. Her eyes were locked on the fiery figure now towering over them. "He's stopped moving. That's something."

Indeed, the Gambler's massive steps had come to a halt. He was simply standing, a dozen stories tall.

"Makes that dragon we faced really look like nothing at all, doesn't it?" Finch said, shading his eyes as he craned his neck to look up at the Gambler.

"All of you, shut up," Mulligan hissed. "If we have to depend on the snotty god to do this, the least we can do is be quiet and let them."

At long last, the Gambler noticed them all. Or, at the very least, he became aware that something stood in his path. His head tilted downward, face barely discernible in the raging inferno. Gloucester thought he could make out the vague shape of a nose, the glowing line of a mouth. There were no eyes to be found, but then again, even in the Gambler's normal form, those were a feature he lacked.

"Come on, big guy," Zane whispered. "Recognize us. We're your friends."

The only sound was the fire's crackle. Then the Gambler opened his mouth.

What came forth was like the roar of the wind, a howling, haunting noise. Gloucester had no idea what it meant, but it felt like a bad omen.

"Angus! Shut him up!" Mulligan's demand was shrill with fear, his hands clamped over his ears as he leaped for cover behind Harrison. "Can't you calm him down? Use your powers!"

"He's my brother, idiot!" A high edge sharpened Angus's retort as well, but fear had nothing to do with it. "He's immune to my powers."

"He's *what*—"

"I may as well use them on myself for all the good they'd do." As Angus shouted over the spluttering Mulligan and the Gambler's gale, they shook out their arms, bending their knees into a crouch. Power was building around them. Gloucester sensed it like an itch in his mind, the sound of feathers rustling in his ears.

"Okay, time to get out of the way," he decided. Grabbing hold of Zane and Finch, he pulled them toward the cover of the houses to their left. A few meters away, Harrison did the same with Mulligan and Antimony. Hyena was already there, beckoning Gloucester urgently from where they were crouched—rather pointlessly, given their size—behind some patio furniture.

"You're always one step ahead," he told them, a wild laugh escaping his lips as adrenaline rushed through him. Hyena laughed too, high-pitched with fright. Perhaps they were simply trying to tell him off for joking around at a time like this. Gloucester decided it wasn't really worth worrying about.

He took refuge behind a four-foot garden wall encircling the nearest lawn, its brickwork twined in ivy. Finch and Zane crouched at his side. Harrison stopped a few meters further onto the lawn, depositing Antimony and Mulligan behind a neatly tended flowering bush. Gloucester and his friends peered cautiously over the cement top of the wall.

Out in the street, only Angus remained in the Gambler's path. They hadn't flinched in the face of their brother's roar. They were still crouched, a fighter ready to spring into action.

"Don't try that with me," they said, cutting smoothly through the din. "Just snap out of it, you freak." If anyone had doubted the title of Siblings, Angus's impatient derision would do away with that now. Only siblings could muster that precise tone.

The power of which was not to be underestimated. The Gambler's mouth snapped shut. Visibly hesitating, he stared down at Angus, an elephant put at odds by the mouse at its feet.

"We need your help, Joujou." Though it still carried, Angus's voice softened. "We can't do this without you. So, you need to wake up, all right? Come on."

For a moment, Gloucester thought their cajoling was going to work. The Gambler stood motionless, and Gloucester imagined him struggling against his own consciousness, pulling himself back to reality. Or whatever this in-between place was.

Then he opened his mouth again, and this time what came out was a scream.

Gloucester clapped his hands over his ears, but that did nothing to mute the deafening noise. As was always the case with immortals, he heard a lifetime of experiences and sensations in the singular note as it surged through his skull. It stirred up old memories, old choices, like a tornado through photographs, mixing them with a thousand other thoughts and feelings he knew weren't his own. In that instant, everything ceased to be except the raucous roar of the Gambler's war cry.

"What the hell is this?" Mulligan's shouted fury paled beneath the onslaught, barely audible. "I thought the whole point of siding with the damned god was because they could fight against each other!"

In spite of the dire circumstances, Finch managed to look derisive as he rolled his eyes at Mulligan. "The Siblings' specific abilities only work on mortals. That's how we caught the Gambler in the first place—he can't see his own futures, so he couldn't clearly see us coming for him. But unless *you're* gonna leap into the fray, I wouldn't criticize the Love god too much."

And then the Gambler's bellow was joined by another. More of a screech, it sliced through the Gambler's terrible howl like a blade. If Gloucester hadn't been staring straight at the personification of Love, he might have taken it for the call of some mighty raptor, like the giant eagles who hunted in the mountains back home. But this was no mere bird.

Angus was fighting back.

Chapter 23

Fury

Angus was screaming. Or at least Gloucester could only assume it was Angus. After all, the creature making the horrible sound stood where Angus had been and appeared to be wearing the demigod's clothes.

That and the shock of white hair were where any similarities ended.

Great wings unfurled, covered in the brindled feathers of some huge predatory bird. Again, Gloucester's mind went to the eagles up north. Yet even those great hunters were nothing like this. Angus's wings sprouted from their shoulders, where arms had been only moments before. Their feet shifted, elongating grotesquely into scaly talons. Though their face remained roughly human, there was something newly sharp and angry about it, shedding the usual round curves of their cheeks and jaw.

"Bloody hell!" shouted Mulligan, all decorum forgotten as he abandoned the flowering shrubbery and leapt behind the meager cover of a small corkwood tree slightly further away. "What's going on now? Do you think they're joining him?"

"No!" Unlike Mulligan's distress, Antimony's increased volume was simply to be heard over the cacophony. "Look!"

Angus ascended through the air, wings beating steadily, until they were level with the Gambler's head. Each wingbeat bore them up and down several feet, but their attention never wavered from their brother. The unintelligible scream tearing from them began to alter and change, a symphonic calamity in a language only the Siblings understood.

"Yikes," said Zane, still peeking over the garden wall. She clamped her hands over her ears. "And I thought arguments with my sister were bad."

"I'm so glad I'm an only child," said Finch.

Half-deafened by the demigods' furious exchange, they had no choice but to stand by and watch, hoping they were far enough out of the way should the situation deteriorate. Gloucester wished he could discern whether things were going well or not. Though the Gambler had yet to lash out at his hovering sibling, neither immortal was calming down at all. The Gambler's fire still blazed, and Angus's wrath screeched on. In the back of his mind, an anxious whisper fretted over how much noise was being made and what it might attract.

"Is it a distraction, maybe?" suggested Harrison. Leery of standing too far from Mulligan, he loomed behind the politician, his size further emphasizing the corkwood's inefficiency as a protective barrier. "Maybe we should be taking the chance to attack?"

"Tempting." The effect of Finch's sighing demeanor was ruined by the pitch at which he had to shout to be heard. "But nah, this isn't a distraction. It's a negotiation."

"I don't think many things are actually solved by two people shouting in each other's faces," Gloucester said. His gun felt heavy in his holster, but he fought the urge to draw it. Ever since he'd tossed it aside in the false Maze in favor of reasoning with the thought-beasts, the weapon no longer felt like his best option. What if, in spite of appearances, this was another moment where the non-violent route was the better one? They had to trust Angus to know what they were doing.

"Bit of an understatement to call that 'shouting,'" said Harrison.

"And a bit of an overstatement to call them 'people,'" added Finch.

"Quit snarking and pay attention," Gloucester told them both. "Unless you want to get stomped on because you were too distracted being witty to notice the danger."

"You know you love my witty snark." Finch grinned but left it at that.

The angry confrontation between the demigods finally seemed to be going somewhere. The Gambler's roar ceased, and for a moment that stretched indefinitely, only Angus's cry remained. It was as powerful as ever, and all the more shrill without the foghorn blare of the Gambler to counter it.

"Do you think that means they've won? Can we—oh shit!"

Zane's hopeful question curdled into alarm. Angus had stopped screaming, but not by choice. The Gambler moved quickly, lashing out one enormous arm to swat Angus away like a fly. The smaller immortal tumbled through the air, colliding with a house on the other side of the street in a crash of glass and feathers.

"Oh shit," echoed Gloucester.

Zane was almost vibrating with dismay. "There's got to be something we can do." Peeking through the ivy leaves, her eyes darted from the Gambler to Angus, who was pulling themself slowly to their feet. The demigods' strength was undeniable; Gloucester was sure the blow Angus had been dealt would have killed anyone else instantly.

"Right. There's gotta be something." Finch half-turned from the street, regarding the rest of the group from within the wall's shadow. Intense determination shone in his eyes. "And here's what it is. While the Gambler is distracted beating the shit out of his sibling, we're going to move back into the fray and get him under control. Enough so that Angus can talk to him without getting smashed to bits. I'll do my best to rein him in with spells. Mikalai, d'you reckon you can use your shield to impede his movements? Trip him up?"

Gloucester bit his lip, glancing from Finch to the Gambler. The demigod's attention, such as it was, remained entirely focused on Angus, who was still gathering their wits about them. The idea of going up against the formidable form of the Gambler was daunting but so was crouching here uselessly. He clenched his hand into a fist, the rings' chains brushing against his knuckles.

"I dunno," he said. "Maybe? But this isn't some imagination monster, is it. How do we know this'll work?"

"You sound like Zane," Finch told him. "C'mon."

"Smart and sensible, you mean," said Zane. She winced, then added, "I've gotta, ugh, agree with Finch, though. Better to try something than just sit here like lumps on a log."

"And I've got to agree with Gloucester." Mulligan sounded as displeased with this as Zane. "This could get us killed."

"Look," Finch said. "If there's one thing I've learned traipsing around with you idiots—sexy company excluded," he added with a wink in Gloucester's direction. "It's that sometimes the only way you can win is by trusting the people around you. The people on your side. I'm trusting you lot, so just...trust me. Please."

He stared around at them all, green eyes earnest.

"Wow." Zane reached out and patted the magician on the arm. "I think that's the most reasonable thing I've ever heard you say." Then she scoffed. "Minus the 'sexy' part."

"I thought that bit was nice," Gloucester said to no one in particular.

"Whichever way you see it, we're running out of time." Antimony's eyes were on the Siblings. "Finch is right, and we haven't the time to argue this. Let's go."

Having said her piece, she pulled herself to her feet and strode out of the garden with hip-swaying purpose, never looking back.

"Well, that settles it." Zane sighed. "Leave it to Antimony to make me choose between sanity and, well, her."

Without any further hesitation, she hopped over the wall onto the sidewalk and after her friend. Gloucester looked over at Finch.

"Trust isn't always easy," he said quietly. "But I trust you. Let's do this."

Finch nodded, his eyes saying everything his tight-lipped smile didn't, and together they followed after Zane. Hyena, Mulligan, and Harrison joined reluctantly in their wake.

Antimony was already in the middle of the street, her head tilted back, resting against the glass of Gear's constructed skull. Gear caught Gloucester's eye, questions filling her gaze that she didn't have the time to ask, let alone he to answer.

"Gambler!" Antimony shouted. "Stop this."

At Gloucester's side, Zane muttered under her breath. The words were too quick and quiet for him to hear clearly, but they sounded a lot like "please don't get stepped on" repeated over and over.

The Gambler's head slowly turned, following the sound of Antimony's call.

"Right," said Finch. He gave his arms a loosening shake, then held them out to his sides. "Everyone, latch on."

The others gathered close and laid their hands on his sleeves. Already Gloucester could feel the magic gathering, buzzing into his fingers.

"Mikalai, get that shield up between her and him."

He drew in a breath, and with it, the familiar sensation of Finch's magic. Raising his free hand, enchanted rings on his splayed fingers, he imagined the invisible barrier.

He conjured it up more easily this time. Gloucester was growing accustomed to the feel of magic and what it took to pull it into place. Though he could see no visible sign of the shield, he could sense it materialize between Antimony and the immortals.

"I don't know how long I'll be able to hold it," he said. "Or how well it'll hold up against him. But it's in place."

"Good," said Finch. "Right, the rest of us—"

"Gambler!" cried a different voice, interrupting. "Gambler, it's me."

Though she couldn't look at him from where her head was lashed to the rucksack, Gear's shout called the Gambler's attention to her like a beacon. Silence fell over the street, save the whirring *click-click* of Gear's clockwork moving quicker than usual, almost a hum as the gears spun in her skull.

Also audible in the newfound silence was the long sigh Antimony released. It shook slightly, betraying her fear more than her face ever did. When she spoke, however, the words were steady.

"Gambler, when we first met, I asked you why you showed yourself to me. Do you remember?"

The Gambler didn't answer, didn't move, but Antimony carried on without waiting for a reply.

"You didn't tell me then. It was only later, when I kept asking, that you told me there was something in my futures that drew you. Something you couldn't see, no matter how hard you tried. My futures were a mystery, muddled so you couldn't read the odds, and that intrigued you." Her slim figure stood tiny before the titanic flames, white dress painted orange in the firelight, yet she didn't waver. "I like to think we've become friends since then. I believe we have. But I know what it was you couldn't see. What it was that drew you, Gambler. It was her."

Then, showing more bravery than Gloucester could ever hope to possess, the scientist turned her back on the Gambler, letting Gear face him instead.

"Shit," muttered Finch. "I completely forgot about her. What're they playing at?"

"I'm here," Gear called. "I know I look a bit different, but it's still me. I'm just all in pieces. Don't worry, though. People get all worried when they find that out, but I'm okay. Are you okay? You're different now too."

If a face made of flames could convey hesitance, Gloucester reckoned the Gambler had just managed it. He was motionless, a skyscraper of fire looming over Antimony and the automaton on her back. The scientist was even paler than usual, but she didn't retreat or turn to protect her precious creation from danger.

Trust, thought Gloucester. He kept his hand raised, drawing magic from Finch to keep the shield in place.

"What is she doing?" Finch's arm twitched under Gloucester's hand, as if he were tempted to lunge forward. "This isn't the plan. This isn't—"

"You wanted us to trust you," Zane said. "Maybe now you need to trust *her*."

Firelight reflected off the clear dome of Gear's skull, half obscured by Antimony's head. Gloucester could still hear the mechanical clicking of her clockwork, the delicate complications that brought her to life.

"Gambler," she said. "I know you're scared. I didn't even know what scared was until I saw you hurt back at that Maze place. But it wasn't a good feeling. I don't want to feel that, and I don't want you to feel it, either. Please don't be scared. Please listen to us. To me."

In a pile of debris on the other side of the street, Angus stared at the automaton. Their wings had furled back into human arms, and confusion wafted off them like heatwaves. Gloucester prayed they wouldn't interfere. Perhaps what they all needed right now wasn't immortal power or complex magic spells. Maybe what they needed was love, pure and simple.

"Well?" Mulligan hissed. "Are we going to attack? He's distracted, this is the perfect opportunity."

"It is," agreed Gloucester. "But not for an attack. Let her talk."

Finch let out a quiet growl but remained where he was. "Let's just see how this goes. But be ready. If it goes sideways, we need to be able to react instantly."

Gloucester could only imagine how difficult it was for him, letting someone else take the lead in a moment like this, when he was surely keen to use his trusted magic instead. He gave Finch's arm a squeeze.

"The shield is still in place," he reassured him. "It'll be okay."

Please, please let it be okay.

"Don't let the fear win," Gear said. "I know it feels easy to let it take over. That's how it was for me. But it wasn't good, I don't think. I didn't like how it made me. I like how I am better when I fight it. Even like this. Please, Gambler. Please let it go." Her voice shook a little but was filled with an earnestness nearly as palpable as the Love god's emotions.

The Gambler opened his mouth, a gaping maw in the midst of the flames. Gloucester winced pre-emptively, expecting another ear-shattering roar.

Which never came. Instead, a great, hot wind blew through the street, swirling dust off the pavement and scattering purple leaves and pink flowers from the crab-apple trees shading nearby gardens. Gloucester's shield blocked it from reaching the group, but across the street, Angus staggered under its impact. It was a sigh unlike any Gloucester had ever heard, and not just for the sheer size of the lungs it escaped.

Slowly, the Gambler began to shrink. The inferno of his form dimmed, a blazing fire tempered into coals, and then into flesh and bone and an eyeless human face. From the vanishing flames whirled two pale spheres, rolling through the air before returning to their orbit around the Gambler's head.

After what felt like ages and no time at all, the Gambler stood before them as Gloucester remembered him: a tall, slender man with golden-brown skin and pale blond hair, his features solemn and angular. Smooth skin stretched over his eye sockets. The eyes themselves continued to spin around him, amber and unblinking. He looked dazed and ruffled, as if he'd just woken from a long, deep sleep.

His impossible stare was fixed on Gear. Gloucester could imagine the bright smile the automaton aimed back at him.

"I have *so many* questions," Harrison said.

"I'm finding it best not to question too much when it comes to magic." Gloucester let the shield disappear as he dropped his arm back to his side. When Zane scoffed openly, he looked over at her in surprise. "What?"

"Oh, come off it," she said with a laugh. "You ask more questions than anyone I've ever met." The confrontation's peaceful ending had left her blatantly relieved. A broad grin spread across her face. "Not that I think it's a bad thing," she added. "Nothing wrong with a good question."

"Right, well then, here's one," Mulligan said. "What now? Is he all...fixed? Better? Whatever?"

Finch rolled his eyes. "Yeah, that question would win awards for its gravity and eloquence."

The look Mulligan offered him was icy. "And yet it stands."

"I am...better than I was," the Gambler said, speaking for the first time.

With Gloucester's shield dropped, he moved toward Antimony and Gear. He raised a hand to the automaton's face, brushing gentle fingers across her cheek. She giggled, while behind her, Antimony smiled. Though he'd sounded exhausted, the Gambler wore a small smile of his own as he let his forehead rest tenderly against Gear's brow. The sight was both heartwarming and deeply unsettling, Gloucester reflected. The Gambler then pulled Antimony around into a wordless hug.

"That's not a great answer," Harrison said after several beats of expectant silence, when it became apparent the Gambler wasn't planning on saying anything more. The bodyguard's words were stiff, as if he wasn't sure what tone to take with the demigod. "How do we know you won't burst into flames again? How do we know we can trust you?"

Antimony cast him a faintly scandalized look over the Gambler's shoulder, and Gear sputtered, but Gloucester noticed that they didn't actually offer an argument. It was a valid question. Like everyone else, they turned to the Gambler, waiting for an answer.

"You don't," he said simply, releasing Antimony and taking a step back. "You can't. Because even I don't know for certain I won't fall sway to it again." He gave a haunting sigh. "More than ever, the futures elude me. They're too wild, too changing, too wrapped up around Denken."

He shook his head from side to side, brow creased. Gloucester wondered what it was he saw.

"But I have to believe I won't," he went on. He fixed his eyeless gaze on Harrison. "You wish you were anywhere else but here, Mr. Harrison, yet do you not believe in yourself enough to remain staunchly at your employer's side?" He looked next to Finch. "You fear and dislike me and my kin, yet you do what you can to help and not hinder. Does that not require faith in your own judgment? And Gloucester, who feared for so long that you had gone mad, do you not trust yourself now?"

He wasn't sure what to say to that. Next to him, Finch frowned, but he didn't seem angry so much as indignant, likely affronted at being used as an example. Gloucester, on the other hand, considered the Gambler's words and, rather to his surprise, found them to be true.

"Yeah. I do." He turned to the others. "And I trust him."

"Good," said Angus. They were back to their usual form, unharmed beneath a layer of dust and annoyance. They came to stand beside their brother. "So how about we get a move on before Denken finds us and we have to put it to the test?"

Chapter 24

The Body

"So, what now?"

It was Mulligan, unsurprisingly, who asked the question, leaning against the back of Gloucester's old armchair.

The group had retreated back to the storage unit. Outside, the sky betrayed no change in hour, stuck in the same stormy twilight it had been since they first arrived in Frettchen. Gloucester supposed it was his own need to cling onto time in this now timeless place that made him feel like the day had come to an end.

For once, Mulligan wasn't demanding an answer out of impatience or annoyance. Even he wasn't immune to the feeling of victory that had settled over the group. Reuniting with the Gambler was a major win, no matter that the demigod himself had been quiet since returning to the safety of the unit. He sat in a corner, Antimony at his side and Gear's head in his hands, conversing with them quietly as Antimony caught him up to speed. The rest of them left her to it.

Angus watched from across the room, watery eyes unblinking. They'd barely spoken to their brother, but the emotion wafting off of them wasn't anger so much as awkwardness. Gloucester guessed that the pair of demigods hadn't spent much time together in a long while. Perhaps Angus felt guilty for not recognizing the Gambler's year-long absence for what it was. Imprisonment.

He was hardly about to open that can of worms, however. He had enough trouble parsing through his own issues, let alone those of immortal personifications.

"Good question," said Finch. Like Mulligan, he seemed willing to forgo his usual sardonic air. He sat on the floor, sorting idly through Gloucester's photographs. The novelty of the old pictures was no longer enough to distract him from the challenges at hand. "Normally I'd say, 'Get some sleep,' but I'm not tired. Not more so than I normally am, at least. I'm not sure we could sleep even if we wanted to."

"I wouldn't recommend trying it," Angus said. "Worst case, you succeed and vanish into the same limbo as all the other living beings who were here. Best case, it's just a waste of time."

"Fun." Finch sighed, dropping a stack of photos back into the box and closing the lid. "But good to know. Back to brainstorming, then."

"Our best move is to follow through on Hyena's tip," said Angus. They'd taken up their seat on top of the dresser again. "Find Denken. Or more specifically, his body."

Gloucester had almost forgotten about Hyena's encounter with the oracle. He pushed away from the wall he'd been leaning against. "Is that what Orange Ianto was showing Hyena? Where Denken is? What do you mean 'his body'?"

He glanced over at the thought-beast, who chuckled uncertainly. They were sitting on their haunches near the closed door, curled in on themself as much as possible. They always seemed to be hunching, as if constantly trying to make themself as small and unobtrusive as their size would permit. Occasionally, they pressed the side of their head to the metal, listening for any indication of Denken's approach. None of them were confident they'd have warning of an attack, but it was still a comfort to have someone on guard.

"Denken's mind is like a boat that's come untethered from its anchor," the Gambler explained, speaking up from his corner. He gently handed Gear over to Antimony and got to his feet. "If we can resecure that line, he'll be—"

"Sane again?" Zane asked hopefully.

But the Gambler shook his head. "No. Not that Denken's ever been what you might call sane. But subduing him will be...easier."

"As in, he might not be a ginormous marauding shadow shark who would eat us as soon as look at us," Angus chimed in. "Remember, that's where his consciousness is now. Back in his body, we may be able to get him under control, maybe even get him to a point where we can talk to the silly prick. As long as he's stuck in the shark, there will be no reasoning with him. Sharks are, famously, not great at reasoning."

"Getting him back in his body sounds like an improvement to me, then," said Gloucester. He looked over at Hyena again. "Do you remember where you saw it? The body?"

Pleased at the prospect of being helpful, Hyena nodded their skull-like head emphatically. They chortled an answer, eyes darting from Gloucester, who they were most at ease conversing with, to the demigods, who could translate.

The Gambler listened calmly to Hyena's laughter.

"They're not sure exactly where it was," he interpreted. "The woman with red hair—Orange Ianto, I presume—only showed them a brief glimpse. Denken in a place, falling, and the shark rising out of him, but Hyena wasn't physically there themself." The Gambler's brows climbed as he spoke, and when he'd finished translating, he turned toward Antimony. "Orange Ianto is here?"

Antimony shook her head. "No. Not in the corporeal sense. It's...a long story. You haven't sensed her, then? She was never able to reach your consciousness?"

"There wasn't much consciousness to be reached. I remember fighting Denken in his false Maze. Then...darkness." The Gambler frowned, contemplative. "There are bits and pieces of feelings more than anything. Impressions. But the next thing I remember clearly was Gear calling out to me."

His frown vanished as he turned a glance toward Gloucester's desk. There, Gear grinned back at him from atop a stack of folded bedclothes.

For once, Antimony paid her creation's mood little mind. She tapped a thin finger against her lips. "You really were out of it, then. She told us she'd tried to reach you several times. She's stuck in limbo like everyone else mortal who was in Frettchen when Denken's power surged. Difference is, she's conscious."

"More like she's conscious*ness*," Finch said. "As in, *only* consciousness, no body. When she isn't snatching someone else's."

The Gambler regarded him for a moment but apparently decided against questioning this. He turned back to Hyena. Picking his way through the clutter, he approached the thought-beast and laid a hand on their arm. Tall as he was, he could only reach Hyena's bicep. "Can you describe exactly what you saw in the vision she showed you?"

Another vehement nod. The laughter spilling from Hyena was long and complex, and the two demigods listened with rapt attention.

"A big dark room," the Gambler related. "Full of stone and shadow. Candles burning in sconces on the walls and..."

He fell silent, realization hardening his features. Gloucester knew why, as he'd reached the same conclusion in his own mind.

If he closed his eyes, he could see it: the vast chamber, its insides impossible in scale compared to its outsides, stone walls shrouded in shadows and an uncanny quiet. And in the center, an expansive web of faintly glowing cords, stretched between the floor and ceiling. A lonely figure caught in their embrace, held captive for so long.

"The High Minister's Cathedral," he said. "He's in All Saints bloody Shrine."

"How fitting," Antimony mused. "Back where this all began."

"Where it all went wrong," Finch muttered, getting to his feet.

Gloucester laid a hand on his elbow. A tightness around his eyes hinted at the guilt Gloucester knew he felt. The magician might not like to admit it, but he'd played a large role in the Gambler's capture. Together, he and his father had designed the demigod's prison in All Saints Shrine.

"Why would his body be there?" Harrison asked. "Wouldn't it still be at the Maze place?"

Hyena shook their head, gibbering a laugh.

"They say they know that place well and it definitely wasn't there," said Angus, lounging against the wall behind the dresser. "And it really isn't that surprising," they added dryly. "Stumbling into the most dramatic location he could think of before losing control of his corporeality sounds exactly like something Denken would do. He's such a diva."

The Gambler sighed, donning the weary exasperation of a sibling. "I might not word it that way, but it is very Denken-like. And setting aside his dramatic flair, it was probably a last-ditch attempt on his part to try and make things right. All Saints is the epicenter of this mess. Maybe he thought he could do something there to stop it, even raging and crazed as he was."

"Do you think he would try to do that?" Gloucester asked. "Try to stop this destruction?"

The Siblings stared at him. While Angus looked typically irritable, the Gambler's voice was as gentle as it could be.

"Denken never wanted any of this to happen. He is capricious and mischievous and dangerously whimsical, but he isn't evil. His actions were misguided at best and catastrophic at worst, but he never acted out of anything but desperation and raw emotion."

From someone else, this might have felt like chastisement. From the Gambler, it was simply an explanation. Gloucester thought back to the conversations he'd had with Denken when he was his prisoner.

Sure, yes, having been a captive made it a little difficult to try and see things from the demigod's perspective, but it was true that Denken never appeared to truly relish the wild power of his violent acts. That violence had only been committed because of the Gambler's abduction. It didn't excuse his crimes, but it did lend them context. The Gambler made a good point: Denken hadn't wanted this. Was it really so far-fetched that he might seek to undo the damage if he could? If they returned him to his body and offered him aid, would he respond to that? Or was he too far gone no matter his form, his desperate efforts to right wrongs forgotten in his madness?

Finch crossed his arms. "Motivation is great and all, but let's not forget everything that's come of it, yeah? A lot more people than just the high minister have died because Denken lost his temper and his goddamned mind. And I'm not just talking about my dad. People who really were innocent. So don't go giving him too much heroic credit, please. He's still an ass."

"Oh, undoubtedly," Angus replied, sneering at him. "But maybe the pot ought not call the kettle black here, eh?" They tutted when Finch gestured rudely in return.

The Gambler sighed.

Zane offered him a wry, sympathetic smile from her perch on a stack of boxes. "Missing being a giant, mindless fire monster?"

"A little," he said, his own smile strained. "My siblings bring that out in me."

"Family, am I right?" she joked. Her next words were directed to the whole group. "So, we know where Denken's body is. That's great. But, uh, what do we do with it? Is there...I dunno, some sort of...of spell we can do to pull him back into it?"

Finch chuckled humorlessly. "That'd be bloody nice, wouldn't it? Certainly would make things easier."

"That doesn't sound all that promising," Gloucester said.

"Spells are generally invented to deal with situations we've, you know, come up against before. This whole 'return a mad god to his body in a city frozen in time limbo before the effects of it spread through the entire known world and we're all lost to the Void' thing? A bit unprecedented."

The group digested this point.

"Could you hazard a guess, though?" Gloucester asked eventually. "You said you and your dad were able to catch the Gambler because he couldn't see his own futures, right?"

He cast the Gambler an apologetic look for bringing up an undoubtedly sore subject. Standing in Hyena's shadow, the demigod's face was more unreadable than ever, but his eyes, usually orbiting his head, hung motionless over each of his shoulders, reflecting, cat-like, the light from Finch's recast illumination spell. They stared directly at Finch.

"I knew something bad was likely going to happen, but I couldn't see what," the Gambler said. "That made things worse, distracting me. I should have returned to the Crossroads, where I would be safe, but I was curious. Foolishly so. I thought I could discover for myself what was going to happen. And that I would be more powerful than whatever danger awaited me."

"Right." Gloucester tried to ignore the mounting tension. "But, Cassus, how did you actually *catch* him? Could we use that sort of magic again, to overpower Denken?"

Finch's freckled nose wrinkled, green eyes narrowed in consideration. "I wish I could say it was easy, but it wasn't. It took months of preparation and my father's lifetime of research." Though he spoke of the kidnapping with an impassive air, he was staring down at a closed box of photographs, conveniently avoiding the Gambler's gaze. "It all came down to the Cat's Cradle. Those ropes he was tangled up in, remember? Dad might have been a bastard in a lot of ways, but he knew his way around magic. The net was woven with as many wards and magic-dampening charms as we could work into it. Something like that would work on Denken too, but it would take ages to create again."

"Maybe the original ropes are still there," Antimony suggested. "Or would their spells have been broken when we cut the Gambler free?"

He shrugged. "I can't speak for the state they're in, but I don't see why they wouldn't be there. Unless Mr. Government cleaned things up." He shot Mulligan an interrogatory glance.

Mulligan crossed his arms and glowered. "I haven't been back there since the day that—" He looked away, clearing his throat. "Since that day. No one has."

"Right then," said Finch, paying Mulligan's grief no mind. "So, the ropes should still be there. Wonderful. And if they're in good shape, they would definitely work to contain that godly bastard."

"And if they're not?" Gloucester asked. "Would you be able to reactivate the spells?"

"Maybe," Finch replied.

Zane lifted a dubious eyebrow. For extra measure, she followed it with the other. "*Maybe*?"

"Would you people please stop acting like I know what I'm doing here?" Finch demanded, throwing his hands up. "All I know is, Denken's too powerful to fight in the form he's in. It's probably the whole reason he got tossed out of his own bloody body. If we want to get him back *into* that body—which we might stand a chance of actually beating—we need to get his power level down. If the ropes are salvageable, then maybe we can use them to do that. Catch him like a *really* big fish in a net."

"It sounds stupid, *but*," said Angus, raising a hand when Finch started to argue, "it isn't totally idiotic. Surprisingly."

"Couldn't resist that, could you?" Finch muttered.

—

It was tempting to immediately make for the High Minister's Cathedral now that they knew where to find Denken's body. Even in Frettchen's temporal weightlessness, Gloucester could feel the ticking clock in the back of his mind. Not literal, of course, like the clicking gears that kept Antimony's creation alive, but his own pressing anxiety. How, in this place with no time, did he feel so certain they were fast running out of it? He felt like any moment, his ticking worries would reach some fatal hour, and their tolling would be deafening and horribly final.

I spend too much time with Zane.

Except the clock technician would probably be soothed by the thought of her precious timepieces.

Unfortunately, "use the magical ropes that may or may not still work" wasn't all that popular a plan, as plans went, no matter the pressing sense of urgency.

"We have to think of the next step," Mulligan kept insisting.

This was, all considered, very obvious, and Gloucester struggled to hold himself back from snapping at the politician. Mulligan was just voicing his worries aloud, not trying to be a nuisance.

"So, we rope Denken back into his body," he said, mentally skipping over some stressful hurdles to land as best he could in the semi-comfortable realm of the optimistic hypothetical. He paced back and forth across the small open space in the middle of the storage unit. "Then what? Presumably we'll still have to fight him. It wasn't like he was all sunshine and rainbows before he went full shark."

He paused mid-step to look at Finch. "Say... That room in All Saints Shrine, will it still have your enchantments cast on it?"

"Would have to," Finch said. A foil to Gloucester's anxious energy, he'd sunk into the armchair, chin propped on his hand. "Otherwise, it would revert to normal size. Why—Oh!" His eyes grew wide, creasing the sun on his brow. "Mikalai, you genius!"

"Hardly," said Gloucester, bashful. "Just retreading what Denken probably already thought of. It would still have all the spells limiting his powers, then?"

Finch grinned and sat up straight, re-energized. "I reckon so. Some magic, like my phone number on your hand, is designed to fade over time. But those spells were worked to last. They had to. The high minister didn't plan on letting the Gambler go any time soon."

"Hm." The Gambler's displeasure was palpable.

"Which was very, very bad of him," Finch added. Though the words were snide, he looked sincerely abashed. In so much as he ever did. He took a deep breath, then faced the Gambler. "Look, I'm sorry for the part I played in all that. I know it's too little, too late, and not worth much, but that's the truth. We should have left you alone."

Though Angus scoffed, unmoved by the apology, the Gambler gave a slow and solemn nod.

"Your regret is appreciated," was all he said.

"Right," Finch said. This seemed to be enough for him. Perhaps he recognized it wasn't his place to ask for anything more. "So...the enchantments should still in place. That, at least, we can count on. Even if we can't get the Cat's Cradle to work, those spells might be enough to whittle down Denken's power."

"What enchantments are these, then?" Angus asked, pale brows scrunched. "What are we talking about here, exactly?"

"My prison." The Gambler's response weighed on all of them. "The Finches wrought it with spellwork to limit our abilities within its walls. We are not powerless, but we are the closest thing."

If the bewildered anger buffeting Gloucester's consciousness was anything to go by, Angus found this nothing short of horrific. They turned a furious glare on Finch, but whatever vitriol they'd planned to unleash was halted by their brother's hand on their wrist. He'd flitted across the room in the same manner Angus so enjoyed using.

"Yeah, yeah, I know," said Finch, his earlier contrition depleted. "I'm wretched. *Moving on.*"

"If Denken was hoping to get himself back in control of his powers, maybe that's why he went back there," Gloucester mused.

Antimony pulled her braid over her shoulder, tugging on it distractedly, eyes distant as she thought it over. "It's also possible that's what separated him from his body in the first place. All that raw power balking at the spells trying to contain it."

"The only one who could tell us is Denken himself," said Angus. "The notion is a good one, though." They leveled one of their rare approving looks Gloucester's and Antimony's way. "If Denken was left in the false Maze, suddenly alone, brimming with volatile energy and not knowing what to do, it makes sense he would go to the one other place in Frettchen that might curb his powers."

"The place where it started," said the Gambler. "Where maybe he could end it."

"Where we *will* end it." An odd resoluteness burned in Gloucester's chest. It felt good to see a way forward, even uncertain as it was. "Maybe he couldn't do it alone. But if all of us are there to help him...then maybe there's hope."

As far as he was concerned, his words weren't all that comforting, but one by one, the others smiled and voiced their agreement. To his surprise, Angus abandoned their perch on the dresser to lay a warm hand on his head, ruffling his hair fondly.

The gods, he thought for the millionth time, were weird.

Chapter 25

Old Haunts

The last time Gloucester stood outside All Saints Shrine, it was a warm spring day, the sun beating down on the church's white stone walls and reflecting off its many windows. It had been beautiful, weather-wise, and horrifyingly stressful in every other regard.

That day felt like a walk in the park compared to now. Gone was the nice weather, sunshine replaced with the perpetual storm clouds and twilight of the frozen city. Stained glass flowers seemed to alter whenever Gloucester wasn't looking, warping into strange, unfriendly faces that stared balefully down at them. The carved figures of saints lining the ornate main doors, in contrast, no longer had faces at all. The stone melted like old candle wax. Gloucester shivered.

Even setting aside Frettchen's nightmarish state, the stakes of that previous day, so dire at the time, paled in comparison to the mountain of misgivings now threatening to crush him as he stared up at the High Minister's Cathedral.

Behind him, the street solidified in the wake of their shifting travel from Fredson's Storage. Gloucester felt a pang of déja vu as Antimony, Zane, and Finch moved forward to stand at his side. When last they stood here, they'd worn matching black suits, disguised as the high minister's security team.

Now they were a ragtag group, as mismatched in appearance as they were in so much else.

At the storage unit, Gloucester had taken the opportunity to change into one of his own shirts, keeping his gun holstered under one arm, though he had little intention to use it. Despite the fear worming its way through his heart, he shied away from the idea of more violence than necessary. Violence had led them here, had made their problems worse at every turn, had twisted love and desperation into chaos. If he could avoid adding more, he would. He hoped the others felt the same.

Next to him, Finch was in shirtsleeves, octopus tattoo on full display, spreading its tentacles down his bicep and around his elbow. Zane had gathered her hair up in the orange head scarf she'd acquired in the south, her face set in grim determination. And Antimony had hoisted Gear onto her back again, her blonde bun brushing against the glass of the automaton's skull.

Gear's ticking clockwork counted the minutes refusing to pass.

Gloucester glanced to his other side, at Harrison and Mulligan, at the Gambler and Angus, and beyond them, the hulking form of Hyena. The thought-beast offered him a toothy grin he was fairly certain they meant as an encouraging smile. He offered them one in return.

In the middle distance, he caught a sudden flash of something red, but it disappeared as quickly as he'd spotted it. Orange Ianto, perhaps? He imagined her ghostly astral projection, lending them support in whatever meager way she could. Immaterial as it was, he appreciated it.

All together, they were the most bizarre team he'd ever been a part of. He wasn't sure how to feel, thinking that they might be the world's last chance.

Oh well, you can't choose your heroes. If that's what we are.

"Here we go again," said Zane. Like Hyena, she exchanged a strained smile with him, a hand placed on his arm in momentary, bracing encouragement.

"We can do this," Gloucester told her. A reassurance or a promise, the words were for both of them. She chuckled nervously but nodded. So did everyone else.

The sky rumbled overhead.

Inside, the church was quiet. High stone walls muffled the sound of thunder, and the air was unnaturally still. Unlike the confined space of the storage unit, which had kept Frettchen's unworldly atmosphere at bay, here the halted passage of time hung oppressively over everything. Not even the sound of Gear's cogs turning could sway the feeling.

The dark nave sent fear creeping up Gloucester's spine. It would be all too easy for Denken to sneak up on them here. Even Angus, with their immunity to darkness, shed no helpful light on their surroundings. If anything, all they did was highlight how shadowed everything and everyone else was. Zane held forth her pocket watch, but it did little in such a large space.

Then light flared to life. Gloucester flinched in its sudden brightness.

"Sorry," said Finch. A sphere of light hovered above both his palms. These orbs were larger than the ones he'd cast in the storage unit. "Figured we could do without standing around blind as bats."

"Technically, bats are in their element in the dark," Antimony pointed out. "But it's appreciated by us humans. Thank you, Mr. Finch."

"No point in hiding our presence now," he said with a shrug. "Still, let's get to the room, eh? I'd really rather not face old Sharky outside of its enchantments."

They hurried down the nave, shadows dancing across marble columns and the arched ceilings high above. Their footsteps echoed in the quiet of the church. Gloucester's imagination ran amok, casting every movement in the corner of his eye as a lunging enemy. He did his best to keep his breathing slow and even. The last thing he needed now was to jump at every step.

At the far end of the grand space, the flagstone floor split in two directions. Behind the altar, looming windows of stained glass extended toward the ceiling, framing the end of the main space. The imagery depicted there had changed from what Gloucester remembered. In place of the best-known saints this church was dedicated to, black glass swirled unnaturally. Though the form darted in and out of sight, there was no denying what it was. The shark swam through a stormy, obsidian ocean, Finch's spell streaking like lightning off its waves. Trying not to dwell on the image, the group turned to the left.

At the end of the corridor stood three doors. Gloucester paid two of them no mind—they only led to the priests' dormitories and the bell tower. Both would be as empty as the rest of Frettchen.

It was the central door he made a beeline toward.

A screech of laughter halted him in his tracks. Hyena's gigantic hand closed around his upper arm and spun him around. Startled, Gloucester stared up at the thought-beast, whose many eyes were rolling in obvious terror. It pointed frantically back the way they'd come.

"What?" he asked, stomach roiling in alarm. "We can't go back now, Hyena. We've got to—"

"That's not what they're saying." Angus's words were an urgent whisper. They, too, were looking back in the direction of the nave. On their other side, the Gambler silently pulled Antimony and Gear behind him. "Probably should have waited a little longer on that spell, magician."

Something was seeping across the floor of the church. At first Gloucester thought it was water, black in the dim lighting. But no, its surface held no reflections. This wasn't water—it was simply darkness, which now crept around the corner toward the altar.

Finch swore and flicked his wrists. The lights hovering over his palms vanished, dousing the group in more natural shadows.

Zane's pocket watch still cast pale illumination over them, but when she moved to stow it under the neckline of her shirt, the Gambler warned, "Don't. We don't want to be caught completely blind here. Get to the door. *Quickly.*"

"Come on." Antimony waved them all forward and dashed the remaining distance to the door at the end of the hall. "The sooner we've the enchantments on our side, the better."

The others ran after her without delay. Gloucester moved to follow but was stopped short unexpectedly.

Hyena's hand still gripped his bicep, fingers clenched in fear. Trying not to panic, Gloucester reached up and patted the back of it, hoping to offer both reassurance and an indication that the grip was a little painful and *more* than a little inconvenient.

"C'mon!" he urged them. "We'll be safer inside the room."

But Hyena didn't move. They shook their head, all six eyes locked on the direction of the creeping shadows, now invisible in the darkness.

Shattering glass punctured the air, the dreadful window exploding inward over the altar. Outside light made the flying glass glitter as it fell, until the darkness swallowed it too. Angus and the Gambler each jolted in response. Yet not out of fear or surprise—instead their forms changed, flames bursting to life around the Gambler's body as Angus's limbs morphed into wings and talons.

Preparations for a fight.

Desperate, Gloucester tried to pull away from Hyena's grasp again, tried to tug them toward the door and whatever crumbs of safety lay beyond. Hyena gave a near-silent chortle and let go. Then, to his surprise, they moved away from the door, back the way they'd come. Toward the oncoming monster.

"What are you doing?" he demanded in a whisper. "Denken's almost on top of us!"

Hyena gave him a push that would have been gentle were it not coming from someone ten feet tall, and then laughed, short and sharp. The Gambler and Angus glanced back at them.

"They say to go. They'll stay here and slow Denken down." Angus turned to Hyena. "Are you sure?"

Hyena nodded, the motion jerky with fear but resolute. They rolled their skeletal shoulders and stood taller, looming over the rest of their companions.

"We can stand with you." Fire crackled over the Gambler's words. "Perhaps the three of us can keep him at bay until the humans are prepared."

Hyena laughed again and shook their head.

Gloucester didn't need a translation to know what they were saying. He stepped closer to Hyena, opening his mouth to argue, to demand that they all stop being silly and get into the safety of the enchantments—

Something moved in the dark. Its shape was impossible to make out, but Gloucester saw the glint of teeth and the terrifying silhouette of a leviathan swimming through the inky shadows of the church. Hyena stood up on their hind legs, as they once had in the false Maze. They gave a final, blazing laugh, wild and free, and lunged toward Denken's spectral shark.

Instinctively, Gloucester moved to follow them, but a fire-wreathed pair of hands latched onto his arm. The Gambler's flames didn't burn, but the demigod's grip was strong as he dragged Gloucester through the door, ignoring his protests. Angus hurried behind, their sharpened, birdlike face steely and their brindled wings spread, a shield blocking Gloucester's view of Hyena's last stand.

They were halfway down the hall before the Gambler released his hold. Shadows blanketed the tapestries on the walls, every stained glass window above them murky and opaque. The others stood by the far door, staring at the trio.

"What's going on? Why do you two look like that?" Zane was a flurry of fearful questions. "Is Denken here already? Where's Hyena? We heard them making an awful racket. Are they okay?"

"They're buying us the time we need." Despite their battle-ready appearance, Angus's voice was surprisingly soft. "Let's not waste it."

Furious, Gloucester said, "We can't—!"

"It's too late," the Gambler interrupted with solemn certainty. "And their sacrifice will be in vain if we don't keep going. Hyena will lead Denken away for now, but they won't be able to waylay him forever. They're no match for his power."

He caught the look on Gloucester's face and shook his head. "I'm sorry, Gloucester. But don't weep for them. Hyena's sacrifice is courageous, but it isn't tragic. Not really. Even Denken cannot kill imagination. When they fall, they will finally be free to return to the Maze. The real one. They'll be home."

Gloucester fought the need to argue further. The Gambler's assurances provided some bitter consolation, but he still wanted to go back to help his friend. No more laughter echoed out from the nave. Yet the others, somber, only turned toward the intricate, carved door at the end of the hallway. Finch pulled it open and everyone stepped through.

Gloucester cast a final look behind him, the silence filling his gut with ice, then let the Gambler usher him into the room beyond.

The last time he'd passed through this door, it heralded the return of his memories, the answer to the mystery of his imprisonment at the hands of the high minister. He'd been swept away in a deluge of recollection, brought back to the fateful day he discovered the Gambler in his prison. Trying to rescue him, a failed act of heroism, had cost him his freedom and very nearly his life.

Now he stepped through it in the wake of a friend's sacrifice. He did not have fond associations with this door.

Denken's Interlude

Chaos

Darkness whirls dizzy, delirious headspin, blind and angry. Light streaks through, there and gone again in milliseconds that don't exist, neural pathways firing and dying in instants. Decades. Eternities. No time at all. No time. No more.

Movement through the dark. Or dark moving through him. Nothing is certain. Nothing is real. Everything and nothing. Everything is him. Spreading. Diminishing. Becoming one and nothing and everything and all. In a moment and never and always and now. Consciousness, fleeing and fleeting. No more.

Alone. No more laughter or words of kin or thoughts. No more of what he is or was or could be or never will. Thought was what he was. What he did and spoke and created and loved. What composed him and was composed of and by and for and through. No more.

Change. Something new in the dark. Something separate. Not him. Not timeless, not diminishing. Presences sparking a shift. Time remains still. The darkness still looms. Loneliness rages on, yet the change persists. Pinpricks of light. Angler lures in the depths. Threats. Fears. Heralds and harbingers and broken promises of hope. Hope has no place here. No more.

Yet there it is. The scent of blood in the water. Drawing him. Calling out. Lure or hope or prey. No way to know. No way to fight instinct and anger and fear. He lets it all pull him, torpedo body riding the waves. Pulled by their sway. In the deepest, furthest reaches of the dark, something sparks. Neural pathways. Faint hope. Dreadful fear. He won't resist.

No more.

Chapter 26

The Last Stand

Hyena ran. Darkness surrounded them on all sides, rendering their many eyes completely useless. Not that it mattered. Where they were running to didn't matter. The laughter bursting from them with every footfall was high-pitched with fear, yet wild with elation. They were scared, yes, but they'd also never felt braver.

They'd never before felt brave, period. Not back when they risked everything to save Gloucester, when the concept of bravery hadn't even occurred to them yet. Not when they stood up to their kin to help the humans escape the false Maze, when desperation had made them think nothing at all. Not when they ran through the frozen city to find Gloucester, when they'd sensed his return, and joy had swept all other emotions away in its current.

Now, though, they did feel it. Bravery. It didn't banish the fear by any means, but it burned alongside it. Maybe it couldn't exist without the terror, Hyena considered, the thought darting through their mind at the same breakneck speed as their galloping limbs.

They gave another shriek of laughter, purposefully loud. The loudness was key. No point being a distraction if they weren't, well, distracting.

And it was working. They could sense their pursuer, shadowy teeth snapping at their heels. The Guardian wasn't himself, wasn't in control of his powers or his body or even his own thoughts. It made him more dangerous than ever, but it also made him predictable. Entangled in his bestial form, he was a slave to the simplest of predatorial rules: if something runs, chase it.

Hyena wasn't sure they completely understood what Gloucester and his friends were trying to do, but they knew the end goal was to make things right. Back there, following along after the humans and the Guardian's kin, what help could they really offer?

But this, *this* they could do. They could give the others the one thing they desperately needed. The one thing this city—this world—didn't have. Hyena could give them *time*.

Spectral jaws scraped one of their legs, driving a fresh shriek from their lungs, laced with pain. They tried to ignore the agony, panic gifting them a fresh burst of speed. Somewhere ahead in the pitch black was the door out of the church. Hyena would lead the Guardian back outside. Lure him on a chase through the city for as long as they could. It wouldn't be forever. It wouldn't even be for long. But maybe it would be for just long *enough*.

They collided with solid wood, but they'd expected that. They braced against the door and shoved with all the strength they could muster. The door swung open, and darkness spilled out, waves of it flooding onto the street beyond, sweeping Hyena out with it. They tumbled, long head over bloody, bitten heels.

Knowing without looking that the shark still followed, that the chase was still on, they rolled to their hands and feet and kept running. They tried to imbue their laughter with taunts, wanting to keep the Guardian's attention, but mostly they knew they just sounded scared.

It'll be okay. It will all be okay.

Though the desperate, hysterical thoughts were their own, Hyena imagined them in Gloucester's voice. Picturing the odd little human made them feel braver. Gloucester had risked his life over and over to help his friends, including Hyena. All the little humans back in the church had. They bickered and made lots of noise and rarely made sense, but they were doing everything they could to save their world.

Thinking of the Maze—the real, proper one, not the facsimile the Guardian had made here—Hyena could understand why. Their own home was beyond reach, but this place was the humans' home. They didn't want to lose it. Hyena could understand that well.

Hyena dashed down the street, rounding the corner at an angle more horizontal than upright, spurring themself forward off the side of a motionless car, then rebounding against a lamppost. They were successfully making a ruckus, but that wasn't hard when there was so little competition for noise. They repeated the goal over and over, threading it through the fear and pain. Keep the Guardian distracted as long as possible.

You can do this. It'll be okay.

In their mind, Hyena tracked their best course. The plan, loosely formed as it might be, was to lead the Guardian on a lengthy loop eventually ending up back at the church. They'd done enough running around Frettchen that they had a good idea of the city's layout, so it was easy enough to visualize all the nearby streets to plot a route.

Humans, Hyena had come to realize, seemed to have trouble with their memories, struggling to recall what they'd seen or heard with any reliable detail. Bizarre, really. How could they experience things yet not remember? Maybe it was just their little organic brains. Only a handful of details seemed to stick in their minds, and then they'd stand around and argue about it until even those got all muddled up. Hyena found it oddly charming, but not very helpful.

All these thoughts ran through their mind instantaneously, mental background noise as they moved from street to street. The Guardian was gaining, darkness nipping at Hyena's heels. The shadows swallowed up what little sound was left in Frettchen, drowning out the thunder with its dreadful silence.

Hyena laughed as loud and as long as they could, rebellion jolting through the fear. They wouldn't let the Guardian win. They wouldn't—

Sharp pain snapped their ankle, yanking them to a violent halt. Their laughter shattered into a screech, alarm and agony, and they fell, careening forward onto the pavement. They knew immediately that the foot was gone but couldn't stop themself from looking anyway. Horror turned their stomach, a sick mix of pain and cold shock at the sight of their own mangled limb.

Darkness was all around them in seconds, as if they'd plunged into the depths of the ocean out beyond the harbor. They could feel another presence moving within it. The Guardian.

I'm sorry, Gloucester. This is all the time I can give you. I just hope it's enough.

They'd never really thought of themself as an "I" before. They found they liked the sound of it. As the darkness pulled them down, away from the street and the pain and the corporeal world, they clung to that.

I am me. I am Hyena. A creation of Thought, but also a person. A me. An I. A friend.

The darkness changed, shifting from oppressive to whirling. Hyena still couldn't see, couldn't really perceive anything beyond themself, but familiarity struck. This was the Void Between Worlds. They'd experienced its chaos only once before, when the Guardian's mistakes had torn them away from their home, but the memory of it would stick with them forever.

And then, as the last vestiges of pain dissipated, they felt stillness once more. A cold, hard surface materialized beneath their body, and they slumped blindly against it. Stone? A creaking echoed faintly. Were those doors?

Too tired to open their eyes, Hyena breathed a quietly elated laugh.

I'm home.

—

Back in the High Minister's Cathedral, the Gambler closed the door to the hall with an audible click. As he did so, the flames encompassing him petered out. This was accompanied by a rustle of feathers and a mutter of indignation, as Angus's form shifted against their will.

The enchantments of the room held.

A few meters away, Finch and Zane surveyed their shadowy surroundings, the latter holding her watch aloft like a lantern. There wasn't much to see. The gloom surrounded them as much here as it had in the church proper—more so, in fact, without the Gambler's fire or even windows to let in the drab light of outdoors. The pinpricks of candlelight Gloucester recalled were gone. So too were the glowing cords of the Gambler's enchanted rope bindings.

"Just as we left it," Finch whispered. "It should only be the internal enchantments left. Unless you brought another magician in, Mr. Interim High Minister?"

Mulligan shook his head, face lost in shadow. "Like I said, no one has been back here."

As the group stepped further into the cavernous chamber, guided by the light of Zane's pocket watch, Gloucester searched for the ropes of the Cat's Cradle. What little he could see of the stone floor was bare. Had the broken spells degraded them into nothing? Tendrils of hopelessness threaded through his chest.

He drew in a deep breath, trying to banish the treacherous feeling.

"I hate this place." The Gambler's statement was flat, his presence heavy.

"Yeah," said Gloucester. "Me too."

This room had ruined both their lives.

"Does anyone see Denken?" asked Mulligan. "His body, I mean."

"It's hard to tell in the dark." Zane peered around. "I can hardly see anything. If only he was all glowy, like Angus. Speaking of... Can either of you, I dunno, sense him?" she asked the demigods.

Angus wrapped their arms around themself. "This whole stupid city feels like him, especially with his big stupid consciousness stalking about. It's like trying to find a needle in a stack of needles. And this room is awful. It's hard to concentrate."

"Let's get looking, then." Murmuring an incantation, Finch conjured more orbs of light. He passed one to Gloucester, who took it tentatively. It floated above his palm, not dimming in brightness despite Finch relinquishing control to him. A faint warmth emanated from it.

"Neat," he said faintly. "But will magic draw Denken back to us too quickly? We still need to find his body. And those ropes, if they're still around here somewhere."

Finch passed the other orb to Harrison, then conjured another pair for himself and Antimony. "I don't think it matters much at this point. Hyena bought us the time we needed to get in here, and now we have the enchantments on our side. Still, let's move quick-like, eh?"

Mostly wordlessly, the group split up to continue the search. Zane, Antimony, and Gear ventured in one direction, Harrison and Mulligan in another, and the two demigods strode away side by side, without need of illumination. This left Gloucester and Finch alone together. Finch's orb hovered beside his left ear, casting the side of his face in dramatic lighting. His eyes narrowed, not from the brightness, but in searching concentration. Gloucester followed his gaze around the dark room. He had expected—or hoped—that Denken's body would be as easy to spot as the Gambler had been, strung up directly in the center of the room, highlighted by the spells holding him prisoner.

Alas, it was not to be. Mimicking Finch, Gloucester guided the orb to hover by his shoulder, then drew his gun from its holster. He still wasn't sure if it would be useful at all, nor even if he *wanted* it to be, but he'd rather be prepared for whatever might be lurking in the shadows.

"You wouldn't think this part would be difficult," he said. Focusing on the task at hand made it easier to keep his storming emotions in check. "Except I'm not sure how big this room actually is."

"Big enough," Finch replied. "And more complex than it looks. Magic like this sometimes makes things...confusing. The original room and the enchanted space can sort of overlap. Especially when the enchantments haven't been maintained."

"Oh, great." Gloucester started off into the dark, waving for Finch to follow. "What exactly does that mean?"

The room, while impossibly large, wasn't a complicated layout as far as he could tell. From what he remembered, it was just a big hall. Now, of course, the shadows made it difficult to tell. And he didn't like the sound of "overlap." It brought to mind the way Denken's false Maze was affecting the human world.

Finch's grimace was eerie in the light of the orbs. "I'm not great at explaining this. Hmmm, think of this room as two separate places, as it appears now and as it was before the spells transformed it. One laid over the other. Two different rooms with two different layouts. One looks like a big bloody atrium, right, but the other might be more complex. With nooks and crannies, alcoves and the like. If the spells were maintained, it wouldn't matter, but as the magic gets rusty..."

"The layout of the original room could start bleeding through," Gloucester finished. He glanced around. The dark, as far as he could perceive, contained nothing but empty space and stone columns. "So could we suddenly bump into a wall or fall down stairs we can't see or something?"

That certainly wouldn't make a battle with Denken any easier. He took a few more steps forward, his movements distinctly more cautious than before.

"Hopefully not," Finch said. "Our spellwork was good. Dad was one of the best magicians in the business. It should be holding up fine. I'm just floating it as a possibility. And from what I remember of the room before we worked it over, it didn't have any steps or walls in weird places. I just can't remember exactly what its layout was."

"Good to know." Gloucester puffed a sigh. "D'you think anything could just be easy for us for once? Just for novelty's sake, at the very least."

"Pffft," scoffed Finch. "We'd get bored. Wouldn't know what to do with ourselves!"

Chapter 27

Darkness

Several non-minutes of fruitless searching passed. Occasionally Gloucester heard the faint murmur of conversation, his companions' orbs bobbing through the blackness elsewhere in the room. Yet there remained no sign of Denken's body or the remnants of the severed Cat's Cradle.

As hopelessness began to bubble up in his mind, one of the orbs approached through the murk. It drew close, revealing itself to belong to Antimony's group. Zane looked as frustrated as he felt.

"How is it this difficult?" she demanded. She gestured angrily around, the pocket watch swinging in a wild arc around her. "There's nowhere here to hide!"

"Maybe he's not here." Antimony held her sphere aloft, its light glancing off the glass of Gear's head and highlighting the intricate workings within. "Maybe Hyena got it wrong."

Stung, Gloucester shook his head. "If Hyena was sure, I trust them. Denken's body must be here. Or it was at some point. Could it have moved somehow? Maybe he woke up or something?"

The others were dubious, but before anyone could offer an answer, a cry came out of the gloom.

"We found something! Over here!"

"That's Mulligan," Gloucester said, hastening in the direction of the shout. "C'mon."

They came upon Harrison and Mulligan, the former holding his orb of light with one hand and waving energetically with the other. Mulligan was crouched beside him, and for a moment, Gloucester wasn't sure why. What had they found? All he could see was more darkness.

Wait...

It was *too much* darkness. While Harrison's orb illuminated the two men, the stone slabs beneath their feet were curiously obscured in pitch black. Gloucester glanced down. The light from his and Finch's orbs spread across his own feet and the floor around him, revealing the intricacies of the stonework without much trouble. Taking a few steps closer to Mulligan and Harrison, he stopped and looked down again.

"What the—?"

The details of the floor were gone. It was as if he'd stepped onto an impossibly black carpet. He could still *feel* the stone beneath his soles, but the light no longer touched it, the bottom edges of his shoes strangely blurred. He hastily raised one of his feet to take a look at it, but it was free of any residue.

"Huh," said Finch. "Well, that's something."

"Yeah," Zane agreed, stepping up beside them. "Something really weird."

"We wouldn't have even noticed," said Harrison. "Except, well, Mr. Mulligan, he, um..."

"I only bloody tripped over it." The red in Mulligan's face was difficult to see in the imperfect lighting, but his scandalized tone was blatant. "And let's all be grateful that I did, all right? Otherwise, we would never have found it."

At their confused looks, he huffed and pointed emphatically at the concealed ground over which he was crouched.

"You found the ground? Well done," said Finch. Gloucester suspected it was more a case of low-hanging fruit than a genuine desire to mock, as he was quick to add: "Something seriously wrong with the floor, though."

"That's an understatement," Mulligan snapped. Nose wrinkled in distaste, he reached down and grabbed something from the floor.

At least Gloucester assumed that was what he did. His hand vanished into the black, and when he raised his arm a moment later, the appendage was still swathed in impenetrable shadows. As if the limb were draped in a blanket of midnight.

"Oh wow, what the hell?" Zane said. "Is your hand okay?"

"Perfectly fine, thank you, Miss Zephyr." Mulligan dropped whatever was causing the effect, revealing an unscathed hand. Then he repeated his earlier action. His hand disappeared again.

"What are you holding?" Antimony asked. Uncharacteristically animated, she leaned forward to peer at Mulligan with open curiosity.

"Scientists," muttered Finch.

"Come feel for yourself," said Mulligan. "I'm not sure you'll believe me otherwise."

"I don't think there's much any of us wouldn't believe at this point, Mr. Mulligan."

As she spoke, Antimony eagerly moved forward, the others shuffling closer behind her. With far less reluctance than Mulligan, she reached down and took the whatever-it-was from his hand. Her thin brows rose in surprise. Then, to Gloucester's amazement, she smiled.

"Brilliant." Gazing up at the others, she held her hand aloft. Like Mulligan's, it had disappeared into unnatural darkness. "It's Denken."

Gloucester stared. Yet no matter how he looked at the void cloaking Antimony's hand, he deciphered no hint at what she meant. He crouched by her side, tentatively reaching out to touch the shadows. His hand passed into them without resistance. He'd expected to feel something, a thickening of the air or a drop in temperature, but no such thing happened. His hand simply vanished from view, and a moment later, his fingers brushed against the familiar texture of skin: Antimony's fingers, gripping...

A wrist. Slim and limp, but definitely a human wrist. He could feel the bones beneath the skin and, following its contours, a hand. Moving his fingertips in the other direction, he traced the shape of an arm and finally a shoulder, then a chest. No heartbeat stirred.

"It's definitely a body," he said, the words oddly distant and emotionless in his ears. A thought struggled toward the forefront of his mind, mumbling about how unbearably strange his life had become, but he pushed it back. *Not helpful.* He forced himself to look up from the seeping blackness, back at his companions. "And unless there are some other shadow-exuding bodies lying around Frettchen, I think it's safe to say it's Denken's."

As if summoned by their brother's name, Angus and the Gambler appeared out of the shadows behind Harrison. The bodyguard twitched but otherwise contained his surprise. The Siblings stared down at the blanket of darkness concealing Denken's body, silent and solemn.

"He doesn't seem to be breathing," Gloucester told them reluctantly. From his angle, they were intimidatingly tall. "Is that normal or...?"

"It is just his physical form," the Gambler answered. "Without his mind and essence, the body isn't really him. It's not alive. Once we return him to it, he will be fine."

Gloucester thought he detected a worrying note of uncertainty in that final statement. His hand still rested against Denken's motionless chest, and as he began to move it away, his fingertips brushed against something else. "Hang on... There's something wrapped around him." His hand followed blindly along the unseen object. It felt like—

"I think it's a rope." Falling to his knees next to the body, he used both hands to trace the hidden binding. It seemed to wrap around Denken's torso like a constrictor before trailing away through the darkness. "He's tangled up in the Cat's Cradle!"

"You're kidding." Finch stepped forward, crouching to join Gloucester. The two of them followed the rope past the edge of the unnatural darkness, where the orbs' light finally revealed its twisted, fraying cords. No ethereal glow surrounded it now. Finch straightened up, holding the seemingly mundane rope in his hands. "Denken must have had the same idea we did. He wrapped himself up in this, trying to get himself under control."

"But it didn't work." Mulligan, too, had gotten back to his feet. He glared down at Denken's hidden body, shoulders sagging. "The ropes are useless."

"Oh, ye of little faith," said Finch. He gripped the length of rope and looked around at the rest of them, his grin flashing in the golden light. Unlike Mulligan, there was renewed determination in his eyes. "If there's a spark of magic left in this, I can bring it back. I'm not gonna give up now. None of us are. Not when we're this close." He laughed with a manic edge, pulling enough rope loose to drape it over his shoulders and free up his hands. "That bloody thought-beast got to be all heroic, leading Denken away on a merry chase until we're ready for him, and I'm not going to let them have all the glory."

He shooed Gloucester and the others back. Then he shuffled his feet a little and winked at Gloucester's questioning look.

"Don't want to stand right on top of the bastard, but he's a little hard to see," he explained. Spreading his arms wide, he rolled his neck one way, then the other, and let out a loud breath. "All right, let's start with a little better lighting."

In a grand sweeping gesture, Finch swung his arms up over his head. His hands clapped together, and a miniature sun blazed to life from between his palms.

Within seconds, it filled the entirety of the immense hall. Their orbs paled in comparison. Warm sunlight chased the shadows away, the grand room properly illuminated for the first time. Its stone walls and candles in their few and far-between sconces were thrown into sharp relief. Tall window frames, filled in with austere brickwork in place of glass, towered between columns extending to arched ceilings. Everything was cast in a daylight as unnatural as the shadows it had replaced.

Everything but the floor right at their feet. A circle roughly six feet across remained in shadow as thick and impenetrable as before. Squinting in the sudden brightness, Gloucester tried again to see something—*anything*—within the patch of dark, but to no avail. The only indication of anything hidden within were the ropes of the Cat's Cradle, trailing out of the black and up across Finch's shoulders.

As the magician lowered his hands to the draped cords, everyone's orbs blinked out of existence. The daylight he cast remained, diffused throughout the room.

"Right, now that I can see what I'm doing..." Finch muttered, attention zeroed in on the ropes. He closed his eyes, words changing smoothly into the flowing language of an incantation. Magic whispered through the air. The ropes glimmered.

"Wonderful," Mulligan said. "Nice to have something go right for once."

Before any of them could voice fervent agreement, they were interrupted by the arrival of Denken.

He didn't slip in subtly, a darting shadow of his former self, nor did his hidden body surge suddenly back to reanimated life. Instead, a tidal wave of living shadows exploded through the wall behind them, a torrent of darkness and rage, torpedoed into jaws and fins and massive, *massive* teeth.

The shark was bigger than Gloucester had ever seen it. Bigger than he could have imagined. It swirled through the too-big, suddenly too-small room, bearing down on the group in an instant.

Just as quickly as it appeared, it stopped. The tip of its pointed snout was mere feet from them, and though its eyes were scarcely visible from where he stood, Gloucester knew it was looking directly at Finch. The magician opened his eyes, face pale in the weak shimmer of the rope around his shoulders.

"Ah," he croaked. "Oh dear."

Chapter 28

Into-Body Experience

Denken's shark hung motionless in the air, the size of one of the storm clouds surely still rumbling outside. The humans and their companions stood just as still, no one daring to be the first to move. There was no sign of Hyena anywhere in sight. Grief added a bitter chord to the fear coursing through Gloucester's mind. Time, non-existent as it was, had run out.

"What was the next part of the plan again?" Zane's hushed voice trembled.

"Use the ropes to trap it," Gloucester murmured back, trying to move his lips as little as possible. "Hope that the room weakens him."

Zane slid a sideways look at the bit of rope glowing feebly in Finch's grasp, the rest of its length consumed by the shadows pooled at their feet. Then back at the huge shark, seemingly unfettered by its enchanted surroundings. "Right," she said. "Death it is. Cool."

They both startled at sudden movement at their flanks. As one, Angus and the Gambler launched themselves forward to stand between the group and the shark. Though neither could shift into their more monstrous forms, Gloucester sensed power simmering below the surface. The contours of their bodies began to alter, a ghostly mirage of wings and flame.

"We'll hold him off as long as you need to prepare," the Gambler called over his shoulder. His hands clenched into fists, eyes spinning in a frantic whirlwind. "Get those ropes working!"

Relief to have the immortals between him and the shark flooded through Gloucester, but it was quelled by the worrying realization that the very enchantments they were depending on to curb Denken's abilities were also rendering their most powerful allies rather moot. What could they actually do to hold the shadow beast off? Was this another sacrifice?

"Denken," the Siblings said together. "Listen to us."

Gloucester staggered back under the strength of their combined voices. If this was them with their powers muted, the full effect would have blown his eardrums out. Some hope flared anew, even as he flinched.

Fingers brushed his elbow. Risking a glance down to the side, he caught Antimony's eyes. She was watching him with admirable serenity from where she crouched on the inky floor, half of her body veiled in Denken's blanket of shadows. At her back, Gear watched the demigods with wide, fearful eyes, biting her lip in dismay.

"Help me with this," Antimony whispered. "We need to get him out of the black. I think it must be acting like a sort of ward. Even if we manage to weaken the shark, it could keep his consciousness from returning to his body."

Gloucester cast a nervous look up at the immortals. They were successfully distracting the shark for the time being, calling out to it in booming voices and waving their arms. Whether due to the enchantments cast over the room or simply for ease of movement, the beast had shrunk a little in size, but it still stretched longer than any natural fish. It circled the Siblings, swimming through the air, as they subtly distanced themselves from the humans.

Leaning down beside Antimony, Gloucester reached into the darkness. Zane hurried to help too.

With the room's newfound brightness, the shadows hiding Denken's body were more obvious than ever, and his limbs were easy enough to grab hold of. Gloucester felt along until he was clutching the body under the armpits, with the others gripping Denken's wrists and ankles. They heaved, but the darkness clung, weighing the body down.

"C'mon," Gloucester grunted. "C'mon!"

Harrison and Mulligan joined in, crowding on either side of him to grab each of Denken's upper arms. Together, they gave another mighty pull.

With a bizarre squelching noise, Denken's body yanked free, as if from thick mud. *Success!* Gloucester and the others fell back, knocked off-balance by the sudden reward for their efforts. As soon as the body was free, the shadows receded, slithering back into the body itself and vanishing. Gloucester recalled the way Denken had exuded shadows like that when angered or injured. Maybe Antimony was right in calling the blanket of darkness a ward. Some sort of bodily defense mechanism, protecting him from further harm.

Alas, the shark noticed this change of circumstances. Angus and the Gambler had led it away from the group, but now it gave a great flick of its tail and surged toward them. The immortals dashed ahead to cut it off, moving so fast that they were nothing more than two blurs. It wasn't quite their usual ability to shift like shadows from one place to another, but it was close. Gloucester remembered Denken moving such a way in this very room, in that fateful moment right before he murdered the high minister.

Now the immortals' uncanny speed was on their side. The Gambler and Angus stood once more between humans and shark. The beast's mouth gaped open, a wide maw full of teeth, and white flashed amid the darkness as its ghostly eyes rolled back for the attack.

The Siblings spread their arms wide, voices rising in a chorus of unintelligible protestation. The flickering contours of their bodies grew more frenzied, but they still couldn't break into their fully powered forms. The Finches' enchantments remained a double-edged blade. Glancing back over his shoulder, Gloucester saw Finch had his eyes squeezed shut once more, lips moving as he continued his hasty incantations. The ropes were definitely gaining power, the unearthly glow he remembered once more present.

Whether rebuffed by the Siblings' verbal dismay or its own limitations in the spelled room, the shark's attempted progress was halted. At the last moment it altered the course of its charge, veering upward and swirling around to face them again.

Gloucester's heart felt like it was trying to escape out his throat, but he did his best to shake the terror from the forefront of his mind. He recalled the way the shark had attempted to consume Finch the last time they were here, and how the enchantments had rendered the act harmless. Surely it would be the same now, right?

Much as he wanted to be certain of that before putting it to the test, he doubted they would have the chance.

"Safe to say he's interested in his body," said Zane, no longer bothering to keep her voice down. She pulled a face. "Ergh, I really hate how that sounded. But you know what I mean. So now what? Does he *just* want the body, or does he also want to eat us?"

"Dunno. Let me just consult my Shark-Frettchennian dictionary." Finch's retort held the shrill edge of panic. He dashed in front of them, dragging the magical ropes behind him. The light surrounding them was now bright enough to make Gloucester squint.

"Do they have those?" Gear asked, earnestly interested.

"Sarcasm, automaton!" cried Finch. "Now, get the body untangled from the rest of the rope. I'll need as much to work with as I can get. Hurry!"

Without question, they followed his command, pulling the ropes from around Denken's limp torso. As soon as the cords were free, Finch gathered them up in his arms, the glimmering magic washing the color from his features. He roared another spell, loud and musical, and threw the ropes into the air.

To Gloucester's amazement, that was where they remained. Floating as if weightless, the ropes twisted into a net extending several meters in all directions. On the far side of this sudden barrier, the shark took notice. It circled through the air, gaining momentum.

As the great beast lashed its tail, Finch glanced over his shoulder and met Gloucester's eyes. Time hadn't moved since they arrived in Frettchen, yet in that bare instant, Gloucester truly felt it stop. The other man's expression was so openly vulnerable, free of its usual bravado and smirk, that he was struck by how scared he really must be. A thousand unspoken words passed between them, fears and confessions and hopes. Then something hardened behind Finch's eyes, and he gave a single sharp nod.

Banishing the fear to the back of his mind. Gloucester knew the feeling well.

The shark attacked. Surging through the air toward Finch, it barreled past the Siblings, throwing them from their feet. Its mouth gaped wide, and its eyes rolled back, ghostly white points in the inky blackness.

And then it stopped.

The magical net thrummed, its many knotted cords vibrating violently as the shark struggled. Finch shouted another spell, hands sweeping in complicated arcs, guiding the ropes to further entangle the creature. They wrapped around its fins, its tail, its mouth full of gnashing teeth. For all its seeming intangibility, it was caught.

"Will it hold?" The Gambler sounded out of breath as he picked himself up from the floor beneath the thrashing shark. He helped Angus to their feet, both of them watching the embodiment of their brother's consciousness fight against its imprisonment.

"Not for long." Finch's reply was distracted, his eyes still focused on the shark, his hands still gesturing in calculated movements. "I'm draining as much power from him as I can, though, so it might just be long enough. Look!"

No need to ask what he referred to. Before their eyes, the shark was shrinking further. Every angry flick of its tail reduced its size. The ropes, in turn, gained brightness as it struggled. They clearly weren't designed to hold the amount of power Finch was siphoning into them, however; Gloucester could hear them creaking under the strain. Knots began to fray, threatening to snap. Sweat shone on Finch's brow.

"Right. Lay the body down and then everyone get back. Except you." Finch paused his gesticulations to point at Gloucester. "You're gonna be my channeler again, okay? Be ready to raise that shield. Last resort only, though, 'cause I can't cast through it. Everyone else, fall back as far as you can. No telling how nasty this could get if those ropes give out."

"What are you going to do?" Gloucester asked.

Finch jerked his head at the shark caught in the net. "I'm gonna drag him to his body. If he's weakened enough, his consciousness *should* return to it."

Zane looked to Gloucester, an argument in her eyes, but he shook his head. They didn't have time for questioning the plan now, no matter how desperate it might be.

"If things start going really badly, get Antimony and the rest out," he told her. "Get back to the storage unit."

Digging into his pocket, he pressed the key into her hand. Though she still looked like she wanted to argue, Zane closed her fingers around the key and retreated. Antimony and the others set Denken's prone form down and followed suit.

Gloucester half expected the pervasive shadows to bleed out of Denken's body again, but they didn't. Whatever magic had obscured it before, the spell seemed to be broken. Or perhaps it was simply no longer necessary with the demigod's ferocious consciousness so close at hand. Either way, one less thing to worry about.

Which is good, because there's still an awful lot to worry about.

"Right," he said. "Now what?"

Finch's attention was back on the netted shark. "We get out of the way, for starters."

Side by side, they retreated until they stood a few meters behind the body. A clear path lay between it and Denken's captured consciousness. Drawing in a deep breath, Finch began another incantation. This one was quieter, a low melody instead of a bellowed war song. As he murmured the incomprehensible words, he caught Gloucester's eye, an unspoken request for assistance.

Gloucester took a steadying breath of his own. He'd helped Finch channel magic a few times now, even managed to take control of it the last time, and though the experience was still bizarre, he knew how it worked. He took hold of Finch's arm and immediately felt the presence of gathered magic.

Here we go.

Compelled by Finch's spell, the magical net moved toward Denken's sprawled body, dragging the shark along with it. The beast tore at the ropes, knots catching between its teeth, and Gloucester winced as several snapped. Pieces of broken cord fell to the floor. Unlike last time, when Antimony had freed the Gambler by severing a single knot, the rest of the ropes maintained their power. For now.

"Come on," he whispered, watching the net inch closer. "Almost there..."

Finally, the net came to a stop, hovering over the body. The shark grew still.

"If I'm right about this," Finch said, slightly breathless in the wake of so many incantations, "he's lost too much wild power to keep separate from his physical form. Once I sever the net, he *should* be pulled back into it without us needing to do anything else. There's a connection within all of us, body and soul. They *want* to be together. It's how dream-walkers can always find their way back to themselves. It should apply here. But just in case I'm *not* right, I also want to be ready."

Fresh magic stirred, buzzing against Gloucester's fingers. Bracing himself, he let it in, let it travel through his hands and up his arms to burn electric at his core.

"Hold steady." The echo of Finch's magic carried in his words. How much of a spell was specific incantations and how much was unspoken intent? Was it different depending on the type of spell? And how much did Finch's heritage play a part in it, his blood running with his mother's innate magic, combined with the inherited knowledge from his late father, who had learned so much from books and other magicians?

Here's the deal, me, Gloucester thought. *If we don't die, you can ask him all the questions you want.*

Finch spoke a single word, and the magical ropes fell away. As they dropped to the flagstones, the light infusing them dimmed, and they hit the ground with a mundane thud.

The shadow shark became a swirl of furious darkness, exploding into motion the instant it was free of the cords, and Gloucester flinched in spite of himself, eyes squeezed shut in the face of what was surely imminent death. In the split second before he closed his eyes, he thought he saw a streak of red dart across the room.

A rush like a strong wind blasted over him. Still abuzz with magic, Finch's arm clenched in his grip, Gloucester struggled to remain upright. He heard a gasp from Finch, or maybe it was from his own mouth, and then—

Silence.

Chapter 29

The Return

Someone coughed. A quiet noise, but in the surrounding silence, it echoed like the church bells up in the tower. Gloucester opened his eyes.

From the floor a short distance away, Denken stared up at him. His wide black eyes were bleary with confusion, and he blinked several times, as if chasing away sleep. Knotted ropes were strewn across his chest and limbs, glowing weakly.

"Get back," Finch hissed in warning. He pulled free of Gloucester's hand and grabbed hold of his shoulders, urging him further away from the suddenly conscious god's body. His fingers still hummed with magic. Gloucester could feel it still gathered in his own body, an unmissable warmth in his chest spreading out through his veins with every heartbeat. It was a reminder that things were far from over. They retreated several more meters in the direction of Zane and the others. His fingers brushed the gun holstered under his arm, ready to draw at the first sign of a threat, now that Denken was in physical form.

Alone in the center of the room, Denken sat up with a jolt. The ropes fell away, their power too spent to hold him back. In the wake of his cough, he gasped, long and loud.

"Epiphany..." Like Denken's cough, the Gambler's murmur carried like a shout in the quiet of the room. An unspoken question followed, hanging in the air with the same weighty presence as the shark who had so recently disappeared back into Denken's body. Gloucester wasn't even sure what the question was. Maybe the Gambler didn't know either. If he was anything like Gloucester, it could be any of a million queries swirling around his head.

Whatever it was, they all waited on the answer with bated breath.

Denken's dark eyes found the Gambler. Then, with a twitch of his head, he spotted Angus. With dreadful slowness, he turned to look at the rest of the group. The distance between them suddenly felt like not nearly enough. Gloucester's hand closed around the gun.

Denken blinked once, opened his mouth, and screamed.

The sound blasted through the air. Gloucester felt his feet leave the ground. For a brief, timeless non-moment, he was airborne and weightless. Then his shoulder blades struck the stone floor and pain lanced through him. He felt the gun leave his grip, heard the clatter of it skittering away from him, out of reach. The world winked, momentarily black before returning with spinning confusion.

"*Denken*!"

The Gambler's and Angus's voices, once more melded in overwhelming alarm, were little more than meaningless noise in Gloucester's ringing ears. He rolled onto his side, dazed, his shoulders screaming in agony. Finch groaned at his side. Gloucester met his eyes and read the breathless question there.

"I'm okay," he panted. He clumsily clapped a hand on Finch's chest. "I'm okay."

He didn't feel okay. His upper back was stiff with pain, and when he stumbled to his feet, the pain jolted through his left arm, which resisted every movement.

Broken or just sprained? thought his stumbling, dizzy brain. *Doesn't matter. No time.*

Getting to his feet was made more difficult by Finch, who had fallen across his legs. The magician was slower to pull himself up from the ground, having caught the brunt of Denken's wrath. He rolled off of Gloucester's legs and onto his back with an oath.

"Well, we can thank the saints the bloody enchantments are still in place," he said, coughing as the air returned to his lungs. "Reckon that might've killed us."

"No doubt."

Reasonably sure that Finch was all right, Gloucester looked around for the others. He spotted them in a huddled group near the wall behind him. Blonde hair a windswept tangle, Antimony clutched at the bag containing Gear with uncharacteristic panic. Maybe she'd landed on top of it in the blast and feared for the state of her automaton.

Zane crouched beside her, peering urgently at the clockwork visible in Gear's head before offering Antimony a relieved nod, lips moving in apparent assurance that the complicated movement was undamaged. She caught Gloucester's eye and sent him a quick thumbs up, a silent confirmation that everyone over there was okay. He breathed a little easier, the knot of tension in his chest loosening. On Zane's other side, Harrison was in full bodyguard mode, crouched protectively in front of Mulligan. The group as a whole appeared unscathed.

For the time being.

Denken was on his feet now. His thin frame stretched and quivered, as if his newfound return to corporeality wasn't sticking well. The remaining ropes had been blasted away from him, laying in tangles across the floor in every direction. His siblings stepped over them as they circled him slowly, predators unsure whether or not they were looking at a threat.

Denken jittered his shoulders, an unnerving, sputtering motion. Darkness darted along the lines of his body, lightning in negative.

Threat, shouted Gloucester's instincts. *Threat threat threat threat threat—*

He gave his head a sharp shake, the pain elicited by the motion enough to jar him out of the descending curtain of panic. Part of the buzzing in his skull, he realized, wasn't fear, but rather the persisting presence of Finch's magic. In the chaos, the thrill of it was almost easy to forget.

"I've still got a lot of magic, feels like," he whispered, as he steadied the magician on his feet. "Is there anything we can hit him with? Something to contain him or calm him? What about the rope?"

The idea sounded simplistic, but he had no idea what else they could do. His gun lay uselessly on the flagstones several meters out of reach. He was certain any move toward it would provoke Denken. And he didn't like the idea of using it anyway. The thought of killing Denken, if that was even possible, brought him no pleasure. If Denken had truly come here to try and set things right, he deserved the chance to be saved.

Some pieces of the broken net had landed nearby, however. Would it still hold enough magic to be of use? It still carried the hint of a magical sheen, but Denken had shaken it off before with no apparent trouble. Gloucester's hope for it dimmed, and he cast around for another idea. "Or maybe my barrier? Trap him in a corner or something..."

Denken had turned his body and attention back to his siblings. He opened his mouth again and let out a loud hiss. After a moment, Gloucester realized there were words slithering through the sound.

"I—" The word dragged across the air, nails on a chalkboard. "I—can't—I don't—"

Fingers like claws clenched and unclenched. He seemed dazed, but no less dangerous. Perhaps more dangerous than ever.

"Gamblerrrrrrrrrr." The 'r' rolled like a growl. "Angusssssssssss."

"He recognizes them," Gloucester said. "That's good, right?"

Denken's hands lashed out, shadows moving in tenebrous whips. The attack against his siblings was so swift that neither demigod dodged, and the pair of them cried out in distress as the darkness snapped at them.

"Denken, you idiot!" Angus's shriek carried an eagle's edge, but without the ability to shift their form, they could do little more than lift their arms to try and shield themself as best as they could. The wings tattooed across their skin shifted, as if trying to unfurl into proper form, but to no avail. Something pale and shining ran down their arms, like liquid light.

Angus's blood, Gloucester realized. Beside them, the Gambler fared no better, steam rising in hissing clouds where Denken's darkness had struck him. Though the flames of his unleashed powers still couldn't emerge, they clearly lurked just beneath the surface.

"Leave me aloooooooone!"

Denken's protest crescendoed into a roar. He lunged at his siblings, and as he moved, he doubled in size, stretching upward like a shadow. The unbridled power of his rage seemed more successful at battling the enchantments of the room than the Gambler or Angus were.

He's going to kill them. We've got to stop him.

The thought had scarcely barreled through Gloucester's head when Denken stopped short. With a scream of fury, he rebounded off the air itself, which fluoresced blue on impact, illuminating a wall that had appeared in his path.

As quickly as it became visible, it disappeared again. Yet Gloucester knew it was still there. He could feel the power of it thrumming through his arm, his raised hand, the splayed fingers between which spanned the chains of Lucienne's enchanted rings. The sensation of magic threaded through the pain in his arm, which protested the sudden movement strongly enough to bring tears to his eyes.

Finch stared at him, dumbfounded.

"Sorry," Gloucester grunted, trying not to lose concentration. "It was the only thing I could think to do."

His other hand clutched Finch's arm in a vice grip, and he knew he was pulling magic from the magician, as he had back in the false Maze. Exactly *how* he was doing that, he still had no idea. Magic seemed to be largely intuitive.

"Sorry," he muttered again. This was probably considered very rude among magic-users. "Desperate times..."

"Forget that." Finch gaped at him. "You just *aimed* a defensive spell. With no training."

"Is that good?" Gloucester said through gritted teeth. His outstretched arm was starting to shake. The magic felt like a balm to his injured shoulder, a buzzing massage as it passed through, but the ache persisted.

"Is that—Saints, Mik! Remind me later to explain how impressive that is. For now, just hold on. Zane, come help us!"

A moment later, Zane was at Gloucester's side, eyes wide. Finch jutted his chin at Gloucester's arm.

"Help him hold it up," he said, and for once Zane didn't argue. She took hold of Gloucester's elbow, offering him support to keep his arm raised.

"Thanks," he grunted.

Zane offered him a weak smile, though her eyes kept darting back toward Denken. The demigod took another run at the barrier, scattering pieces of rope as he once again rebounded. "Least I can do, eh? You can do this. Just hold it in place as long as you can."

Gloucester wasn't sure what else he *could* do. Angus and the Gambler stood on the far side of the barrier, both still in one piece, but if he didn't lower the enchantment, how could they combat their brother? But if he did lower it...

"Can they beat him?"

While the question had crossed his mind, it was spoken aloud by Zane, who had turned her full attention back to the demigods. Denken raked his claws across the invisible wall, and Gloucester felt the reverberations in his fingers. The barrier held. For now.

"These enchantments of yours, Finch," she said. "Will they be enough to let the Gambler and Angus stop him? Their powers are inhibited too. So is the magic even helping or just making things worse?"

"Well, none of us are dead yet, so yeah, I'd say it's helping," Finch growled back. His brow was slick with perspiration as Gloucester continued to draw magic from him. "You want to help, then join in. Mik's a good channeler but maintaining a spell like this for so long is difficult enough for a practiced magician, let alone a complete newbie."

"Hey now," panted Gloucester. "Can we lay off the whole 'newbie' thing? I've known about magic for, like, two whole months now."

Zane laid her free hand on his shoulder, a mirror to the way his own hand clutched Finch's, while her other maintained its supporting grip on his outstretched arm. "Even longer, if we count all the time you just couldn't remember that you knew about it. Balls, I hate the feeling of magic." She shuddered and drew in a shaky breath, fingers spasming against Gloucester's shirt as she drew magic into herself. "I hope you both know I have no idea what I'm doing here."

In spite of her words, her presence immediately helped, lessening the magic's burn in his own body. He let out a grateful sigh of relief, able to breathe easier once again. The shaking in his outstretched hand eased a little.

Beneath the slight relief, panic still boiled in his chest, mixing with the channeled magic. What was their next move? What now? His head spun in growing exhaustion, searching for solutions.

"Speaking of ideas, I've just had one. Possibly a really dumb one, but bear with me."

Gloucester hadn't realized he'd squeezed his eyes shut until Zane's declaration made him open them again. Her hands were still a comforting presence on his shoulder and elbow, but her eyes were narrowed in consideration, focused on Denken.

Or rather, on the floor at his feet, where the glowing bits of rope lay strewn.

"Just hang in there for a minute, Gloucester," she said. She flashed him a shaky smile, and in that instant, he saw her plan as if she'd projected it into his head like one of the immortals. He opened his mouth to protest, but she cut him off. "Back in a tick!"

She took a deep breath and dashed forward. The moment her hands broke contact, the magic flowing through Gloucester surged and he gasped, almost dropping his arm and the shield along with it. He heard Finch swear, felt him dive to his other side to take Zane's place, supporting his elbow, but all of his attention was on Zane as she darted across the flagstones toward Denken.

In the god's shadow, she looked tiny. Gloucester's heart, already aching with Hyena's sacrifice, threatened to beat out of his chest at the thought of losing her. Yet it was too late to do anything but watch as she ran full tilt toward the nearest length of rope. It flared in her hands as she snatched it up, and Gloucester wondered if she'd managed to hold onto a little of the magic that had flowed between them moments before. His brief flash of curiosity was curdled by fear as she looked up from the rope in her hands to survey Denken, head tilted to one side. The demigod, intent on getting at his siblings, had yet to notice her behind him.

"Zane, please don't—" Gloucester dared not raise his voice above a whisper, terrified of drawing Denken's attention to his friend. The clockmaker had made her decision, though, and before he could even finish his useless protest, she lunged forward, the rope gleaming between her hands.

Stretched like an evening shadow, Denken was too tall for Zane to reach higher than his chest, but she made a valiant leap, wrapping the length of rope around his torso and upper arms. The demigod lurched in surprise, and Zane let out a desperate, triumphant yell as she deftly tied a knot, securing the rope in place.

Startled, Denken yowled like a wet cat. He clawed at the rope looped around his chest, the struggle made difficult by the pinioning of his biceps. Were it not for the magic infused into it, the simple binding would have been easy for him to shake off, but even his deadly claws couldn't slice through it now that the spells had been reawakened. He screeched in rage as Zane stumbled away. She returned breathlessly to Gloucester's side, grinning from ear to ear. Victory made her laugh, loud and wild, as she laid her hand back on his shoulder, reconnecting the channel of magic between them. Gloucester could feel her fingers trembling through his shirt fabric. He realized he was laughing, too, the relief tumbling through him as heady as magic.

"Thought that might slow him down a little," Zane said, watching Denken struggle against the rope, distracted from his assault on the barrier. "Not exactly much in comparison to what Finch did before, but it's better than nothing, eh? I figured it might at least stop him from tearing us apart while the other two can catch their breath or whatever."

"Again, you strive to protect my children."

A new voice echoed from every corner of the huge room. It wasn't loud, but neither was it even sound in the regular sense. It flowed like music caught in Gloucester's thoughts, appearing in his skull seemingly independent of his ears. Unmistakable.

The air in the room grew still.

Purpurrot.

Chapter 30

Goddess

Like marionettes controlled by a single puppeteer, everyone in the room looked around, searching as one for the goddess. The light from Finch's spell held strong, keeping any shadows at bay. Gloucester wouldn't have thought Purpurrot would be easy to miss, whichever form she was in. Yet there was no immediate sign of her.

"Purpa?" called Antimony. "Where are you?"

"I am here," said the goddess's voice. Lovely as ever, it sounded like it came from everywhere at once. Which wasn't entirely helpful.

"Er," said Zane, mystified. "Are you?"

Movement behind Antimony caught Gloucester's eye. A form, slim and russet orange, trotted forward from the window frame, where the red brickwork had camouflaged it. Purpurrot was still a fox, only her unusually large size and purple eyes marking her as an animal out of the ordinary. That, and the fact that most foxes didn't speak. Especially not in notably apologetic tones.

"I'm sorry," she said, looking around at their dumbstruck faces. "Hiding is beneath me, but this room is...difficult. Gathering what strength I have is challenge enough without the magicians' spells hindering me."

No one seemed more surprised to see the goddess than her children.

"What are you doing here?" Angus demanded, arms akimbo, feathered tattoos bristling. Beside them, the Gambler gaped in open bewilderment. "I thought you'd given up. Hiding wasn't so beneath you when we tried to get your help before. What changed?"

"Motherrrrrrr," growled Denken, before Purpurrot could reply. His hands dropped away from the rope looped around his chest.

Though its power had pulled the demigod back down to his usual height and stature, its magical blue luminosity had diminished considerably. Strands frayed around his sharp talons. Gloucester dared not drop the wall yet, just in case Denken's distraction and the fading magic didn't last. Not that he was sure how much longer he could maintain the barrier.

If Purpurrot was here, if she had changed her mind, maybe he wouldn't have to. Despite her misgivings, she'd gotten the upper hand with Denken before.

Denken turned his back fully on his siblings, and the intensity with which he eyed Purpurrot served as a chilling reminder that, while it protected the Gambler and Angus, Gloucester's barrier now effectively walled the personification of Thought in with the rest of them.

The fox stepped forward, up to where Gloucester stood with his shaking arm still outstretched, Zane and Finch at his sides. She seemed bigger now than she had back in the pie shop. Perhaps she was now garnering her power in a way her earlier hopelessness hadn't allowed. Standing on all fours, the black, pointed tips of her ears were level with Gloucester's head.

"Nothing changed," she said, answering Angus's question. "And everything."

On Gloucester's other side, Finch made a quiet sound, the strangled offspring of a grumble and a laugh. Purpurrot paid him no mind.

"I was so afraid. And I still am. I look at how my children suffer, how my world suffers, and I am *so* afraid. And yet, when you left me to my fears, I couldn't get your words out of my head."

To Gloucester's great surprise, she craned her neck to look at him. His arm trembled, starting to go numb from the strain of maintaining the shield, and sweat tickled the sides of his face, and yet the goddess gazed upon him with earnest admiration. Galaxies swirled in her purple irises, as easy to get lost in as the void haunting Frettchen's borders. He could only hold her gaze for the passage of a few heartbeats, but it felt like an eon. His head spun.

"What, me? I mean, mine? My words? Why?" The questions stumbled out of him, dumbly human.

"Your fear is as great as mine, perhaps even greater, and yet you fight. All of you. I have grown so comfortable in this world, forsaking my powers. I love the little life I made for myself. And yet, curled up in my shop after you left, your words stuck with me. You said we stand a chance *together*. I realized, all this time I have been living amongst you humans, I never really thought of myself as anything other than alone."

The fox turned her eyes away, not in embarrassment or shame, but to survey her children. The three of them stared back at her, astonished, temporarily united in the face of their mother.

"I thought there was nothing I could do, because I thought I had to do it alone. And that is terrifying. But no one can live in this world alone. Not even me. And no one can fight alone for its survival. So, we do this together."

She moved forward. Her tail brushed Gloucester's leg as she passed him, and she glanced back, the universe in her eyes.

"You can drop the shield, Mikalai," she said. "You saved my children. Again. Thank you, truly. But now it is my turn."

Despite the tension in the air, she did not sound upset. In fact, her words carried only calm gratitude. She turned away again and padded toward Denken, undaunted. The fur on her back bristled. Gloucester let his arm fall back to his side, aching from fingertips to neck, and he nearly collapsed as he felt the magical wall dissipate. He was out of breath, a stitch digging at his side like he'd just run a long distance. Finch's arm snaked around his waist, and Zane's grip on his shoulder and arm tightened, both of his friends keeping him from falling.

In front of them, Denken squared off against Purpurrot. A growl filled the air, and Gloucester, dragged back several hasty steps by Finch and Zane, couldn't say for certain if it was the demigod or the fox who made it. Then Denken tore the rope from his arms in one savage movement, its cords snapping with a loud *crack*, and he lunged. His silhouette stretched upward, growing like a shadow on a dying day. Any lingering humanity vanished from his features, obliterated by wild rage.

The two beasts charged each other, gaining momentum as they crossed the space between them. The odd big-small stretch of the room seemed to lend them time that didn't exist, and for an instant, eternity pulled between the two like an elastic band.

Then the elastic snapped. The demigods clashed, huge and vicious. The last thing Gloucester saw was a fox the size of a grizzly bear locking its teeth around Denken's neck. The personification of Thought loomed as tall as his bestial mother, talons piercing into Purpurrot's fur, sharklike teeth snapping in rabid fury.

At the impact of their bodies, the air exploded.

Then Gloucester's back hit the floor.

—

"This whole 'getting knocked out all the damned time' thing is starting to really peeve me."

Finch's mumbled complaint brought Gloucester back to his senses. Head spinning and thoughts a jumbled mess, he simply laughed in response. Then memory settled back into place and chased the humor away.

His eyes snapped open. Sitting up too quickly, he battled a wave of nausea that nearly flattened him again.

"What—?" he started, raising a hand to his smarting head. It came away bloody, a cut above his ear sticking the curls to his skull. "Ow. Fuck."

His muttered oath was barely audible, but it sounded loud in the chamber's silence.

The silence...

Urgently blinking away his dizziness, Gloucester looked around the room. His friends were in much the same condition as he was, lying in various places around the hall, in the stunned, unruly state of the recently-returned-to-consciousness. Nearby, Zane was picking herself back up, chin bloody from a split lip. Uncaring of the injury, she stared past Gloucester toward the center of the room, where the godly clash had occurred.

Gloucester stumbled to his feet. He moved unsteadily toward the spot where Purpurrot and Denken had launched themselves at each other.

Two giant forms lay on the stone floor, motionless. An odd scent filled the air, the sharp tang of ozone lingering like the aftermath of a lightning strike. On the opposite side of the bodies, the Gambler and Angus stood frozen like statues. They appeared unhurt, physically unswayed by the blast that had upended the mortals in the room. Yet their slackened faces betrayed the depth of their shock. Angus's emotions, even numbed by the room's enchantments, were a presence as claustrophobic as the fried odor clinging to Gloucester's nostrils.

"Are they..." Antimony limped to his side. Sweeping tangled hair from her eyes, she stared down at the fallen gods. She sounded as stupefied as the remaining immortals looked, and though she didn't finish the question, Gloucester knew they were all thinking the same thing. Neither body was moving.

"Are they dead?" asked Mulligan bluntly. He was squinting, his glasses lost at some point in the chaos. "That'd sort out our problems..."

He tried for a laugh, but everyone ignored him, even Harrison.

"I'm just saying," he muttered, abashed.

Would it, though? Gloucester stepped cautiously toward Purpurrot's and Denken's bodies. If they had perished in some sort of mutual destruction, would that fix everything? Would it fix *anything*? Or would it make everything worse? Considering the unchanged purgatory of their surroundings, it didn't seem to be the solution.

Or they aren't dead.

"Purpurrot?" he asked, approaching the fox's flank. He couldn't see any rise and fall of breath in the great beast's chest. He peered past her at the shadowy form of Denken. "Er," he said, unsure if he wanted to attract the demigod's attention. "Denken?"

No response. Not daring to get any closer, Gloucester raised his eyes to the Gambler and Angus.

"What happened?" he asked.

"What never should have," the Gambler said slowly, as if the words were difficult to get out. He had never sounded so dazed. Not when Gloucester first discovered him in his prison, nor when they'd finally rescued him six months later. Not even earlier this not-day when Gear had reached him through his feral rage, pulling him back to consciousness. Now he sounded like he really, truly didn't know what was going on.

He lowered to his bloody knees beside his fallen kin. The lines of his face were haggard, the empty sockets beneath his brows full of shadows. His eyes rotated around his head, solemn moons circling a mournful planet. "They're both...gone."

"Gone?" echoed Gloucester. Behind him, this word echoed amongst the others. He felt light-headed. "How?"

"Their powers were both great, but tremendously unstable," said Angus, when the Gambler didn't reply. "Maybe it was just too much for either of them."

The personification of Love sounded toneless and weary. Their grief seeped off of them, flooding the room. Yet Gloucester felt oddly numb to it. This couldn't be how this ended. He sank to a crouch beside the motionless bulk of Purpurrot and laid a tentative hand on her fur.

Only to flinch away when he discovered faint stirrings beneath his fingers.

"She's alive!" he shouted, shocked into high volume. "She's breathing. I...I think I can feel a heartbeat."

Do immortals have hearts?

No time for that!

"Purpurrot!"

Antimony rushed to Gloucester's side, throwing herself at the fallen goddess. Her face was wet with tears as she lay her head on the fox's side. "He's right. I can hear a heartbeat. It's weak, but it's there."

The Gambler lurched forward, half-kneeling still. "Angus, help me." His words rumbled with relief and urgency. "Lend her some of your power. Perhaps between the two of us, maybe..."

He didn't finish the sentence. No one needed him to.

Stepping carefully over Denken's still form, purposefully not looking at it, Angus settled on their haunches beside their brother, their motions less eager, more uncertain.

"Do you think it's possible? But the enchantments...?" they asked, the questions full of quiet terror. Gloucester was reminded sharply that, in spite of the immortals' bizarre appearances, Angus was, in a way, just a person. A person kneeling at their dying mother's side and scared of losing her. He felt a great pang of sympathy for the Siblings.

The emotion was followed unexpectedly by another, fainter but just as present: grief. Grief for the other loss the Siblings had just accrued.

The two gods laid shaking hands on their mother's side.

"I think we can work around the room's enchantments. If we siphon our power, our magic, directly into her. We just have to be careful. Steady. Please move back, Mikalai," the Gambler told him gently. "I can't pretend to know what we're doing but suffice to say it isn't safe. You too, Antimony."

Gloucester and Antimony shuffled back, falling mutely to Zane's side. She watched the scene with tears sparkling in her eyes.

"Do you think they're going to make it?" she whispered.

As they watched, Angus and the Gambler bowed their heads, as if in prayer. Gloucester couldn't feel magic gathering the way it did around Finch when he prepared a spell, but he could tell something was happening. It was as though all the air in the room was drawing closer to the immortals, lending them their own field of gravity. Gloucester felt like, if he wasn't careful, he would tumble across the room into their orbit. He braced himself and took a deep breath.

"I don't know about Purpurrot," he murmured back. "Whatever they're doing, maybe it'll be enough to revive her. Denken, though..."

"He's dead," Finch said beside them, face pale. Though there was no victory in his statement, there was no doubt there either.

Chapter 31

Death

"He can't really be..."

Zane was incredulous, but in a battened-down way, too tired to lend her incredulity much enthusiasm. She stared at the body. "I know we had to defeat him, but I guess I never really thought he could..."

She shook her head, drawing in a deep breath. Her headscarf had been pulled askew when they were buffeted by Denken's fury, and she carefully fixed it now, fingers trembling against the vibrant cloth. When she spoke again, her words had gained a measured edge, like she was putting significant effort into rationality.

"If he's...if he's gone, then shouldn't all this, I dunno, go back to normal?" She gestured around at the grand hall. "Shouldn't Frettchen wake up? It's hard to tell in here, but it doesn't feel any different. I still have that, uh, that timeless feeling, you know?"

As he watched the immortals try and work their magic over Purpurrot, Finch looked wearier than Gloucester had ever seen him. He shrugged, shoulders slumping like that simple movement weighed the world. “Maybe it was all too far gone. Maybe we never had a chance.”

“No.” Gloucester shocked himself with his own conviction as the word burst out, loud and fierce. The others gaped at him. “I refuse to believe that.”

“I don’t think that’s how it works, Mikalai,” Finch said, but Gloucester ignored him.

Striding forward, he skirted around Purpurrot and her remaining children. They were utterly engrossed in their desperate ministrations, hands buried in her russet fur. They didn’t speak, didn’t move, yet Gloucester knew they were hard at work; the power they drew from themselves and the room still tugged at him.

He paid it no mind. He crouched down next to Denken’s body instead, back aching in protest, his earlier apprehension forgotten.

The demigod certainly *looked* dead. He’d shrunk back to his regular size, and though his fingers were still talons and the teeth in his slackened jaw were still sharp, he seemed distinctly humanoid again. Mortal. Unlined by visible age, his face was youthful, and despite the violence of their confrontation, neither Purpurrot nor he appeared bloodied. He may as well have been sleeping.

“Wake up, you son of a bitch!” Gloucester snapped, before tossing a guilty “No offense” toward Purpurrot. He returned his attention to Denken and told the body, with ferocious adamance, “You don’t get to just *die*.”

When no reaction came, he gripped Denken’s shoulder and gave it a firm shake. Still no response. “C’mon, you bastard!”

“There’s no point.” The Gambler didn’t spare a glance at his fallen brother, didn’t break away from his efforts to save their mother. His words were cold in the forced, choked way of grief suppressed. "He's gone. That isn't him anymore. Just an empty husk again." Then, whispered and disbelieving, "He's gone..."

Gloucester stared at the Gambler's downturned face, emotions thundering through him like the gathered magic of a spell, strengthening with every beat of his heart until they threatened to overwhelm him. Before that could happen, he gave himself a shake.

"No," he said again.

Turning back to the body, he gasped in horror. It was diminishing before his eyes. The smooth features of Denken's face grew gaunt, cheeks hollowed and closed eyes sunken. His arms were becoming more and more skeletal, body mass crumbling into nothing. As if the false Maze overtaking Frettchen was now consuming its own creator as well. Gloucester grasped one of Denken's hands, feeling fragile bones break beneath papery skin at the touch. He swallowed down his disgust and held on. "Don't you bloody dare."

He thought he heard the others protest further, but he pushed their words to the back of his mind. Staring down at Denken, an overwhelming emotion swept over him, stronger than the fear and the confusion and the bone-weighing weariness. He knew it wasn't Angus's or anyone else's. This emotion was his alone.

Anger.

"You don't get to just die," he growled again. "Not after everything! Not if it means the rest of us get stuck here! This is your mess, and you don't get to just swan off and leave everyone else to clean it up for you. After everything you've been through, everything you put us *all* through. I know you; you're tougher than this. Look!"

Thrusting his hand into his pocket, Gloucester yanked out Denken's tooth and waved it in front of the corpse's skull-like face. The lack of response, though expected, only made him angrier.

"The stubborn idiot who barely even flinched when I knocked this out, he wouldn't go down this easy." Gloucester clenched his fist around the tooth. Panic simmered beneath the anger threatening to break through.

If Denken was gone and Frettchen still wasn't saved, then what did that mean for the rest of them? What did it mean for the world?

"Where did you get that?"

There was enough sharpness in Angus's question to pierce through the fog of his anger. Or maybe it was the surge of surprise and hope accompanying it. The emotions caressed Gloucester like a spring breeze, unexpectedly pleasant. He half-turned where he knelt. Angus was staring at Gloucester's hand like he held a miracle. The demigod sat up from where they'd been lying across Purpurrot's side, and though they were blatantly exhausted, a newfound brightness shone in their eyes.

Gloucester opened his hand again and held the tooth out for the others to see. In the light, it looked unremarkable, a bone-white triangle between his fingers.

"It came from Denken," he told Angus. "I, er, punched him. In the face."

His anger startled away, Gloucester now felt a wave of inopportune fretfulness. "He'd kidnapped me," he added, somewhat defensively. Would the other immortals, raw with grief, take kindly to the news that he'd once struck their brother? Probably not, even if he had deserved it.

Except apparently, they would, as Angus's face broke into a broad, gap-toothed grin. Beatific, they resembled more than ever the cherubs of the Blue Church, rosy-cheeked and joyful.

"Mikalai Gloucester, you genius!"

"Uh..." said Gloucester, who didn't know how to respond to this emotional roller coaster. "Thanks." He looked from Angus to the tooth. "Why?"

Angus leapt to their feet and snatched the tooth from his palm, holding it aloft like a priceless gem. "This is a piece of him. A piece of his essence, separate from his death. It's not much, but it might be just enough."

Behind them, the Gambler watched from Purpurrot's side. Though fatigued, he too wore a smile. Gloucester wasn't sure if this was because of the tooth and whatever it signified...or because the Siblings' efforts had paid off.

Next to him, Purpurrot was stirring.

And shrinking. The red fur of the fox fell away, vanishing as soon as it was shed. In its place were drapes of violet silk and long dark hair. Soon, the beautiful woman Gloucester had met in the pie shop lay before them. She blinked awake in a flutter of ebony lashes, leaning heavily on the Gambler as he supported her gently upright. She smiled at him but didn't speak, clearly still only semi-conscious.

Caught between Purpurrot's recovery and Angus's fascination with the tooth, Gloucester struggled to focus.

"Just enough for what?" he asked the giddy personification of Love. Angus, however, had spun back toward their mother, distracted. They left Gloucester's question hanging in the air alongside his hand, still outstretched from passing the tooth over to the demigod.

In spite of his confusion, hope inflated like a balloon in Gloucester's chest, swelling with elation, but fragile and ready to pop. The feeling expanded through the chamber, drawing everyone closer. Finch rushed ahead of the rest to stand at Gloucester's side, grabbing his outstretched hand and pulling him to his feet.

"Are we sure we want to bring him back?" he hissed in Gloucester's ear, a protective grip on his arm. His eyes darted to the haggard, hopeful gods fussing over Purpurrot.

"Feels kinda like we're stuck here if we don't," Gloucester whispered back. "Whatever this is," he added, gesturing at the body, "it doesn't seem to have changed anything for Frettchen. And if someone else here could fix it, they already would've, right?"

A few weeks ago, that would have felt like an insurmountable degree of trust to lay on anyone else. But Gloucester, looking around at everyone in the room, no longer felt those doubts that had once plagued him. Everyone here had proven themselves.

Finch wasn't as convinced. He crossed his arms, glaring down at his feet. He might not have had literal clockwork in his head, but Gloucester could practically hear the gears turning.

Finally, he met Gloucester's eyes again. "If he comes back and still wants to bloody well kill us, I'm holding you accountable," he said wryly.

Gloucester laughed. "Fair enough." Raising his voice again to recapture Angus's attention, he asked, "So how does the tooth help?"

The personification of Love was still grinning ear to ear, their tear-stained cheer edged in manic desperation. "Right," they said, leaving Purpurrot in the Gambler's capable hands. They closed the distance between themself and Denken's shriveled corpse with renewed focus. "It's sort of like when you think a plant has died."

Silence followed this explanation.

"Is it?" Zane said eventually.

A modicum of Angus's usual derision returned, dampening their smile. "What I mean is, a plant that appears dead can sometimes be brought back if you still have some essence of it left. A good root. An offshoot. A seed." They gestured emphatically with the tooth. "This is our seed."

"Ew," she murmured.

Gloucester turned the metaphor around in his mind. "So will it bring him back to life or...Saints, this sounds dumb...grow a new Denken?"

"Now there's a mental image," Finch said. "Valid question, though."

"And one I wish we had a definitive answer to," said Purpurrot. She drew herself slowly to her feet, the Gambler at her side. Though she'd regained her usual imposing height, it was belayed by her obvious unsteadiness. "All we have is hope."

Gloucester sighed. "Well, we've been running on that practically since the beginning of this whole mess, so why stop now? What do we have to do?"

"Maybe I can infuse the tooth with my own power..." the goddess mused. Her hair hung loose like dark, coiling vines, and her feet were bare where they poked out from beneath folds of purple cloth, the fabric frayed along its edges like torn spider's silk. She looked more like a wild goddess of Nature than Gloucester had ever seen her.

"No," the Gambler said immediately. "You've barely the power to keep yourself present. And I'm the same. I drained most of what I can access in this place to heal you. Angus?"

Uncertainty rolled off them. "I can try."

"Oh, for pity's sake," grumbled Finch, throwing up his hands. "I'll help too."

The immortals stared at him. And they weren't the only ones.

"Really?" said Gloucester.

"Yes, really." Finch looked thoroughly infuriated with himself. He dragged both hands through his hair, making the short red strands stand on end. "I don't know how much good it'll do, but I'll set up an Amplification spell for these fools"—he gestured at the demigods—"and see what magic I can siphon off of Dad's enchantments. It's a lot of powerful magic, so it ought to lend us a fair bit of firepower, so to speak. We'll need the spells dismantled anyway, at least the ones limiting their powers, so might as well not waste the magical energy."

Following along with that logic, Gloucester still had to ask, "You'd do that, though? Try to save him?"

Out of all of them, Finch had the most reason to want Denken to remain dead.

The magician huffed a laugh and laid a shaking hand against the side of Gloucester's face. "Don't worry, I can hardly believe it myself. You're a goddamned bad influence on me, Mikalai. Now, let's see if we can save the Big Bad Shark."

Chapter 32

Resurrection

"Look, I get why we're doing this, not wanting to be trapped in purgatory and all that, but are we *sure* about this?"

Mulligan's raw anxiety slipped through the imperious tone he was trying for. The group had all gathered in a loose circle around Denken's body, which was now scarcely more than a skeletal husk in tattered clothes. The interim high minister, standing with blatant reluctance a few feet from Denken's shriveled back, looked like it was taking all of his courage to voice his concerns.

"No, dipshit, we're not sure," Angus snapped, their annoyance lancing out from them. "Would you rather we just stood around and did nothing? Waited for this bubble of timelessness to spread over the whole Lower Lands? Does that sound fun?"

Mulligan did his best to draw himself up indignantly, but he was pale in the wake of the demigod's anger.

"I was just asking..." he muttered, dropping his gaze.

"He's got a point, though," Antimony said. "If this does work, we don't know what state Denken will be in. He could well be vicious and deranged still. More so than he normally is. We have to be prepared for that."

Zane sighed, long and loud. "Yeah, if we bring him back just to kill us, we're all going to feel really stupid as we die."

She crossed her arms tightly over her chest, worrying at her lip as she stared down at Denken. Gloucester reached out to pry one of her hands loose and take it in his own, giving it a reassuring squeeze.

Finch and the immortals discussed their options for several minutes—or the approximation of that, with the clock around Zane's neck still frozen—and came up with a rough idea of what they were about to try. Tension filled the air, but for once the magician and the gods managed to avoid arguing. Gloucester might have been impressed if he weren't so terrified of what they were about to attempt.

Could it work? If anyone could be brought back from the dead, it made sense it would be one of the demigods. But *was* it possible, even for them? They'd just borne witness to Purpurrot's return, but she hadn't actually been dead, just nearly so. And if it was possible, what then? Would he be healed? His mind soothed? His powers back in check? Or were they just bringing their vanquished enemy back once more to destroy them and the world along with?

Too late to worry about it now, he told himself. Of course, such stern words did nothing to actually stop the worries, but he pretended they had strengthened his resolve and did his best to refocus.

"Right," Angus said. "I'm going to siphon my magic into the tooth, to try and encourage the lingering essence there to grow. Magician, get these bloody enchantments dismantled and start your spellwork to boost it."

"Bossy prick," muttered Finch.

Then he huffed and offered his hand to Gloucester. "Shall we see what mischief we can wreak?" he asked, roguish grin chasing away the storm clouds in his eyes. Gloucester found the smile did quite a lot more to keep his fears at bay than his self-recriminations had.

Mustering a smile of his own, he clasped Finch's hand. "Beats hanging around here for the rest of eternity."

"Bloody hell, maybe you two *are* perfect for each other," Zane griped from his other side. She let go of his hand and moved to stand beside Finch. "C'mon then, Finch, give me your other hand and I'll help too."

"Much as I like the charming imagery of us all holding hands, love, I do need to keep one free." If Gloucester wasn't mistaken, there was actual fondness in Finch's reply. "But grab a hold of my shoulder. That ought to work just as well."

Zane did so.

And she wasn't the only one.

Antimony, with Gear watching from atop her knapsack, moved forward and laid a slim hand on Finch's other shoulder. The automaton's transparent skull was scuffed, the stitching that bound the skin of her cheek frayed. Yet her clockwork beat steady and determined, as if, without a hand of her own to offer, she could aid the spell with sheer willpower alone.

Maybe she can, Gloucester thought. Gear's will and enthusiasm had done wonders enough before, and anyway, what did he know about the science and spellwork that powered her?

Mulligan and Harrison joined as well, leaning in to each put a hand on the magician's back. Finch blinked, glancing at all the people now standing around him. He was suddenly rather pink in the face.

"Well, uh, the support's appreciated," he said. "I'd make some snippy remark about being crowded, but I reckon we need all the help we can get." He cleared his throat. "Let's get this party started, then. I'm beginning the spell. Humans, get ready to channel some serious magic. Immortals, do what you can with it and try not to end the world any more than it already has."

Closing his eyes, he began an incantation. As usual, Gloucester didn't recognize the words. Finch spoke in an undertone, a melodic hum more song than speech, that was echoed in the building thrum of magic.

The spell felt different from any other. Though Gloucester's experience was limited, he'd grown accustomed to the almost electric sensation of Finch's spells, humming through the air and his own veins on the occasions he'd channeled it.

This wasn't like that. Though it still coursed through Gloucester's veins, it lacked the usual buzzing sensation. Instead, it felt deeper, more fluid, as if it weren't tingling through his bloodstream but gently infusing into his blood itself. The magic was a comforting presence, in tune with his body instead of overwhelming it. Perhaps it was the type of spell, one he hadn't experienced before. Or maybe it was the fact that Finch was making use of his father's lingering spellwork, coloring the new incantation with the late Finch's own flavor of magic. Finch had told him once that every magician could recognize their own magic, after all. That it was unique to each caster. Curiosity bubbled through him, temporarily distracting him from their dire situation.

And then the thrum became something much stronger. Gloucester's ears popped, and abruptly the magic was not only audible but rushing so loudly he felt like he'd stepped under a waterfall.

"What in the world?" Mulligan yelped, knuckles white against Finch's back.

"He's breaking down his father's enchantments and feeding them into the Amplification spell," Antimony explained over the noise and Finch's incantation. "The Siblings won't be limited in their power anymore. Just be careful not to break the one keeping the room as it is, Mr. Finch," she added. "We don't know where we are in the original layout of this place."

Finch didn't reply beyond a silent tilt of his head. His eyes were closed, his free hand sweeping back and forth through the air in front of him, gesticulating in time to the spell. His other held tightly onto Gloucester's, who could feel magic traveling through the connection. Though the spell seemed unusually intense, the power channeling into him wasn't any worse than the other times they'd done this. He wondered if it was because so many of them were helping.

He felt a pang of gratitude for all his friends.

Angus stepped forward. Standing directly over Denken's body, they pressed their hands to their chest, the tooth still within their grasp.

"All right," Gloucester heard them mutter. "For once, Denken, don't make things difficult."

They drew in a deep breath.

Everything shifted. If the magic's sudden change in volume had been like his ears popping, this was like the whole world turning sideways. There was a mighty jolt, and Gloucester had to stop himself from falling to his knees, tightening his grip on Finch's hand for support.

"What's happening?" he shouted over the now-roar of the unfolding spell.

Finch's face was a rictus of pained concentration. His free hand still moved, each motion more fraught than the last. The tattoo on his brow flared blue, bright as the sun it depicted, the full circle of it shining through his hair. More magic than Gloucester had ever felt coursed through the connection of their grasping hands, all-consuming.

"Angus, be careful." The Gambler's warning rang clear over the din. "You're reaching beyond just the magicians' spells. You're drawing in all the magic locking Frettchen out of time!"

"It might just be enough." Angus's weeping eyes were closed. They looked strangely peaceful, standing in the eye of the storm.

"Or it might destroy us all!"

"It won't," they insisted. The tooth was glowing now, so bright that it shone through Angus's hand, pressed against their chest, as if their heart itself was aflame. The bones of their hand stood out like shadow puppets in the center of the shining light. Their shirt crumbled away, fabric burned to ash. The tears on their face turned to steam. "This place was born of him. It will restore him."

"Wrong."

Purpurrot moved into the golden aura. Silver streaked her hair as it whipped in the gale of the spell. She ran a gentle hand across Angus's cheek, brushing away their steaming tears.

"It was born of both of us. Denken and myself. The state of this city, this world, is my transgression too."

Her touch moved to the spot on Angus's chest where they pressed Denken's shark tooth against their skin. Slowly, Angus lowered their hand, letting Purpurrot take the tooth. In her palm, it tempered slightly, casting warm illumination across her face. It was quite possibly the most beautiful thing Gloucester had ever seen. Purpurrot pressed a mother's kiss to Angus's round cheek, then softly pushed them back.

"Before, I wasn't ready," she said. The admission was but a murmur, the vibrato hum of building strings, yet it carried over everything else. "I wasn't ready to face the power I had left behind. Nor the children I had abandoned. I failed you all. In spite of all that was at stake, in my heart I clung to the life I'd made for myself in this city. I resisted. And that almost doomed everything I ever created. Again, and again. But no longer."

The gold highlighted gentle lines tracing down her cheeks. She was weeping. "I must become once more what I was. What I have always been."

"Purpa..." Antimony, too, was crying.

Purpurrot closed her fist around the tooth and the golden light flared brighter, a tiny sun in her grasp. Gloucester shut his eyes against its beams—he could feel the warmth of it against his skin, while all around, the room surged with power. It flowed through Gloucester's bones and blood and every thought.

For a moment, he wasn't a person at all, but a piece of the light, the magic, the life energy of the very universe, wielded by this beautiful, tragic goddess as she gave up a piece of the world she had made for herself. In the midst of it all, he heard a laugh of bright, pure relief. Though it carried little of the madcap power he'd heard from the demigod in the past, he knew it belonged to Denken. Hope, reckless and wonderful, barreled through him, as powerful as the magic swirling all around.

If I don't make it through this, he thought, *it seems a sublime way to die.*

Then the moment ended. Gloucester was grounded back in himself once more, keenly aware of his body: the pinch of Finch's fingers, the aching pain of his injuries, the winded shortness of breath in his chest. He gasped and opened his eyes.

The room remained impossibly proportioned and lit by the fading magic of Finch's spell. The magician and his bevy of impromptu channelers stood huddled together, windswept and weary. A few meters away, the Gambler and Angus gaped in a distinctly ungodly way at the empty space in front of them.

Purpurrot and what had remained of Denken were gone.

Chapter 33

Frettchen Awakened

"Did it work? Something happened. Was it a good something? I couldn't see!"

Gear's questions broke the silence, accompanied by the frantic whirring of her clockwork. The automaton's head jostled in place atop Antimony's bag as she tried to get a better look at the magic's aftermath. Murmuring reassurances, Antimony stepped away from Finch to let Gear survey the scene. This action broke the contact of any further channeling, yet it felt clear that the spellwork was no longer needed. Finch had ceased the incantation, bent double as he panted to regain his breath.

But had it *worked*?

Gloucester stepped back as well, extricating his hand from Finch's and looking around. The chamber appeared much the same as before. Yet something did feel different in the wake of Purpurrot's sacrifice. The air was lighter. The thick presence of magic was gone, leaving Gloucester feeling strangely weightless in its absence.

"Hey!"

Zane's exclamation made them all jump. Gloucester whirled to face her. She was holding her pocket watch aloft and grinning widely.

"Listen," she said with a relieved laugh.

Gloucester listened, unsure what he was supposed to be hearing. The watch sounded normal, ticking just like any other timepiece Zane owned.

Wait. Ticking...

"Time has started up again!" Zane bounced on the spot, delighted. She hugged the ticking watch to her chest. "Oh, this is the best sound ever!"

Another gasp interrupted the happy moment. The Gambler lifted his head, mouth agape. Angus turned to him in alarm, but before they could say anything, the Gambler laughed. A smile cracked his stoic exterior, rare and rather alarming in its broadness.

"They're back," he said breathlessly, as if he couldn't quite believe it. "The futures. I can see them again." His eyes spun around his head, more boisterous than they had been in a long while. He sagged against his sibling's side. If he could have, Gloucester imagined the Gambler would be weeping. "I can finally See again."

Something had definitely changed, then. Desperate for more proof, Gloucester launched himself toward the door out of the hall, where light and windows would give a better indication. The others tromped at his heels.

Through the doorway, the corridor was warm, sunlight streaming in through the high-up windows and illuminating each and every lush tapestry. Gloucester glimpsed blue sky beyond the glass. Birdsong filtered through from the gardens behind the church, nature's accompaniment to the distant sounds of traffic.

"No more storm clouds," he said, pointing giddily. "No more thunder. C'mon!"

Like children racing from their beds to find presents on their birthday, the group dashed down the short corridor leading back to the church proper. Even before he wrenched open the door, Gloucester could hear noise on the other side, where before there had been only the final strains of Hyena's laughter. Still, it was with bated breath and hammering heart that he stepped through.

Church-goers milled about in the light of the nave. Several people were scratching their heads and everyone appeared bewildered, but otherwise no worse for wear. A priest leaned against the altar, godly decorum forgotten as she slumped forward on her elbows. Three children sat on the floor in front of a nearby window—once more depicting a saint, surrounded by birds and flowers—loudly discussing their confusion with animated good cheer. Their faces were cast in technicolor by the sunlight shining through the colored glass. The church rang with dozens of voices, as if the eerie silence was nothing more than a bad dream. No one paid the group emerging from the doorway any mind.

Out of the corner of his eye, Gloucester saw Antimony slide her bag off her shoulders and quickly stow Gear's complaining head back inside, out of sight. Beside her, the Gambler pressed a kiss to his fingertips then brushed the digits against the bag, murmuring words that Gloucester couldn't hear.

"Everyone seems to be okay," Gloucester observed, looking out over the parishioners. In an instant, a thousand questions bubbled to the surface of his thoughts. "What do you think they remember? Anything? And how are we going to explain everything to—"

"We're not," Finch said firmly. "Or, at least, I'm not, because that sounds tedious and annoying. But maybe we should get out of here before the confused crowd notices the eyeless man and his white-haired sibl—oh, nope, nevermind, they're already gone."

Gloucester turned around. Sure enough, the Gambler and Angus had vanished. "They really do like doing that."

"We'll see them again." Antimony hefted her bag up onto her shoulders. "We should get back to mine, though. Even with those two gone, we're not exactly an inconspicuous group."

It was a fair point. Regardless of the Siblings or Hyena, they stuck out, everyone's hair and clothes mussed from the fight. Zane's chin was bloody from her split lip, Gloucester cradled his sprained arm, and more than a few of them bore visible bruises and scrapes from getting tossed around by Denken's rage. Besides that, it would only be a matter of time before someone recognized Mulligan, who was squinting around in the absence of his glasses.

In spite of his dishevelment, the politician was grinning more widely than Gloucester had ever seen. He kept clapping Harrison on the arm while repeating, "We did it!"

"Yes, sir," replied Harrison, smiling down at him.

"We actually did it!"

"We certainly did, sir."

"There's a back door," Gloucester said, pointing across the nave to the far side of the altar. "It leads into the gardens. Let's get out of here."

He knew he ought to be overwhelmed with relief. Yet, as his initial giddiness faded, his muddled emotions felt distant. As if Angus had taken them with them when they disappeared. The world was saved, but he couldn't yet find the energy to celebrate. He thought of Hyena, the fading sound of their laughter, and hoped that the Gambler was right, and that in their sacrifice the thought-beast had finally found their way home to the Maze. He wondered if Denken himself might have found his way back there too.

No certainties came miraculously to mind. He sighed and beckoned for the others to follow him, heading for the door and the sun-filled city beyond.

—

Their trip back to Antimony's was surprisingly quiet.

The moment they stepped into the garden, Harrison's radio started buzzing with panicked voices trying to contact him, and soon he and Mulligan disappeared into a van of extremely frazzled security agents, leaving everyone else to catch a cab.

Though he said nothing, the driver kept glancing at them in the rear view. They were crammed into the backseat, all save for Antimony, who sat primly in the passenger's seat, demurely ignoring the cabbie's curious looks as she finger-combed her hair into some semblance of order. Outside the car windows, Frettchen was full of noise and movement once more. Beyond a few fender-benders where drivers hadn't been quite quick enough to regain their wits upon reappearing in the mortal realm, and a general air of mild confusion, the city seemed to be in surprisingly fine condition.

"It's as if no time has passed," Zane remarked as they watched the cab drive away from the sidewalk outside Antimony's home. "Everyone's in a bit of a stupor, but not, you know, panicking. Not like they should be after a fortnight in existential limbo."

Antimony's neighbors were out in droves, chatting with each other over garden fences and congregating on porches. The sounds of dogs barking and children playing filled Gloucester's ears. People waved to Antimony, calling out greetings and questions, which she waved off politely. The street was alive once more, abuzz with noise and activity.

"Maybe that's exactly it," Gloucester posited. The afternoon sun was warm on his face, and he fought the overwhelming urge to yawn. "Maybe time didn't pass for them. Maybe it all just passed in a blink of an eye."

"They're all going to be really confused when the rest of the Lower Lands gets back in touch." Finch's laugh was slightly hysterical. "Bloody hell, I'm tired. Anyone else want to have an extremely strong drink and then sleep for a month?"

"That sounds deeply tempting," Antimony said, leading the way up the steps to her front door. In the full light of day, her face looked thinner and more angular than ever, her usually neat hair a mess despite her best efforts, and streaks of tears dried on her cheeks. None of them looked any better. No wonder the neighbors eyed them all with such curiosity. A reminder that victory hadn't come easily. "Before I do that, I want to get Gear safely downstairs and get everyone patched up. You're all welcome to stay as long as you need."

Despite being in unusually rough shape, Antimony's smile was the warmest Gloucester had ever seen her aim at anyone other than Gear. She laid a hand on Zane's arm, then made her way down the front hall in the direction of her basement lab.

"Am I going to be in one piece again?" Gear asked, muffled by the cloth bag and the growing distance.

"Yes," came Antimony's reply. "Everything will be okay now."

"Do you think it will?" Zane asked Gloucester and Finch, the three of them left standing together in the entryway.

"Be okay?" Finch scratched his chin and stifled a yawn. "Saints, I hope so. We've saved the day enough times now that it'd better stay saved for a bit. I need a lie down."

Gloucester leaned against the kitchen doorway, watching the birds in Antimony's front garden through the window. They darted to and fro in dappled sunlight, offering no sign of their recent imprisonment in limbo. It was like all of Frettchen had woken from a nightmare, but he and his friends were the only ones who remembered it. Them and...

"What about the immortals?" he asked. "The Gambler and Angus and...and the others?"

Zane shrugged, her frown sad yet thoughtful. "I dunno. What happened back there...it didn't really feel like a...a death, you know? But it definitely didn't go the way I expected."

Finch huffed and flopped back against the pale wallpaper of Antimony's hallway. His chuckle soon morphed into another yawn. "It never does where that lot is concerned. But Zane's right. I don't think it was an ending for them. Not in the deadly sense, anyway. Who knows, maybe they really can't die after all. But things *have* changed. For the better, it looks like. I guess we have to—*ugh*—trust them."

Eyes narrowed, Zane's lips spread into a smile. "Who are you and what did you do to Finch?"

"You lot are just a bad influence on me, I keep telling you," he replied plaintively, a smile sneaking onto his face too.

Gloucester joined in their laughter, and as he did so, he finally felt something akin to relief creep back into his chest. Things weren't perfect, but then, nothing ever was. Time was moving again, and the sun was shining, and he was alive. It struck him as something not to take for granted.

Chapter 34

Two Months Later

Summer in Frettchen settled in dry and dusty, far different from the muggy heat of the south. Desert-baked winds gusted in from the east, coating everything in a thin layer of sand.

Every morning, shopkeepers could be spotted out in droves, yawning and chatting as they swept it away from their doorsteps. Boats filled the harbor, where the sun glittered off cerulean waters. Sailors frequented the pubs and small businesses down by the waterfront, bringing a seasonal boost to sales. Nordish and Southern tourists alike filled the streets, taking in the sights. More than usual this year, with the curiosity of the entire Lower Lands driving them to explore Frettchen for themselves, in the wake of The Incident.

Very few Frettchennians recalled what had transpired in the mysterious weeks when a storm held sway over the city. The population as a whole was bewildered by the news of so much time passing. Or, in fact, that any time had passed at all. To them, one moment had simply passed to another, nothing more than a minor odd blip in their perception. Yet, according to their friends and relations in other regions, that moment had contained a significant portion of time.

Some, mostly magic-users with loose tongues, claimed to remember fleeting images and emotions, half-remembered as a long-ago dream: dark streets and a lightning-filled sky, beasts of shadows and flame looming overhead. These tales fed into several weeks of bluster and hysteria.

And then, unexpectedly, things calmed down again. The Incident was still discussed, of course, but the tirade of speculation tempered, both within the city and without.

"Enchanters everywhere are running themselves ragged," Finch explained to Gloucester and Zane over lunch at the clock shop, two weeks after time had resumed its usual pace. "In all of the Lower Lands. Mollifying people, modifying memories, offering explanations for things that can't be explained."

"So everyone's just getting bamboozled?" Zane set her teacup down with enough force to spill some of its contents over her hand. She bit back an oath as she swiped away the hot liquid with her sleeve. "That's awful!"

"Maybe so," Finch said. "But better that than people rioting in the streets, isn't it? And it's fewer people than you might think. Most of the magicians and other magic-users know some version of the truth. Word travels fast. Probably half of them don't believe a word of it, and there are about seventy different versions I've heard, most of them absolutely ridiculous, but they know what's what, more or less. Folks who know about magic will be able to comprehend what happened, at least to some degree. And I think there are a lot more of the latter now than there were before."

"So, people know about what we did?" Gloucester asked, surprised. "And about Purpurrot and the Siblings?"

He would have expected more fanfare if that were the case. It wasn't every day that you found out the creator of the world lived in your neighborhood.

"Welllll..." Finch tapped the side of his nose conspiratorially. "I kept our names out of it. I knew you wouldn't appreciate the attention, and I figured Zane and Antimony and the rest could probably do without it and all. Mostly, word's out that some really powerful magic ran amok. The stories of the Brothers—the Siblings, sorry—aren't all that unknown, so a fair few in the community accepted that they had something to do with it. No one knows how to deal with that, though, so it's generally being agreed upon to leave them alone. Helps that no one knows how to contact them anyway."

"Maybe we're moving toward a new age," Gloucester said, before chuckling at the unintentional grandeur of his own wording. "I just mean, maybe sooner rather than later we'll reach a point where magic isn't hidden anymore. It didn't used to be, right? When the sorcerers were still around or whatever. Maybe the Lower Lands will go back to that."

He liked the idea. A world where fewer secrets were kept, where fewer people had to hide who they were...that sounded pretty nice.

In the following weeks, his gratitude for Finch's discretion mounted. Gloucester wasn't sure what anyone would have made of their adventure, or whether anyone would even believe it, but the idea of having to explain it to people, to have all their eyes on him and everyone asking questions, was exhausting to even imagine. He'd much rather let them all come up with their fanciful stories and keep his true part in it out of the limelight.

One thing everyone—whether bamboozled or in the know—*did* agree on was that things felt better now, better than they had since the high minister's unexpected death. Desperate to cling to something cheerful if not explainable, everyone decided this was a Good Thing. The sort of Good Thing, in fact, that was best focused on without too much question.

In the end, Frettchennians and outsiders alike shuffled awkwardly away from the mystery of The Incident. While the scientifically- and politically-minded continued to argue and hypothesize, the general populace concluded that they really didn't want to know.

Hundreds of weary enchanters breathed sighs of relief.

For Gloucester, the whole thing often felt like a bizarre dream. There were still many mornings he awoke with an anxious start, fearful he would open his eyes to the bare white walls and cracked ceiling of his cell. Everything that had happened since his release felt too strange to be real, yet too certain to be imagined.

But real it was. As Zane had once said, now that he'd noticed it, Gloucester could see the hints of magic everywhere. Little glimpses of spells by magicians too impatient or cocky to hide. Technology that ran a little too smoothly. Shops he'd always assumed to be tourist traps selling *actual* good fortune and garden-variety spellwork. He found himself smiling at such sights, feeling like a part of the secret, finally not the person perennially out of the loop.

Less subtle was the occasional visit from one of the immortals, whether it was the Gambler stopping by Zephyr Clocks to say hello or, more boggling by far, Angus appearing unannounced to bring Gloucester a morning tea. The latter had happened three times since time resumed. Angus never stayed long, nor seemed interested in much conversation, but they did inexplicably know exactly the flavors Gloucester preferred.

Baffled, he mentioned it to Zane and Finch, unsure why the normally stand-offish demigod was giving him the time of day, let alone being so nice.

"You did save their brother," Zane reminded him. "Both of them, in fact. On multiple occasions. I reckon that's a big part of why all the immortals like you so much."

"Like me?" This gave Gloucester pause. He supposed when he thought about it, they all were quite amiable with him. Even Denken had expressed regret over hurting him.

His surprise amused his friends.

"Typical of you to not think twice about why someone might like being around you," said Finch with a snort. "Like Zane said, you went out of your way to help them. Often at great inconvenience to yourself. A few cups of tea are owed, if you ask me."

Gloucester joined in on their laughter, a warm feeling in his chest. Part of him wanted to question their reasoning, but he pushed it down. Maybe he'd earned the right to a little pride in his actions. And who would be fool enough to turn up their nose at the friendship of a demigod? Maybe he'd earned that, too.

—

Today, Gloucester was awoken not by nightmares, nor the anxious fear of imprisonment, nor even a tea-bearing demigod, but rather by the slobbery nose of a dog snuffling across his face. He grumbled and rolled over, his sleepy protests turning to laughter as the wet nose ruffled the hair on the back of his head.

"All right, Zedley, all right. I'm getting up." He gently batted the dog's snout away and sat up. "Zane," he shouted, rubbing sleep from his eyes. "Come and get your dog!"

Zane appeared in the doorway to the break room, which was still Gloucester's temporary abode. She yawned, the sound turning to a groan as she stretched, but she wore a grin as she took in the scene.

"I can't help that he loves his uncle," she said with a chuckle. "C'mon, Zed! Walkies!"

She held up a bright orange leash. Zedley bounded to her side, shaggy tail wagging.

"We shall return," Zane called over her shoulder as she headed toward the front of the shop. "Put the kettle on, eh? This dog is like you, a—*ugh*—morning person." She shook her head in mock despair. "He gets up inhumanely early. But I will prevail! May the prospect of caffeine sustain me through this walk!"

Yawning, Gloucester got out of bed, smiling to himself at the sounds of Zane and her recently acquired canine leaving the shop. The tinkle of the front door chime marked his solitude.

Or perhaps not. He'd only just pulled himself to his feet and shuffled sleepily up the stairs into Zane's kitchen when he heard someone calling his name from the floor below.

"Mikalai?" came Finch's voice. "You here?"

"Just a moment," he called back. "Just putting the kettle on."

Hastily trying to tame his bedhead using the frankly unflattering reflection on the side of the kettle, he added another mug to the table and made his way back downstairs.

Finch waited for him in the doorway to the break room. "Morning, love," he said, leaning in for a quick kiss. "I passed Zane and that bear she calls a dog on their way out. What's its name again?"

"Zedley." Gloucester gestured for them to sit down on the edge of his pull-out bed. "Zane says she 'enjoys a multitude of Zs.' That aside, what are you doing here so early? Not that it isn't always nice to see you."

To his bemusement, the cheery smirk and flirtation he'd expected didn't come. Instead, Finch scrunched his nose and tipped his head back to look up at the ceiling, as if unsure what to say and hoping to find the answer there. Gloucester eyed him.

"What's wrong?" he prompted. Upstairs, the kettle whistled its shrill song of "morning at the clock shop," accompanied by the usual backing vocals of hundreds of timepieces. Distance made the sound easy to ignore in favor of the enigma that was Finch.

Finch glanced back at him. "Nothing wrong. It's... I've got a sort of proposal for you. Wait, not a *proposal*—" He waved his hands in comical dismissal as Gloucester's brows rose. "A question. Idea, I guess. That I wanted to, erm, ask you. Run by you, sort of thing."

"Oh," said Gloucester, caught between curiosity and amusement. "And were you planning on asking it this century or the next one?"

That garnered the familiar grin. "Cheeky. Right, here's the thing. I've got a job. A contact in the Nordlands reached out to me. Got himself into a spot of bother with some forest spirits and a local curse, and he's asked me to come deal with it. So, I'm leaving Frettchen."

"Oh," said Gloucester again. He tried to ignore the sinking feeling in his chest.

"Shouldn't take longer than a few weeks, maybe a couple of months at most, but—"

"That's great!" Forcing the enthusiasm felt like tearing off a bandage. A necessary pain. "I'll see you when you get back, then, I suppose."

"Or you could shut up and let me finish, you daft bastard." Finch laughed. "The job's up north. Way up. Thing is, I was scoping it out on a map and it's not more than a short drive away from a wee little town, name of Lalune."

"That's—"

"I know. That's *why*, before I was rudely interrupted, I was going to ask if you wanted to come with me."

Gloucester blinked. "You mean..."

"You could go home. I know you've been meaning to, now that things are returning to some form of normal. And I mean, I know your folks have already been down to visit you, but I thought it might be nice for you to, you know, go there." Finch's explanation was starting down a distinctly rambling path. "They were so happy to know you weren't, you know, *dead*, and I'm sure you going up to visit them would be a delight and all."

That was an understatement. In the days after time resumed, Gloucester had finally worked up the courage to call his parents and let them know he was all right. Even now, he could recall with vivid sensation the way his heart climbed his throat as he listened to the ring on the other end of the line. Dozens of potential conversations had scurried through his mind, half-formed and anxious. What should he say? What *could* he say? Would they believe whatever he did tell them? Would they think he was crazy? Would they even believe it was *him*?

Then came his mother's voice, older than he remembered, and for a long moment terror and a thousand other raw emotions choked him. She had been on the verge of crossly hanging up when he finally recovered his capacity for speech.

He needn't have worried so much about explanations, because his mother and father hadn't waited for one. They were on the next train south and then spent a fortnight scarcely letting him out of their sight. He offered up the same hole-filled explanation he'd given Jeb, but they hadn't cared, too relieved to have their son alive and well to question his story. Maybe one day he would fill them in on the whole thing: magic, gods, and all. For now, he just wanted to enjoy their happiness.

"Anyway," Finch said, addressing the ceiling once more. "It isn't all charity on my part, this offer. See, uh, the fact is, I don't really like working on my own. Not used to it, to be honest. And you..."

He dropped his gaze to meet Gloucester's eyes, a blush turning his pale cheeks rosy. "You're a damn good channeler. 'Specially considering you've no training. So, I thought, you know, if you wanted, I could help you with that. Training, I mean. In magic. And we could work this job together. And maybe, erm, future jobs."

Gloucester stared at him. "Are you asking me to travel the Lower Lands with you as some sort of...of magical private investigators?"

Finch ducked his head, a bashful movement so uncharacteristic it melted Gloucester's heart. "Well, when you put it like that, it sounds—"

"Kinda awesome."

"Yeah, I understand, I just thought—Wait, sorry, what was that?"

Gloucester got to his feet, took Finch by the shoulders, and met his gaze as he looked back up. "It sounds pretty great. I'm in. And you'll really teach me how to channel magic better?"

Surprise was still etched across every line of Finch's face, but he broke into a smile, dimples cutting into his freckled cheeks. "Yeah. I mean, if you wanted to learn."

"Might as well, right?" Gloucester laughed. "If it's always getting used around me, it'd be nice to get in on the fun myself."

After everything, it was hard to believe that not so long ago, the idea of him learning magic, real proper *magic*, would have seemed completely mad.

Finch grinned, his usual confident self once more. "What about Zane? D'you reckon she'll hate me all the more for stealing you away?"

Gloucester cast a fond eye around at the clock shop, then shrugged. "Zane will be fine without me underfoot. She was fine before I came trampling into her life. And anyway, she has Zedley to keep her company while I'm gone. Not to mention Antimony and Gear and all that lot."

Remembering the kettle upstairs, which was still whistling its heated complaints, he gestured for Finch to follow him and made his way back up to the kitchen.

"How is Antimony?" Finch asked as he reached the landing. "Did she have any trouble getting Gear back in one piece?"

"Not once she was in her lab again." Gloucester poured hot water into the teapot to steep. "Zane's been over there a lot, helping her out. And she said the Gambler's been there quite a bit too."

A shadow passed over Finch's easy humor. "Oh? And how is he?"

Gloucester shrugged again. "Who knows with him. He doesn't seem devastated, so maybe everything with the immortals will be okay." He hesitated. This was prickly territory. "Have you heard anything in the magical community? Anything that might hint at Purpurrot or Denken?"

The day after Frettchen's return to normal, Gloucester, Zane, and Antimony had gone to Purpurrot's Pies, only to find the bakery locked and empty, its windows dark. A few days later, Bleifrei and Lucienne returned to the city. Neither of them had heard from the goddess either, but they *had* heard from someone else.

"Had myself a really weird dream the other night," Blei told them, after inviting them to the pie shop a week after time resumed. "Orange Ianto was in it, which is how I know it wasn't just nonsense. She told me to come look in Purpurrot's office for purpose. 'What's that mean?' I say. And she just does her oracle thing and smiles all mysterious and away she goes!"

The chef laughed raucously, then held up a slip of paper. "Who am I to argue with the oracle, though, right? So I go and look, and I find this. Ownership of the pie shop, officially passed onto me." Her wide smile slowly faded, and she shook her head. "I guess she really isn't coming back. And she knew she wouldn't be."

Blei was silent for a long moment, before mustering a determined grin. "Lucy and I, though, we'll do her proud with this place."

In the present, Finch's face was pinched as he considered Gloucester's question. "Dunno. I mean, we're all still having thoughts and whatnot. Existing and all that. So, their...you know..." He fluttered his hands through the air in an extremely unhelpful pantomime. "...essence or whatever, it's still around. I wish I could give you a better answer. Saints know I've had enough other magicians and witches ask me to explain what exactly happened. At least you don't try to curse me when I don't have a good answer."

He let out a long sigh as he sank into one of the chairs at the table. Gloucester clicked his tongue sympathetically and passed him a mug of tea. Finch murmured his thanks before continuing.

"I've spoken to a few soothsayers and magicians I know who are prone to visions. A few of them have been having strange dreams this past month or so, but that branch of magic is pretty wobbly. Trust me, I know from experience. But enough of them have been dreaming of sharks and foxes that I think, in the long run, those two immortal pricks will recover."

He didn't sound particularly excited at the prospect. Gloucester, however, felt a wave of relief at the news. Purpurrot's sacrifice had saved the world, but at the expense of her own place within it, so it eased his mind to think that maybe, one day, she would be able to make her way back.

And maybe he ought not be happy, however complicated his emotions might be, to think that Denken might have survived. But emotions *were* complicated, and so were people. Denken's rampage and reign of terror had caused terrible destruction. It had cost people their lives and livelihoods and loved ones. Yet Gloucester couldn't convince himself that the demigod was completely evil. Maybe if he did recover, things would be different.

Downstairs, the front door chimed again, accompanied by Zedley's happy woof. A moment later, Zane's voice rang out from the bottom of the stairs.

"Another bloody pamphlet on my doorstep! If Mulligan thinks just because he helped us save the world, I'm going to vote for him in this election next month, he's got another thing coming!"

Her rant carried her up into the kitchen. Despite her show of exasperation, she seemed as chipper as when she'd left. The second he was off his leash, Zedley bounded over to Gloucester for a pat, then made a beeline for Finch, where he laid his fluffy head on the magician's lap.

"I don't think he has much chance of winning," Gloucester said. "But fair play to him for calling the election in the first place. *Especially* since he probably won't win."

"Not being a despot is kind of a low bar." Zane blew out a breath of laughter, balancing on one foot as she unlaced her shoes. "He grew on me, you know, a little, but I don't like the idea of someone that close to the old high minister being in charge of anything."

Gloucester and Finch chuckled their agreement.

"Lucky for us, we get to swan off and shirk civic duty," Finch said, clapping a cheerful hand against Gloucester's chest.

Zane dropped her shoes by the door and brushed dust from her clothes. "He's agreed to go with you, then?"

Gloucester blinked. "You knew?"

Lowering herself onto another of the chairs, Zane reached for the teapot. "Yeah, he mentioned it the other day." She flicked a sideways look at Finch, smile mischievous. "I think he was asking for my blessing."

"Was not."

Though Finch's counter was indignant, a smile warmed the protest. Gloucester inwardly marvelled at how far the two of them had come.

"Keep telling yourself that. But in any case, I think it's a good idea. Sounds like fun, if magic is your thing. Me, I'm happy here with my clocks. And my baby boy!" Her words turned to cooing as she vigorously scratched her dog's back. Zedley immediately abandoned Finch for her affection.

Wiping dog drool off his knee, Finch leaned toward Gloucester, green eyes sparkling. "You'll really do it, though? You'll come with me?"

Gloucester thought about his life there in Frettchen. What it had been: quiet and small and happy. What it had become: dangerous and confusing and exciting. He thought of all he had lost and all he had gained and all he had learned. The people he'd met, fought, rescued, and been saved by. The person he'd been and the one he'd become. He smiled. For once, no questions plagued his mind. Just happy certainty.

"Yeah. Let's have a new adventure."

Epilogue

The Epitome of Science

And so, where it is able, time spins ever on. Clocks tick, hearts mend, and stories begin and end. Life happens.

It isn't always gentle and rarely is it fair, yet for all the heartache and hardship, it does hold wonders. This is what it's all about, great and mundane, big and small, good and bad, whether you view it with magic or science or some mix of both. It is complex and frightening and so very difficult. But if you live it with thought and love and choice, it is worth it.

In the Maze, a new Guardian stands watch over the doors of their kin, laughing with the joy of home and fresh purpose. They will hold steady until the god of that timeless place may return.

And somewhere in the imponderable depths of the universe, in the Void Between Worlds, Nature and Thought swirl through the chaos. Hand in hand, they heal.

So, the hour strikes and the clock tolls its song, marking not an ending but a moment to be remembered.

Acknowledgments

And here we are, at the end of the trilogy! It's hard to believe; I felt unbelievably lucky to have my first book published and now I have all three. It's an amazing thing. And it isn't something I achieved on my own. Far from it. The following people deserve so many thanks and more gratitude than I can really put into words, but I'll do my best.

First off, to Susan Brooks and the team at Literary Wanderlust, who have brought this and my previous two books into reality in a way I'd only dreamed of. Thank you for taking the chance on my books! The publishing business is a tough one and it means a lot that you decided my stories were worth it.

To Craig Terlson, who has designed such fun, eye-catching covers for the trilogy. I appreciate you taking my opinion into account, and your ongoing encouragement is always lovely.

To Jennica Dotson, who I'm convinced is one of the best editors in the business. You made the editing process enriching, eye-opening and quite often fun. I am a much stronger and more discerning writer for the work we've done together and I can't thank you enough for that.

Thanks as well to my family, whose never-ending encouragement and support can never be appreciated enough. To Mum, Kate, Jess and Libby, all of my aunts and uncles and cousins and relations near and far who took the time to pick up my books and cheer me on.

To my friends, who have watched these stories evolve, have inspired characters and let me bounce ideas off them and ramble for ages.

To my work family at Manticore Books, who not only support me as an author, but as a bookseller and friend, as well. And make life pretty fun and interesting, to boot. Support your local indie bookshop!

Finally (and perhaps predictably, but no less true), thank you to my readers. To every person who took the time to pick up my books and give them a try. I wrote Gloucester's story because it was the sort of tale I wanted to read myself, but I also wrote it for anyone else out there looking for a bit of fun and adventure and queerness and magic. If it resonated with you, then I couldn't be happier. From the bottom of my heart, thank you.

About the Author

Ali Ives is a writer, artist, and daydreamer. She grew up with a love for reading and creativity that hasn't waned with adulthood. Working in a small indie bookshop near where she lives in rural Ontario has only made her love and appreciate the world of books all the more. Her first novel, *The Winding*, came out in October 2022, a fantasy novel about chaotic demigods, nefarious politicians, and one young man searching for answers. The sequel, *The Ticking*, followed in January 2024. *The Epitome of Science* trilogy concludes with *The Tolling*.

When Ali isn't writing or surrounded by books, you're likely to find her drawing, wandering around her property with her dog, or covered in dirt and grass stains from her other part-time work as a lily gardener. The story that would eventually develop into *The Epitome of Science* trilogy started taking form all the way back in her teen years, with the characters filling up many a sketchbook and doodled on the edges of her schoolwork.

Instagram: https://www.instagram.com/aliiveswrites/

Tumblr: https://aliiveswrites.tumblr.com/

Goodreads: https://www.goodreads.com/author/show/29736940.Ali_Ives

www.ingramcontent.com/pod-product-compliance
Lightning Source LLC
Chambersburg PA
CBHW061631190726
48289CB00006B/1557
9781956615524